Treacherous Paradise

COUPLES & CRIME BOOK THREE

LYV LAMERE

Tuxtails Publishing, LLC

Tuxtails Publishing, LLC

www.tuxtailspublishing.com

First Tuxtails Publishing Print Edition December 2025

ISBN: 978-1-957211-36-7

eBook ISBN: 978-1-957211-37-4

Cover design by Lvy Lamere and Tuxtails Publishing, LLC

Learn more about the author at www.lyvlamere.com.

To Love

Josh stretched his arms overhead and smiled at the sight of Ben's shirt riding up while he rummaged through the fridge. When his lover turned around, Josh closed the distance between them, and after taking the ingredients from him and putting them on the counter, he closed the fridge and gently pushed Benicio against the door.

"Hey."

"Hey. You were gone when I woke up." Josh sulked.

"Hmm, yes, sorry. I'm starving, and last night you said I could help myself to anything."

"You can. I just missed you."

Grinning, Ben leaned in for a peck on Josh's lips. "I wasn't far away."

"That's good."

"Is Bonny still upstairs?"

Josh nodded. "Yeah, she was still sleeping when I followed you down here. Guess you'll have to make do with only making out with me for now."

"A true hardship," Ben teased and ran his arm around Josh's waist, pulling him close and kissing him again.

Chuckling, Josh ran his hands over Ben's chest and deepened their kiss, indulging in his boyfriend's taste. They got lost in each other for a while, soft sighs filling the quiet of the kitchen.

Their peaceful moment was interrupted by a sudden, "What the fuck, Josh!?"

Startled, the guys took a step apart and turned to the voice directed at them. Tyler and Scarlette stood in the kitchen's backdoor, carrying grocery bags and staring at the couple, shock clearly written on their faces.

"Hey, leave him alone! He doesn't need your homophobic bullshit," Ben yelled at Ty.

Scarlette and Josh both gasped, then jumped into the argument. "Whoa, calm down there," Scarlette said while putting the groceries on the kitchen island.

Josh put a hand on his lover's arm. "Babe, he didn't mean it like that."

"How can you say that? Look at them glaring at us. You don't deserve that."

"I don't, no. But I also know my brother. Some of his best friends are bi and gay, remember? You being a guy is not the problem."

Following her brother-in-law's example, Scarlette laid her hand on Ty's shoulder. "Take a breath, Link, and let's figure out what's going on," she said to him, before turning to the other men again. "Josh is right, Ty didn't mean it like that. But we're more than a little surprised to find him kissing somebody other than the woman he's been with for the past seven years, the woman who is part of this family and who we thought he was planning to propose to during their vacation."

Josh blushed and scratched his neck, then huffed out a heavy sigh. "Yeah. Look, that was the plan, you're right. And I probably should've said more than 'We have a surprise for you' when I texted you last night to tell you we're home early."

Ty cocked his head. "Yeah, might've been a good idea, little brother. What's going on? Did you and Bonny break up? Or are you cheating on her? Because I don't think Mom and Dad raised you like that, and I know I never gave you an example of it."

Josh didn't have a chance to answer when Bonny spoke up from the kitchen doorway. "Don't worry, he isn't cheating on me, Ty. And we didn't break up." She took a few steps over to her men and gave both of them a peck on the lips, then addressed Tyler and Scarlette once again. "The contrary, actually. We're all three together," she stated simply and snuggled against Ben and Josh, who each ran an arm around her while also holding onto each other.

Scarlette blinked a couple of times. "Ah, wow, I did not see that coming. Okay, you guys put the groceries away, I'm gonna make coffee, and then I really want an update." Looking from Bonny to Josh and then to their boyfriend, Scarlette seemed to remember something. "And sorry for not introducing us, but this is a pretty big surprise. This is Tyler, and I'm Scarlette. Hi."

With all the guys still seeming stunned by the whole situation, Bonny chuckled. "That's Benicio. But we call him Ben. Let me help you with the coffee, Scar."

The women began to move, which got through to the guys. Ty cleared his throat and nodded. "Ah, yeah, hi. And Sparks is right, an update would be nice. You gonna help me here, Josh?"

"Yeah, yeah, sure."

Ben nodded slowly but seemed still to be on guard. "Yes, hello. Uhm, I would help, but..."

"No problem. It looks like you guys were about to make breakfast, Benicio. We also stopped by the bakery after getting groceries on our way back from New York, so if you want, you can just sit down, and we can all have the breakfast we brought along," Scarlette offered with a smile and pointed to the breakfast nook.

"Yeah, okay. And it's okay if you call me Ben, too."

Chapter One

His sister would hate him for showing up, he knew that.

But he had to make sure that she was okay, that she was safe. He trusted her; she was a smart, responsible young woman. Still, she didn't know some of the things he dealt with. He had been holding too many bones in his hands recently, too many girls her age, too many lives brutally lost. But he couldn't tell her the details, not with his job swearing him to secrecy for good reasons. He trusted his sister, yes, but he knew her heart. She would want to protect her co-workers, her friends, and by doing that, she might unwillingly alert the wrong people. He couldn't risk that. This investigation was far too important, as twisted as it was, and he was only a tiny part of it.

So he did the only thing he could think of: after finishing the latest examinations, he explained to his boss he needed time off because of a family emergency. Honestly, it wasn't much of a lie. His mother only knew what the press had covered, which was a fraction of the actual case. Even that had her close to panic, knowing her daughter would be working far away from home for weeks. If she knew what he knew? She would never let her daughter out of her sight.

His sister and his mother had debated about the situation for weeks. With more and more young women going missing from popular tourist spots, their mother had pleaded with her daughter not to go, to stay at home. His sister had listened respectfully, then kissed her mother's cheek and sighed. *"Mamá, I know you worry,"* she said in Spanish. "But last week you almost got hit by a speeding car just down the street. There's always something that could happen to me, wherever I am. I will be fine. I will not leave the hotel grounds, I will be surrounded by people all the time. It is an excellent hotel. You know I need to do this."

His mother had finally accepted, but her pleading eyes had found him across her daughter's shoulder, begging him to look out for his sister. How could he refuse her?

Chapter Two

When Bonny smiled next to him while they waited to check in, Josh felt a wave of happiness roll over him. They had been together for seven years now, and he still seemed to fall deeper in love with her every day.

Years ago, they had been shy teenagers. He, Josh O'Brien, the gangly nerd who had lost his parents not that long ago but was lucky enough to still have his brother. She, Bonny Robins, the smart, beautiful girl he still couldn't believe had started talking to him on a class trip.

Now, they had recently graduated from the university and this vacation in Mexico was their reward for years of hard work. Bonny glowed with joy, ready to finally relax for a few weeks – something they hadn't allowed themselves for a long time. Acutely aware of a small weight in the inner pocket of his jacket, Josh ran his arm around Bonny's waist and pressed a kiss to her cheek. A light flush spread across her dark skin, and her eyes lit up when she turned her head, her smile getting even brighter. *Yes, it's time for us to take the next step,* he thought. Grinning, he pecked another kiss on her lips, which drew a delighted giggle from her.

The sound caught the attention of a guest standing in the line next to theirs, who seemed to also be waiting to check in. The man looked at them with warm eyes and a kind smile before stepping up to the counter when the person in line before him walked away.

"Oops," Bonny whispered and buried her head in Josh's neck.

He gently squeezed her waist before letting her go. "Relax, it didn't seem like he minded. And this is kind of a romantic place, right? I don't think we're the only couple here," he whispered back. Nonetheless, he was careful to pick up the guy's name when he gave it to the clerk during check-in, just in case. You never knew what people would take exception to. He and Bonny hadn't faced any problems back home in Hope or at their university in New York, but he was aware that mixed-race couples weren't accepted that easily everywhere.

For now, though, he decided to let it go with a last glance at the man, mentally filing away some details: about 5'9" tall, lean but trained, dark-brown hair and eyes together with the golden skin tone and facial features pointing to Hispanic roots, mid- to late twenties, high-quality gray t-shirt, dark jeans and sneakers.

With that out of the way, Josh focused back on Bonny and moved to the counter with her.

A few minutes later, an employee led them through the gardens to their bungalow. The hotel was made up of a larger main building with simple rooms, but also offered several secluded bungalows settled into the lush greenery of the vast garden landscape. It was a tropical paradise even now during the rainy season. They had discussed postponing the trip until the dry season to improve their chances to catch some sun, but in the end had shared one look and laughed at the thought – they would spend most of their time together in bed, anyway.

Once they were at their bungalow, they thanked and tipped

the employee, then had a look around. The living room was inviting and colorful, and an alcove offered a simple kitchen area. French doors opened to a covered patio area with a table and chairs next to loungers and a small private pool, all surrounded by large plants for privacy. Back inside, they made their way to the bedroom. Warm, muted colors and a large, comfortable bed were calling for them to take a rest after a long day of travel, and Bonny reached out to take Josh's hand. "As much as I would love to use this bed for something else, right now, I could use a nap. Why don't we freshen up, then rest a bit before we get ready for dinner?"

Josh brought her hand to his lips and kissed it. "Sounds perfect, baby."

A nap had turned out to be a good idea, and waking up to Bonny crawling down his body and taking him into her mouth while touching herself had made it perfect.

Both of them were rested and relaxed when they strolled through the garden to the restaurant, holding hands and admiring their surroundings. Soft lights illuminated the pathways, and even though they could hear people and music from one of the larger pools with a bar, it was far from the obnoxious party atmosphere their friends from the university had been looking for. Of course, they had been out partying with friends while at the university, and they had both enjoyed it. But this vacation was just for them. A time to reconnect without intrusions. They had always been together, had spent as much time with each other as possible, even during their courses. But sitting next to each other studying and working on papers was a far cry from quiet time as a couple with no need to prepare for the next big exam.

The hotel offered several restaurants, and for tonight, they had chosen one of the smaller ones with a cozy atmosphere. It was probably as authentic as you could expect in a hotel catering mostly to tourists, but the food was supposed to be delicious. Since they were near Cancún, the seafood promised to be fresh, so Bonny ordered Shrimp Ceviche while Josh decided to have one of the local specialties and went with *Cochinita Pibil*. And a glance at the wine menu made them both smile when they saw some of the wines Josh's family produced on it. They chose a local wine, though, listening to their waiter's advice on which one to pair best with their dinner. A few minutes later, they were surprised when they were also presented with a bottle of champagne. A card printed along with it and handed to them made them laugh.

Enjoy, you deserve it! Congratulations on your graduation! We're proud of you both!

Scarlette and Tyler

"Your brother and sister-in-law are awesome for organizing this, babe," Bonny said.

Josh nodded. "Yeah, I got lucky. Well, we, I guess. I mean, they're your family, too."

"They are, yes. And I'm happy to call them that."

He was happy to hear her agree with him. He knew she was happy with him and liked his family, but Bonny confirming it helped calm the butterflies in his stomach. He wouldn't ask today, but just the plan to do it during this vacation was enough to make him nervous in the best kind of way. For tonight, though, they would enjoy each other's company, a delicious dinner, and the excitement of a long-overdue vacation.

They were waiting for their desserts when they spotted the guy from check-in earlier that day coming around a corner to leave the restaurant. He recognized them as well and gave them another smile and a friendly nod before disappearing.

Bonny and Josh returned the gesture, and Bonny shrugged. "Well, he seems nice enough. Bit tense, but perhaps he's here for work and not for a vacation."

Josh nodded in agreement. The man had smiled, but he had been walking with a little more purpose than an evening stroll after dinner would usually call for. "I thought you'd see that, too. Yeah, he didn't exactly seem super relaxed. But like you said, maybe he's not here for a vacation."

Enjoying the rest of their dinner, they forgot about the other guest until they were walking back to their bungalow. They took a detour to check out the public pool area, since they had decided to go there for a while the next day. But when they were nearly to it, they spotted the guy again. He stood in the shadows, somewhat hidden from view, and looked at the bar. Josh laid his hand on Bonny's arm, stopping her. They both watched the man observing the bar for another minute, but just when Josh wanted to ask him what he was doing, the guy shook his head, seemingly at his own behavior, and walked away in the other direction, not noticing them.

"That was strange. I get a weird feeling from that guy," Josh told Bonny under his breath.

"I know what you mean. But perhaps we're reading too much into it. Maybe he's really here for work, would like to have a drink but knows his boss or client or whoever would not approve, and he was just having an internal debate whether he should or shouldn't go over there. Or he was looking for somebody he finds interesting but nobody caught his eye, so he left instead of flirting with just anybody. Hell, maybe he's on the rebound and is trying to hook up with somebody but can't bring himself to do it just yet."

"Yeah, or maybe he's stalking his ex and was afraid to be spotted if he walked any closer to the bar."

Bonny desperately bit her lip, but she couldn't hold back the chuckle. "Oh god, I love you so, so much, Josh, but damn, you're already in full PI mode. I'm not saying you're wrong, mind you, but maybe give that brain of yours a little rest. We've seen him, we can describe him; if anything happens, we can come forward as witnesses. Stressing the *if* here. We can even keep looking out, see if we spot him doing any other strange things. But right this moment? He hasn't done anything other than change his mind about going to the bar."

Josh sighed. "Yes, I know. And you're right, Bonny. Just like I know you came up with the other ideas to keep my brain from going there," he told her and gave her a quick kiss for it. Smiling at her, he took her hand. "You're probably right, too, and I'm sure it's any one of your scenarios and not him being a stalker. So, let's go to our room?"

"Great idea," Bonny replied and snuggled closer to steal another kiss before walking to their bungalow with Josh by her side. It took him a few steps, but then he relaxed again. She *was* right – they could keep an eye on him (which would also be a good training exercise for Josh, whose first job working for a private investigator would be starting soon), they could describe him, and Josh had even caught his name earlier: Benicio Pérez.

Chapter Three

Lazy vacation mornings were the best, Bonny was sure of that. After waking up in Josh's arms and leisurely making love, they had eventually gotten out of bed to have some brunch. It had been as delicious as dinner the previous night.

Their plan for the rest of the day involved a lot of doing nothing. They had changed into their swimsuits, had thrown on some shirts for the walk, and were now carrying their towels and books toward the pool where they planned to spend the afternoon. The weather was on their side with the sun shining brightly after a few early clouds had dissipated.

But what should've been a short stroll ending on a lounger was interrupted abruptly when they heard a woman hissing at somebody. For a moment, they were confused where the voices were coming from, until they realized the people arguing must have been hiding behind some of the large plants growing along the pathway. It was a mix of Spanish and English, and it was clear the woman was not happy.

"*¡No chingues!* What are you doing here?"

The reply was barely audible. "Making sure you are safe."

"I told you not to come."

"I know. But..."

"No 'buts!' *¡Déjame en paz!*"

"I can't just leave you alone, you know that."

By now, Josh had heard enough and took a step through the wall of leaves to make sure the woman was okay. A few seconds later, he came face to face with a woman wearing the uniform of the hotel barkeepers and the man he and Bonny had seen yesterday. "Is everything okay here?"

When Bonny followed him, she grumbled, "Okay, I take it back, the stalker theory sounds plausible after all."

Perfect, now people thought he was a stalker! Benicio groaned and let his head fall back, silently cursing everything and every-one. He had known this would happen, hadn't he? He had told his mother his sister would react like this if she saw him around the hotel. Her helpful advice had been, "Then she better not see you."

Now, his sister was mad as hell (he knew she only kept her voice down and her language mostly civil because they were at her place of work, and she had likely used some English hoping her coworkers wouldn't understand all of it, should they hear something), and the couple he had seen yesterday – the couple he had been having the strangest thoughts about just before he had fallen asleep – thought he was a crazy stalker. The guy looked like he was ready to wrestle him to the ground and keep him there until the police showed up, while the woman seemed to be considering whether she should punch or kick him.

Things had been going well until a few minutes ago, but then one of his sister's coworkers had told his sister she might have an admirer – just because he had been caught looking at the bar once too often to make sure she was all right and nobody else was paying her too much attention. She had spotted him across the pool and had recognized him in a heartbeat. Then she had dragged him to a semi-secluded spot and had been quietly yelling at him until now.

His sister switched from angry, snarling sibling to professional in the blink of an eye; he had to admire her for it. "Hello. Yes, everything is perfect. I'm very sorry we disturbed you. Please, let me make sure you get a drink or a snack of your choice on the house."

But of course, the young man didn't let it go just like that. "Are you sure you're okay? If he is harassing you, we will back you up with your boss. Just because he's a guest and you work here doesn't mean he can do whatever he wants."

It was then that his sister brought her hand up to cover her mouth, but her laugh still escaped. She needed a moment to calm down, but then smiled at the couple. "Oh, my... wow. *Gracias.* Thank you. You are a good man. But the situation is not as bad as it looks. He is my brother, not a stalker. He can just be a little overprotective, and I would think also terrible at saying no to our mother."

Her gaze landed on her brother, making him shrink. "*Sí.* You know it, Val. *Mamá* asked me to look after you. What was I supposed to do?"

"Tell her you have a job yourself? Tell her you can't just take time off to check on your adult sister?"

"But..."

Suddenly, the young man interrupted him. "Benicio, word of advice, '*but*' will not help you in this situation. Your sister is understandably furious, even though I am sure she knows her mother – and you – meant well. Let her work in peace for now. And later, you two, and maybe your mother, can talk about it."

At first, Benicio nodded, but then he stared at Josh in surprise. "Wait, how do you know my name?"

Damn, Josh was normally a lot better at this, but after seeing the way the other man had acted the evening before, he had been on Josh's mind. Now that he had an explanation, he had relaxed and let the name slip. He did his best to appear flustered; no need to let them know he had actively been compiling information about Benicio in case anything bad happened. Scratching his neck, he mumbled, "I must've heard it when you checked in."

Knowing exactly what her boyfriend had done, Bonny took the initiative to distract them. "I'd say it's time for introductions all around. This is my boyfriend, Josh O'Brien. I'm Bonny Robins." She held her hand out to Benicio's sister with a friendly grin.

The woman shook it, her professional smile back in place. "I'm Valeria Pérez. And this is my brother Benicio Pérez, as you've already found out. Please, let me thank you for trying to help me. Come with me to the bar, I will make you something special, and you can keep telling my brother why it's not a good idea for him to glare at everybody approaching the bar. If he keeps doing that, there won't be any guests left by evening."

Bonny laughed easily. "Don't worry, we'll distract him so you can get your work done."

Chapter Four

He didn't know how exactly it had happened, but moments later Benicio found himself sitting around a table near the pool with Bonny and Josh and got the feeling he was about to be interrogated.

They gave him a moment, waiting for Valeria to bring their drinks and leave again after they thanked her. He took the time to look at them, to finally see them when he had the chance for more than a glance or wasn't surprised by them and possibly in danger of being detained or beaten.

He thought them to be about the same age, both in their early to mid-twenties, and from the way they looked at each other and their body language, they seemed deeply in love, sharing loving glances and constantly touching in one way or another.

Bonny was a beautiful young woman. She was about 5'6", slim but not skinny, had soft facial features and full lips. She wore her dark hair loosely tied back, her shoulder-length curls untreated, looking soft. Her brightly colored clothes contrasted with her dark skin and warm, dark eyes. Benicio got the impression she was comfortable in her own skin: she carried an air of self-confidence without seeming arrogant with it. He could easily see why Josh would be attracted to her.

As to Josh, Benicio thought he was a great-looking young man. He was a bit taller than Benicio, maybe six foot, lean, but some muscle definition hinted at regular training. His hair was an easy length to style and looked like he had finger-combed it this morning, the color hitting somewhere between dark-blond and warm caramel with streaks that the sun had bleached a bit to a lighter blond. It went well with the kind, rich brown eyes. Studying his face, Benicio thought he could see some finer European features, highlighted by the thin blond beard running along Josh's jaw and framing his mouth, not unlike his own darker facial hair.

All in all, seeing them together, he got the impression of a smart, confident, and loving couple.

Once his sister was gone, Bonny and Josh focused their attention fully on him. It made him nervous, but for reasons he couldn't pinpoint, it wasn't an entirely unpleasant feeling.

After a long moment, Josh cleared his throat. "Okay, we've given you the benefit of the doubt here, because your sister doesn't seem to be the kind of person who would keep quiet if you had truly harassed or stalked her."

"I know, and I thank you for that. You're right about her, she would speak up."

"And you knew this would piss her off," Bonny threw in.

"Oh, yes, I knew. Her mood is no surprise."

"Then why do it? I know how mothers can be, but doesn't she know where your sister works? I mean, this is not exactly some sleezy motel renting rooms by the hour."

"Bonny is right. And yes, we know you don't need to be poor to commit crimes, but still, this seems like a pretty safe place to work."

Benicio ran a hand through his hair, then shook his head. "It's complicated. You two come from the States, right?"

When they nodded, he kept talking. "Well, I don't know how much of this is covered in the news in the US, but for a while now, young women have been disappearing all over the country. Now, before you say anything, yes, it's terrible, and unfortunately, it's not something new. But our news stations have found out and reported that all these women worked in hotels. That's enough for my mother to worry about her daughter."

Josh studied him intently, and to Benecio it felt almost like he was trying to read his thoughts. "But that's not all, is it? If that was all, you wouldn't still be here after the dressing down your sister gave you. You would've packed your bags and told your mom that Valeria is okay but sent you away. But you looked so anxious yesterday after dinner that it's obvious you worry, too, and I think it's because you know there's a reason for it."

Dumbfounded, Benicio stared at Josh until he shook himself out of his stupor. "You are very perceptive. Yes, I admit, I am also worried."

"And why is that?" Josh asked.

"For reasons I cannot talk about."

That comment made Josh sit up straighter instantly, and Benicio held up his hands. "Please, don't get the wrong idea. I'm not involved in anything illegal. It's just information I can't share."

Bonny tapped her finger lightly against her glass before she offered her conclusion. "Because you're investigating the case."

"Why do you... What? And what do you mean by me looking anxious yesterday evening? It sounds more like *you* are stalking *me*."

"Hm, it does, I'll give you that. But it was a coincidence: we saw you staring at the bar after we left the restaurant," Josh explained.

Then Bonny added, "And to the why and what? I know how tense all you investigators are when you're on a case, and if it's personal or could become personal, you're even worse. Josh has studied so he can open his own PI business one day. Some of his brother's best friends are cops. And the mother of his sister-in-law's best friend works for the FBI. You give off this investigator vibe, too." Okay, Bonny knew she was exaggerating her conclusion, but his reaction would give her a good idea if she was on the right track. And if she wasn't and he was indeed involved in the disappearances, he now knew they were well connected to law enforcement. So far, she had a good feeling about him, but it always paid to be careful.

Benicio took a moment to compose himself, then he folded his hands together on the table and looked at them. "You both see a lot. And you're partially right. Yes, I am part of the investigation. But I am not a cop. I supply background insight about information that is not public knowledge. And with you planning to be a private investigator, Josh, I am sure you can both understand the need to keep some things confidential."

They both confirmed it with a silent nod and would've stopped asking more questions, when Valeria stepped up to their table again and set down a fruit platter. "I hope my brother is not grossing you out with stories of his career as a forensic anthropologist. Don't misunderstand, I am proud of him, but it is not a topic most people like talking about," she said with a cheeky wink at her brother before she walked to the next table to bring the guests there their drinks.

Bonny and Josh put the pieces together in seconds.

"Oh. No wonder you're worried about your sister, Benicio," Bonny said softly and reached out to squeeze his hand. She looked confused that she had done it and withdrew her hand quickly, glancing at Josh. He gave her a small smile, wordlessly telling her it was okay. He knew she easily gave comfort to people, and it seemed they both had the impression Benicio was being truthful and honestly afraid for his sister.

Heaving a sigh, Benicio let his head fall back for a second, then faced them again. He had absolutely not planned to let them know this much, but even though it made no sense, he had the feeling he could trust them to keep this quiet. "Thank you. And you can just call me Ben."

Around them, the noise level had risen with more people arriving at the pool. Their table was set a little to the side, so Josh was sure they wouldn't be overheard when he addressed Benicio quietly. "Okay. Now, believe me, I know about confidentiality, and you don't have to confirm or deny anything. But let me just summarize this: there's a presumably large number of young women going missing from hotels – and I assume they were employees, or the US media would've made it a big topic of missing tourists. I would think that is as much as your mother and your sister know. But you are part of the investigation in your capacity as a forensic anthropologist, so at least some women have been found dead. Your sister works in a seemingly secure hotel, and yet you're worried about her, so I also assume the other women went missing from similar places," he concluded.

Ben didn't say anything, but he held Josh's gaze, and his eyes told the couple Josh was right.

"But how did your mother think this could work? Even if she doesn't know about some of the women being found dead or that you are part of the investigative team, you can't take off work indefinitely, can you? Especially not if you're working on this case." Bonny could understand Ben's and Valeria's mother's worry, but she couldn't see how it was practical to do as she had asked.

"Ah, you see, my sister is a few years younger than I am. She has yet to decide what she wants to study. Tourism is one of her choices. But she wants some insight before signing up for classes. This is more of a paid internship. She's only here for a month. With everything going on, I haven't had time off work in a very long time, and although I still feel bad about it, I exaggerated and told my boss I had a family emergency. He wasn't happy, but I'll have to live with that. Anyway. I cannot tell you the details, but I can say, while I am part of the investigation, I am not the only one looking at anything coming up, so I was able to take this long of a vacation."

"I guess that makes sense. Well, do you think your sister will let you stay here? Or will she have you kicked out?"

"I honestly don't know, Bonny."

Now Josh cocked his head, an idea forming. "What about this? I can see why you want to make sure your sister is okay. So tell her you will let your mother know she's safe and you won't bother her anymore while she's working. But also tell her that you *do* have the month off after all, and that you'd just like to stay and relax. Tell her the three of us get along well and you'll just hang with us. That way, you have a reason to stay here, and Bonny and I can help you keep an eye on her, hopefully with her feeling less like she's being watched all the time. With three of us there, it's not like you constantly have to look at her and make it awkward for her. If we take turns, it will be a lot less obvious."

Josh had no idea why he had said that – this was his and Bonny's well-deserved vacation before starting work in six weeks. He could always see this as some extra observation training, but normally, he wouldn't bring this into their time off. And yet, for some unknown reason, he felt compelled to help Ben. And one look at Bonny told him he had done the right thing.

She smiled at him, then at Ben, giving the other man an

encouraging nod. "Yeah, we can totally do that. I'd feel better knowing your sister is safe, too. And with such a case, I'd say you can actually use the time off, too."

"*Sí*, of course. I mean, yes, I could. But I can't ask this of you. This is your vacation, and you don't even know me or my sister."

Bonny shrugged at Ben's arguments. "Yes, we're sure. We might not know you yet. But Josh wouldn't have offered this if he didn't feel the same way I do: that you've been honest with us, that you're under a lot of pressure, and that you could use some help. I might not plan to work in the same profession as him, but I still want to do right by people. We've both learned to listen to our instincts, and they tell us to do this. And about this being our vacation, yes, it is. But, Ben, it's not like we'll stick with you twenty-four seven, right? We'll still have our bungalow, we'll still have the evenings to ourselves."

He couldn't believe this kindness and support from two strangers. "I don't know what to say..."

"Say, 'Thank you. I'll get the next round of drinks,'" Josh offered with a grin.

"I can do that," Ben replied and got up to order another round of cocktails and some water, and used the chance to talk to his sister for a second.

From what Bonny and Josh could see, she wasn't completely thrilled by the idea of her brother staying, but she seemed a bit calmer than earlier.

"You think we're doing the right thing, babe?" Josh asked.

"Yeah, I do. I have a good feeling about him. And just because we're on a couple vacation doesn't mean we can't make new friends, right?"

"Right," Josh agreed and leaned over for a kiss.

Chapter Five

I nitially, Ben had been careful, not entirely convinced that Bonny and Josh weren't looking for some inside information about the case. After all, if anybody managed to look at some of the case files, they could have found his name as a medical consultant. But the more time he spent with the couple, the more he came to trust them. They didn't push for any additional information, only did as they had promised and kept an eye on his sister.

To make things better, he realized he liked both of them. They were great company, and while they were talking, he found out they had a lot in common. They were only three years younger than him, both of them liked SciFi films and comic book adaptations, and it sounded like Josh had an impressive comic book collection at home. They told him about their studies and what they wanted to do with them.

It made sense that Josh had his Master's degree in Criminal Justice and Computer Forensics if he wanted to work as a PI uncovering cybercrime, and the additional Business and Finance courses he had taken would help him a great deal when it came to fraud cases. With the internships he had completed during his studies, and the job with a PI he had lined up to start soon, he was indeed well on his way to his own company someday soon, and to Ben's mind, it sounded like a great idea for him to consider becoming a Certified Legal Investigator.

Bonny's studies didn't sound any less impressive. She had earned her Master's in Management and Sustainable Business Development and had taken extra courses in Marketing and Visual Communications. Hearing that Josh's brother and his wife were working with Bonny to have her run the family wine and horse breeding business in the future spoke volumes as to how much they trusted her. It neither surprised Ben that she had offered to later support Josh with founding his business as well, nor that she apparently had already helped improve her dad's farm business during her studies.

These two were obviously hard-working and had goals they were determined to reach. And when Josh finally told him how he and Bonny had started talking on a class trip back in high school, then had become a couple amidst a blackmail scandal involving Josh's family – that even threatened his life when explosives had been placed in his car – something clicked for Ben.

All three of them were still sitting near the pool, and Ben slid forward, perching on the edge of his seat. "Wait... O'Brien and this story. Is your brother Tyler O'Brien, the writer?"

"Yes, he is," Josh admitted with a smile that conveyed how proud he was of his brother.

"Oh, wow. I read his book about the story. I couldn't believe it. Your family was really blackmailed for almost a century?"

A sigh preceded Josh's answer. "Yeah. I'm glad we put an end to it, but even now it seems crazy, especially if you consider it all started because our ancestors just wanted to help their friends."

"I remember, yes. We talked about the book at a family

dinner one night, and my *abuela* shocked almost everybody when she told us how proud she was of her sister for doing the same to help one of her friends a long time ago."

"That's awesome," Bonny agreed.

"*Sí*, it is. I kept reading more of your brother's books after that. I think he changed his subjects a little after that, right?"

"Well, kind of. It was because of what happened to our family, but also to the person he wanted to write about after that, Cory Gilbert. The poor guy was killed. After that happened, Ty decided to change his focus somewhat. He had always written biographies, and most of them were about interesting but 'normal' people," Josh said, making air-quotes before continuing, "I mean, mostly they weren't the standard biographies of politicians or rich businessmen. But after what happened to our family, and then to Cory Gilbert, Ty decided to write biographies of victims. He said to me once, 'Everybody knows the faces of Evil. Mention Ted Bundy's name, and most people have a face in their minds. But who can name his victims? He *needs* to be remembered so we can learn how to prevent people like him from killing in the first place. But his victims *deserve* to be remembered for who they were, for the potential they carried and the life that they were robbed of.'"

Josh took a sip from his drink, then kept talking. "It's something that's stuck with me ever since. We're fascinated by what people are capable of doing to other people to the point where there are countless documentaries, shows and movies about pretty much every famous serial killer, giving them a stage and feeding the ego of the ones still alive. We can't change that. Hell, I'm planning to work on fighting crime in my own way, so of course, I listen to true crime podcasts and watch such shows. But Ty, he looks at the victims. And he manages to make even the most ordinary people special. He reminds his readers that those people were mothers, daughters, brothers, uncles. That they were loved. That they were extraordinary to those who loved them. And he makes sure that even with all the attention their killers get, they, too, won't be forgotten or end up a mere footnote in a paper.

"I mean, he also writes about other crime victims, like people who lost all their savings, people who were abducted but lived through it. And he does a great job. But when he writes about a murder victim, it's the most impactful for me because there's no bigger loss than life."

Bonny nodded earnestly and took Josh's hand in hers. Ben studied them both for a long moment, then agreed. "You are absolutely right. And it is clear to me that you respect and love your brother very much. If you are as smart at starting your business as you are at analyzing your brother's work, I have no doubt you will be doing great, and you will help many people."

Humbled, Josh lowered his gaze, a light flush coloring his cheeks. "Thank you, Ben."

In contrast to Josh's quiet reaction, Bonny chuckled. "Yeah, seriously, thank you, Ben. He might not have seemed like it so far, but Josh can sometimes still be shy. And despite knowing he has the investigative skills and the brains to be a great PI, and knowing I'll lend a hand when it comes to the business aspects should he need me, it's good for him to hear people other than his family say that they believe he can do it."

"We can all use some reassurance, I would say. Even more so at the beginning of your career. Although I am sure both of you will be fine; you have obviously chosen careers according to your strengths. And with Josh's family trusting you with their business, even with the gradual transition you mentioned earlier, Bonny, I would say you bring just as much brains and integrity to the table as Josh. That doesn't mean the first steps into a job after you've studied for years to get there aren't unnerving," Ben told them.

"Huh, yes, I think you're right. Was it like that for you, too? I mean, I know you can't tell us about the case, but you can tell us about your studies and your job in general, can't you?" Bonny asked.

It was a relief to realize they truly respected that he couldn't and wouldn't talk about an active investigation. He had already thought they would, but in the past, not even all of his friends had understood that, and it had left him wary. With them not pushing him at all, though, he decided to trust them. Visibly relaxing, he leaned back in his chair. "Yes, I suppose I can tell you about that. You might need to know first that Mexico has been working on restructuring its forensic education system for the past several years. My university collaborated with one in the US, and I attended some classes in the States. My main focus has been Forensic Anthropology, but I had Biology and general medical courses as well. They're still debating if they want to change the title for my degree in the future, so I was even more nervous than others when I started my career, not knowing if employers would risk it. I was lucky and found a good position, and so far, my degree hasn't been a problem. It's enough to work with in Mexico as a forensic technician without problems, and my employer made sure to get something drafted with our legal department and a judge so that even if anything changes in the future, any reports I've done under that title will still hold up in court. He might not always be the easiest person, but he takes his job seriously. Now, my work often has me traveling across the country to consult with medical examiners when they come across a case with skeletal remains. Sometimes I also give seminars, but that's usually only when my boss can't make it and I have to fill in."

"Wow, that's seriously impressive, Ben. Not just the degree, but also that you were brave enough to try the new education path. And it explains why you have less of an accent. Your sister's English is great, too, but her accent is a little more pronounced," Josh said.

"Thank you. Yes, I did my best to become as fluent as possible. When it became clear that I would need to speak at conferences and seminars in the States, I figured people would listen to me better this way. Not only is there still a perceived bias with many people thinking Mexico hasn't yet reached the same investigative standard as the US, but I also remembered a professor I had. He taught here in Mexico, but Spanish wasn't his native language. He was a great teacher, don't get me wrong, but following his lecture could be difficult because of his heavy accent."

Bonny nodded in agreement. "I totally get that. I had one Japanese professor, and her lectures were amazing. But her heavy accent sometimes made it a challenge to understand each and every word. Still, I admire everybody who's learned more than their native language, even more so if they even work somewhere that requires them to use the other language."

"Have either of you learned other languages?"

Bonny and Josh shared a glance, then grinned. "Well," Bonny said, "we both had Spanish in high school, and we still keep learning, but I would think our accents are terrible, and it's not a language we use every day; it usually takes us a bit to talk fluently again. And then there's the bit of Italian and Louisiana French we've picked up, but most of that deals with food."

Ben looked confused for a moment. "Wait, I thought your families lived somewhere in or near New York, at least that's what I remember from the book. Well, your family, Josh."

"Oh, we all do," Josh confirmed. "But... I feel like we might need to draw you a diagram so it's easier to follow. Anyway, so like I said, my brother wanted to write about this guy, Cory Gilbert, about six years back. But Cory was killed, and parts of his body were found in a shark tank. Ty's close friend, Luke, and his boss, Leroy, caught the case. But they needed help to retrieve the body parts. Ty's wife, Scarlette, owns a pet consulting business, and at some point, she sent one of her veterinarians to help the cops. That vet was Michelle. He and Leroy got together during the case. Following so far?"

"Yes, I think so."

"Good. Now, Michelle originally comes from New Orleans, but he studied in New York and stayed there. His mom and his stepdad had a restaurant in New Orleans. But when Leroy and Michelle got married four years ago and started the adoption process, Michelle's mom and his stepdad moved their business from New Orleans to New York, too, to be close to their son and their grandkids."

"It's amazing that they'd do that."

"It is. And it's awesome for us, because now we have even more places to eat. Scarlette's dad and her grandmother run an Italian restaurant together, and it's always been this family meeting place. We've all been included in the Langella family – that's Scarlette's clan – right from the start, and that not only included Ty and me, but friends like Scarlette's best friend, July, who's married to Luke now, and Michelle. They had been coming to the restaurant for years already before we even met Scarlette. And when Michelle's parents moved to New York, Scarlette's dad and her grandmother helped them set up their restaurant again, near their own place, and now we all meet at one of the restaurants for family dinners almost every week. So over the years, we've picked up some Italian and French, and we know a damn good Cajun restaurant in New York and an amazing Italian place. And the best part is that the restaurants get some of their ingredients from Bonny's dad's farm. We all help each other out."

Ben looked at them for a long moment, then laughed. "That's perfect. Your families and friends would get along well with my *mamá*. She owns her own food truck business. She runs five trucks in three cities, and they all offer traditional Mexican food, but she makes sure all of it has restaurant quality: no quick, greasy fast food."

"Your mom sounds amazing," Bonny stated, then chuckled. "And I get why it's hard to say no to her. She's not only your mother, but she must also know how to get people to do what she needs them to when she runs five trucks like that."

Ben couldn't agree more. "You could say that, yes. I love that woman, but believe me, you do not want to cross her."

Around them, it had become quieter, and Valeria came over to their table. "You all seem to be getting along. My shift is over now, just so you know."

It was a surprise to all three of them. They hadn't realized they had been talking for hours. After a glance at Bonny and Josh, Ben stood up. "Would you two excuse me? I think I should have dinner with my sister, if she will let me. Can I try to make amends, Val?"

She gave him a stern look, then rolled her eyes. "*Sí, sí*. Why not? *Vamos*, let's go already, then. I'm starving."

"*Bien*. Thank you both," Ben addressed the couple.

"No problem. We'll see you tomorrow, right?" Josh asked. He and Bonny had stood up as well by now and were gathering their belongings.

"Yes, sure."

"Cool. Then enjoy dinner with your sister. We'll get something to eat now, too."

During dinner, Bonny and Josh talked about a few of their upcoming tasks regarding their new jobs when they'd be home again, made a list of possible presents for a few of their friends from the college whose birthdays were coming up, and several other topics. But they came back again and again to one subject in particular: Benicio.

What struck them both, but what neither of them managed to put into words, was the fact that they didn't even talk about the case all that much. It came up, of course. But the focus was on the man himself. It seemed like he had made an impression on both of them.

Perhaps that wasn't all that surprising. They had been talking with him for most of the day, and the conversation had flowed easily. They shared many interests with him, especially Josh, considering they were both pursuing careers dealing with law enforcement and the justice system. Add to it that Ben appeared to be a nice, dependable, and responsible guy. Of course they were talking about him, comparing their impressions.

On their walk back to their bungalow, they were both silently contemplating their new friend. But once they were inside, Bonny pushed those thoughts aside and snuggled into Josh's arms, her arms running around him, her hands pulling his shirt free and running underneath it to reach his skin. His eyes lit up as they always did when they got together like this, and his lips found hers. Slowly, they made their way to the bedroom, their movements almost a dance. Clothes dropped to the floor, and the quiet was replaced by sighs and low moans.

Seven years had done nothing to make them desire each other any less. But it had taught them that, sometimes, it was nice to take their time. They had been teenagers when they had started dating, and except for their very first time, they had made love like teenagers for the first years of their relationship. There had been a lot of hot kisses, hands landing quickly between the other's legs, a rush for instant gratification. Had it been bad sex? Hell, no. They still loved each other like that often enough. But over the years, they had also come to cherish these intimate moments with each other, to explore and tease, to slowly rise on the wave of their lust and prolong their pleasure before they reached the peak together.

In a tacit agreement, they were gentle tonight. They spread lazily on the bed, hands roaming, lips wandering over skin that carried the lingering taste of sunscreen. Light brushes of Josh's fingertips made Bonny gasp when he trailed them along her ribs. She made him shudder when she ran her nails carefully along his spine. Their mouths met again, and their kiss deepened until Josh finally slid inside of her.

Moving together like this always felt wonderful. Warmth spread through them, the harmony between them a calming force to their rising hunger. The climax that took them over at the same time was a slow but intense fire. It was sheer bliss.

So it was no wonder that Bonny was shocked when, at the height of her desire, an image popped up in her head. An image of her and Josh – and Ben. All three of them lying in bed, kissing and panting, their naked skin glistening with a fine layer of sweat.

Chapter Six

It was amazing what women were willing to tell strangers while partying – as long as they were telling it to other women. Calling her higher-ups and flagging the girl after a night of clubbing was nothing. She was exactly what her bosses were looking for.

Now came the tricky part: first, confirming that her suspicions about the woman's identity were true. She sat in a bar and scrolled through her phone for a while until she had found what she was looking for. Yes, perfect.

But how to approach the next step? She shook her head at herself. She probably shouldn't be looking all this up in public. But it was easier around all these strangers than at work with nosy coworkers constantly looking at everybody's screen.

A few taps later, she had found a way to contact the person she was looking for and began taking notes and composing a text on her phone. The girl would be gone by the time things were in place, of course. But it wouldn't be a problem to find another possible mark and present that one as a means to follow their actual target to whoever showed up to save the first girl. She'd get them enough information so they'd have no choice but to reward her helpfulness.

Chapter Seven

Josh woke up confused, achingly hard, and with a feeling of guilt creeping up on him.

The previous night had left him wondering whether he had done something to accidentally hurt Bonny during their lovemaking. She had seemed to enjoy it as she always did. But after, when they had cuddled under the covers after a quick dash into the bathroom, she had been oddly quiet. When he had asked her what was wrong, she had told him she had a mild headache, nothing bad, and some sleep should cure it. Then she had just closed her eyes.

Now she was still sleeping in bed beside him – and Josh didn't know what to do. Not only had he no clue whether he had done something wrong last night, but he had woken from the strangest dream he could imagine, one he could make no sense of, given that he was incredibly in love with the woman next to him. And yet, his body told him it was very simple.

But there was nothing simple about it. How could he dream something like that when he was as happy as he was with Bonny? Unbidden, the images of his dream flashed before his inner eye once more.

Josh lying on top of Bonny, leisurely thrusting into her, kissing her.

Her breath catching, her moan echoing through the room.

Then a hand on Josh's back. But it wasn't Bonny's. Her hands were holding onto the headboard.

No, this was a larger hand, but it was gentle as it trailed up and down his back, then glided to Bonny's thigh to caress her.

A second hand lovingly but firmly grabbing his chin and turning his head to the side.

A pair of lips meeting his, short stubble catching on his own.

And those warm, kind eyes staring into his when he was so close to his climax, quivering with need. Eyes he had looked at for hours during the day. Benicio's eyes.

This couldn't be. He *loved* Bonny; there was no doubt about that. Looking at her sleeping beside him, he knew his feelings for her hadn't changed at all. And yet, he had dreamed of somebody else being with them. That had never happened before. Had he noticed if people looked good over the years? Sure, he wasn't blind. But there had never been anything even coming close to imagining doing something with them. And it wasn't just that they had spent a long time the day before with Ben. Bonny was right when she said Josh could be shy sometimes, but that didn't mean he didn't have any friends – male and female – he spent a lot of time with, talked to for hours. And he had never dreamed about any of them before. Horny teenage fantasies from before he had even talked to Bonny aside, the only person he had ever dreamed of was her. What made it all the more confusing was the fact that his dream hadn't been only him and Ben, but the three of them together. Even in a dream, it should've been weird to have another person in bed with them, to think of somebody else's hands touching him, touching Bonny. Worse, if it had only felt like they had invited somebody to join them for some fun – not that they ever had done so in reality – it would have been something he could understand. But while he had been asleep, while the images had taken over his mind, it had felt like all three of them had a real connection, like what was happening was a lot more than some casual fun. It had felt... *right*. That thought made another wave of guilt rush over Josh, and he shuddered almost violently with it.

It was enough to wake up Bonny. She looked at him intensely for a moment, like she was searching for an answer to an unspoken question, before turning away from him and getting out of bed with a mumbled, "Morning."

It was so completely unlike her, and Josh knew she must have seen the dread on his face. But she hadn't asked what was wrong. Just like he couldn't seem to bring himself to ask her the same. Something had shifted between them. It terrified him; the idea that he might lose her was something he couldn't stomach. He stared at the ceiling as nausea rose inside him. With his hand pressed to his stomach, he rolled off the bed, not sure if he had to run to the toilet or if he would be able to calm himself down. He heard the shower being turned on, but then he caught something that sounded like crying. Forgetting about his own unease, he rushed into the bathroom where he saw Bonny sitting on the floor inside the shower. She had drawn her legs up, her head lay on her knees, and she was wrecked by desperate sobs. The water raining down on her was steaming hot, but she didn't seem to notice.

He reached her in a heartbeat. When the water hit his arm, he hissed at the temperature and switched off the shower before falling onto his knees next to her. "Bonny, baby, what's wrong? Talk to me. Please, please talk to me."

"I'm so sorry! I don't know how... why... I'm sorry!"

Gently, Josh cupped her cheek and guided her face up. The tears streaming down her cheeks broke his heart. "You don't know how or why what, baby? You can tell me. You can tell me anything, you know that."

"But..."

"Anything. I promise I won't be mad. But we need to talk about what's going on. It's tearing us apart, and we don't even know why."

Bonny dragged in a ragged breath, but nodded at last. "Yes, I know. You're right. But..."

Josh crawled from her side to sitting in front of her, both of his hands now holding her face. "I love you. There's *nothing* you can say to change that."

Another small nod. Then Bonny drew in a huge breath, and everything spilled out of her. "Yesterday was so much fun. And we didn't even do a lot. We just talked. It was great to meet Ben and his sister. And he's a great guy. So nice, and he cares so much. We all got along so well. And then you and I had dinner, and we still kept talking about him. Because, yeah, we just spent the afternoon with him, and he's somebody we just met, so that's normal, I guess. But we both seemed to like him so much. And I love you, Josh, I really, really do! I swear I love you! And I love sleeping with you. Last night was as amazing as it always is! But... oh god... but when we both came..." Bonny's voice trembled, and the next part came out almost a whisper. "I... I had this image in my head of Ben being there with us, kissing us, both of us, enjoying our usual post-sex cuddles with us like he had been there the whole time. And the worst part was, I liked that image. It felt like he belonged there with us." She shook her head, seemingly disgusted with herself. "God, I'm a terrible person. I woke up a million times tonight and I felt so guilty; I still do. What kind of girlfriend who loves her boyfriend with all her heart thinks such things?"

Josh studied her for a long moment, his thumbs brushing tears from her face. Finally, he leaned in to press his lips to hers.

When he had her full attention, he gathered his courage and told her, "The kind of girlfriend whose boyfriend dreamed almost the exact same thing. This morning, I woke up from a dream in which I was making love to you. But Ben was there, too. He was touching us, and he was kissing me. Believe me, it's not just you feeling guilty. I have never thought about anybody this way since we've become a couple. I love you so much, Bonny, I really do. But you're not the only one who seems to be drawn to him. Because, yeah, in my dream, it also felt right to have him with us, and it felt like more than a crazy one-night stand. So, first of all, thank you for telling me, for being honest. I don't know about you, but for me it kinda helps to know I'm not alone in this."

Bonny was completely stunned. Had Josh seriously just told her that? Were they both really interested in somebody else? The same person on top of that? Her mind was racing with all kinds of questions until she realized she had been staring at Josh and hadn't said anything to him about his revelation. "Uh, yeah, you're right, it helps knowing it's not just me. But what do we do now?"

"Now we order breakfast from room service because I think we need some privacy, and then I would say we have a lot to talk about."

Chapter Eight

Today promised to be... interesting? Weird? Benicio had no idea. He only knew he had fallen asleep to some very intriguing fantasies involving Bonny and Josh. He probably should have felt bad about that. They had been kind to him and were interesting people. Lusting after them wasn't a nice thing to do. And it had surprised him that he obviously saw both of them that way. Generally, he wasn't interested in more than one person at a time. Perhaps it was because these two were so close, a unit: they complemented each other.

He would have to do his best not to be obvious about his interest. From what he had learned so far, they were open-minded people, so they probably wouldn't freak out. But they probably wouldn't appreciate it either, and he didn't want to make things awkward between them.

He would be friendly and enjoy their company throughout the day while keeping an eye on his sister. And maybe, once he knew Valeria was safe in her room, he would just head out to a nearby club and look for somebody to hook up with. He had been single for too long, too busy to find somebody to date – no wonder he was seeing Bonny and Josh this way.

It was just his luck that his sister was working the hotel's beach rental stall today. Yesterday, they had been preoccupied with getting to know each other and talking for hours, so none of them had been in the pool. He doubted this would last for another day. The weather report promised another sunny day, and Bonny and Josh were on a vacation that had been a long time coming. Surely, they would want to go for a swim in the ocean or rent paddle boards or a jet ski. He would just ignore seeing them shed the shirts they had kept on the day before. There were enough other pretty people around, and he wasn't bothered by that either. How bad could it be?

It looked like he was about to find out when he saw the couple strolling towards him, hand in hand and smiling a little later. They looked around the beach, which was framed by large rock formations on both sides. Loungers and parasols were spread in clusters, and to the right were a small hut where hotel guests could rent all kinds of equipment, and a second, even smaller kiosk for booking of activities. From the look on their faces, they liked what they saw. The beach was secluded and belonged to the hotel. Yet, with the natural borders, it didn't make you feel like you were fenced in.

After greeting them, he showed them to some loungers he had reserved for all three of them, close enough to the rental hut to see his sister but not so close that he'd smother her. She had been very clear about what she would allow during their dinner the previous evening.

When Bonny was pulling the beach dress she was wearing over her bikini up and over her head, Ben cursed internally. *¡Wey, no mames! I'm fucked. She's gorgeous.* She wore a bright bikini, the color hitting somewhere between pink and orange, with a pattern of gold circles shimmering in the sun. It was a perfect contrast to her dark skin, and the cups gave her breasts just a little lift.

He must have been staring, because he heard a chuckle next to him. *Fuck!* "I, ah..." Ben felt the color rise on his cheeks.

But Josh just shrugged, a smirk dancing around his mouth. "It's okay. She *is* beautiful. You're not the first to notice."

Ben turned to him, not believing what he heard. "And you don't care?"

"Why would I? As long as people don't get creepy, neither she nor I mind. Plus, I know my girlfriend." There was a tiny pause, then Josh added, "She wouldn't do anything I wouldn't do, too." He gave Ben a wink, then pulled off his own t-shirt, revealing his light skin and a breathtaking tattoo covering his chest. It looked like ripped skin with the red and black parts of a Spider-Man suit beneath it peeking through, the spider emblem set right in the middle over his sternum. The 3D effect was done perfectly, and the lightly pink edges made it look incredibly real, like the torn skin was fresh.

"Oh my god, that's amazing," Benicio whispered. Before he knew what he was doing, he reached out and ran his fingertips over the ink. After a second or two, he came to his senses and quickly drew back his hand like he had been burned. "Shit, I'm sorry."

When he looked up to see how badly he had screwed up, Ben found Josh watching him intently, his pupils wide, his lips parted. *What the hell?* A glance at Bonny only showed her looking at them with a serene smile on her face.

He shook his head, took a step back. "Guys, what's going on? What's happening here?"

Bonny focused her attention on him, then pointed at one of the loungers. "Have a seat. I think we should talk."

Once they were all seated, with Bonny and Josh sitting on one lounger facing Ben on another, Josh cleared his throat. "Okay, I'll just put it out there, and then you can decide what to do with it. So... Bonny and I had an interesting morning. When we woke up this morning, something was off between us. We were both quiet, distracted. But we didn't talk. That's not us. We talk about everything, and we're completely honest with each other. We were getting ready for breakfast when I heard her cry in the shower." Josh took Bonny's hand and interlaced their fingers. "That's when we knew we had to talk about what was bothering us."

Now, Bonny took over their explanation. "It turned out we were both feeling incredibly guilty. I'm sorry if this is too personal, but you need to know to understand." She told Benicio about the night before, their lovemaking, and about the morning and Josh confessing his dream.

Ben's mind was reeling, but he kept quiet, letting them finish.

When she stopped, Josh nodded. "Yeah... When we realized we are both interested in you, it was a shock at first. But then we kept talking.

"Here's the thing: we know ourselves. We know when something feels right to us. When we got together, it was easy. It was easy, because we talked, but also because we recognized what was right for us and acted on it. You said you read my brother's book about my family."

Ben only nodded in agreement, not knowing where Josh was going with this.

"Well, our families trusted my brother and Scarlette to know themselves, too. Nobody in our inner circle said they made a mistake getting married so soon, changing their lives like that. Only strangers called them crazy and thought they'd get divorced sooner rather than later. They haven't yet, and they won't. Their story, the stories of their friends Luke and July, and Michelle and Leroy have taught me an important lesson: fuck what other people think. As long as you truly know yourself, you also know what's right for you. And then it doesn't matter how long you've known another person. If you fit, you fit. And apparently, it also doesn't matter if it's more than one person.

"Yes, I will admit, Bonny and I never expected we could be interested in anybody else. But we are. You captivate us, Ben. We have no clue where this could go, whether it would only be some holiday fun or if we could build something together. We'd have to figure that out. But while we were talking this morning, we realized we both thought we had seen you glancing at each of us yesterday, too. So we thought, today, we would pay more attention. And if you kept looking, we were thinking about flirting with you, see how you'd react to that. Then I saw you watching Bonny, then you touched me, and we knew we needed to let you know right away." Josh took a deep breath. "And that's a whole lot of rambling to tell you we both think you're amazing, and gorgeous, and we want you. We want you in bed, but we would also love to get to know you better, see if there's potential for more."

"We understand that this is a surprise. And you don't need to answer us right now. Hell, you don't owe us any answer at all. You can just tell us to go, and we won't bother you any longer. We'll still keep an eye on your sister to make sure she's safe, no matter what. But there's no pressure on you to say or do anything," Bonny finished their admission.

Benicio was stunned. He looked from one to the other while he was going over everything they had just said. Thoughts raced through his mind. *Are they serious? Do they really want me? Can we make this work? Did I really check them out yesterday already, without even realizing it? I totally did, didn't I?* It suddenly hit him that, not once did he think this was crazy. Not for one moment was he thinking about how to tell them no — because he didn't want to.

It seemed like it was his time to tell the truth. "Thank you for being honest with me. So... yes, I think you're right, I probably looked at you yesterday already, although I wasn't aware of doing it. But I know that I definitely was thinking about you, both of you, when I was lying in bed trying to fall asleep. You both are very distracting, let me tell you that."

He knew it had been the right thing to say when he saw them visibly relax. "I can say I have also never been in the situation where I'm interested in more than one person at the same time. And it is interest. At first, I thought it was only attraction, because, yeah, you both are stunning. But that's not all. I want to talk to you for hours like we did yesterday; I want to know what makes you sad, and what makes you smile. I want to know your favorite dishes. And yes, I also want to be intimate with you. You said I captivated you, Josh. Believe me, you both do the same to me. So, I guess, what I'm saying is, I would love to give this a shot. But I think you're right, we have a lot of things to figure out."

Bonny and Josh nodded and she asked, "So, where do we go from here?"

Chapter Nine

That was the million-dollar question, wasn't it? Josh knew what he would like to do, but he had no idea what Ben would be comfortable with. Communicating had brought them this far, so he decided to stick with that. "I would love to kiss you. Both of you. But I don't know if you want your sister to see that, Ben," he told them and moved one foot over to Ben's, gently nudging him. Warmth flowed through Josh when a smile spread on Ben's face upon the contact.

"I would like that. But while I usually don't have a problem with my sister seeing whom I kiss, I would like to keep our first kiss a little more private. I get the feeling we might get carried away, and that won't be something she wants to see, nor would it be appropriate for the beach with all the other guests around. If you don't mind, let's wait a little longer. Her break is coming up in a few minutes, and she told me yesterday she'd just sit here with her two colleagues and eat a snack. She will be fine then. And we can walk down the beach and go behind that rock formation. That part of the beach doesn't belong to the hotel; there shouldn't be any people around. Let's see how we feel after the kiss, and if we all are still willing to try this, then I don't care if we show each other some affection when we're in public. I will just let Valeria know not to tell our mother right away. For that, I would first like to see where things are going. Would that be okay?" Ben asked.

It sounded like a good compromise, so Bonny and Josh agreed happily. "Perfect. You two wait here, I'll be back in a minute. I wanted to try out parasailing today. I'll go book something for the afternoon," Bonny said and left the men alone when she strolled over to the booth next to the rental kiosk.

"Don't you want to do that with her, Josh?"

"Not today. I have that planned for later. I was doing our regular self-defense training with Bonny last week and I missed a block. Her kick hit me in the ribs. It's not too bad or anything, but I wanted to avoid the harness for a few more days."

An image of Josh in a different kind of harness popped up in Ben's mind, and he inhaled sharply. Josh smirked and playfully swatted his knee. "I know exactly what you were just thinking of."

"Can you blame me?" Ben's eyes gleamed with excitement, a grin on his face.

"No. And I can tell you, even though Bonny and I are not part of the BDSM scene or anything, we have a few toys, including some rope and a harness or two. They're more for the visual, but you could probably use them to restrain somebody, too. But like I said, it's all light stuff. Honestly, most of the things we have come from a gag gift from Scarlette."

Ben blinked a few times. "Your sister-in-law gives you sex toys as a present?"

"Well, the year Bonny and I turned twenty-one, she gave us an Advent calendar with toys. We were complaining about our coursework keeping us apart from each other, and she told us each to pick half of the toys, that maybe they would distract us when we miss the other. Or we could bring them with us to the university and vall each other during our lunch breaks."

"Do I wanna know what vall is?"

In that moment, Bonny came back to them and giggled. "Oh, you're already indoctrinating him? 'Vall' is something Josh and Scarlette came up with. It's short for 'video call.' I mean, if you check websites like *Urban Dictionary*, there are some other weird meanings for it, but what don't they have weird meanings for? And yes, at first, we all laughed at them. But I have to admit, over time it has spread, and many of our families and friends say it now."

Ben chuckled at that. "I can see how it would spread. Did you get your booking?"

"Yep. I'm scheduled for later this afternoon. And your sister just left for her break. She asked me to remind you that you are not supposed to interrupt her lunch break in any way," Bonny said with a wink. "So, can we go now?" She was clearly as eager as both men, and her smile got even wider when they stood up from their loungers.

For now, they all ambled along next to each other but refrained from touching. Even Bonny and Josh kept their distance, both feeling that if they wanted to do this right, they should wait until all three of them could connect. Now that they had talked, things had changed.

It wasn't a long walk, but by the time they finally turned around the corner of the rock formation, they were all buzzing with excitement. A quick look around confirmed that they were indeed alone. Then they turned to each other, and for a second, uncertainty surged through Benicio. "Are you both sure about this? Absolutely sure? I don't want to ruin anything for you, I don't want to come between you."

Bonny had been looking forward to this ever since she had seen the look Ben had given her when she had taken off her beach dress earlier. In that moment she knew where they would end up, and that it would be amazing. But she couldn't deny that she was also a bundle of nerves. She knew she wanted Ben, yes. But she had also never been with anybody other than Josh. He had been her first and only in so many ways. Her first kiss. Her first boyfriend. Her first lover. No matter how right this felt, it was still all new and a little scary. That was, until she heard Benicio ask them so sweetly, showing how much he already cared.

It untwisted the small knot inside her, and she reached up, gently putting her hand on his cheek. "We're sure." Then she turned him around so he would face Josh and stood behind him. "And we very much want you between us. Now, kiss him, so you can kiss me after."

Oh god, this is really happening, Josh thought nervously. He knew he and Bonny were feeling the same about this. They were both equally nervous and thrilled. He had gotten a lot better when it came to overthinking. But this was huge. *And I want it.* He was sure about that.

He felt the sand under his feet shift when he leaned closer to Benicio to let his fingertips run along the short beard. Dark like Benicio's hair but styled almost exactly like Josh's. It was different from Bonny's soft skin, but by no means unpleasant. Slowly, he ran his hand around Ben's neck. He felt Ben's hand landing on his hip, gently tugging him closer.

And then their lips met. A shock ran through Josh's whole body. He was truly kissing somebody other than Bonny. *And it doesn't feel wrong.* In the back of his mind, he had been terrified that after all his talk and after thinking he knew what he wanted, he would end up feeling terrible, like he was betraying Bonny. But that wasn't the case. He opened an eye and saw Bonny looking at them with awe in her eyes. Yes, she was all right with this. And knowing her, Josh knew she wouldn't mind if he dragged this out a little longer.

He slowly opened his mouth, his lips catching on some stubble and adding a new thrill to the kiss. And when he felt Ben's tongue meeting his own, when he tasted him for the first time, he groaned. The kiss wasn't rough, not even all that different from kissing Bonny in terms of mechanics; both men found their rhythm instinctively. But other things were different. Instead of soft curves meeting his chest, he felt a hard plane, felt arms with a sharper edge to the muscles enveloping him. Those parts were different – and utterly glorious. Josh groaned again, digging his fingers into Ben's back and hair.

"God, you two are hot together," Bonny panted next to them.

It broke their spell, and Ben playfully nipped on Josh's bottom lip before turning to her and dragging her to him. His mouth closed over hers, and Bonny moaned into the kiss. For a second, it was the strangest feeling to kiss somebody else. But then Bonny tasted Ben, and her mind blanked the same way it always did when she kissed Josh. She had worried that she might feel jealous seeing Josh and Benicio kiss, but there had not been even the tiniest spark of jealousy. All she could think about was how amazing they looked together. Given the approving grumble she heard from Josh, she was sure it was the same for him.

Both Ben and Bonny felt a hand on their waists, guiding them into a slightly different position. And then suddenly Josh joined their kiss. It was like nothing any of them had ever experienced. Three pairs of lips caressing each other, three tongues meeting, their unique flavors coming together in an intoxicating mix. They took and took, until they eventually broke apart panting, in desperate need of air.

Bonny and Josh shared one glance. It was all it took to know they had felt the same thing. Each of them laid a hand on Ben's cheeks, looking him in the eyes, and Josh told him, "You're ours. It will be a pain in the ass, we will likely get a lot of shit, and we have a ton of things to figure out. But you are ours, Benicio. You need to know: nothing has ever felt so damn right before than kissing you two. I love Bonny with all my heart, and I never felt like I missed something. But this was something else. It completed me, completed *us* in ways we couldn't even imagine before."

He drew in a sharp breath and stared at them. "Are you sure? How do you know this is not just lust talking?"

Bonny sweetly laid her lips on his, then drew back to look him in the eyes once more. "We are sure. And yes, there's a lot of lust running through all of us. But I can tell you why *we* know: because our first real kiss on our class trip all those years ago felt exactly like this. Like a promise. Like coming home. If you tell us you want us, too, that you felt something even remotely similar, then we're yours, too."

"God, yes. I can't explain why, but I start to understand what you mean by knowing when things feel right. I have never felt like this when kissing anybody else, no matter how turned on I was. There's more than lust to it when I kiss you both. A want, a need for more, but not just something physical."

"Then we're gonna make this work, baby," Josh said and leaned in for another small kiss.

All Benicio could do was nod and huff out a happy sigh.

Unfortunately, they had other plans for the rest of the afternoon than hiding from everybody to make out. "I hate to say it, but I think your sister's break is almost over, babe. If you want to keep an eye on her when she's manning the hut alone, we'll have to go back," Bonny said.

Ben nodded, his fingers trailing through her mass of dark, soft curls. "*Sí*, you're right. So, we are all okay with this, yes?"

Both Bonny and Josh nodded in agreement.

"Then, does that mean I can hold both your hands on the way back? Can I kiss both of you even in front of people?"

Josh studied him for a long moment, then took his face in his hands. "Of course. We don't care if people are weirded out. If they have a problem, they can just look away. If they come up with stupid comments, we'll just ignore them," Josh shrugged, then continued, "we'll just behave like any other couple. I don't have to make out with you in public to the point where we almost rip our clothes off – I never do that with Bonny, either. But holding hands? A kiss? Of course, that's okay for us. Is that okay for you, too?"

"*Sí*, yes, yes, that's very okay for me."

"Perfect," Bonny chipped in. "Then let's go."

When they came back to the part of the beach belonging to the hotel, all holding hands and cheerfully discussing dinner plans, they were aware of a few glances, though most of them seemed to stem from curiosity. And the one or two unhappy people huffed and turned around, apparently deciding that their beach tan was more important than stirring up trouble.

Of course, Valeria wasn't blind, and Ben's phone pinged with a text from her before they had even gotten to their loungers. "Val ordered me to come to her and explain what's going on. No surprise there," he told Bonny and Josh.

"Want us to come with you?" Josh asked and ran his thumb over the back of Ben's hand.

"No, not right now. I will talk to her first. Perhaps all four of us can have dinner together tonight, though. That way, you will have a chance to get to know her as well."

"Excellent idea. Go, then," Bonny said and gave him a quick peck on the lips.

Josh drew him in for a quick kiss as well, then pulled Bonny down to one of the loungers that they had reached by then. Benicio left them with a last look and a smile, maybe still a little bit in shock but with a feeling of lightness suffusing him. Val would likely declare him insane but right that moment, he couldn't care less. He was glad that she was currently working, though. It might stop her from yelling at him. Perhaps.

Oh, she wasn't yelling. But that didn't stop her from hissing a tirade filled with colorful curses in Spanish at him. "Have you lost your mind? What the hell is going on? Tell me I didn't see what I think I did. Did you seriously just come walking down that beach holding both their hands? Did you really kiss them both? What are you doing? You met these people *yesterday*, Ben!"

Benicio scratched his neck, a sigh escaping him. This was very much what he had been expecting. But even just the memory of kissing Bonny and Josh, and especially that three-way kiss they had shared only a few minutes ago, had him straighten his back and look at his sister seriously. "Yes, Val, I am well aware of when I met them," he replied, also in Spanish. "But yes, you saw exactly that. There's something about them, I can't explain it."

"I can explain that: it's called thinking with your dick," Valeria told her brother with a smirk. It seemed she began to come around and see the humor in it and had found a way to tease him, probably thinking he was only talking about an easy summer fling. It made Ben chuckle.

"Sure, I want them, I'm not denying that. But it's more. I want to get to know them, I want to spend time with them."

Now Val observed Ben with a serious expression, concern shimmering in her eyes. "And then what? They're from the US, yes? I don't want to see you get your heart broken. I don't know them, but Ben, what are you to them? Did you talk about what this is? Are you some fun distraction, a vacation fling, something they can't have at home?"

His sister could be a pain, but she had her sweet moments, too. "No, that's not it. Look, I still have a lot to talk about with them, I know that. So far? We have told each other that we're interested in each other, that we want to spend our time here together, and for now just see how things develop. We shared a kiss. Separately, at first. Then all three of us. And it was mind-blowing, Val. I will admit to that. It felt like no kiss I had before, but not just because they're both so hot."

His sister snickered and leaned her arms on the counter, looking over to Bonny and Josh on the lounger quietly talking and cuddling with each other. "I'll give you that: the guy is hot, yes. And that tat is epic." She sighed heavily. "I guess you're old enough to know what you're doing. Go have fun, then. Just... don't get hurt, okay?"

"I won't. You are a good sister," Ben ended their discussion and gave her a kiss on the cheek. Before he left, he asked her to join them for dinner, but she declined for that evening since there was a team dinner scheduled.

He strolled back to Bonny and Josh, warmth flowing through him when they smiled at him. *This is crazy. I don't even know them. How can they make me this happy already? But that kiss...*

Some of his thoughts must've shown on his face because they both sat up and made room between them.

"Come, sit here," Bonny said and patted the lounger they were sharing.

"What happened? Did your sister not take it well?" The concern was clear in Josh's voice.

Benicio shook his head. "No, that's not it. I mean, she was a little shocked at first. But she started teasing me soon enough. She just pointed out that I only met you yesterday and what this was supposed to be. And then I came back here, and you smiled at me, and I was a little shocked how happy that made me. I mean, she's right. We only just met. How can that be?"

Beside him, Josh nodded in understanding and took his time formulating an answer. "I hear what you're saying. It sounds unbelievable, I know that. But believe me, you're not alone. We're happy to have found you, too. Let me tell you something that my brother didn't state that plainly in his book, even though he also didn't exactly make it a secret. He and Scarlette? They met in a bar, talked for a while, and then all they planned was to have a fun one-night stand. He didn't go into detail, thank god, but that's what they did. Have some fun. Then Scarlette left. They didn't exchange numbers or anything. And they both cursed themselves the next morning when they couldn't find the other. Something had clicked for them, and when they met again, they concluded that it would be better to try and see where things would go rather than regret later not giving it a chance at all. None of them was ever the person to believe in love at first sight, but they knew things were different between them than with others before." Josh threaded his fingers with Benicio's. "And their friends? They recognized that the same thing happened to them, too. July and Luke were both unlucky when it came to dating. But when they met, it just worked for them. Leroy and Michelle, too. I know it seems so unlikely that something like that can happen..."

Bonny picked up Josh's thought. "You know, we're told so often that we can't 'just know' when we meet the right person. Society now tells everybody, especially women, but it's pretty much the same for guys, that something like love at first sight doesn't exist, that you can't just know somebody fits you just like that. There are no movies or books like that anymore. We are taught that it takes countless dates, maybe a background check, vetting by friends and social media and who knows what to just 'be allowed' to call somebody your boyfriend or girlfriend. We're told to be wary of our own judgment. But tell me, how are your friends or anybody else able to tell you whether you fit with somebody you met? They don't know your feelings or what your instincts tell you.

"And the paradoxical thing is that, at the same time, we're told that 'the right' relationship just works and takes no work or anything. So people dump each other all the time because they think it can't be right if they come to a point where they might have to compromise in a relationship. It's terrible, but for me it sometimes feels like fast fashion. It's cheap, so it doesn't matter if you throw it away. Same for a relationship: it's not been going on for long, you were careful not to get too involved, which makes it easy to break things off. I'm not saying *dating* has gotten easy – but finding a person to meet has. There's always somebody on an app you can meet up with. And with that rush – and the input, sometimes from complete strangers online – people have stopped listening to their own hearts. So, when somebody does and recognizes a connection and goes with it, they think that can't be, and they tell that person it's not real." Bonny took Benicio's other hand before she went on. "And yes, it's something even fewer people understand when it comes to poly relationships. Look, I'm not declaring my undying love to you right now, and neither is Josh. But we both think it's worth trusting our gut over the opinions of others. Which is something many people have forgotten how to, or are too afraid to, do. It's just easier for us to do because we've seen the positive outcomes more than once; that's why we're ready so quickly to see if this can be more than a crush."

Benicio considered their arguments for a moment. "Hmm, I think you both make valid points. And even without them... Yes, it sounds like something that's not 'normal' anymore, but I look at both of you, and I cannot deny how you make me smile and how much I want to be with you. It's that simple. A little terrifying because I've never experienced something like it before, but nothing I want to turn away from."

Josh broke into a bright smile and leaned into Ben. "Perfect. Then get comfy with us. We'll probably have to push the loungers together, though. They're not made for three people."

Bonny checked her watch, then looked at the guys. "Take your time with that. The two of you can share one. I'm off for now. It's time for me to meet the guy for parasailing."

"Okay. Oh, uh... One thing before you leave, baby," Josh stopped her.

"Sure, what is it?"

"How do we wanna handle things between the three of us when one person isn't there? Things like kissing and more?"

Bonny cocked her head and studied them. "Good question. So, for me, it would be okay if we kiss, hold hands, cuddle a little, or tease the others a bit, even if one of us isn't there. When it comes to more, I would say the first time we really have sex, it should be the three of us. If it feels like the kiss and just like this after, like all three of us belong together, then I don't think I'll care if we're all together or if it's just two of us, no matter who. What do you two think?"

Both men nodded, and Ben gave her a kiss. "Sounds perfect. And I agree, the first time we sleep with each other should definitely be the three of us. I can't wait to get you both in bed," he told her with a grin.

Bonny grumbled. "Not fair with your sister working for a few more hours."

"Sorry." But the glint in his eyes told an entirely different story.

"Yeah, I don't believe that." But she grinned at him, too. "Make him pay, Josh. Okay, I'm off now. I'm gonna go flying," she said and jumped up and vanished.

Benicio looked from her retreating back to Josh. "You sure you don't want to go with her? I can keep an eye on Val."

"Nah, all good. She'll need to get ready and everything. I'll just walk to the water once they're good to go and film it then."

"Okay."

"And until then, I get to punish you," Josh told Ben with far too much glee in his voice for Ben's taste.

He narrowed his eyes. "What are you up to?"

"Me? Nothing. *You* will be doing the work. Here," Josh said and reached into the bag Bonny had brought along and pulled out a bottle of sunscreen. "You should totally help me, you don't want me to get a sunburn, do you?" Mischief was written all over his face when he flopped onto his belly on the lounger and looked at Ben over his shoulder.

"Weren't you supposed to be shy?" Ben asked with a laugh as he opened the bottle and squeezed some lotion into his hand.

He had to give it to Josh: it was a special kind of torture. After warming the lotion in his hands, Ben began spreading it on Josh's back in gentle circles. He felt Josh inhale sharply, then go pliant under his hands. Ben's fingers began trailing the outlines of Josh's shoulder blades, then carefully massaged his neck before wandering down along his spine. As he got farther down, Josh's breath quickened, his muscles tightened.

Ben could imagine all too well what he would do if they were alone and not on a public beach. *He could picture his hands sliding even farther down, his lips following the path.*

Shorts would be pulled off, revealing the enticing flesh beneath. Then he would slowly run a finger between...

Yeah, that did it. The smell of a hot summer day, the ocean, and sunscreen would now cement itself in his mind as an aphrodisiac. And going by the barely audible moan from Josh, Ben wasn't alone.

Then he figured two could play. Josh had pushed him this far; now it was Ben's turn. And it would help hide the fact that his blood had already rushed south. Moving from sitting on the edge of the lounger, he straddled Josh's thighs, his hands gliding up again. When he leaned forward and his hard length settled between Josh's butt cheeks – the perfect position to discreetly slide up and down to create some delicious friction while he kept rubbing the sunscreen into Josh's back – Josh groaned beneath him, a little louder now, his hands grabbing the edges of the lounger.

Ben leaned forward and whispered into his ear, "Relax, *bebé*. Just imagine how amazing it will be tonight without all these pesky clothes in the way."

Josh gasped, his knuckles turning white where he held on to the lounger. Yes, he could absolutely imagine that. And the images in Josh's mind were glorious. "Oh god..."

After a glimpse over his shoulder, Ben figured he had tortured them both enough. He pressed a kiss between Josh's shoulder blades and smiled when he could feel a shiver run through Josh. "I think Bonny will be up in in the air a few minutes."

"Huh?"

Chuckling, Ben got up from Josh's legs and lay down on the lounger next to them, also on his belly. "You wanted to film her parasailing, right?"

"Yeah." Josh took a few calming breaths. Who would've

thought Benicio was such a damn tease? "Yeah, okay. Well played. I need a minute."

"You know, just think..."

It was as far as Ben got before Josh clamped his hand over his mouth with a chuckle. "No more putting pictures in my head." After a few more deep breaths, he grabbed his phone and got up. "I'll be back soon."

Josh focused on the hot sand under his feet just so he would stop himself from remembering Ben sitting on top of him, his hands exploring him, and the proof of how much he wanted Josh pressed... Yeah, better not go there with so many people around.

Were they crazy? Perhaps people on the outside would think so. But for Josh, nothing had felt so perfect since the day on that class trip back in high school...

He and Bonny had been talking more and more in the previous days, and she had given him a peck on the lips a few times before. But that evening, they had stolen some time away from their classmates and were planning an actual date for when they were back home. Then one of her friends had called her. But before she had left, she had taken his face in her hands and pulled him closer. The kiss had been soft and sweet at first, but they had quickly begun to explore each other, tasting each other, like the eager teenagers they had been. Nothing more; they had stopped at the kiss. But it had been enough for Josh to know he could fall for her.

And fallen he had. Back then, he had noticed other girls, yes, found them cute. But he had never had a huge crush on anybody before her. With Bonny, though, he was almost desperate to see her, to be near her. And it hadn't only been teenage lust. He and Ty had talked a bit, and his brother had told him the first girl he slept with might not rock his world. That it might be good, but once he found the right woman – like Ty had with Scarlette – there would be a deep connection. The first time Josh and Bonny had made love in her treehouse, he had known exactly what his brother had been talking about. Ever since, Bonny had been his everything.

Yes, it was this unexplainable thing to others. You had to experience it to even believe in it. But Josh was a hundred percent sure of what he felt, of what he had felt even back then. And he knew he and Bonny had found this amazing connection once again with Ben.

He understood why it was harder for Benicio to simply accept it, because it hadn't happened to him before. But Josh wasn't worried. When he saw the way Ben looked at them, when he felt the way he touched him, kissed him... Damn, he needed to stop thinking about this, at least until the three of them were alone.

Seeing his girlfriend in her bikini smiling brightly when he reached the shore did not help. He had meant it with every fiber of his being when he had said to Ben she was beautiful. And it was more than just her looks. Oh, she was gorgeous, no doubt about it. But she was incredibly smart, and there was a kindness shining from within that added to her whole being. He knew she could be all rational and make tough decisions. But she also always saw the people who were impacted by said decisions. She looked further than just the next paycheck or quarterly report, and she made sure everybody understood why she was doing something. He knew she also would make sure everybody in their family's company – of course it was their family, she was an important part of it, whether they were married or not –

would be taken care of. It had been the easiest decision he, Scarlette and Ty had ever made when they'd offered Bonny the chance to take over running the company. Yes, she had just graduated, and she wouldn't take it on all at once. But she would work with Scarlette and Ty (since they were currently doing most of it) and their advisors so she would learn the ins and outs until she would finally be the one taking the reins. Mentally, he chuckled over the unintended pun. His family did run a winery but also a racehorse breeding business, after all.

When she spotted him, Bonny waved over to him but then focused again on the guy giving her some last instructions. Josh took a few pictures, and just before she was lifting off the ground he switched to record a video. He grinned when he captured her excited squeal, her happy laughter. From his vantage point, he could see her mouthing something that might have been "This is awesome" but the noise of the boat canceled out most of her voice, and even for the rest she was too far away to actually hear anything. What he was sure of, though, was that she enjoyed every second of it. The grin never left her face, and when she touched the ground again she erupted in a bright laugh. God, he loved her and would do everything to keep her this happy for the rest of their lives. And he had the feeling a big part of that happiness in the future would be connected to the man back on the beach waiting for them.

He stayed put until Bonny came over, and they strolled back hand in hand.

The rest of their afternoon was filled with Bonny telling them how much she had enjoyed parasailing and, for once, doing a lot of nothing. They pushed the loungers together and were all lying close together, trading soft kisses, and dozing in the sun but always keeping an eye on the rental stall until it was dinner time.

Chapter Ten

At the end of Valeria's shift, all three of them would've walked with her but she was being picked up by a colleague. It relaxed Ben, and he let her go alone. And even if they wouldn't admit it, it also calmed Bonny's and Josh's nerves. They knew what they wanted – but they would feel a bit more settled to have one more evening with just Benicio before they were interrogated by a family member.

Unwillingly, they had parted ways before dinner to get changed. But beachwear wasn't exactly restaurant attire. And once they laid eyes on each other again, they knew it had been worth it. Ben stared at them when they met in front of one of the hotel's restaurants, his eyes roaming over them. Bonny wore a long, floating green dress made from a light fabric. Josh had opted to go with black jeans and a burgundy-colored dress shirt, of which he had left the first button open. After a compliment, Bonny only thought Ben looked just as great. He had chosen some dark-blue jeans and a white dress shirt but had rolled up the sleeves.

Josh had one hand at the small of Bonny's back, the other trailed up Ben's forearm. His stomach chose that moment to remind them why they were here. "Damn. I was tempted to say 'Let's skip dinner' but I think something to eat would be good."

Ben smiled and pressed a kiss first to his then Bonny's mouth. "It would be. You'll need your strength later tonight."

Josh exploded into a coughing fit, which made Bonny laugh. "Oh my god, we're gonna have so much fun. Come on, guys, let's eat."

And while dinner had indeed been fun, it was getting into Bonny's and Josh's bungalow that they were all really looking forward to. Bonny walked between the guys, Ben's hand running up and down her back, Josh holding one of her hands. The air was still warm but heavy with humidity now – the weather report promised rain for the next day – and the sweet fragrance of tropical flowers surrounded them. Combined with the attention of two stunning men focused on her, it was a heady feeling.

It wasn't a long walk, and Bonny expected to feel a little nervous given that this was something they had never done. But any nerves dissipated when Josh drew her in once they were in their room and kissed her lovingly while Benicio sweetly laid his lips on her shoulder. This was heaven. She sighed and lifted one hand to cup Josh's cheek. Her other arm reached back, running around Ben's neck and holding him in place. Both men stepped even closer to her, and she felt their hands roam over her body. Slowly, carefully, they maneuvered her toward the bedroom.

There, Josh gently pulled on the ribbon holding her dress in place. When he tugged it free, and her dress fell open, she heard both men draw in a sharp breath and knew she had chosen wisely. Josh hadn't seen her lingerie when she had gotten dressed earlier, but she knew this was one of his favorites on her. It was an ivory-colored strapless bra partially covered in black lace with small pearl highlights, and she wore it with a pair of panties that completed the set. Behind her, Ben drew the dress away from her shoulders, then leaned in again and whispered in her ear, "You are incredibly beautiful."

Her head fell back onto his shoulder, her eyes closed. She knew the hands tracing the swell of her breasts belonged to Josh; she knew the feel of them by heart. She shivered when those hands wandered down her ribs, then followed the seam of her panties.

She would have complained about Josh's hands leaving her skin, but she stayed quiet when she saw him unbuttoning his shirt. Both she and Ben observed him, heat crawling through them with every button Josh undid. Bonny could feel her own pulse deep inside her and knew she was already wet. Then she realized Ben's hands were hardly moving, like he wasn't sure where he was allowed to put them. She wiggled back, her butt pressing against his hardness. So he *was* enjoying this. She would just have to show him that everything he wanted to do with them was okay. She grabbed one of his hands and leisurely guided it over her stomach, then further down, her fingers covering his and pressing them between her legs. "Touch me."

A deep groan reached her ear, and then Ben's mouth landed on her shoulder again, his teeth gently biting her while he began to rub a finger over her still-covered clitoris. Bonny moaned, and a second later she heard Josh do the same. When her eyes managed to focus on him, she saw he had shed his shirt and was running a hand over the bulge in his jeans. She indulged herself in Ben's touch for a moment longer, but then took a slow step away from him. Looking from one to the other, she told them, "You both need to get out of your clothes," and proceeded to climb on the bed.

Sitting on her knees and facing them, she reached behind herself and unclasped her bra. She carelessly threw it off the bed before settling back against the pillows and oh so slowly pulling off her panties. Josh and Benicio were entirely under her spell, and her laughter flowed through the room when she saw them staring at her – both completely motionless, only breathing rapidly. "Move! I wanna see you both, too."

Josh knew Bonny inside and out, and yet she still could make him forget about everything. But her demand got through, and he looked over to Ben, who was still drinking in the sight of the stunning woman on the bed. Josh could understand why, even more so when she ran her hand over one of her breasts, cupping it. She didn't have huge breasts, more a nice handful, and he wouldn't want her any other way. But she was right, Josh wanted to see more of Ben, too.

So he closed the distance between them and ran his hands up Ben's torso and began opening his shirt. "You heard her," Josh told him, his voice heavy with lust. In response, he was dragged down for a passionate kiss. Once the shirt was gone, Josh leaned further down, his lips and tongue exploring Ben's pecs for a moment before his fingers found Ben's jeans. At the same time, Ben's hands started to undo Josh's jeans. It ratcheted up his anticipation, and as soon as he had Ben's pants open, he decided he didn't want to draw this out any longer and pushed the jeans and the boxer briefs down his thighs at the same time. His fingers curled around Ben's length. He was rewarded with a huffed-out curse. "Fuck, Josh."

"You better catch up and get my pants off, too, or she's gonna kick our asses. God, you look amazing, baby."

A moment later, Josh's pants and underwear were pushed down as well, and he gasped at the hand enveloping him. "So do you, *bebé*."

From the bed came a hum full of approval. "You have no idea how stunning you two are together. Now come here, will you?"

The guys pushed their pants further down, but when Josh was about to pull Ben to the bed, the other man stopped him. "Wait, we need to discuss one thing. Well, probably two."

"Okay, what is it?" Josh was buzzing with excitement but he could see the seriousness in Ben's eyes.

"Well, one thing goes for all of us. That's the question of condoms. And then maybe more between me and you, do you have any preferences when it comes to topping or bottoming?"

Those were important questions, Ben was right. Josh pulled him to the edge of the bed and sat down with him while Bonny sat up straighter as well.

She was the first to answer. "So, when it comes to contraception, I can tell you I have an IUD. And Josh and I don't use condoms because we don't need them between just the two of us. But given the situation, it would probably be a good idea to use them until we've all been tested just to be safe regarding any STIs and so on."

Josh nodded. "Yes, Bonny is right. We both don't mind being tested and using condoms until then. When it comes to your second question, let me first make clear that neither Bonny nor I expect you to refrain from sleeping with her, which also means penetrative sex. We both want you; that includes pretty much all forms of sex in all combinations between the three of us that you are comfortable with. When we talk about my preferences specifically, I can tell you that I don't think I have any."

Ben drew his eyebrows up in question. "You don't think?"

"Well, you are the first guy I've ever been with. I've only ever been with Bonny, and she with me."

It was almost comical how huge Ben's eyes got. "What? You two have never..."

"No. We told you we've never been interested in anybody else. That didn't mean only romantically. We never played, we never invited anybody into our bed."

"Wow... I'm not sure whether I should be honored or terrified about the implications. But how come you think you don't have a preference, then? Aren't you kind of anxious?"

From the head of the bed, Bonny chuckled, and Josh leaned his shoulder against Ben's and grinned at him. "Pegging is a thing, you know," he told him with a wink. "So perhaps the more important question is: do *you* have a preference?"

To that, Ben shook his head. "No, when I'm with a guy, I'm vers; I very much enjoy both topping and bottoming."

"Nice, more ways for us to have fun. Now, tell us your opinion on the condom topic so we can get back to enjoying each other."

"Right. Um, I'm with you. Condoms until we get tested sounds good. I mean, you both are most likely okay, so I would say you don't need to use condoms between the two of you. And I usually use condoms, and even though I got the new HIV vaccine, I'm still using PrEP to be on the safe side. It's not like I'm constantly hooking up with people. But..."

Ben was rambling, and Josh took pity on him. "Hmm, maybe let's talk about that later. For now, we know you're safe, but we all agree to use condoms with you. Everything else we discuss after. Okay?"

Ben nodded. "Yeah, sounds good. Sorry for ruining the mood."

Josh and Bonny both shook their heads. "Never, ever apologize for wanting to keep us safe," Bonny told him.

Ben nodded. "Okay. I guess after what you told me, that means you don't have any condoms and lube here?"

Josh shrugged. "We've got lube, but no condoms. I think the care package in the bathroom has some, though."

"No, it's okay, I brought some." Ben bowed down to grab his pants from the floor and pulled a few foil packages from his back pocket.

"Good thinking," Josh told him and took his mouth. He could get lost in this man. But there was so much more fun to have. So he broke the kiss and pulled Ben further onto the bed with him.

They bracketed Bonny between them, their hands stroking her body. Her skin was almost fever-hot, and she was quivering under their fingers. Her breath quickened with every brush over her skin, and when Josh took Ben's hand and brought it between her legs again, then guided one of Ben's fingers inside her and gently pushed in one of his own, she arched up with her head thrown back into the pillows, gasping, "Oh god!"

Josh loved seeing her like this, lost in her own passion. Bringing her to this point together with Benicio? He couldn't even begin to describe how perfect it felt. His gaze caught Ben's, and they didn't need words to know what they both wanted. Leaning in, both of them brought their lips to Bonny's. Sharing another kiss between all three of them, the men captured her moans in their mouths. Their tongues tangled, and Josh got more desperate. They would have time to go slow soon, but this first time, he just needed to feel them both.

He broke the kiss and cupped Ben's face with one hand, the other still making Bonny crazy along Ben's. "Take her while I get myself ready for you."

Ben drew in a ragged breath while Bonny groaned at Josh's words. When he saw the question forming in Ben's mind, he nodded. "Don't ask. Yes, I'm sure. I want you to feel her. Once I'm ready, let me get inside her before you take me."

All Ben could do was nod in agreement – and hope he wouldn't explode from the images in his head alone. He gave Bonny another kiss and made his way between her legs while reaching for one of the condoms. Josh was sitting beside them, observing them with shallow breath and blindly rummaging in the nightstand next to him. He came up with a bottle of lube but threw it onto the bed for now, his eyes instead following every one of Ben's movements.

With the condom finally rolled over him, Ben leaned down on one arm and studied Bonny's face. "Are you sure, too?"

"Hell, yeah. Wanna feel you," she breathed out.

Ben took a deep breath. *This is real. I never imagined something like this.* He completely lost track of his thoughts when he slowly slid inside Bonny for the first time. Her heat surrounded him, and he groaned when she clamped around him with a deep moan. *God, she's so hot, so wet.* He pushed further into her, then withdrew a little only to slide back inside. And all the time, her eyes were locked with his. One of her hands had found Josh's, though, and she intertwined their fingers, bringing him into the moment with them. Ben already didn't think anything could top being with them. But when Bonny started to move her hips, meeting him thrust for thrust, it only got better.

Ben was aware of Josh next to them lazily stroking himself, watching them for another moment. Bonny stopped him, though, and turned her head to the side to take his length into her mouth. It was a glorious sight, her dark lips closing around full, hot flesh. Her moan was evidence of how much she enjoyed herself. It didn't take long to feel her contract around him. He had to focus to stop himself from coming with her. The visual of Josh reaching back and prepping himself absolutely did not help. Luckily for Ben, he wasn't the only desperate one.

Josh bit his lip hard to stop his climax. He had worked up to three fingers and hadn't touched his prostate on purpose. Seeing Ben sliding in and out of Bonny, his hands reaching out to knead her breasts, his lean muscles taut and covered in a fine sheen of sweat, was already driving Josh wild. Not to mention Bonny's hot mouth sucking him deep, her tongue playing with him. *I can't wait any longer.* "Baby, stop."

She let him go with a smile and the glazed eyes she always

had after an orgasm. Josh planned on giving her at least one more. He leaned down to kiss her before crawling closer to Benicio and taking his mouth as well. Josh ran his fingers through his dark hair and let his lips wander to Ben's neck, nibbling and lightly sucking. His nose teased the line beneath Ben's jaw, and Josh drew in a deep breath. "You smell so good. Will you take me now?"

"*Sí, sí, bebé.*"

They changed positions, and Josh leaned over Bonny. "Hey, baby. All good?"

"Uh-huh. Need you. Please!"

He had never been able to say no to her pleas. He slid deep inside her, feeling her heartbeat in her pulse all around his length. It was a feeling he knew and cherished – familiar, yet always exciting. Once he was seated, he stopped moving, though, and looked over his shoulder. There was no fear, no nervousness. He had told Ben he was used to pegging. He hadn't mentioned how much he loved it. So he repositioned himself a little, spreading his legs further, and nodded at Ben. After seeing him take a deep, calming breath, Josh felt Ben's tip pushing against his entrance. A bit more pressure and Ben entered him. It was a different feeling from a toy. Hotter. More texture. The knowledge that it belonged to Ben, that he got as much pleasure from this as Josh – that was mind-blowing. And as perfectly as Bonny did it, a toy didn't allow for easily adjusting the angle like Ben did now. Benicio easily slipped deeper inside Josh, and when he hit his prostate, Josh cursed in ecstasy. Josh knew it would be one of Ben's favorite things to do in the future, if his smug chuckle was anything to go by.

Finally, Ben was sheathed completely in Josh's body, and all three managed to look at each other. They were together. All of them, connected in a way they had never been with another person. It felt like so much more than sex. It felt completely and utterly right. It felt like... "Home. We're home," Bonny whispered, and both men nodded. It was the only way to describe what they were feeling in that moment. And when Ben's hand trailed up and down Josh's back and over to Bonny's thigh, and Ben stole himself a kiss, it was just like Josh's dream. It was perfection and had him close to tears from the wave of emotion swamping him.

Slowly, they began to move, to find their rhythm. Moments later, Josh eagerly worked himself between his lovers: sliding into Bonny, pushing himself back onto Ben, over and over. Passion swamped them, and none of them was able to think clearly. Instead, they let their bodies rule. Hot breath ghosted over skin, teeth nipped here and there, nails scratched along skin, leaving their marks.

It didn't take long until Bonny exploded beneath Josh again, screaming both her lovers' names and her body forming another tight arch, her muscles squeezing him inside her and dragging him over the edge with her. His climax had him clutching around Ben as well, and when he felt the throbbing of his hardness in the perfect spot, he yelled their names, too, just like Ben did with theirs.

All of them collapsed, barely conscious and blissed out. The guys were left with just enough thoughts to roll onto each side of Bonny once more so they wouldn't squash her beneath them.

Bonny wanted to focus on what she was feeling, wanted to take in every moment and commit it to memory. She wasn't sure it would happen; her mind was blank, and she felt like all the blood had left her brain.

Looking from Ben to Josh, she thought she wasn't the only one feeling like that. Then Ben stirred next to her, likely to take off the condom. And Bonny knew a trip to the bathroom would be good for her, too. She moved and followed him out of bed.

Behind them, Josh patted the empty space. "No, come back here."

"Babe, bathroom. And I was thinking about a quick shower with both of you," she told him. His head burrowed deeper into the pillow, and he groaned, decidedly unconvinced. *You look like I feel: like you have no bones left in your body.*

From behind her, Ben laid his chin on her shoulder. "Or did we wear you out, *arañita?*" he asked in a playful tone.

"Hmpf... Yeah, yeah, I'm coming. Wait, did you seriously just call me 'little spider?' You know I'm taller than you, right?"

Ben's only reply was a loud laugh as he took a quick step back when Josh tried to grab him.

A few minutes later, they were standing under the water. Their movements were a little more coordinated, but their minds were still caught in the rest of their post-coital haze. It showed when Bonny looked at the guys' hands soaping her up. "We make a nice color gradient now," she stated, then buried her face in her hands. "Oh god, I did not just say that."

It took about three seconds until the guys burst out in laughter.

But as much fun as it was to explore each other under the shower, the bed was calling to them. The sex had been amazing, and even though they hadn't physically done a lot that day aside from making love, they were all emotionally exhausted, albeit incredibly happy.

It had been an eventful day, to say the least.

Chapter Eleven

It should be no problem at all to grab their next target. The thought was easy to read on all their faces, even as they discussed the plan for the night for a final time in a café where nobody paid them any attention.

The little bird they used to look for new people had used her day off from her regular job wisely and had scouted the clubs in Cancún for girls. According to her, this one would be perfect: a young woman, apparently from somewhere in the UK, working on a cruise ship that would be docked in Cancún for a few days; far too trusting, far too happy to share too many details with a stranger. It was a perfect combination. The cruise company would try to keep things quiet, and even if her people started looking for her, it would be too late. She'd be long gone before the authorities finished dancing around each other.

For being so close to the harbor, the night was surprisingly quiet. Life and laughter were happening nearer the heart of the city. But away from all that, they were waiting. Some of them in the shadows of alleys leading to the cruise ship terminal, two pretending to be in a friendly conversation – just winding down before heading home after a night of clubbing.

One of them spotted her from his hiding place and texted the rest whom to look out for. She was easy to make out with her bright clothes and her colorful make-up. She looked to be around twenty, pretty enough, with blonde hair, dark eyes, and a figure that would allow for what they had planned for her. Fortunately for them, she was also alone. Then again, most employees weren't allowed to bring just anybody back to their cabin on a ship.

Everything unfolded just as they had planned.

The girl, on her way to the cruise liner, neared the two men leaning against a low stone wall. One of them had a cigarette in his hand, his fingers digging into his pockets, seemingly looking for a lighter. He came up empty, of course. He gestured to his friend, who shook his head. A resigned huff, then he spotted the girl and put on a bright smile. For a second, she hesitated, but then stepped over to them. Her hand was in her purse, and a moment later, she came up with a lighter to help out the man. They engaged her in some meaningless conversation while another of their group snuck through the shadows, creeping closer and closer. He had to cover the last few feet in the open, but the girl hardly took notice of him when he appeared behind her. She probably thought he was just passing by them. That was, until the needle pierced the skin of her neck.

It didn't take long for her to lose consciousness. Carrying her away wasn't a problem, either. Should anybody ask, they could always say they were taking her home because she partied too hard. In a city that lived from tourists flooding it for just that, it was something everybody would believe.

. . .

As soon as the girl was in a car and her belongings dumped into the water, the group met up again to exchange a few last details. They would split up; the next means of transport was smaller than usual. And you never knew when another opportunity would arise – it was only smart to always have somebody close to all those marks.

Chapter Twelve

Ben woke up to two people wrapped around him. Somehow, he had ended up in the middle last night, sandwiched between soft, subtle curves on one side and lean, strong muscle on the other. *I could get used to this,* he thought.

Last night had been extraordinary. Exciting, thrilling, passionate. But also sweet, gentle, delightful.

They had made love again in the middle of the night. Slow, sensual, and ending with Ben and Josh sliding their fingers into Bonny again while she was stroking them both until they shuddered and came under her hands.

After that, they had talked some more. Ben had gone into more detail about what he had hinted at, telling them that he sometimes hooked up with women or men, but always used protection. That he just wanted to be as sure as possible to be safe, even though he hardly had time these days to meet anybody. But it wasn't just the sex that had him careful. One of his colleagues from another department had been consulting on another case with the police, and the crime scene had been a mess from what Ben had heard. He still wasn't sure how, but his colleague had come in contact with contaminated blood and had contracted HIV – even with post-exposure prophylaxis. She was doing well, luckily. But it was something Ben didn't need, even if – given his own field of work – it was less likely for him to come into contact with anything dangerous in the first place.

Bonny and Josh had understood Ben's need to be safe, though. He was taking on a lot of responsibility when it came to looking after his mother and sister. His father was a long-haul truck driver working in the US. He loved Ben's mother, but his job simply didn't allow him to be home very often.

Still, they had decided to look for a physician to get tested right away to make sure all of them were safe because, as Bonny had put it, "as much as we promise to always remember, look at us, we're likely to get carried away at some point."

She wasn't wrong. It was also why they had decided that it wouldn't be a problem for any of them if they had sex with each other even if they weren't all together. Their chemistry was too much to ignore, and they had already learned that there was no jealousy from any of them. So none of them saw a reason to torture themselves with waiting if one of them wasn't there. Although Benicio thought that it would always be the most special when it was all of them making love together. Even just looking at them sleeping next to him made his head swim, not to mention his blood pool south. With light crawling into the room, he knew they would wake up soon. Perhaps they could enjoy each other again before breakfast...

His phone chose that moment to buzz on the nightstand. He silently cursed and carefully freed his arm from underneath Josh's head. He checked the text from his sister. She might not be ecstatic about him staying at the hotel, but she kept him updated on her schedule nonetheless. And her message meant he could settle back into the pillows.

"What has you smiling like that?" Bonny asked and snuggled even closer.

"Val let me know that there was a change and she'd be in the kitchen helping out for now. Which means we can take our time and don't have to rush through breakfast."

"Nice."

"Hm, yes. I just think I'll need to get to my room to change into fresh clothes before we go eat."

"Maybe, yeah. Let's head to your room after breakfast again and grab more clothes, though. I understand if you wouldn't want to give up your room after one night. But I can tell you, Josh and I would be happy to have you here during our stay."

Beside them, Josh woke up as well and pushed himself up on one arm. "Bonny is right, we would love that. But we also get that everything has happened extremely fast." Which was true but didn't stop him from leaning over to first kiss Bonny then Ben.

"Then let's say this: I get some clothes, but for now I won't check out of my room. We see how this goes, and in a week or so, we can decide whether we talk with the hotel to move me in here with you."

Bonny and Josh nodded in agreement and settled in for a few minutes of cuddling before the day would start for them.

It turned out the weather forecast hadn't lied. After a few rays of early morning sun, clouds had taken over and it had been pouring for most of the day. Usually, none of them would describe that as perfect weather for a vacation. But for once, it worked in their favor. It meant Valeria's schedule had changed, and she was currently only working in the background with her colleagues. It allowed them to make some calls and drive to a clinic to get tested.

What they hadn't expected was that the rainy day would lead to Val putting them to work. Guests couldn't do a lot in the hotel's garden and pool area and had to be entertained indoors. When it had come up in one of her staff meetings that Val and her brother had both been going to dance school in their youth, the decision had been made to offer free dance lessons that afternoon.

Valeria had sought them out as soon as they had gotten back from the clinic and sat them all down around a small table in one of the lounge areas. She declared they would not only help round up guests, but Ben would also help out as a teacher. "See it as your punishment for showing up here in the first place," she told her brother. Then Ben and Val had found out that Josh had also been to dance school. Which obviously meant he got drafted as an instructor, too.

Bonny thought she would get out of it, but Val cocked her head, studying her. "What about you?"

"I've never formally learned dancing."

"But you can?"

An evil smirk showed on Josh's face. "Oh yes, she can. She has been to enough official functions and galas with me over the years. She knows how to dance."

"Perfect. Do you have a dress that works, Bonny?"

"I'm not sure. The shorter dresses I brought are more of a tight fit, and my flowing ones are all floor length."

"Hm, don't worry, I think I have a knee-length one that should fit you and work well for all kinds of dances," Val told her, her gaze intense. "Come with me, you can try it on. And then we all should get ready. We want to start the lessons soon, and we will get more people on board if we look the part when inviting them."

Bonny got the feeling it wasn't just the dress Val wanted to get her alone for and thought it might be a good idea to lighten the mood. "Am I the only one who thinks this is turning into an odd version of *Dirty Dancing?*"

The others laughed, and when they all got up Josh and Ben both kissed her cheeks. Josh added, "Don't worry, nobody puts our baby in a corner," then left hand in hand with Ben to get changed. *Our baby.* Warmth rushed through her. It was a marvelous thing to hear, but after what they had shared the night before, the moment they all had been connected, there wasn't a shred of doubt in her mind that she was exactly that. *Theirs.*

Unfortunately for Bonny, they had barely left when Valeria guided her to her quarters and began the expected interrogation on the way. She wanted to know more about Bonny and Josh, their personalities but also their job prospects. Benicio might have told his sister a little bit, but seemingly not all of it. And when the woman's questions drifted toward more personal topics, Bonny had an idea why she was asking all this. "Valeria, please don't worry. Josh and I are secure financially, and we're seriously not trying to get me pregnant expecting your brother to pay for a kid. Or even for me to get pregnant and then not let him know that he has a kid. I don't know how I can explain it in a way that makes sense to anybody. But with Benicio, I feel just like I felt when I started dating Josh." *I'd better keep it at that. No need to tell her that I'm pretty sure I can easily fall in love with her brother, too.* "It's the same for Josh. I mean, you've dated before, right?"

"Yes, I have. But that was one guy at a time."

"Sure, I get that. Here's the deal, I dated only one guy for seven years. I love Josh. I know how it sounds and looks. But there's nothing missing for Josh and me; we never looked at anybody else. With your brother, it's different. It's like we both didn't even know there was room for another person in our hearts. Then we met Ben, and things... fell into place. It's like you would meet somebody you're interested in; with us it's just Josh and me both liking the same person."

Valeria huffed out a heavy sigh. "*Sí*, I can see that when you both look at my brother. But what are your plans once my internship is finished, when your vacation is over?"

"I'll be honest, we haven't talked about it, yet. We need to see how we fit together, first."

"I guess I can understand that. Just... don't hurt him, okay?"

It warmed Bonny's heart to see the obvious concern Valeria had for her brother. It reminded her of her own siblings. She would do what she could to protect them as well. "Don't worry. I can tell you one thing: we have already established that communication is key. We will always talk, all three of us, and we will respect everybody's wishes."

"I think I cannot ask for more." She stopped in front of a nondescript door. "*Aquí es.* This is my room."

Armed with a pretty blue dress, Bonny finally made her way back to her bungalow, grateful for the hotel's foresight to have some covered pathways as well so she wouldn't get soaked.

She was just getting her keycard out to let herself in when she heard soft moans through one of the open windows. Seemed like her men were having fun; she couldn't wait to see them enjoying each other. Not wanting to interrupt them, she did her best to open the door as quietly as possible and slipped off her shoes in the small hallway. The dress found a place on the living room couch, and Bonny tiptoed over to the bedroom.

Oh yeah, seeing them like this was worth sneaking in. Ben and Josh lay on the bed, their clothes scattered everywhere, their eyes closed in ecstasy. Their moans were muted only because they had their mouths full, cheerfully sucking each other, their fingers digging into the other's butt. Bonny knew from experience Josh was great when it came to oral sex with a woman, and from Ben's shivering muscles she assumed he was equally great at giving blowjobs. Knowing they might soon both be able to taste Ben without a condom – and for him to taste them – gave her another thrill. She bit her lip and slid her hand into her soft, wide pants to pleasure herself. Soon though, she couldn't stop her own moans from escaping. Two pairs of eyes found her, and the sight of her – one hand down her pants, the other kneading her breast through her shirt while she leaned back against the doorframe for support – was enough to send both men over the edge. The intensity of their orgasms was palpable, and it did incredible things to her, pushing her to climax as well.

"Hey, baby," Josh greeted her when his breath had returned to almost normal.

"Hey, *bebé*. Were you okay with what you walked into?" There was an almost inaudible anxious quiver in Ben's voice.

Bonny chuckled. "What gave you the impression that I wasn't?"

But he didn't seem entirely convinced. So she took the few steps to the bed and knelt on the floor, pressing her lips to his. There was a hint of latex, and she couldn't wait until she could taste Josh on Ben's lips instead. But for now, there was something more important to be said. "Benicio, sweetheart, we agreed we're all okay with it. Josh and I meant that, and I hope you did, too, and didn't change your mind. So, trust me, I enjoyed every moment of what I walked into, I swear," she reassured him.

It was a relief when the shadow finally cleared from his eyes, and he smiled at her before he told her, "I meant it, too, and I didn't change my mind."

"Perfect. Now, I would love to crawl into bed with you two, but we promised your sister our help. And after she already put me through an interrogation, I don't want to give her any grief."

"I'm sorry about that," Ben said, caressing Bonny's cheek with gentle fingers.

"All good. I would do the same with my siblings. I totally get where she's coming from. So, let's get ready, shall we?"

The dance lessons turned out to be a big success. People even laughed when, at one point, Ben let go of his sister and reached out for Josh. *Goodness, he's breathtaking. And he can fucking move,* was all Benicio could think. The same went for Bonny, but she was currently dancing with a man whose wife had to take a break and fix one of her shoes. Thus, Josh had taken the time to sip some water before ending up in his boyfriend's arms.

With Ben's hands holding on to him – the thumb of one hand brushing circles over Josh's hip, his other hand intertwining their fingers more intimately than the standard handhold the dance called for – Josh grinned at his lover. "You keep touching me like this, people will think we're dating."

"We are, aren't we?"

In response, Josh pecked a kiss on the tip of Ben's nose.

There were a few murmurs going through the crowd, but nobody dared to say anything.

And when the evening got later and the more formal dances and music were replaced by club music after dinner – the hotel had set up a buffet along one wall of the ballroom they were using – nobody seemed to care anymore when Josh and Ben were dancing closely, their arms around each other, with Bonny wrapped up in their embraces as well.

Chapter Thirteen

Josh woke up with Bonny snuggled to his back and Ben against his chest facing him, his arm lying over Josh's waist with his hand on Bonny's hip. They were both still dead to the world. Not that Josh could blame them; not only had Valeria roped them into some trivia game night the previous evening, but when they had come back to the bungalow, they had also made love for half the night – which didn't surprise him at all.

The evening before, they had finally gotten the results from the clinic. It had taken five days, and the clinic had apologized once again for it, even though they had warned them from the beginning that it would take time due to the hospital's high workload. It didn't matter. What mattered was that all their test results looked good. And with nothing to worry about, they had indulged in tasting each other, in loving each other with no barrier between them anymore. Josh smiled brightly at the memory.

Careful not to wake them, Josh reached for his phone. He checked the time and decided to let his lovers sleep a little longer. Benicio's sister had the morning off and had told them she'd sleep late, which meant they didn't have to watch out for her for a bit. Enjoying a quiet morning in bed sounded perfect to Josh. *Although I don't think "quiet" would be the best word to describe our times spent in bed together so far,* he thought with a mental chuckle. For now, he was grateful that the hotel offered an exclusive app for its guests. He used it to cancel house-keeping for the day and order breakfast from room service.

It struck him that he knew precisely what to order for each of his lovers. That he did for Bonny wasn't a surprise. But even with Benicio, after knowing him for eight days and dating him for a week (he didn't count the current day, since it had barely started), he already could pick his favorites from the menu. He *knew* Ben. Yes, they had spent a lot of time in bed together the past week. But they had also been talking for ages, learning more about each other on a deeper level. Josh already knew whether Ben had any allergies, Ben could name Bonny's most-loved band, and Bonny would be able to pick Ben's favorite perfume. They enjoyed some of the same hobbies, they shared the same values. This thing between them *worked*. Ben just *fit* with them. Thinking about all of it made Josh realize his own feelings. It sent a thrill down his spine, making him shiver. He would have to talk to them soon, especially Bonny.

A hand traced over his tattoo, the fingertips caressing the inked skin. "You are thinking too hard for this early in the morn-ing, *arañita,*" Ben whispered before placing a kiss onto Josh's tattoo.

"You like that nickname, don't you?"

"*Sí,*" Ben answered, then replaced his lips with his tongue. It had quickly become one of Ben's favorite things to do. Not only was the tattoo amazing and he constantly found new details, fine lines he hadn't seen before, but he loved the taste of Josh's skin as much as Bonny's. Where she tasted sweet with just a hint of salt – almost reminding Ben of salted caramel – Josh tasted almost like a breeze of sea air, salty and fresh. Mixed with their scents – something close to peach and vanilla for Bonny, something light like mint and citrus with just a tiny bit of musk for Josh – it always drove Benicio wild.

He was gradually making his way further down Josh's body, lips and hands exploring, caressing, when a soft knock on the door interrupted his fun. He huffed out a frustrated breath.

Josh kissed his hair. "Damn, they're fast. I'll go, baby. Why don't you wake up our woman?"

"Okay." *Our woman* sounded like heaven to Benicio. They had told him right away that if he wanted them, they were his just like he was theirs. In the past week, they had done everything to prove that. It was surreal, but it felt so wonderful that he had a hard time imagining how he had felt before meeting them. He hadn't been *unhappy*. Frustrated with his job, or rather the higher-ups, sometimes. Too busy to meet even friends regularly, let alone somebody special. More worried for his sister with every new consultation. Bothered by the lack of progress that, to his mind, largely stemmed from egocentric idiots too full of their self-importance to work together. But even with all that, he wouldn't have described himself as lonely or miserable.

Then he had met his lovers, and things had fallen into place like never before for him. Hearing Josh say things like "our woman" so easily and without hesitation was all the confirmation he needed to know he wasn't alone. They both thought this was something special, too. And he had begun to understand that *not unhappy* was something entirely different from *happy*. He would make sure to cherish every moment he had with them. And when he kissed Bonny awake, her lips answering his, a thought crossed his mind: *That's what my future tastes like.* It was an unshakable knowledge and came with another realization, leaving him overjoyed and maybe a little terrified at the intensity of it all.

· · ·

Shortly after breakfast, Bonny had hurried them out of the bungalow. Valeria might not be working for another couple of hours, but Josh had finally booked his own parasailing spot.

When they came to the beach, Bonny walked over to the meeting point hand in hand with Josh. She was thinking about making a fun memory and wanted to ask if there was a chance they could get three people up in the air together.

Ben had stayed behind to get them some sodas and waters from the beach bar. The weather had changed once more, and after a few rainy days, the sun was now already scorching hot – and it was barely noon. Then he got lucky and managed to get them one of the few Bali beds on the beach for the day. He was surprised when Bonny joined him on it a few minutes later. "I thought you wanted to film Josh's flight."

"Sure. But they have a new trainee there, and the poor guy was nervous enough with Josh standing there when he was supposed to explain the safety instructions to him. The main guy told me it would take about another fifteen minutes. And I can see when they'll get started from here. So I decided to wait here with you," she explained and rolled onto her side, indulging in a long, slow kiss.

"Excellent decision, *bebé*."

Bonny left the bed again when she saw them getting ready to get Josh up in the air. She was excited and hoped to see him enjoy the activity as much as she had. Given his loud laugh as soon as he lost the ground beneath his feet, she didn't think she needed to worry.

She waited for him with a smile and was picked up and twirled around as soon as Josh reached her after his flight. "Oh my god, that was so much fun. We have to do this together with Ben."

"Yeah, let's see if they can get a harness and a canopy for three people, then we totally will."

They were both laughing and walking with their arms around each other's waist when, halfway between the water and their Bali bed, a woman stepped in front of them. She was maybe in her late sixties or early seventies, and her expression did not bode well. Bonny steeled herself for a lecture about unmarried folks being too cozy in public or perhaps even some racist tirade about them dating. You never knew what was going on in people's minds.

The woman frowned at them, and it left her face with even more wrinkles. She already looked beyond her age, her probably light skin tanned to the extreme with a leathery look to it, her heavy make-up doing nothing to help improve her features. "Young man, is this your wife?"

Ah, here we go, Bonny thought.

"She's my girlfriend, ma'am."

"Good."

That stopped Bonny in her thoughts. Where was she going with this? But before she could ask, the elderly woman spoke again. "It's not too late, then. You should break up with her right away."

Josh shook his head in disbelief at what he was hearing. "And why would I do that?"

"Because she's clearly only looking for a man who'll pay for everything she wants. You cannot trust such girls."

Bonny couldn't believe the audacity of some people. "Excuse me? What makes you even think that? You don't know either of us."

The woman tsked, looking her up and down. "You be quiet. This man deserves better than you."

All right, enough was enough. Josh might have been raised to respect the elderly. But to his mind, that only applied to people who were showing respect themselves. Just because you were older didn't mean you couldn't be a dick. "Ma'am, please leave us alone. You have no right to talk to her like this." Out of the corner of his eye, he could see that the tense stand-off not only had Ben on his way over to them, but several people filming them. *Good thing I'm not as prominent as Ty, or this would end up online with our names sooner rather than later.*

"Boy, I can talk about a hussy like her any way I want."

"How dare you call her that?!" Josh's voice rose, taking on a harsh tone. He wasn't yelling, yet. But his fingernails dug into his palm with the effort to keep some semblance of calm.

Bonny clearly was too shocked to speak; her eyes were wide, and her whole body shivered.

"If the shoe fits. That slut has her arm around you when she had her tongue in another man's mouth just a few minutes before that!"

Bonny's head snapped back like she had been slapped, and Josh laid a steadying hand on her back. Rage boiled through him, then reached the point where he was completely and utterly calm once again. "You better stop talking *right now*. This woman is the love of my life, just like the man she kissed earlier. The next time you even consider sticking your nose into other people's lives, make sure to know what you are talking about. I love her, and I love him. All of us are together. Not that it is any of your business. Now, leave. Us. Alone," he told her, stressing every word carefully.

Next to him, Bonny realized what Josh had just said. Calm-ness flowed through her. *Fuck other people's opinions.* Josh had told her what she needed to know – that she wasn't alone when it came to her feelings about Benicio. When she had kissed him on the Bali bed earlier, she had been sure of what she felt for him, and that it was just as strong as what she felt for Josh – she just had wanted to wait until they were all together to tell him the first time. Looked like Josh had beaten her to it. Ignoring the old woman, she framed Josh's face and pressed a kiss to his mouth. "I love you, too."

Ben had reached them a few moments before and had looked like he wanted to rip the woman's head off. Josh's confession had stunned him into silence, though, and Bonny took the chance to give him a kiss as well. "I love you."

Josh sidestepped around Bonny and turned Ben's face to his, finding his lips with his. "I love you."

For a second, Benicio stood there, panting, the blood pounding in his ears, then he drew them into a three-way kiss. "I love you, too. Both of you."

Half the beach around them cheered, and there was more than one "Aww." But the old woman wouldn't give up. "How dare you! You are sick, all of you! Get away from us good people!" she screeched.

While the three of them did their best to ignore her, for a moment only basking in the knowledge that they belonged together, some of the other guests yelled at the agitated woman, "Lady, shut up and leave them alone." "Who the heck cares?" "They look happy, let them be."

By now, the scene had caught the attention of one of the lifeguards, who apparently had called hotel security, and they were both coming over. "*¿Qué pasa aquí?* What's the problem?"

Of course, the old woman yelled first. "That whore and these two degenerates corrupt the people around here! Take them away!"

None of them managed a word before a guy in his early thirties stepped in, handing his phone to the security guard. "Here, I caught everything on video. Had a feeling she wanted to stir trouble when I saw her first observing the girl earlier, then getting up when she and one of her boyfriends came back this way. The three of them did absolutely nothing wrong. They were way nicer than the old ha..." He caught himself before he finished calling her a hag and covered it with a small cough before continuing, "...woman deserves. I think I speak for most of the beach when I tell you we would be happy to see her removed."

Bonny hoped the guard wasn't as conservative as the woman, or even if he was, that that he would understand the hotel would lose more money throwing three people out than one. The disdainful look he shot at the woman let Bonny breathe a little easier. The security guard handed back the phone and thanked the man. Then he focused his attention back on the woman. "Collect your belongings, please. You will come with me."

It was a prospect she wasn't keen on, and she exploded, yelling more profanities at the poor man. She was so frantic that he had to call for one of his colleagues to help him. Meanwhile it seemed like the other guests had had enough of her. A woman packed the woman's things and handed the bag to the guard. "Please, get her away from here."

The lifeguard had also watched the video and was stepping over to Bonny, Josh, and Benicio. "*Vamos*. Let's go. You heard enough of her, you don't need that."

"Just a second," Bonny said and quickly ran over to the guy who had helped them with the recording. She held out her hand. "Thank you." Behind her, Josh and Ben waved and mouthed the same.

The guy shook her hand and genuinely smiled at her. "No problem. Ignore her. From what I see, most people here are either totally fine with it or just don't care. If the three of you have some time over the next few days, come and find us. My mates and I are here most of the time, and we're always looking for people to play some beach volleyball with. I just don't think you'll have time today. I'd think they'll want to talk to you again."

"Probably. Thanks for the offer, though. It sounds fun. We'll see if we can make it," Bonny said with a smile of her own before turning around and taking her men's hands while the lifeguard accompanied them to their Bali bed.

Once the lifeguard had left – after asking again if they were all right – they drew the sheer curtains for some privacy and all sat facing each other on the bed, holding hands. Now that they were alone and the adrenaline had worn off, they truly processed what they had said to each other.

Chapter Fourteen

Ben was the first to quietly ask, "Did you mean it?" The hope in his voice was tangible, and his eyes pleaded with them not to take it back.

Bonny crawled closer to him until she was almost sitting in his lap, her hands cupping his face, and her thumbs brushing over his cheeks. "Listen to me. We meant every single word we said. We don't say something like that lightly. We love you, Benicio Pérez. We love you so much. I felt myself falling for you for the past week, and I was completely certain of my feelings when I kissed you right here earlier. I just wanted to have Josh with us to share the moment when I told you."

Josh leaned over Bonny's shoulder, his face next to hers, and ran a hand through Ben's dark hair. "What she said. I knew for sure this morning when I woke up to you two sleeping next to me. I didn't say anything right then because we had somewhere to be and we still have a lot to discuss."

Relief was written all over Ben's face. "I really love you both, too. I never thought this possible, and then I thought you couldn't really both love me back. But your eyes tell me it's true."

"It is, sweetheart," Bonny said and gave him a whisper-soft kiss that caused a shudder to run through him.

"So this is more than simple dating; it's serious for all of us. Does that mean we are a throuple now?"

"It's serious, yes. And I think we can live with that term, right Bonny?" Josh asked and pecked a kiss on her cheek.

"Yep, that's okay. *Ménage à trois* or anything like that always sounds more like some short-term thing to me, even if it's not always meant that way, or sometimes people use it with a meaning that's not working for us, because we're all involved with each other and are all equals in this relationship. Throuple is good with me."

Their following kiss to seal it was interrupted by a soft knock on the bedframe. "Whoops, *perdón*. Sorry to interrupt your fun there, brother."

Ben turned around, surprised to see his sister standing there with three drinks on a tray. "Val, why are you here? I thought you had a shift at Reception starting in a couple of hours."

"Oh, *sí*, that was the plan. Then the manager who was supposed to train me was called to help with an unruly guest. I'm not trained yet, so I couldn't go there. But one of the bartenders here helped out there before. She took over the front desk, I was called in for the bar. Then I was told to bring the people who were apparently yelled at by the guest some complimentary drinks. So these are for you," she said and handed over the drinks. "Now, from all I have heard, this could take quite some time, so I think you can all enjoy the afternoon here. But you know you must tell me what happened, Ben!" Clearly now that she had seen they were okay, Valeria couldn't wait to hear the story.

They gave her the quick version so they wouldn't keep her too long from work, but she made them promise to give her more details over dinner.

When she was gone, Ben looked at Josh. "I guess that means we have time to discuss those things now. We can see the bar from here, and I don't have to go to the front desk and spend time in the lounge area there."

"That's true. Okay... So one thing is easy enough: we haven't managed to cancel your room yet and book you into ours."

"Right, because my sister came up with ways to keep us busy."

"Well, I can't blame her," Bonny chuckled. "We basically spy on her, I think it's fair that she doesn't want to just watch us lounging around all day for that. And she wanted to get to know us, let's not forget about that. But I'm with Josh, if you want it too, we will happily share our bungalow with you, officially."

Ben goofily grinned at them. "I'd like that a lot."

"Then we'll do that later," Josh told them and stole himself a quick kiss from Ben. But he got serious after that. "Now to the not-so-easy topic. We love each other, and to me, that means it doesn't matter if I've loved Bonny for longer. I want to be with both of you in the future.

"How can we make this work? Normally, I'd be the first to agree that a relationship sometimes means compromise, and maybe people have to move for each other. The problem is where our family business is based, and that Bonny is supposed to take over at some point. Even with some of it being possible to be handled remotely, not all of it is. And while I could still decline my first job, it's not exactly easy for me to work in every state, far less every country, because many of my courses and the licensing I have applied for differ from state to state. It was already a hassle making clear to the authorities that my main residence is in New Jersey but my job will be in New York. I'm not even sure I could get licensed in Mexico at all."

They were silent for a moment, studying the ocean and all brooding about the dilemma at hand. Then Ben cleared his throat. "I might have an idea. I've actually been thinking about this for a few days, ever since I realized I wasn't just crushing on you two but falling in love with you. This is nothing that will work forever, but it would give us time."

"Tell us," Bonny encouraged him.

"I could talk to my boss and try to convince him to give me more seminars than consulting jobs. Specifically, seminars in the US, on the East Coast. With my degree being partially gained in the US, I might also be able to find a second job near you, so it could be easier to move to the US."

Both Bonny and Josh gasped. "You would really move for us to the States?" Bonny asked in awe.

"*Sí*, of course. From what I just heard, you would consider moving for me as well, but our situations mean it is easier for me."

Josh nodded. "Yeah, that might be. But what about your family? You look after your mother when your dad is on the road, you worry about your sister."

"Ah, I think *mamá* would understand – after she's recovered from the surprise that I'm moving for two people, not just one. She moved from one end of Mexico to the other when she met my father; she supports him when it comes to his driving. And there is more family around, she won't be alone. And Valeria, she's smart. I only worry so much about her right now because of this internship. But even if she decides to study some form of tourism, this case that puts her in danger will hopefully be solved by the time she'll have finished with her studies. Or she might decide to study something different. Nothing is set in stone, yet."

"All right, these are good points. But what job could you imagine in the US? Does it have to be forensic anthropology, or could it be something broader?" There was hope shining in Josh's eyes, like he might have an idea.

"What do you mean?"

"Well, you told us you had some biology and med courses, too, right?"

"*Sí.*"

"Okay. So, the guy I'll start working for takes on cold cases, or even open cases where the police have given up, pretty regularly. Those are often some murder cases, and even though he has picked up a lot, he sometimes hires a medical consultant. But his usual consultant is currently on parental leave for the foreseeable future. Maybe I could put in a good word for you."

Ben couldn't believe it. He grabbed Josh's hand and tugged him closer. "You would seriously do that?"

"To have you close to us? Hell, yeah. I mean, you'd still have to go through an interview, show your qualifications and all that. And if anything ever goes to court, we'll likely have to have somebody else with the right certifications check it again to verify – but we have to do that with our current consultant, too. But it would be a lot easier to get your visa and permanent working permit and so on with a job offer in hand, right?"

"Yes, yes, it would be. Oh god, this could truly work, right?" Ben was so excited and happy that he didn't even notice when a few tears ran down his cheeks.

Josh brushed them away. "Not only *could* it work, it will. We'll *make* it work."

That declaration ended in another long, sweet kiss between all of them until Josh broke it with a sigh. "Okay, that's almost everything I wanted to discuss with you right now."

"What else is there, baby?" Bonny asked curiously, her fingers playing with a strand of Josh's hair that hadn't fallen in place since he had been parasailing.

"It's more of a *what isn't there anymore.* Bonny, baby, I love you, you know that."

"Of course I do."

"Yeah... Interesting choice of words right there," he told her with a meaningful tone in his voice.

"Why... oh."

"Oh..."

It seemed like Bonny and Benicio had both understood the implication. Josh nodded slowly, "Yeah. Look, I wanted to propose to you during this trip. I want to spend the rest of my life with you. But I don't think I can still ask you to marry me. I don't want only two of us legally bound to each other. All three of us belong together. To exclude Ben would feel wrong to me."

"Josh, don't worry. Had you asked me on our first night here, I would've said yes in a heartbeat. Now? I agree with you one hundred percent. We can't exclude Ben, he's part of us. We'll find another way; perhaps a ceremony in the future for all three of us, and then we look at what we can set up legally in terms of taxes, insurances, permits to give information to all of us in case of emergencies. There are ways around a marriage license. Who cares if the state sees it as a marriage? We will. That's important. That is, if you both want the same."

"Of course I want that with both of you," was Josh's immediate answer.

Ben, on the other hand, stared at them, perplexed. "Did you just ask me to marry you both?"

Bonny looked at him, completely serious but with love radiating from her. "Yeah, I guess we did. It wouldn't be something that would happen next week – I'll leave *that* to Scar and Ty – but at some point down the road. And I would say we'll do a proper proposal then. For now, let's just agree that we look forward to the same things. But you don't have to agr..."

She couldn't finish the sentence before Ben crushed his mouth to hers. Eventually, he gave her a chance to breathe and said, "God, yes, I want that in the future."

Chapter Fifteen

The three days after had been absolute bliss. They had spent a lot of their time alone making love, and whenever they had been making sure Valeria was safe they'd kept planning their future in more detail. And although the throuple had sent pictures – for now of all four of them rather than only of Bonny, Josh, and Benicio together – to their respective families, all they had said had been something along the lines of, "*We met some great people and are having a great time,*" deciding that it would be better to tell their relatives in person about the situation.

Now they were all panting, their blood pumping through them. They finally had found some time to look for the guy who had helped them out with the video, and after inviting him and his friends to some drinks, they had played beach volleyball with them. It had been an intense match. In the end, Bonny, Josh, and Ben had lost, but it had been a close call. The guy who had taken the video came over to high-five them. "You were damn good. That was fun."

All of them agreed, then wished him a safe trip when he

told them a change of plan for his group meant they'd have to leave earlier than planned and it was their last day at the hotel.

Which only meant there were fewer people to interact with and more time to enjoy as a throuple, Benicio thought a little guiltily. But he knew, even with all their plans and knowing they all were serious about making their relationship work, that they wouldn't see each other for a bit once Bonny's and Josh's vacation (and his own) were over. Convincing his boss, applying for the necessary permits and visa, even just terminating the rental agreement for his apartment and packing his things, would all take time. So he vowed to enjoy every moment with them that he could.

From where he was lying on his lounger, he briefly checked the hut for rental equipment that his sister was manning that day. She was currently speaking to one of her colleagues, and although Ben could see a frown on her face for a second, she soon nodded and her colleague left again, and Ben figured it was nothing serious. He rolled onto his side and snuggled closer to Bonny, looking over her shoulder and reading the postcard she was writing. His hand ran up and down her back, his fingers tangling with Josh's, who was lying on Bonny's other side and doing the same. All three of them grinned.

"Bea is Scarlette's *abuela*, right?" Ben asked with his eyes still on the postcard.

"Yep. She asked us to send her an actual postcard she can put on the wall in her restaurant. She got a postcard a few years ago from a family who had eaten at the restaurant while on vacation in New York. They thought it was a fun idea to reverse things and send postcards from their home to places they had visited, kind of a family project with their kids once they were back home. Bea loved the postcard and hung it up, and some of her regular guests started sending postcards, too. Soon after that, everybody in the clan started sending postcards whenever they were traveling. The wall is huge by now," Josh explained.

Ben chuckled. "I love how you just call it a clan."

"It is, believe me. Bea sometimes also jokingly calls it 'the mob.' The Langella family alone is quite large, especially on the side of Scarlette's dad. Then there's Scarlette's friends and employees and their families who visit the place regularly. And with Ty marrying into the family, his friends joined. Which means another large family on Leroy's end. With me, Bonny came into the clan, and she has her parents and siblings, who visit the restaurant whenever they're in the city, and some cousins who studied in New York. I swear, sometimes I don't know what's more impressive: Bea always finding a seat for anybody of the clan dropping in spontaneously – or for guests who aren't part of it."

Bonny finished her postcard and looked up at Ben. "It's true. I've never seen anything like it. It's amazing. Here, sign," she said and held out her pen to him.

"I... what? You want me to sign? I have never even met her. Wouldn't she think it weird?" Ben asked her incredulously.

Josh snorted. "God, no. And believe me, once she finds out that we're together – and have already been while writing this postcard – and she can't find your signature, you'd be in trouble. Maybe we should have warned you. But being with us means being part of a huge group of amazing and sometimes crazy people."

Benicio nodded. "Yes, I'm starting to realize that. But it's all right – it's almost the same with my family. Which means it's good that you already are familiar with such chaos and won't run away as soon as you meet them."

"It takes more than that to make us run, believe me. I mean, you read Ty's book, and I told you I almost got blown up by those crazy blackmailers pretty much right after Bonny and I got together – in her family's driveway. And she never even considered leaving."

"Are you crazy? Of course not! I know life will never get boring with you, baby. Though I will say, I could've done without you lying bleeding on the ground. Maybe not make it a life-and-death situation with a safety margin of barely two seconds next time," Bonny agreed with Josh and pressed a kiss to his lips.

Both of them heard their boyfriend gasp and saw the color drain out of Benicio's face. "That... your brother didn't write about that in his book, not that it was *such* a close call, that you actually got hurt."

"Well, yeah, he only wrote I was attacked. But I was underage when it happened, and I admit I was also still working on processing it entirely when he was finishing up the first draft. That's why he didn't go into detail. I'm okay now, though, and Bonny and I both realized over time that a little dark humor helps us deal with it."

Slowly, Benicio nodded. "*Sí*, I can understand that. And we also use dark humor when we're dealing with an especially hard case. It does help. I just..."

"Realized how close you came to never meeting Josh?" Bonny asked gently when Ben seemed at a loss for words to explain his reaction.

"Yes."

"I get that, believe me," she replied and leaned in for a soft kiss. Ben closed his eyes and felt Josh run his finger through his hair. "But he's okay, he's here with us," she told Ben when her lips left his.

"Okay," Ben sighed and stole another kiss from his lovers. "Okay. Now, I still need to sign this postcard..."

Their conversation shifted back to happier topics after that, and when dinner was getting closer, they packed their things and meandered between towels and loungers toward the equipment rental hut.

Valeria was closing up for the day and smiled at them. Bonny stopped her from pulling the shutter closed so she would have a surface to write on. "Wait a sec. We want you to sign, too."

"And what will I be signing?"

Bonny showed her the postcard, and upon Valeria's questioning look Josh shrugged. "Family greetings. I'll tell you about it on the way. You have a staff dinner, right? I'll walk you there, then put this in the mailbox at Reception on my way to our bungalow. You two okay with me making a detour?" he addressed the last part to Bonny and Benicio.

"Sure."

Walking side by side, Ben had his arm around Bonny's waist, his hand reaching up and playing with her curls. "I love your hair, *mi amor*."

"Thank you," she said and snuggled closer into his side hug. "Josh loves it like this too. And so do I, or I'd braid it or straighten it more often. Although I think I'll take the time tomorrow, it's supposed to be even hotter and more humid. If I don't braid it, it can be a pain to comb through after a day like that."

"Hm, yes, good idea. If you show me how, I'll help you."

"Really?"

"Sure. I have several young cousins who easily get bored at family meetings. I sometimes go mountain climbing in my free time. So somehow my family thought it made total sense that me knowing how to tie a few different knots also means I know how to braid."

Cocking her head, Bonny asked, "How..."

"Don't ask me. I have no clue how that makes any sense. And I am glad they don't know I also took a *shibari* class a few years back and still practice the knots. Not sure if you know it, but that's Japanese rope bondage. So who knows what they'd come up with if they knew about that. Anyway, I watched a few videos, and the girls were young enough not to complain when the first braids weren't perfect. Over the years, I've gotten better, and I'd be happy to help you."

They were standing in front of their bungalow, and Bonny turned to face Ben and smiled at him. "I'd like that very much." She quickly opened the door, then focused her attention back on him, now smirking. "So, about that *shibari* class..."

Ben threw his head back and laughed. "Why am I not surprised that you came back to that?"

"Baby, let's face it, you mentioned it for a reason, even if you did it unconsciously."

That stopped Benicio mid-step and had him think about why he had actually brought it up. "I... huh, yeah, maybe you are right. But it's nothing we have to do or anything. So, while I think some light bondage can be fun, I think I mostly brought it up because you might see me with rope in my hands sometimes. You told me you two aren't into BDSM, and honestly, neither am I. It was something that started as a fun idea between a friend and me. Over the course of the class, I came to appreciate the artistic part of it, not just the erotic aspects. And for me, it's almost a form of meditation, tying the knots helps me relax when work has been crazy."

"Huh, yeah, I can see why it would be calming to do that. Have you ever been tied? I have a friend from university who made some money working as a model for a *shibari* class. She told me the money was nice but that she also liked being bound – that, if done correctly, it triggered a huge endorphin rush for her. I think that could be interesting to experience. Which is the main reason I came back to it. Although, yes, while we're not really into BDSM, we told you some light bondage is fine and fun for us, too," Bonny said with a wink.

Grinning, Benicio ran his arms around her waist and drew her in for a kiss. "I'll keep that in mind. But to answer your question, yes, I have been tied once or twice. I didn't reach such an ecstatic state, but I also wasn't tied completely or for a longer amount of time. But we can keep it in mind and look into it in more detail in the future."

"Yeah, I'd like that. But right now, we should get ready for dinner. Wanna join me in the shower?" Bonny asked and ran her hands down her boyfriend's sides before tugging on the hem of his shirt.

"I hope that was a rhetorical question," Ben replied with a smirk and made her squeak in surprise when he picked her up to carry her to the bathroom.

After setting her back down, he leaned in for another kiss. Her full lips were soft, and she opened them pliantly when his tongue teased her. The happy sigh that escaped her was music to Benicio's ears, and he deepened the kiss, indulging in her taste. His hands ran up her back, gently pressing her even closer against him, his tongue tangling with hers in a lazy dance.

They teased each other with tender hands and wandering lips. Bonny pressed small kisses along Ben's jaw, her nails teasingly dragging up the back of his neck, leaving him shuddering with the sensation. Ben brought his mouth to her ear, kissing the soft, sensitive spot right behind it before playfully nipping her earlobe and making her whimper, all while his fingertips whispered up and down her spine, causing goosebumps all over her body.

What started soft and slow soon got more passionate. Bonny swore Ben's taste got darker when their mouths met again, and she moaned. Shifting slightly, she hooked her foot around his ankle, pulling his leg between her thighs so she could rub against it. She dug her fingers into his back and dragged herself closer, pressing her hot and throbbing center hard against his muscles, and trembled with need. "Ben..."

"Shower, *bebé*. I want you wet on the outside, too," Ben whispered into her ear with a rough voice, drawing a groan from her. While Bonny nodded desperately, still grinding against his thigh, Ben reached into the shower to turn on the water. Then he made short work of her clothes, pulling her dress over her head and loosening the ribbons holding up the yellow bikini she wore that day. He loved the contrast between it and her dark skin. But it was nothing compared to her standing in front of him naked and shaking with need for him, her eyes unfocused, her breath hot against his skin. "You are so beautiful, *mi amor*."

Bonny seemed incapable of answering and just smiled dreamily at him.

Not that he was doing any better. He shoved off his own clothes with trembling hands, then did his best to push her carefully into the shower stall, but his legs were far from steady. So he ended up with his body against hers once more, his forearms resting against the wall above her head to steady himself while he pressed her back against the tiles and took her lips again, his hard length sliding between her thighs.

The friction was driving Bonny wild, and yet, it wasn't enough. Her hand found the soap dispenser, and she filled her palm with the liquid while squirming between her lover and the wall behind her. Ben's hot skin and the initial coolness of the tiles had only driven her higher, her body unable to make sense of the contrast and having her nerves fire all over her body in reaction to the mix of pleasure and mild discomfort. Through it all, her only thought was, *More.*

She wiggled so she could slide her soap-filled hand between them and began spreading the liquid all over Benicio's skin. It would never stop to amaze her that she could make him – and Josh – quiver like that. Soap suds ran down his chest and stomach, and she traced them with her fingertips, reveling in the feeling of his pecs and abs, smiling at his gasp when her hands followed his happy trail until she curled her fingers around his shaft. His deep growl was delicious, and she closed her mouth over his, swallowing the sound. "Need you inside me," she managed between kisses and moved a step to the side where a small bench was built into the back wall of the shower. It allowed her to put one foot up for some leverage while she guided Benicio into her. He was hard steel wrapped in satin skin, and she felt his blood pumping deep inside her. Sparks raced along her limbs and up her spine. Her eyes fluttered closed, and her head fell as far back as the wall allowed.

It was so much like when Josh entered her – and completely different at the same time. Each had a unique feel; Josh was a little longer and could reach her a little deeper, and Benicio had a wider girth leaving her feeling fuller; they both paid attention to her every reaction and adjusted their movements to what she needed, and yet the angle of their thrusts was different for each of them. It didn't matter, though, who was inside her. It was perfect every time whether it was Ben or Josh.

At that moment, she enjoyed the feeling of hot water running down her body, soap-slick skin sliding against skin, and one of Ben's hands cupping her breast, teasing her nipple between his fingers. His pinch sent a light pain through her. The sensation traveled under her skin down to her center and brought her nearly over the edge. Her hips eagerly met Ben's slow thrusts, and her hands held on to his shoulders.

Benicio felt drunk from Bonny's kisses and her heat surrounding him. The easy slide in and out of her was amazing. She gave herself to him without hesitation, and her moans crept under his skin, leaving him with only one thought: to make sure she would fly. It didn't matter how close he was. He loved feeling her clench around him, so he wouldn't come before her.

And she was getting closer, too. He knew her now. Her breath came shorter and shorter, her moans turned deeper, and her nails nearly broke the skin on his shoulders. He began thrusting harder, faster, his arm around her waist shaking with his restraint. They were both panting; the steam hovered around them, enveloping them and clouding their senses.

Suddenly, a bubble of cooler air washed over them, and they both heard a long groan floating through the steam.

"Damn, I love seeing you two like this," Josh told them before pulling the shower door shut behind him and stepping over to them.

Josh had already expected to find them getting lost in each other, and hearing the shower and their moans when he had entered the bungalow had him greedy and hard in seconds. He had shed his clothes on the way to the bathroom, then had enjoyed the view for a little while, his hand slowly pumping the evidence of his arousal. Sometimes it was enough to watch them. But on that day, he wanted more – especially with the steam obscuring the view more and more. And he had something on his mind that he had wanted to do for days. It seemed like the perfect time for it.

Moments later, he stood behind Benicio, pressing against his back. His boyfriend moaned contentedly and leaned back, careful not to go too far and making sure he kept Bonny safe in his arms. Josh pressed a kiss between Ben's shoulder blades, then leaned over to also kiss his girlfriend. She sighed happily into it, and Josh could see her glowing even more. She loved them both, enjoyed being with even just one of them. But when they were all together making love, she lit up like the sun, completely and utterly happy to be with both her men. He understood her – it was the same for him. Being with them both gave him a sense of completeness he hadn't even known existed before they had met Benicio.

Josh ran his fingertips up and down Ben's ribs, then further down to where he was joined with Bonny. They had stopped moving when Josh had joined them, and now Josh's hand found its way between them, first gently pressing against Bonny's clitoris, then his fingers sliding along the parts of Ben's length that weren't buried inside their girlfriend's hot body. Their groans were intoxicating, and Josh leaned in to steal himself more kisses from both of them before moving his hand back.

"Keep moving. Slowly," he told them in a voice heavy with desire. His hand moved over the planes of Ben's back, his teeth scratched along the side of his neck. Then Josh's lips followed the path of his hands, all the way down. Sinking to his knees behind Benicio, Josh dug his fingers deep into the muscles of his boyfriend's butt, his mouth pressing kisses against it before playfully nipping at the skin and following the small bite with a gentle, soothing lick of his tongue.

Beneath his hands, Josh felt Ben moving again and he heard Bonny sigh in response. He kept up the slow massage, his fingers creeping closer to the middle until he could spread the cheeks and run his thumbs along the seam, carefully pressing against the edge of Ben's entrance. It wasn't the first time he moved to prep Benicio, and his lover reacted like he had the times before, eagerly pressing back against Josh's fingers.

This time, though, Josh leaned in closer, the tip of his tongue circling the rim before pressing a kiss against Ben's opening. He felt a full-body shudder running through Ben, heard a grunt from above. Taking it as an invitation to keep going, Josh ran the flat of his tongue from Ben's taint all the way back up to his entrance, then circled the edge once again before pressing the tip of his tongue oh so gently inside.

Ben's head fell back. "Oh, fuck," he groaned loudly, one of his hands reaching back to sink into Josh's hair.

"Whatever you do, baby, keep doing it. Ben's so, so hard inside me," Bony told Josh, then dragged Ben's mouth back to hers, feasting on his moans while moving herself up and down on his arousal until she came for the first time, her yell mixing with Ben's growl when he felt her muscles squeeze him inside her.

As if Josh had any intention of stopping. Ben's musky smell, the taste of his lover, and the clench of his muscles around Josh's tongue overwhelmed his senses; by then, he was pretty sure he could come without even touching himself.

But then Ben's fingers let go of his hair, moving to where Josh was spearing his tongue inside his body over and over. Ben pushed a finger inside himself and managed to mumble, "More... need all of you... fill me."

It might not have been Josh's original plan, but who was he to deny his boyfriend? He hadn't brought any lube with him, though – pleasuring Ben with his mouth and using his hand on himself would've been enough. But luckily, they had some in-shower body lotion from home sitting next to them on the bench. Not ideal, but it would work. Reaching over, Josh covered his fingers and, after gently pushing Ben's hand away, began prepping Ben in earnest with his fingers and his tongue. Looking up, he saw Bonny looking over Ben's shoulder down to what he was doing, panting and her pupils blown wide with passion. He winked at her, and she groaned, resting her head against Ben's shoulder.

Ben relaxed quickly, pushing back on Josh's fingers and then into Bonny. "*Bebé*, now... please!"

So Josh got up, used some more lotion to slick his shaft, and positioned himself against Ben's back again. He guided his tip against Ben's entrance and unhurriedly pushed inside. God, the tightness was amazing. Even more so were the cries from both Ben and Bonny when Josh began moving inside Ben, making him drive deeper inside Bonny and slide out when Josh pulled his hips back against him.

Worked up as much as they all already were, Ben soon begged for more. "Harder, Josh, faster."

Bonny whimpered in agreement, one of her hands now clutching Josh's hair, the other still clinging to Ben.

Josh grunted, then did as he was asked. He thrust into Ben hard and fast, wet skin slapped against wet skin. His hardness dragged over Ben's prostate on every move. None of them was able to speak, and their moans were getting louder and louder, their breath coming in short pants. There was no way they were going to last much longer.

Proving it, Benicio dragged in one huge, ragged breath. Caught between his lovers, his mind and body were swamped with sensations, and when Josh thrust against the perfect spot once again, Ben's muscles went taut, and his eyes felt like they were rolling back. Explosions went off in his head and in his body. He screamed toward the ceiling when his climax rolled over him, and his world focused only on the feeling of Josh inside him and Bonny surrounding him. Hard and soft a perfect combination, both of them giving off an incredible heat. Their lips landed on each side of his neck, sucking the skin and no doubt leaving their marks there.

A couple of seconds later, they moaned against him, and he felt Bonny tighten around him once more, her muscles contracting and releasing and dragging the last of his orgasm out of him, while Josh pulsed inside him, his release so hot, filling him.

All three of them sagged against each other, panting heavily and waiting for their brains to regain their function. It was Bonny who managed to speak first. "That was incredible."

Josh nodded with his forehead leaning against Ben's shoulder. "Yeah, it was."

Slowly, Benicio agreed. "*Sí*, it really was. Where on Earth did you learn to rim like that, *arañita?*"

Snorting, Josh playfully but gently smacked Ben's butt. "Babe, you're bi, I thought you knew hetero pairings have all kinds of sex, too. And it's not like Bonny and I haven't tried things, you know that. That includes things like rimming and anal for both of us as well."

Bonny cuddled closer against Ben's chest and hummed happily. "Josh is right. And I think lots of women would be happier if they realized that they're allowed to enjoy stuff like that, too, without being seen as super kinky or dirty or something."

"Yeah, you're both right. I just didn't meet a lot of women who were into any of it, and the guys I've been with who were more into women and only rarely into guys usually weren't as experienced in it."

Bonny grinned cheerfully at Ben. "Well, you're in luck with us, then. Hmm, and this actually seems like the perfect time to tell you two that I want you both inside me at the same time at some point."

Benicio gasped, and Josh ran his knuckles gently over her cheek. "You sure, baby?"

"Yes, absolutely. Perhaps not tomorrow, but in the future, yes."

Seeing the honesty in her eyes, Ben cupped her other cheek with his hand and pressed a soft kiss to her lips. "That sounds amazing, *mi amor.*"

Josh smiled blissfully at them before pecking a kiss against their skin. "It does. But as much as I like discussing future fun times, I think we should get ready for dinner."

· · ·

They were barely out of the shower after rinsing off again when they heard a knock on the door. Benicio wrapped a towel around his waist with a frown but told his lovers he'd go see who it was.

When he opened the door, his sister stood in front of him. She cocked her head and, after looking him up and down, bit her lip for a second. "Nice hickeys, brother," she informed him with a smirk in Spanish.

One of Ben's hands fluttered to his neck, touching first one then the other side. But then he rolled his eyes with an irritated huff. "Shut up, Val. Not that I'm not happy to see you, but what are you doing here? Did your dinner get canceled? You could come with us, we're just getting ready to head out."

Valeria stared at him in disbelief for a few seconds before she guffawed. "Oh god, you're serious. Benicio, I have no idea what you've been doing... Forget that; I can imagine exactly what and whom you were doing. You guys have seriously lost track of time. My dinner is over, and although I suspect you could still get a table at one of the restaurants, I need to talk to you, so maybe you could consider ordering something from room service."

"Ah, wha... Seriously?" Benicio was flustered for a second, then opened the door further. "Oh... Uhm, yeah, okay, come in, I'll let Bonny and Josh know. And stop grinning like that."

"Nope, not happening," Valeria answered, laughing again at her brother while stepping inside.

Chapter Sixteen

A little while later, all four of them sat in the living room of the bungalow, and Ben counted himself lucky to have such amazing partners as he did. They had both only laughed when he'd told them how long they'd all spent under the shower, and they had no problem at all dressing more comfortably and eating in their room with his sister.

They had quickly placed an order with an extra dessert for Valeria, and now were cuddled on the couch with Ben between Josh's legs and Bonny on Ben's lap. Val was sitting on the smaller couch opposite of them and grinned. "You guys are disgustingly cute together."

Bonny giggled and snuggled even closer into Benicio's arms. "Thanks. So, Ben said you wanted to talk about something. Do you need us for another trivia night? More dance lessons? You know we're happy to help, and that's not just because we're dating your brother."

Valeria smiled at the other woman but shook her head. "I know, and it's appreciated. But it's nothing like that. There was a larger change of plan. I wasn't initially scheduled to do this at all, but some of the lifeguards got sick and had to take some time off. Management knows I swam for the school team. There's an off-site training pool, and I and a couple of employees have to go there tomorrow and stay a few days. We'll get some training. We won't end up certified lifeguards, but we'll be taught the basics so we can fill in until they find a proper replacement. And before you ask, no, there's no way for you to come along. It's a private training facility."

Both Bonny and Josh felt Benicio stiffen between them. "I don't like this, Valeria," he told her slowly.

His sister ran her hand through her hair and sighed. "I didn't expect you to. What do you want me to say? This is my job, even if it's just an internship. But come on, I'll be with my colleagues the whole time. And yes, I know how many girls have vanished. But don't you think if it was at the hands of one of their coworkers, they'd have caught the guy? It would be obvious to hop from hotel to hotel and have girls vanish, and then somebody quits, right? And let's be totally honest: nobody even knows what happened to those girls. Which is scary, sure. But who knows, they might have left on their own. It's not like they've been found."

Josh and Bonny stayed quiet. They knew Benicio couldn't just talk about the case, even with his sister. With her not knowing that he was involved in the investigation, they couldn't fault her logic. What Josh could do, though, was offer something to ease his lover's mind a little.

"Can I make a suggestion?" Josh asked and gently ran his fingers through Benicio's hair, pressing a kiss to his temple before looking at Valeria.

"Of course," Ben answered, while his sister only nodded.

"All right. I know this will sound intrusive at first but bear with me, please."

Valeria's eyebrows rose, and she possibly couldn't look a lot more sceptical than she already did but she gestured for Josh to go on.

"Thanks. So, my future boss is currently testing new GPS trackers, and he gave me a couple. We each have one in our luggage, and he gave me access to the portal to check how accurate they are. It's a new generation and they're really small, but the battery lasts for a while. We could lend you one. You couldn't wear it in the pool, but in case these women were indeed abducted, I seriously doubt anybody would do that to you while you're in the water surrounded by others."

Valeria's expression as she answered him was so stoic that Josh thought she had to be an amazing poker player. "I love how you make it sound like a favor to *me* to lend me a tracker when we all know it's just to lessen my brother's worries."

"Val..." Benicio began, but she held up her hand.

"Stop. Brother, you cannot expect me to be happy about this. I understand why Josh offered. And as much as I hate it, I will agree to it. Otherwise, you'll just show up there, too."

It was in that moment that Ben understood how worried his sister actually was. Aside from all her placating words to their mother and her current effort to seem nonchalant, he knew she would never agree to this if she wasn't acutely aware of the situation in the country and possibly even had an idea of what the media wasn't saying.

"Thank you, Val. It will indeed help me knowing where you are. It's not that I don't trust you, you know that."

"*Sí, sí.* I know. Doesn't make it easier but whatever."

Ben only nodded. But Josh dared a small smile. "For what it's worth, it's not just for Ben. Bonny and I like you, too, Val. It will ease our minds as well."

"I like you guys, too. And you make my brother happy and care about him, so I get it. Let's just get this over with, okay? I'll give you the damn thing back once I'm back here."

"Sure. I'll get one of the trackers," Bonny said and got up from Ben's lap.

Once their dinner had arrived, they had talked some more, making plans for Valeria to also check in by text. But now she was gone again to pack her things, and Josh and Bonny flanked their boyfriend on the couch. "Thank you for not saying anything to her about the case."

Bonny took Ben's hand and kissed his palm. "Of course. I mean, we don't know a lot, but still. Although I want to say, I think she has a rough idea. Your sister is smart; she knows you wouldn't be this tense for nothing."

"*Lo sé*," Ben sighed and leaned his forehead against Bonny's shoulder. "I know, and you're right about her."

Josh ran his hand in soothing circles over Ben's back. "Sweetheart, listen, I know you are not supposed to talk about any of it. But you know we'll be a vault. Do you want to let us know more about the case? Sometimes talking about it helps."

Ben lifted his head and looked from one to the other. "I know you wouldn't say anything. I trust you. I've trusted you right from the start, or I wouldn't have told you even the little that I did. And I really, really shouldn't tell you anything else. But... I don't know, I just have a bad feeling. And for some reason, I have learned to listen to my gut recently," he added with a sad smile, which earned him a kiss on the cheek from Josh and one on the lips from Bonny.

"So, yeah, I will tell you what I know. Let me get us coffee first; this is going to take some time."

Each with a mug in hand, they soon sat facing each other, and Benicio began talking. "First of all, sorry for this in advance. It's your vacation, it should be a happy occasion. But this will not exactly be a cheerful story."

"You know you make us happy, no matter what. And when it comes to the case, it might not be happy. But it's not something you caused. Don't worry about that, Ben," Bonny assured him, and Josh nodded in agreement.

"You make me happy, too. Okay... Things started probably about three years ago. At least that's what I know from the files I've seen over time. I wasn't on the case right from the beginning; I had barely started my job. And frankly, I'm not sure my department has even been called to every find of remains that might be related to this. The communication between different police stations is also a mess. So I don't think I have all the information there is. I'm not even sure *anybody* has all the information in one place. But it's enough to paint you a picture.

"About three years ago, skeletal remains were found in a national park near Mexico City. Often, these cases are people who either got lost while hiking, or sometimes they committed suicide. There would be an examination by an ME, but our department is not always called in for a consultation. In this case, though, an American tourist had gone missing a while before, and they wanted to confirm whether it was him or not and what might have happened to him. But when one of our forensic anthropologists arrived, she could tell that it was not only not the American, but also that the skeleton belonged to a young woman. Markings on the bones indicated that it might not have been an accidental or natural death. The investigation that followed indicated multiple deep stab wounds with the knife scraping over the bones, and there were other signs of physical violence close to her death. In the end, there was no way to determine whether the stab wounds were what killed her; the cause of death remained undetermined."

Josh nodded. He might lean towards cases involving technology and offenses like cybercrimes, but people hurt each other over those as well, so he had made sure he had a rough understanding of medical processes and evidence in criminal cases. "But even with the COD undetermined, was it treated as a murder case?"

"Yes, it was. But it went cold. The national park covers a large area, and there are no cameras along the trails, only the occasional wildlife camera, and without a more exact time of death than my colleague's best estimate, there was no chance to look for surveillance footage on the trail cams or of people entering the park at the gates. The skeleton also didn't offer a lot more to go on. It had been found after a particularly bad storm season. A lot of possible evidence had been lost to exposure to the elements."

"Could she be identified?" Bonny asked quietly.

"No, not her. She has remained a... how do you call them in the US... a Jane Doe."

"Yeah, that's the term we usually use," Josh confirmed. "But you said 'not her,' so I assume there were more and you could identify them."

"You're right, *arañita*, there were more. Seven more cases we've been called to consult on since then. All of them young women, and their remains were found all over the country. Out of these seven, we could extract DNA from five of them, and out of those could match four to either missing person cases or, in one case, to one of the ancestry databases people send their samples to."

Bonny sadly shook her head. "So four out of eight. I guess, as terrible as it is, at least the families of those four have some kind of closure even without all the answers. Have those other cases given you any more to work with? Are there any speculations about what's going on? Is it a serial killer killing somewhere before moving on to avoid getting caught?"

"Frankly, we don't know," Ben admitted with a heavy sigh. "It's crossed our mind, yes. But then again, there's not much to go on. What these cases seem to have in common is the fact that any soft tissue was removed from the bones by maceration. Somebody cleaned them chemically, and from what we could gather, it's likely the same chemicals were used for all of those that we could test for it. That has made it harder to find any other evidence; it also prevented us from getting DNA from the three of the unidentified victims because the DNA had deteriorated under the chemicals. Then, in some cases, we can't be sure there were chemicals used because the bones lay outside for too long to be absolutely positive. Not all cases show the same knife marks; one woman had a broken neck, another a bullet wound in her skull. It doesn't scream serial killer to me, but..." Benicio didn't know how to put into words what his gut told him.

Josh seemed to feel something similar, though. "But it feels strangely organized and meticulously planned at the same time, not like different cases coincidentally showing the same results."

"Sí, that's exactly what my mind and my gut tell me. But given some of the differences, not everybody thinks these cases are connected. So there's no pressure to start a larger investigation. And that's another problem: there's no collective case file. All of them are investigated separately by the respective police departments. And I'm not always called to the cases; sometimes it's a colleague and I hear after the fact. Although I have to give it to my boss: he tries to send me when he thinks it's a case that could be connected. In that aspect, he's actually helpful and supports my theory. It's his boss who's blocking everything."

"I hate all that hierarchy thinking sometimes," Josh mumbled.

"Not just you. But you'll find a lot of that here, depending on where you look. Lots of things work well, others are stuck in old structures, and a lot of it also comes from a strong macho culture, and everybody needs to prove they know what they're doing and don't need help from anybody."

"Some guys just don't outgrow the dick comparison phase, do they?" Bonny commented sarcastically.

"No, they really don't. And it's not just my department. I tried to convince the cops on the cases I consulted on to reach out to others. All but one told me they knew how to work a case and not to try to interfere with their investigation or give them any opinion other than what I could get from the bones. The one cop who tried it was blocked by the other departments. They reminded him none-too-kindly that he'd better focus on his own case and not make them look like they had no clue what was going on."

"Damn it," both his lovers grumbled.

"Yes. Now you see why I'm worried. It's not only that I'm scared for Valeria in the first place. On top of that, I'm worried that, should anything happen to her in relation to this, her case might not even be properly investigated, and we never would get any answers."

Bonny circled her arm around Ben's waist and let her thumb caress his skin under his shirt. "I totally get that. Can you tell us why you're so worried Valeria might be targeted? Don't get me wrong, she's pretty and catches people's attention to begin with, and she's smart and kind. But is there something that makes her stand out, that could connect her to the other women? Were there similarities that you know of between them in the first place?"

Ben smiled at her. For somebody who wasn't planning a career in anything remotely linked to crime investigations, Bonny still knew to ask the right things. "Excellent question, *mi amor*. Yeah, I've looked into that, into the cases as much as I could, like I told you. My boss and I have an unofficial file where we keep all relevant information in one place. We might get in trouble for it but it's too important not to do it. To come back to your question: yes, all the women we could identify had a few things in common. Like you said about Val, they were also all pretty, so it's no surprise they'd catch somebody's eye. Even though they all looked different. They were all between eighteen and twenty-four years old. As you know, they all worked in high-class hotels. On top of that, they all spoke English fluently and well, and they all had some form of connection to the US – either because they had once worked or lived there themselves, had studied at a US university, or some of their family had done one or more of those things. All of them had no criminal records and a clean bill of health. At least, that's all I know of them."

Josh cupped Ben's cheek and softly pressed their foreheads together. "No wonder you're afraid for her. Most high-class hotels will do a background check on their people, making sure they don't accidentally hire a paparazzi pretending to be somebody else to protect their guests. That check would tell them all they'd need to know." He left out that a thorough check might even have brought up Ben's name, and, depending on what people were looking for, that his involvement could show up and make her even more of a target. If this hadn't occurred to Ben so far, then Josh thought his boyfriend didn't need to feel like this could be his fault in any way. Instead, Josh tried to focus on things Benicio might actually be able to tell him. "Do you know how or from where the other girls vanished? Did they just not show up for work one day, were they taken mid-shift from the hotels?"

Benicio sighed heavily. On the one hand, it was amazing to feel the love and support from his partners, to see them believe in his theory and try to understand what was going on and what had led him to his conclusions. On the other hand, it meant that he was probably right to be afraid for his sister. Yes, the country was large, there was no pattern, no rhyme or reason to when and where the women had vanished. Still, he had a gut feeling – and it wasn't telling him anything good. Hearing that Bonny and

Josh could understand his worries was a relief and terrifying at the same time. For a moment, he leaned into Josh's touch, enjoying the warmth and the flutter it caused in his stomach. Then he faced the sadder topic of the evening once more. "From what I could find out, nobody ever really saw anything. One girl didn't come back after her lunch break, another never arrived home at the apartment she shared with a roommate after her shift. There wasn't a hotel guest who conveniently left that day. And in some cases, the police didn't investigate a lot in the beginning because it was a woman just leaving, nothing pointed to a crime. And when the remains were found, it was too late for a lot of things that would've helped with the investigation. People had quit, guests had long gone home, you know how it is."

Josh nodded, his hand running through his boyfriend's hair in a soothing motion. He shared a look with Bonny over Benicio's head, an unspoken conversation passing between them. They both knew what was going on in Ben's head and they shared his unease. Unfortunately, there was nothing they could do about it at the moment.

Bonny joined Josh in comforting Ben, her hand running in slow circles over his back. "We know, yes. And it's good that you told us what you did. We can't be there for you without knowing what's going on. We get you, sweetheart. We honestly do. But I also wanna say, your sister is smart, she's capable. And she agreed to the GPS tracker. Even if anything happens to her, we'll be able to find her, to get her back. For tonight, let's put it aside. If not, you'll only make yourself crazy."

"I know... I... yeah, I think you're right. What would you like to do?"

"Hmm, I think there's supposed to be a meteor shower going on tonight. Why don't we all get into our private pool and observe that? We should have a great view of the sky, and you know the water is nice and we have a place to sit and relax."

That drew a tired chuckle from Ben's lips. It wasn't like they had ever used the built-in bench seat beneath the surface on one end of the pool to actually sit on when they'd been in the water. But it was a nice leverage to stop yourself from drowning while you were busy making out with the people you loved. "Yeah, okay, let's do that."

"Perfect," Bonny said and gave first Ben and then Josh a soft kiss before getting off the sofa.

She didn't plan on anything happening. But the water had the perfect temperature to make you sleepy when you spent some quiet time in it. Which was what Bonny was counting on. She wanted to make sure Benicio could sleep tonight, and right now he was too troubled for a good night's sleep.

Chapter Seventeen

The light flooding the room told Benicio it was already late morning when he woke up the next day. He had fallen asleep in seconds, caught in the drowsiness from the warm water and the warmth of his lovers surrounding him. The night before, Bonny had taken care of him so sweetly, running the shower to rinse off the pool water, then had guided him to bed and cuddled him under the covers, holding up the other side for Josh to join them. It had been exactly what Benicio had needed. It was just his luck that a few hours later, somebody had thought it a brilliant idea to walk through the garden with a crying baby, singing lullabies to try to get the child back to sleep. It hadn't been right in front of their bungalow, and Bonny and Josh had slept through the fairly quiet interruption of the silence of the night, but Benicio had woken up and after that had tossed from side to side until exhaustion had dragged him back to sleep when the first light of the day had barely been visible.

It seemed like he had gotten a few more hours of sleep after all. Not that he felt full of energy. But at the very least, he wouldn't be dead on his feet once he got out of bed. The very empty bed. Bonny and Josh had probably been awake for a bit and had wanted to let him sleep a little longer. Now that he was waking up more and more, he could make out faint but distinct sounds in the living room through the closed bedroom door. With a soft smile on his face, Benicio got out of bed and grabbed some lounge pants before quietly opening the door.

The living room was flooded with sunlight, the air full of the sounds of slow kisses and low moans. He spotted Bonny and Josh wrapped up in each other's arms. They were sitting in a tight embrace, facing each other on the couch, and moving sinuously together. The sunlight reflected from several colorful glass decorations in the room, painting vividly glowing spots on the glistening skin of the loves of his life. It was an amazing picture, and for the moment, he lost himself completely in watching them and forgot about his fear. He knew their body language, knew their expressions – they were both so close. He loved seeing them light up with the pleasure of their orgasms, and he would have happily stayed where he was, watching them tumble over the edge together.

But Josh spotted him, and somehow his smile got even brighter when he held out his hand towards Benicio. "Good morning, baby. Come, join us."

It was an invitation he would never refuse, even if he knew he wouldn't participate this time. Still, he wandered over to the couch and knelt next to them on it. They both leaned in for a deliciously sweet, slow three-way kiss. But when Bonny skimmed her hand over Ben's chest and further down, he stopped her and brought her fingers to his lips, kissing each of them. "Go on, you two. I'm fine, just not awake enough, yet."

"Are you sure?" Josh asked with concern in his voice, his fingers combing through Ben's hair while he studied his boyfriend's eyes.

"Absolutely, *bebé*. I'm still a little tired, that's all. But you two are so beautiful together, and I want to watch you making each other happy. That's enough for me for right now."

"Okay," Josh accepted and stole another kiss from Ben before turning to Bonny again.

She leaned in for one more kiss from Benicio as well, then brought her attention back to Josh. They began moving again, their lips meeting. But with Ben's hands running up and down each of their backs, they were smiling too brightly to truly kiss. And when they exploded, they both held on to each other with one hand, the other reaching for Benicio and dragging him into an open-mouthed kiss, their moans floating into him, filling him with their ecstasy.

It took them a few minutes to all come down. Benicio might not have actively had sex with them this time, but it was heady enough of an experience to just be with them in the moment. Finally, Bonny scooted off Josh's lap and dragged her men to the bathroom for a morning shower.

When they were dressed, they ordered some breakfast, and Ben shook his head with a small smile. "You two could've gone to the restaurant. It would've been okay."

"Yeah, and let you wake up alone in the bungalow, all worried and after what was probably not an exactly restful night. Sure, that's gonna happen," Bonny commented dryly.

"She's right. You know we wouldn't do that to you, baby."

The best part? Yes, he knew that. They hadn't known each other for long, but he knew them. He nodded, his expression grateful. "I do. And I thank you for that. It's amazing to know you care about me as much as I care about you. So, yeah, back to what you said, *mi amor*, yes, the night wasn't that restful. But I checked my phone after the shower. Val texted me that they left early and arrived at the training facility according to plan. She knows the people she's with, except the guys giving them the lessons. But she says she won't go anywhere alone, and she has to share the room for their stay, so she won't even be alone there."

"That's good news, I'd say. And to make you feel better, come here," Josh told Benicio and picked up his phone from the couch table. He settled on the sofa and held his arm open for his boyfriend to snuggle close, then opened an app. He held his phone so both of them could have a look while Bonny was getting them all a water from the minibar. A dot on a map showed up right where Ben's sister was supposed to be. It was moving slowly but only to turn around again, then repeating the pattern. "She might be training right now, could be a warm-up run or something. The tracker is pretty precise, you can see even small movements. She's okay," Josh said and pressed a kiss to Benicio's hair.

"Thank you, love. This does help."

"Anything for you. Do you have anything you'd like to do today?"

The three of them spent the day on a city tour and just enjoying the time together, doing some gift shopping and people watching from a small coffee shop, every once in a while glancing at the location ping or getting a text update from Valeria during her lunch break.

Time away from everything was something they hadn't known they had missed. Even now, the worry wasn't gone completely, but they could focus only on themselves for a while, planning dates and how to get Ben moved to the States as soon as possible. When Josh studied his boyfriend and finally asked him whether he could give up the case, Benicio took a long moment to earnestly consider the question. Then he nodded, telling them he knew there was – for the moment, with the road-blocks he was facing – just nothing he could really do, and that it would no doubt eat more at him being called to more possibly related cases without being able to make people see what was going on. Leaving it behind was far from ideal, but he didn't want to spend his career fighting something he couldn't change when he had a chance to work with people who would listen to him and make an actual difference. His answer brushed away a worry both Josh and Bonny had been having ever since Ben had told them all that he knew about the case.

In the afternoon, it started to rain, and the three of them visited a museum before heading back to the hotel. Val commented that they looked "again: just so annoyingly sweet together" when they sent her a selfie they had taken while snuggling close under one umbrella waiting for their ride back to the hotel.

Their evening ended with lazily making love.

It had been a perfect day.

And if fate wanted to balance the scales, it did a terrific job when the next morning turned out to be a nightmare.

Chapter Eighteen

A dark alley behind some warehouses. The first flashes of lightning harbingers of the coming storm.

"Such a cliché," a young woman muttered in Spanish.

Several men stepped in her way, and she held out her hand. "Give me my money, then get out of here. I have no idea where you're going, but I want to be back in my room before the storm hits."

One of the men reached into his pocket and pulled out a bundle of banknotes.

Another pointed a finger at the woman. "You'd better hope she's worth this. You had us go through a lot of trouble for that one. Coming up with this whole scheme, drugging people, only to get her away to some training facility."

"She's exactly what you are looking for," she told them with a glance at the car at the end of the alley with a slumped figure sitting inside. "It's not my fault her brother and his lovers were watching her all the time."

"That is indeed not your fault, I will give you that. What *is* your fault, though, is how long all this took. And we know precisely why," the guy replied.

His colleague gave up the pretense of counting money and looked at her. "We do. And we hate rats, no matter how far down the ladder they are," he said and pushed the money back into his pocket.

Color drained from her face, her skin stark white when the next lightning bolt raced over the sky. "What... I have no idea what you're talking about."

"But you do, don't you? We found out about you getting paid to sell information. I'm not sure what's so special about that girl from the ship, and I don't care. Your plan to get people to follow us as we deliver this one won't work. We cannot be found just like that; you should have known that. Now you will pay for your greed."

A third man had been quiet so far. Now he nodded. "You will. Grab her," he told the others as he drew a gun and began screwing on a silencer.

They reached out for her before she could run, their fingers digging hard into her arms.

Terror crept into her eyes, into her voice as she desperately tried to break their hold. "No, please, no. I didn't! No!"

"You can stop lying; it won't save you."

"I... please, no! I'm sorry! It won't ever happen again, I swear!"

"You're right, it won't," the man with the gun said, aiming at her with a steady hand as he pulled the trigger.

The woman collapsed between the men, her last cry dying abruptly. The shooter glanced at the sky, then back to his colleagues. "I will take care of this. You leave with the girl now before you can't get away before the storm anymore."

They nodded, and after their departure, the clean-up began, the first drops of rain already washing away the blood from the pavement.

Chapter Nineteen

Benicio, Josh, and Bonny were startled awake by the sound of shattering glass from the living room. Outside, a storm was raging. The wind howled between the bungalows; fat raindrops drummed loudly against the windows. It was still early, and the thick clouds made the darkness even more oppressive. There was a beauty to it. An eerie reminder that, no matter what you did, nature was just so much more powerful than humans.

Benicio was closest to the door and slid out of bed to check what had happened. A quick look told him that a giant leaf of one of the palm trees close by had been ripped off and had crashed into a window in the living room. The glass had shattered in one corner, but luckily most of the window was still intact. With a frustrated grunt, he called for his lovers to stay in bed, then reached for the phone and called Reception.

But when he came back into the bedroom, he found both Bonny and Josh getting dressed with dread written on their faces. "What's wrong?" he asked warily, already reaching for his clothes as well.

Josh knew this would be a shock no matter how he'd deliver

it. So he went for direct and quick. Benicio needed to know, and they needed to act quickly. "I checked Val's GPS location. I wanted to make sure they're good with the storm going on. She's not at the training facility anymore. From what I can see, she's likely in a car and being driven south-west. It's five now, the location history tells me she's been on the move for about an hour and a half."

"I tried to call her. She's not answering her phone, either," Bonny threw in.

Benicio froze for a second, the color draining from his face. It flooded back with a vengeance a second later, and he exploded. "Fuck! Fuck, fuck, fuck."

"I know. It gets worse. They're close to a private airfield now. Call the police. You'll be quicker to explain it in Spanish. I'll give you the details. Bonny, will you get the door when somebody comes for the window?"

She nodded, just as Ben who picked up his mobile phone and immediately placed the call. He was talking too rapidly for Josh and Bonny to understand everything. But from his rising agitation, it was obvious that the call didn't go well. Ben grabbed a fistful of his own hair in desperation, almost yelling at the phone.

Next to him, Josh kept his eyes on the screen of his own phone, following the dot moving across the map. Bonny left them both when she heard somebody knocking on the door.

After showing the tired-looking maintenance guy the damage, she moved back to the bedroom and closed the door behind herself. She saw Josh catching Benicio's wrist right before he could throw his phone against the wall, an angry growl coming from him. She rushed over to them and placed her hands on Ben's face. "Hey, hey, what's going on?"

"They said they can't do a lot right now. She's an adult, and there's no sign of an abduction."

"Excuse me, what?"

"They said she probably left on her own accord. They'll be nice enough to call her employer later in the morning and possibly send somebody to the training facility to check."

Both Josh and Bonny shook their heads, and Josh asked, "What about the tracker? The drive in the middle of the night to an airfield?"

"Oh, they only think it's concerning that I would track my sister. They said that it wasn't even sure she'd be going to the airfield, and even if she did, that maybe she met somebody and he offered to take her on a flight in the morning, hoping the weather would improve, and that's why they left so early. Apparently, there's a guy in the area who actually does that to score with women."

Bonny's blood began to boil over the ignorance of these police officers. "Did you tell them about the other women?"

"*Sí*, I did. That's when they told me something like this doesn't happen in a popular area like here, and I should better not start any rumors, and hung up."

Bonny seemed speechless, and Josh cursed. "What the actual fuck." A glance at his phone had him fist the hand that had only just let go of Ben's wrist. "Shit. They're at the airfield."

"We have to get there! Now!" Benicio's voice was full of panic.

Josh could absolutely understand why. And he hated to be the one shoving the reality of the situation into his face but he had to – the faster they got through to him, the faster they could start on an actual solution. "Babe, I know this is hard. But we can't get there on time. This is all planned out; their plane will be ready and waiting for them, especially if they want to get away from the storm."

Ben stared in disbelief at his lover. "You want to give up on her? How can you?"

But Josh shook his head. "I'm not giving up on her. But we need a plan. They will very likely be in the air shortly. Even if we could mobilize the cops to drive there now, they would not make it in time. And even if they did... The kidnappers could be rushed to take off. You don't want that in this weather. Here's what we'll do instead: call the cops once again, try to convince them to act now. And I know this is the hardest part, but try to stay calm. It won't help to have you written up or arrested or something. If they still refuse, call Reception again and demand to speak to Management. Ask them to contact the training facility and to check on Valeria."

"What good will that do us?" Ben knew it wouldn't help at all. Why would Josh ask him to do that?

"It will hopefully get *somebody* to move their ass and try to help. But at the very least, it will show how desperate you are. Which could save our asses later," Josh confessed.

Bonny's eyes snapped from Ben to Josh. "What do you have in mind?"

"Our own rescue mission. While Ben is busy raising hell, you pack the essentials for us. Pack lightly, use our backpacks. I will make use of my education and try to find out where they'll be going."

Bonny nodded, but Benicio looked confused. "What is that supposed to mean?"

"It means he'll put all his cybersecurity knowledge to the test and hack the flight plan for the plane."

Josh nodded. "Yes. It's a private airfield. My guess is they chose it because it comes with fewer security checks, which makes it easier to hide things like kidnapping a person. But the small airports usually come with less security protecting their own systems. They still log their flights, though, including the planned flight path and destination. There are so many planes in the air nowadays that it's a safety measure almost every airport takes. I will just have a look. This time of the night, there won't be many flights; we'll know which plane Val's on."

"Wait... isn't it illegal to hack their system?"

"Well, the hack is, yes. Normally, I could look up a flight tracking website that also shows private flights. But those often have a little delay after take-off, especially for private flights, because of all the data coming in every second. Just looking at the destination in the airport's system is... let's call it a gray area. I could theoretically get the data later legally. But right now, I want it asap. Once we know where they're going, I'll work on getting us a plane to take us there, too. I cannot promise you it will be just as quick, though," Josh cautioned after another look at his phone. "We'll have the best chance of finding a plane at Cancún Airport, and they just grounded all flights due to the storm. Your sister's kidnappers are lucky because they're on the fringes of the weather front, but we'll have to wait it out for a little while. But if the police are doing nothing, I promise you, we will do everything we can."

Benicio was overwhelmed for a moment, then shook himself. "But... you can't do something like that. What if it comes out and you can't do your job... And what do you mean, 'getting us a plane?'"

Josh took his lover's face in his hands and looked him in the eyes, love and determination burning equally bright in his own. "Don't worry about it. I doubt it will be a problem, and even if so, I can probably claim I got the data a little later. But this is an emergency, and the police aren't doing their job. I will not let your sister suffer the consequences of that. Let me worry about that, okay? And as for the plane, Cancún Airport is large enough to offer several charter airlines. We'll get us a plane that can bring us to exactly where they're going."

"I…" Ben desperately wanted to argue – he couldn't let Josh put his future at risk like that. But he also couldn't let his sister vanish. Finally, he sighed. "Okay, yes, I'll trust you about the hacking. But… Look, I want to get to Val as quickly as possible, but I won't be able to afford a private plane. I might be doing well enough, but that's out of my league. We'll have to look into regular flights."

"We won't," Bonny told him firmly. "You are part of our family. Josh and I would do anything to help you. We might not usually spend money like that – hell, even this vacation was more of a gift from our families than us picking such an expensive place – but we, *have* the money. Well, Josh does. We'll get a private plane to follow those bastards. No discussion."

"But…"

"No discussions, you heard her."

"I… uh…" Benicio struggled to get a grip on the situation in general and on the complete and unquestionable support. Finally, he sighed deeply. "Thank you."

"Of course. Now, get moving, both of you. I have to get on with this so I know where we need to go," Josh commanded and finished the argument with a quick peck on the lips for both of his partners before sitting down on the bed and getting to work.

And somehow – he still wasn't entirely sure how exactly it had happened – two hours later, Benicio found himself pacing up and down the aisle of a small plane Josh had organized along with a pilot to fly them to Guatemala.

Earlier, he and Bonny had followed Josh's plan. But as much as Benicio had pleaded with the authorities, not a lot had been done. Yes, the hotel had reacted. They had even talked to the police as well, who then had grudgingly agreed to send somebody to the training facility right away. While Josh had still been working, Ben had gotten a call back from the cops telling him that the whole group of trainees and trainers had been out for dinner and drinks the evening before, and that his sister and her roommate had been talking to some guy nobody could describe properly. With Ben's sister and the roommate both gone from their room, the police figured they were right and the women were just enjoying a reckless night with a stranger. Ben should give them another call if his sister didn't get in contact within the next twenty-four hours. They had hung up after that and ignored all of his other calls. The hotel had gotten the same response. They had then promised to keep trying to talk to the police but had also been careful not to acknowledge any responsibility for the situation.

Then things had moved swiftly. Josh had gotten the information he had been looking for, and all three of them were in a car on the way to Cancún and the city's airport barely ten minutes later.

As it was, they still had to wait for their clearance to take off, but their pilot had told them a few minutes ago that it looked like they would get it soon and that the storm had almost passed. It should have been a relief, but all Benicio could think about was that the kidnappers had a big head start.

Finally, Bonny took his hand and gently tugged him into his seat. "It's gonna be fine, baby. We'll get her back. But you have to sit down so we can take off as soon as the pilot gets the okay. I know this is hard, but we have an advantage nobody else ever had. We know when she was taken, and we know where she's going. We can track her movements. And hopefully, we'll have better luck with the authorities in Guatemala. Hopefully, they'll do their job and help us get her out of there."

Ben just nodded sadly. He had tried to tell himself exactly the same things, and both Bonny and Josh had laid out these arguments for him multiple times before. He *knew* they had a point. Still, he felt like he was going crazy, like he had failed his sister somehow. To make matters worse, he had decided not to text or call his mother to let her know right away. He knew he should. But he couldn't deal with a frantic call from her at that moment (let alone imagine one of his lovers taking the phone from him and letting them deal with her panic), or worse, have her jump into her car and drive for hours to get from her home to the hotel just to find him and her daughter both gone. No, Benicio was not doing well at the moment.

But then he realized Josh was reaching over him and fastening his seatbelt for him, taking care of him, while Bonny made sure all their things were put away for takeoff. Their care grounded him like nothing else ever had. He wasn't at his best – but he wasn't alone. They were with him, and they'd do every-thing they could to help him. That thought brought him a sense of calm he hadn't felt since the moment he had seen Josh's agitated face staring at the map on his phone hours ago. Looking from one to the other, he reached for both of them and sighed a heavy, "Thank you," seconds before the pilot let them know they'd been cleared for takeoff.

Chapter Twenty

Josh was relieved they were all three experienced fliers. A nervous traveler would no doubt have panicked. It had not been a pleasant start. The rain had battered against the hull and windows, and the storm had shaken the small plane left to right and up and down, forcing the pilot to prolong their ascent to avoid climbing through the severest part of the storm clouds. Lightning near them had illuminated the cabin despite the dimmed lights more than once. And that had only been the last edge of the storm.

Then they had finally left the storm front behind, and the sky had become calm, the sun shining around them. And had they not been on a desperate rescue mission, they could have admired the view. Most of the flight path had them cruising over lush forest areas and some national parks.

As it was, Josh instead handed Bonny and Benicio his phone with the tracking app open for them to keep an eye on Valeria's movements while he opened his laptop. First, he sent an email to his future boss explaining the situation and why one of the man's trackers showed up somewhere far away from where it should have been. He was vague about how he had known where to go, but he knew, should he ever have to explain why he'd bent the rules, his boss would understand. He had founded his PI business after his own niece's disappearance and the cops' useless investigation two decades ago, after all. Josh knew he could count on his boss to offer him any tips he might have for a case like this, and he made sure somebody knew where they were and what was happening so there was somebody to send help if he didn't hear back from them with updates. The man had more far-reaching contacts than Josh, and some of those contacts weren't as bound to bureaucracy and the regulations of their positions as the law enforcement contacts Josh had.

Bonny looked over to Josh and scanned his screen. "Babe, are you sure you don't want to let Ty and Scarlette know? Or Luke?" It wasn't that she didn't trust Josh's boss. She did, or she would have voiced her concerns before he had signed the employment contract. But it felt strange not to inform the people she knew had solved more than one mystery and were family. It was hard enough not to tell her own parents and siblings – but she shared Benicio's thoughts when it came to panicked family members. But Tyler and Scarlette would keep their heads, and Luke would be able to possibly mobilize the FBI or maybe even somebody from the CIA.

Josh shook his head. "Usually I would, you know that, baby. But Luke would have to tackle far too many bureaucratic hurdles to act fast enough, and with Ty and Scarlette, I'm not even sure they'd get any message at the moment. I haven't heard from them in a while, so I don't think they're anywhere near a place with constant reception or internet access. We all knew we'd probably lose contact for a few days during our vacation and their trip. It looks like that's the case right now. My last text from yesterday didn't even go through," Josh replied.

Months before, the brothers had talked about this before booking everything, but had agreed that a few days without being able to reach each other wasn't anything to worry about. Josh and Bonny would enjoy their downtime, and Ty would accompany Scarlette on a trip to Madagascar where she would meet with one of her former fellow students who worked at a wildlife sanctuary there now. With a recent new wave of people keeping exotic pets, Scarlette wanted hands-on training handling different lemurs so she could help the authorities better when they were seizing illegally owned pets. Ty would use the time to write his next book uninterrupted.

It had been a great plan. But it also meant that, even if Josh contacted his brother now, the message might only reach him a few days later – which wouldn't do the throuple any good in case they needed help quickly.

"Okay, yeah. Then let's put a plan together for when we land," Bonny decided. She removed a notebook from her backpack and flipped it to an empty page to create a list.

Josh took one look at her and smiled despite the bleak situation. Her face showed pure focus, and he knew her attention to detail. They wouldn't miss a thing. Her determination to achieve a goal would intimidate any future business competitors.

"All right, we'll need maps of the area. Under other circumstances, I'd say a car as well, but I have no idea if there will even be any roads. Seriously, who flies to the middle of nowhere in the Guatemalan jungle? Anyway, full camping gear. And is there a chance we could hire a guide? I know it's a risk. It's a sparsely populated area, the guide could work for them and warn them. But as much as I loved going camping with my dad when I was younger, I have no idea how to survive in the rainforest, and that's where we'll be from the looks of it," she told the guys so they could talk about it while she kept scribbling down her points.

Benicio looked at her in awe for a moment but then he spoke up. "Actually, I know how to do that."

Josh cocked his head with curiosity in his eyes. "How?"

"When I was still studying, I had a friend who studied ecology. One of his projects had him working in the rainforest. I had a month without courses to study for exams, and I decided to join him to get away from the constant distractions. I loaded everything I needed for the exams on a tablet and joined him. We camped in the jungle for weeks with him working on his project and collecting data and me helping with the camp, and as soon as that was set up and the daily chores done, I had hours to myself to study. And, as you know, I also know how to climb, which could be helpful. From the quick glance I had of the map around the airport they're landing at, it looks like we'll be in mountainous terrain. So you better add climbing equipment to the list, too, *bebé*," Ben finished with a glimpse at her notebook.

"Excellent point," Bonny agreed and wrote it down before leaning over and pressing a kiss against Benicio's cheek. "You're amazing."

They spent the rest of the flight planning, and Josh looked up a small store offering adventure packages and adventure tours nearby. He contacted them right away and got lucky when they said they could organize everything on their list and deliver it to the airfield.

The throuple's plane would land at a different small airport to the east near the kidnapper's destination. It was a gamble, and Josh hoped they wouldn't lose some miles depending on which direction the kidnappers would go from the airport. But choosing the same airport without knowing whether the kidnappers controlled it or had contacts there informing them about unusual activities was too risky. Luckily, with the dense jungle in the area, a lot of traffic was done via planes, and small airfields were scattered all over and close to each other.

It turned out that "airport" or even "airfield" were generous descriptions for the short patch of flattened dirt on a narrow plateau between two smaller mountains. From the cabin, they could only see the ground shortly before touching down; before that, they had been enveloped by thick clouds and fog hanging between the mountains. Josh suddenly realized how lucky he had been to find a pilot who knew the region – not every pilot would be able to land there just like that. He made sure to get the man's contact information so he would be able to ask him to pick them up again.

Once the pilot opened the door for them, the throuple stepped out into the moist air. They were high enough above sea level for it to be mild but not too hot, and the air held the promise of chilly temperatures once darkness would fall. Bonny was glad she had checked a weather report before packing their backpacks back at the hotel.

They spotted a young man waving at them from a jeep with the logo of the shop Josh had contacted and made their way over to pick up their gear and get going after the kidnappers right away. They had given up on the initial plan to involve the local police first.

Benicio had tried to talk to the local authorities while they had still been in the air but had been almost as unsuccessful as with the Mexican police. The young woman had sounded like she wanted to genuinely help them at first. Then he had heard her supervisor in the background. She had talked to the man and Ben had heard him grumbling about not having resources, and if it was a Mexican woman missing, he'd expect a call from their authorities. If they didn't even know whether the missing woman was or would stay in their municipality, he couldn't do anything anyway. After apologizing, the woman had hung up. It hadn't come as a surprise, but it had frustrated all three of them, nonetheless. On top of that, they hoped they hadn't tipped anybody off by making such a call. An organization like this could have contacts everywhere. But they had to try – who knew what they'd be faced with once they caught up with the kidnappers.

When they reached the jeep, the guy greeted them cheerily. "Hi there, y'all. I'm Mike. I hope you got here all right. We've gotten some storms over the last few days. But I think the worst is over for now. We'll make sure you've got everything you need in case another bad weather front rolls in, though, don't ya worry."

The man looked to be around Josh's and Bonny's age and was all smiles and enthusiasm when he shook everybody's hand. He didn't give them a chance to even say hello but kept on talking, "If you're wondering about the looks and accent, I'm originally from Texas. Met my wife on a backpacking trip 'bout three years ago, her family runs the shop, and I moved here and help out now. I love it, can't imagine goin' back. We're a small community here, sure, but everybody helps each other, and now that I've been here a while and gotten to know the area, I talked my family into offering tours. They weren't sure before that their English would be good enough to guide people through the jungle. They did well enough with the shop. But just sellin' a few items is easier, ya know? I started the tours for English-speaking tourists, and now my brother-in-law even started doin' the same for Spanish speakers. So if you guys decide you want a guide, just let me know. I love showing people around, and it's amazin' how many interestin' people ya get to meet that way. Actually, I was surprised to hear from another group comin' here just like that and lookin' to go explorin'. We just had some guys, I think from England, goin' by their accent, who asked for almost the same things you did. Y'all got lucky we recently got in a new order in preparation for the next tourist season. It's usually not that busy this time of the year with the rainy season goin' on, so we get everything in order for later right around now. The only thing we didn't have is more tents. You didn't say how many you needed, but we only got one left after the guys took the other three single tents. This one here is only a double with a little extra room for storage. I s'ppose you can share it with three people, but it'll be a tight fit. Hope y'all don't mind. Sorry about that," Mike told them, still with a smile on his face as he scratched his neck.

He was babbling like a waterfall, and Bonny thought this would be their best chance to interrupt him. "Oh, don't worry, that's totally fine. I love cuddling with my guys," she told him with a wink and ran her arms around Josh's and Ben's waists. Maybe it would stun him into silence.

It did not. Instead, an even brighter smile bloomed on Mike's face. "Oh, you three are together? That's cool! You should've told me. I would've looked for something romantic to throw in there, like a few solar string lights or something. Well, the tent will definitely have y'all cuddlin' together, at least. Now I don't feel too guilty the other guys got the tents. Pretty sure they're not together; they all gave off more of a military vibe, all beefy and muscled and tanned. Bit like the guys in the old *Top Gun* movie playing volleyball on the beach, though one of them was seriously sunburned. Hmm, thinking about it, guess they still could be together, of course, but they didn't seem like they had any chemistry going. They were more like friends or a friendly team going on a trip together, not a romantic getaway. But they didn't say a lot other than that they came here after spending some time in Mexico and wanted to see something other than the ocean for a bit."

The more Mike was saying, the more Josh felt a tingling at the base of his skull. Most likely, it was only the mention of a volleyball game and the ocean, but he got the feeling he might know who Mike was talking about. This was just too strange a coincidence to ignore. But he didn't want to give away too much to a person with no filter whatsoever who just told complete strangers too much without prompting. On the one hand, Mike could be a fount of information about the area, but on the other hand, Josh knew they'd just end up at the guy's family dinner table if he asked too many questions. He decided to keep it low-key instead. "Well, this certainly is a change of scenery for them, I'd say. Do you by any chance know in which direction they wanted to go? Just so we don't accidentally surprise them by stumbling into their camp."

The guy nodded eagerly. "Gotcha. They didn't say they had a specific goal in mind, so I gave them one of our maps that high-lights different attractions like caves and waterfalls. I added one of the maps to your gear, too. There's tons of stuff to see around here, so I think even if you run into each other, it won't be a problem. Anyway, they thanked me and left. I was driving around a little later and saw them leaving the village toward the west. Which is kinda weird cause there's not a lot in that direc-tion, mostly another small village a few miles from here. Person-ally, I'd rather go north or south, there's more to see in any of those directions. And with the gear you ordered, you're prepared for pretty much everything, so you shouldn't have any problems reaching anything worth seeing as long as you know a few things about adventuring in the jungle. Your list was quite comprehensive, so I think you'll be fine. Still, please be careful. There are radios, though, so you can call for help should anything happen. And I put a card in there with our shop's number and my personal number for when the shop is closed. You won't have reception everywhere but sometimes you get lucky, and if you have any questions that aren't urgent, try calling or texting."

Josh recalled the map he had studied during the flight. No, there was not a lot to see west from where they were, but there *was* the airport. And a glance at his phone currently in his boyfriend's hand told him that the signal from the tracker was moving south from that airport ever since the kidnappers had landed. It at least gave them a reason to start south as well without making Mike wonder what was going on (and possibly getting the terrible idea of following them). Still, given the situation and Mike's constant happy chatter, Josh was beginning to get a headache. Mike was a nice guy, but if they didn't stop him, he'd keep talking for the next few hours. And he could feel Ben and Bonny both getting more anxious to leave soon. He shared their feelings. "Uh, that's awesome information and very kind of you, Mike. Thanks so much. Please don't think we don't appreciate it, but we'd actually love to get going. There's still some daylight we'd like to make use of. Our girlfriend loves nature photography, and we want to make sure she can make the most of the time we're here and take as many photos as possible."

Yes, Josh was extremely glad Bonny had come up with that cover story to keep people from asking too many questions. One of her visual arts courses back in college had gotten her hooked on photography (albeit that usually included product photography and shooting for ads, not nature photography) and she had a camera with her most of the time. She held said camera up now with a grin. "They spoil me to make this possible, and I'd love to get some pictures for our place."

"Wow, that's awesome. I'd love to do that, too, but I just don't have the talent for it. None of my pictures ever look great. But I totally get you, and your boyfriends are great for supporting you like that. Don't let me stop you, then. If something comes up, don't hesitate to reach out, y'all," Mike told them once again, then accepted the payment from Josh and hopped into his jeep after a few last words about any dangerous flora and fauna and a round of goodbyes.

Chapter Twenty-One

As much as they hated the delay, they knew it was necessary to go through their gear and get prepared for a walk through the jungle. It seemed like Mike had done an exceptional job of providing them with whatever they might need. Benicio huffed out a relieved sigh and added quietly, "For all his..."

"Enthusiasm?" Bonny threw in.

Josh smirked, Ben chuckled. "Yeah, let's go with that. He at least knows what he's doing. We should be fine."

By the time they were done checking and dividing everything into their bags and adjusting their clothes, their pilot was taking off again. Alone, they looked around once more, this time truly taking in their surroundings. The plateau wasn't much: the short dirt runway, a shed with a few tools and a gas pump for the planes, a few lights, and at the edge of the plateau one tiny house with some equipment that supposedly functioned as a control tower on busier days but was currently empty, and a dirt road leading to the village that hugged the gentler slopes of the mountain east of the plateau. They could make out a few roofs from where they were standing, but most of the village, just like the rest of the plateau, was surrounded by thick rainforest. Luckily, the fog and clouds had mostly cleared since their landing.

Josh checked his phone again. "Okay, it looks like the kidnappers are making their way southeast now with Valeria. If we go south in as straight a line as possible and they keep their course, we'll be making up some of the time we've lost due to the storm. They have a head start, but they're moving toward us. Let's go and see that we can get closer to them."

Once they reached the tree line, they stopped walking side by side. The jungle didn't allow such a wide passage. Instead, Benicio took the lead, with Josh behind him and Bonny following. Ben would know best what to look out for when it came to wildlife and treacherous terrain. Josh followed him, keeping an eye on his phone and the GPS signal. Bonny was last in line and would leave trail markers behind. They had briefly discussed whether that was a good idea, but in the end, the pros had outweighed the cons.

Around them, the forest was alive with the sounds of birds singing, insects buzzing, and the calls of several different species of other animals. It was a cacophony of sounds unlike anything they were used to, but it held its own beauty. A dangerous beauty, admittedly. Benicio took a deep breath to sharpen his focus and bring back everything he had learned when he had been in the rainforest before. "Okay, remember what Mike said. I know it's contrary to our wish to be as quiet as possible, but try to step firmly on the ground. We might be lucky and not have a jaguar population near us but there are plenty of snakes. Usually, the vibrations are enough of a warning and most of them will leave. We want to avoid all of them, but most importantly any fer-de-lances – their bite is nasty and can be quite dangerous."

He got a murmured agreement and a quick squeeze on the shoulder from Josh.

They kept walking in silence for a long time. Going by the GPS signal, the kidnappers were still far away, but the throuple wanted to get used to the jungle so they'd all be able to pick up on new sounds like people walking or making camp more easily.

A few hours into their hike, Josh stopped them. "Wait, they seem to be taking another break." So far, they had tried to time their breaks with the ones the kidnappers took. Whenever the signal would stop moving, so would they. They had debated getting closer during the kidnapper's breaks instead, but in the end had decided against it. Not only did they want to get a better idea of the kidnappers' possible hideout so they could report it to authorities, but also, with no knowledge of what they'd be facing, they wanted to manage their own resources so that they could keep up and not be forced to rush at some point when they were out of strength. For what it was worth, the three of them were glad they were all in good shape and trained regularly, and the kidnappers stopped more often than the throuple had anticipated. Which, come to think of it, shouldn't have been a surprise. Hauling your kidnapping victims through the jungle wasn't the easiest task.

There were still several miles separating them from the group. And when the dot on the map didn't move any further after their usual resting time, Benicio concluded the kidnappers were setting up camp for the night. Despite their plan, it was tempting to keep pushing, to try reaching the group. But he knew it would be a terrible idea. The little light that reached the forest floor in the first place was fading fast with the sun disappearing behind the mountain ridges around them, and even though he might be able to guide them during the day, Ben knew he couldn't promise his lovers' safety should they attempt hiking through the night. As much as he wanted his sister back and safe, it was a risk he couldn't take. And that was not even considering that an injury and necessary rescue would only slow them down further.

So, they only walked a little farther until they reached a small clearing. Bonny and Josh cleared the floor and set up their tent while Ben collected some firewood.

A little while later, they sat huddled together near the fire, waiting for their dinner to be ready. Among the things Mike had packed for them were a water filter and a bag to collect additional water during the day, and some powdered soup. It wasn't the most delicious dinner but it filled their stomachs and the ingredients were easy to carry.

When they had finished, Bonny looked at Josh and an unspoken message passed between them. Ben looked into the flames, and they all were quiet. They needed rest and time to process. Josh pressed a soft kiss to Bonny's temple and reached over to give Ben's hand a squeeze. "You two go get some sleep. I'll keep an eye on the fire and the surroundings and wake one of you later."

The next morning, it was Bonny who gently woke the guys up after her own watch. She found them arm in arm just like she had slept first with Ben then with Josh the night before. Their sleeping bags allowed them to zip them together, and it was a comfort to be able to cuddle like this. She regretted having to rouse them from their peaceful sleep, but they had all decided the previous evening that they wanted to get up just before sunrise to get ready for the day. The kidnappers would likely get moving early in the day as well, and they didn't want to fall behind just because they still had to pack up their camp when the other group was already moving.

They were on the move soon enough, and just a few

minutes into their hike Josh let them know the GPS signal was moving again, too. They could only hope that they'd keep making better progress than the kidnappers and their victims.

The jungle soon became just as loud as the day before. The bird songs now were accompanied by the loud, resonant calls of a group of howler monkeys, and all around them, leaves were rustling and branches were snapping when some small animal or another ran from them. It was comforting and scary at the same time to know they were surrounded by so much wilderness with no human noise anywhere near them.

Several hours later, more light began to filter through the trees in front of them. The signal told them they needed to keep walking in that direction, so they stayed the course. It didn't take long for them to find themselves on the edge of a steep cliff. The ground fell away in front of them and some hundred and fifty feet below, a river snaked along a canyon formed by the wall of dirt on their side and the cliff on the other side about forty feet away. With the sun glistening on the water and thick clouds hanging among the trees in the distance, it was a stunning sight. It got even more magical when a sudden an explosion of bird cries hit them and a flock of colorful parrots flew out from countless holes in the cliffside across from them, quickly climbing high into the sky. What should have been utter chaos was instead a perfectly coordinated ballet of wings and tails, each large bird seemingly knowing exactly how to move to avoid a neighbor. It was a breathtaking, beautiful spectacle.

"Wow," Bonny whispered and remembered to actually take a few photos, just in case.

"You never know when you might need proof for your cover story," Josh had told her early into their hike the day before, and ever since, she had taken a moment to snap a picture or two whenever they were taking a short break.

"I wish we could actually take the time to enjoy this. We

should come back one day and bring Scar. She'd love this, babe," Bonny said to Josh.

He nodded. "Yeah, you're right. Let's keep it in mind for the future. For now, we need to figure out a way to get to the other side."

Benicio hummed his agreement to both statements, then set down his backpack to check their position and get out and study one of the maps Mike had given them. "Okay, let's see. Mike drew an addition on this map, too. Looks like there's supposed to be a bridge a little to the east."

It took them about half an hour of walking between the trees to reach the point where Mike had marked the crossing for them. They could have been faster, but didn't want to risk anybody from the other side of the river seeing them walking along the edge of the cliff where the vegetation was less dense.

When they finally stepped out from the trees again, Bonny crossed her arms and drew in a heavy breath. "That's gonna be fun," she huffed out sarcastically.

There was indeed a bridge in front of them – a narrow, ancient-looking wooden suspension bridge. The deck was held up by fraying ropes of plant fibres, and some of the worn-out planks used for the walkway were either broken with splinters protruding from the edges or missing completely. One larger gap was patched up with some flimsy-looking branches that somebody had laid across and roughly tied to the ropes beneath the deck. The light breeze blowing through the canyon made the bridge swing from side to side; the old ropes creaked alarmingly with the movement.

"*Mierda*. I guess Mike has not seen this bridge in a while," Ben cursed and meticulously inspected the bridge's anchor points. "I don't like this. I don't trust the construction will carry all of us without further breaking apart."

There was no arguing that point. But it left them facing the fact that they'd likely lose a couple of hours if they were to turn back to use the bridge that had been farther away to the west from their previous location. Given that the GPS signal showed Valeria to be on the other side of the river by now, that bridge was very likely intact.

All three thought about it for a moment before Bonny spoke up. "What about this? Let me cross the bridge. Just listen," she told her men, holding up a hand when they were about to disagree. "I'm not stupid. Ben, you help secure me. Mike packed climbing gear for us. We have several ropes and also some guide pulleys. You can make sure I'm safe. If we also lay some rope double and fix it so that I can take that with me and we create a pulley system between both sides, I can wait on the other side for you and get our backpacks across without any of us carrying additional weight. Then you secure Josh and send him over. You secure yourself, too, and cross last. You both will have the pulley rope to take further stress off the bridge if you use it to hold on to instead of the frail guard rail."

None of them was a fan of the plan, not even Bonny, but they knew they couldn't waste too much time looking for alternatives. Making this endeavour as safe as possible would already eat away some of the ground they had previously gained on the kidnappers.

After some more detailed planning and looking for the right trees to use for their pulley system, Ben finally helped his girlfriend into a climbing harness, his hand caressing her as much as possible without giving in to the temptation to touch her more. Josh would have loved to help them, too, but he knew Benicio was more experienced. Thus, he was focusing his attention on the other side of the river, looking out for any suspicious movement. Bonny would be alone for a little while, separated from them by a dilapidated bridge that wouldn't allow them to get to her quickly if anything happened and she needed their help.

Then it was time for Bonny to cross the bridge. She checked her gear and the few tools she'd be carrying with her once again, attached the rope for the pulley system to her belt to drag behind so she would have her hands free, and made sure she had a good grip on the safety rope connecting her to Ben and Josh. Should the bridge collapse, Bonny would likely fall down a few feet as well. They couldn't set up everything as perfectly as on an actual climb, but it would do. The rope – and Ben – would catch her. Depending on where the bridge might collapse, she still could end up with some bruises, though. *Well, it won't protect me from crashing into the cliff, but at least I won't fall into the river.* Pushing these thoughts aside, Bonny gave both her guys as reassuring a smile as she could muster right before she turned her back to them and faced the bridge and the abyss below.

Gingerly, she took the first step onto the swaying footbridge. It felt like an eternity, like she was crawling as slow as a snail, but she wouldn't rush herself. The sun had managed to fight its way through the clouds and carried a sweltering heat with it. The light was blinding, just like its reflections on the river. As much as Bonny cursed the wind for the bridge's movement that it caused, at least it brought with it a little relief from the moist heat and stopped the sweat from running into her eyes; she needed to see where she stepped. But even more important than her sight was her feeling for the ground beneath her feet. She tested every plank anxiously before stepping on it, only slowly putting weight on it and trying to always have more than a single point bearing her full weight.

She had passed even the patch of branches without trouble and was some twelve feet away from the other side, when – even after her prudent testing – a board suddenly broke in two beneath her foot. One half stayed attached to the bridge, falling to the side and swinging loosely, the other half fell into the water. Bonny managed to stop herself from falling down by reaching further ahead on the rope railing. Her heart hammered in her chest, and she huffed out a surprised, "Fuck!" Her hold on the railing meant she was leaning forward a little, looking directly at the water and seeing the plank land in it. The current swept it away in a heartbeat, making her realize just how treacherously calm the river looked from up here when in reality it was a fast-moving waterway. She swallowed down the anxious tension bubbling up inside her. Despite the worried calls from her boyfriends behind her, she made the conscious decision to move forward, not back to the safety of the plank she had been standing on before. They needed to get to the other side, and even with the rotten planks, the bridge had been holding up so far. She only had a little further to go. She could do this.

With shaking hands, she righted herself and took a large step to cover the gap and put her foot onto the next board. To her relief, it held, and she managed to move further along the bridge until she finally reached the other side and the solid ground. She took a steadying breath, then turned around. "I'm fine, I swear," she called to Josh and Benicio as quietly as she could, hoping that the wall of trees behind her would swallow her voice before it was carried in that direction.

In minutes, Bonny found a tree that would support the pulley and began to set everything up. Not long after, Josh was clipping the first backpack onto the rope and then helping her to get it to her side. He repeated the motions for the other two bags, and all three of them were glad the system worked flawlessly. Meanwhile, Benicio was untangling the other harnesses and then worked around Josh to put his boyfriend into one of them. His hands gently lifted first one of Josh's feet then the other, then pulled the straps up until the belt sat at the right height and the thigh straps framed Josh's legs and butt. Ben's fingers slid along each band to straighten out any twisted parts and make sure everything was correctly in place. Any other time, he would have loved to explore Josh's skin below his shirt as well for a bit and maybe run his palm over his lover's groin. Not on that day, though.

Once the bags were on the other side with Bonny, Benicio turned Josh around. "Are you good? Anything too tight?"

A grin lit up Josh's face for a split second but then he turned serious again. Oh, how much he wished they had some time for teasing each other. But that had to wait until later. Now he just shook his head, "No, all good."

"Okay. Remember, if anything should happen, trust me and the equipment. You will fall into the harness, and you won't fall for long. Just try to make sure to keep your head clear of the wall should you crash into it for any reason. *I will not let you fall*, I swear, *arañita*," Ben told Josh and cupped his cheek. Bonny had some experience from sometimes going indoor climbing with a fellow student in the past. But for Josh, being wrapped up in a harness like this one and trusting the gear and somebody else – even somebody he loved – was new. Ben wanted to make sure Josh started the walk across as confidently as possible.

"I know, love. I trust you. I will be fine," Josh replied and snuck in a quick peck on Ben's lips.

Josh crossed the bridge as carefully as Bonny had, his hands holding on to the rope overhead rather than the bridge's side ropes. When he came to the spot where the plank had broken beneath Bonny, he slowed down even further and stepped over the gaping hole in his path. He wasn't afraid of heights but seeing the river far below caused a wave of unease to roll through him, even if he knew he would never end up in the water. Instincts were a funny thing when they battled with logic.

He took the last few steps and smiled at his girlfriend when Bonny reached out to him as soon as he was close enough. "Hey."

"Hey, baby. Are you okay?"

"Yeah, all good," Josh assured her and gave her a soft kiss.

"Great. Then let's get Ben over here."

Bonny helped Josh get free of the rope still connecting him to Benicio, then he worked with her to set things up in a way that she'd be able to hold Ben even though he weighed more than she, using a tree as an anchor. "I learned this with a ground anchor, but the soil is far too soft for that here," she told Josh, her unhappiness with the situation swinging in her voice. "And this is not how I would usually belay somebody... It's not even real belaying," she muttered after to herself when she was working on her harness.

Josh stopped her hands for a second and tilted her face up with a finger under her chin. "Hey, baby, I know this is not ideal. But it will work. It's gonna be okay, and Ben will get over here safely. The tree will help, and I'm here to hold on to you, too."

"I know. I just want him to be safe, same as you."

"I know. Check your belt, I'll grab the rope."

Bonny took a deep breath and nodded, and Josh stepped over to the ropes spanning the canyon. Benicio had tied his own safety rope to the pulley and used the mechanism to bring it over to them. They had considered only using the pulley to get themselves across as well, but they had to use trees for the system, too, and wanted to put as little weight on the branches holding the guide pulleys as possible.

Which meant Benicio was now looking at them and waiting for their signal to start crossing the bridge. Bonny felt Josh position himself behind her after securing another rope on his belt and a tree, his hands getting a good grip. Both of them shifted around for a moment, looking for the best footing until they were content with their posture, then Bonny nodded over to their boyfriend.

Benicio took just as careful steps as his lovers had. The bridge kept creaking ominously with his strides and the movement caused by the wind, but he kept walking in a steady rhythm.

He had stepped over the gap and kept moving until only a few feet separated him from the safety of the other side when a strong gust of wind made the bridge swing. Ben had his hands on the pulley rope above his head, but he had to shift to balance out the bridge swaying from side to side. His footfall landed just a little harder than before on a board. It was enough for the rotten wood to crack and shatter beneath his boot. The resulting jolt on the bridge caused the next board closer to the edge to rip away from one of the old ropes holding it in place and fall down as well.

His front foot had nothing to stand on anymore, and when Ben distributed his weight to his other foot reflexively to avoid falling forward, the plank beneath that foot gave way as well. He went from standing on the bridge to falling in the blink of an eye. It was only an arm's length, perhaps a little more with the give of the rope, his hands still holding on to the one above, but his heart skipped a beat and he let out a string of creative curses in Spanish.

Then he forced himself to take a deep breath and focus on getting out of the situation. He still could see part of Bonny and Josh, both now shuffling and swearing. Bonny had her hands on the rope connecting them, and Josh was steadying her. "I'm okay. I think I can even move myself the rest of the way. It's maybe five feet from here."

Bonny's heart raced, and she was glad she had chosen to wear gloves to avoid any possible rope burn – she didn't need to end up with wounds inviting an infection in the middle of the jungle. Her palms were clammy with cold sweat after she saw Ben fall through the planks of the bridge and the gloves supported her grip on the rope. *This can't be happening! He's so close!*

Then she heard him hissing several things she had most definitely not been taught in her Spanish classes. A couple of seconds later, his voice reached them, assuring them he was okay. Relief almost made her legs weak, but she made sure she stood securely and had a good hold on the rope. Then she addressed Josh. "I'm good here now, the break caught, and the anchor helps with the weight. Go check on Ben. It's not far, but five feet can be a pain even on monkey bars; pulling yourself hand over hand along a rope is worse."

For half a second, Josh was tempted to ask whether she was sure. But on top of trusting his woman to know herself he also didn't want to waste any time. "Okay."

He released his hold on her and moved over to the edge of the cliff, then knelt on the ground. The view didn't do a lot to help calm his nerves. Benicio dangled in the air, sitting in the harness with his hands on the pulley rope. Before, he only had two boards left to cross to the other side. When those two and the one he had been standing on had broken, it left him hanging out of reach.

"Fuck. You okay there, babe?"

"*Sí*, I'm okay."

Seeing all of Ben in one piece, no bleeding gashes on his legs, helped. Josh's mouth had been dry but after clearing his throat he sounded normal enough. "Okay. If you can hang on a little longer, I'll help you move along and use the pulley to get you closer faster."

"Good idea, *bebé*."

Josh got up from his kneeling position and walked over to

the tree to which the pulley system was attached, mindful of the ropes everywhere. He gave the others a quick warning, then began to gently move the rope. From his vantage point, he couldn't see a lot of Ben anymore, but he could make out his hands reaching in front of each other in turns, supporting his move toward the cliff's edge.

The combination of Bonny pulling in more and more rope to give a light support to Benicio without dragging him in too fast, Josh's work on the pulley, and Ben's own moves brought him to the edge in no time. Josh returned to him and reached out to help him up the wall. When Ben looked at him with huge eyes and his mouth open to protest, Josh leaned over a little further and kissed him on the nose. "Don't worry, I'm secured, I won't fall dragging you up."

It only took them a couple of minutes to have Benicio back on solid ground with Bonny keeping tension on the rope, Ben using his feet to help himself up the wall, and Josh gripping and pulling him up. Ben collapsed onto Josh in the dirt, and Josh ran his arms around his boyfriend, then opened the embrace for Bonny as soon as she fell on her knees beside them. They ended up in a three-way kiss after which both Bonny and Josh told Ben he better never do something like that again. They all knew it wasn't his fault, but the same relief rushed through all of them, and he chuckled. "I promise. Now, let's pack everything and keep going. All of this took long enough."

In the end, they decided to leave the pulley system in place in case they needed it on their way back, even if it meant leaving behind some rope. It had proven to be solid, and they wouldn't trust the rest of the bridge any longer.

"Oh, but let's use a higher branch on this side. It will create an angled line and give the system a bit more tension. Who knows if we're gonna need it, but I feel like a way to quickly slide to the other side from here could come in handy," Bonny told them.

It would take a few minutes longer to set up, but the guys agreed with her. They'd make use of any possible advantage they could get. It wasn't like the kidnappers would just hand over Ben's sister and send them on their merry way.

Chapter Twenty-Two

They had been walking for a few hours, the jungle's noises of the day fading and the cries of the nocturnal creatures not yet carrying through the air. It was that eerie almost-silence of twilight in which all three of them suddenly heard sounds of a camp being set up – the rustling of a tent tarp, firewood being cut, though it was obviously done by somebody trying to be quiet about it, backpacks opening and closing, soft footfalls on the leaf-covered ground. But no voices, nobody talking.

Josh checked his phone again but shook his head. He showed the display to his lovers, letting them see that it wasn't Valeria's group, or at the very least not all of them, because the signal of her tracker was still moving and already further away.

They listened for another few minutes until Ben took out one of their maps. If they wanted to avoid these people, they had to find a way around them – preferably before it got any darker.

But when Ben showed them a possible path through the thick underbrush, something seemed to hold Josh back. A nagging feeling at the back of his mind, a gut feeling that told him to stay. He lightly laid his hand on Benicio's and looked between his partners, then whispered to them, "I don't know. I feel like we should check this out. Something tells me this could be important."

Benicio shook his head. "What makes you think that? What if it's part of their group? Perhaps somebody got injured and is just going slower."

Unhappy with himself because he couldn't pinpoint what exactly was bothering him, Josh shook his head. "I really don't know, sweetheart. It's just a hunch. But look at it like this: none of the kidnappers would have a reason to be so quiet, and they would make some noise to keep animals away, too, right? Like we do. I don't know," he sighed again. "At the very least, I'd prefer to have a look before we leave – to find out who's close to us."

He could see neither Bonny nor Benicio were happy about it, but they also could follow his reasoning, debating internally what to do. In the end, both of them sighed, and Ben nodded. "Yes, okay. I don't like it. But it's better to know what and whom we're dealing with."

Bonny agreed with a nod as well before speaking. "Then let me go. And before you object, think about it: I'm the lightest, I know how to tread carefully; I'll make the least noise of the three of us. Also, don't get me wrong, you two are pretty. But your skin is a lot lighter than mine. It's getting dark, I'll be harder to spot with my complexion. I'll take our own GPS tracker from you, too, Josh. You'll know precisely where I am."

Oh, her men hated that; she could see it on their faces. They all felt the need to protect each other – but with young women going missing, she understood why they were driven to look out for her even more than for each other in this situation.

The unspoken conversation between Josh and Ben was clear enough for her to read on their faces, as was the moment they both gave in. Josh handed her the tracker, Ben took her backpack so she'd be unencumbered. Before they could change their minds, she gave each of them a quick kiss and moved off into the shadows of the jungle surrounding them.

After a slow, careful walk, Bonny ended up nearly crawling the rest of the way to stay hidden behind the low undergrowth surrounding a tiny clearing. From her hiding spot, she could make out two tents. There was almost no communication at first, only the sounds of a person or two walking around, some wood scraping against wood. She stayed where she was, not daring to bring up her head too high only to get a glimpse.

A long ten minutes later, she could make out a few words by a male voice at last. "... path south looks good," more mumbling and paper rustling, perhaps a map being opened, "... can start the fire."

The smell of fresh flames igniting semi-dry leaves, of smoke from exotic wood wafted over to Bonny. The crackling of the fire swallowed a few words at first, but then she was able to pick up more of the conversation.

"You think we'll find our target at the end of this?"

"I hope so. The intel so far was late but correct."

"She better be there. I hate letting them drag the other girl through here just to see where they're going."

"I'm with you. But even if our target isn't there, we'll have a location to tell the authorities here about, or maybe we'll get the order to step in even without our target there. No matter, it'll be more than we had before. These people will be stopped one way or another. Our team is a bloody good start. And I'm not above calling in reinforcements, if we need them. First, let's work on not losing them until they reach their destination."

Three different voices, all with a distinctly British accent. Those had to be the guys Mike had talked about, right? Listening to them, Bonny couldn't shake the feeling that she knew them. She had no idea from where, but something was oddly familiar about the pitch, the rhythm. She couldn't place it, though; far too much on her mind. But what she had heard had made her heart lighter. She had no clue what some British people – and it sounded like they might be military – were doing here. But it sounded very much like they were following the kidnappers as well and were planning on rescuing at the very least one person.

Still, she wouldn't give herself and her men away without talking it through first. Very quietly, she made her way back to where she had left her boyfriends, this time with a smile on her face.

Back with Josh and Ben, who had been nervously awaiting her, she summarized what she had heard.

After she had finished, all three took a moment to evaluate the situation. Ben ran a hand through his mussed hair. "What do you two think? What should we do?"

That was an excellent question. Josh scratched his neck. "I'm not sure. This could either play out perfectly: they could help us, and we won't have to go in there alone. Or it could go incredibly wrong if they maybe heard Bonny after all and this is a ruse to get us to show ourselves. Or, even if they indeed want to stop those kidnappers, we could still end up being excluded from their operation. If they're military, they most likely won't be happy to have more civilians around to protect. Could be they'll send us back and bring your sister to us."

"If they care to get her out, that is," Ben scoffed.

The negativity wasn't even directed at Josh, exactly – and Josh knew it, the situation just sucked – but he flinched, none-theless.

"Sorry, *arañita.*"

"No, don't worry. I get it. Maybe let me go in first. I can always pretend to be a lone hiker who got lost, got turned around again and again. When I saw their fire, I was hoping for some shelter for the night, something like that. If it's the kidnappers after all, I think it'll be obvious enough. If it's not but instead somebody who could help us, then I can try to steer the conversation in the right direction. Depending on their reaction, I can drop it or come and get you."

Bonny gnawed on her lip. "Damn, now I know how you felt before. I hate this, I really do. But I think it might be our best option."

"I'm with Bonny on this. I hate it, too, but we can't let a chance like this go without even trying. But, *bebé*, promise us to be careful."

"I will be, I promise," Josh replied and vanished just like Bonny after a kiss for his lovers.

Josh did his best to appear like a lost hiker when he got closer to the campsite. It wasn't hard with the unforgiving jungle around him slipping into darkness.

It went against his instincts, but he didn't try to sneak up on the camp, didn't look to stay hidden behind trees. The group wasn't talking a lot, only a few words here and there reaching Josh's ears, which wasn't a surprise because he could smell some soup and heard the sounds of a spoon scraping along a tin.

With the men eating, he stayed quiet until he was closer to them. Perhaps he could get a better look than Bonny now that the guys weren't walking around setting everything up.

It only took him a few more steps until he spotted the bulky frame of a man sitting next to two others. Part of a tattoo was visible above the neck of his shirt, his hair shimmered a golden red in the glow of the fire. But Josh knew it would shine just as bright in the light of day. He was tempted to facepalm himself. Now his nagging feeling made total sense. Instead, he ran his hand over his face with calmer movements and sighed in a mix of relief and apprehension. Then he cleared his throat and stepped from the treeline into the dim edge of the flickering light of the fire. He slowly lifted a hand and waved at the men in greeting. "Hi, guys."

All three men automatically reached towards the weapons leaning close to them but stopped when they got a look at the person intruding on their camp. The bulky guy looked Josh up and down and shook his head. "Well, fuck me."

Beside him, one of the other two snickered. "I don't think he's up to that, boss. He looked quite happy with the two lovers he has."

That got an eye roll and an elbow in the ribs from the beefy guy. "Shut up. And I don't need to ask why you are here, do I?" he addressed the second part to Josh.

"No. Do you mind if I get Bonny and Benicio so we can all talk?"

"Go ahead." The sigh that followed that affirmation came from a man who had resigned himself to the fact that his life – and most likely his mission – had just become more complicated.

Josh's return trip was quicker now that he didn't need to be as quiet as before. When he reached Bonny and Benicio, he gave them a nod. "We're good. And I feel like an idiot."

Both his lovers frowned at him.

"Why?" Bonny asked.

"What happened?" Ben followed up while grabbing their bags.

Josh held his hand out to take some of their gear. He took a moment to adjust the backpack, then told them, "Remember that I said I had some gut feeling? After seeing the men sitting around the fire, I know why. I think it was something that Mike said about the British guys. It's been in the back of my mind the whole time, almost like I had a picture in my mind of them, but I didn't know why."

"So? I'm not sure I follow. How does that make you feel like an idiot?" Bonny asked and ran her hand up Josh's arm, her intense gaze imploring him to explain.

"You'll get it when I tell you the guys sitting around that fire are Kieran, Jack, and Rhys."

Ben stopped walking for a second, staring at Josh. "The guys from the hotel?"

"Yep, them. And I feel stupid because for a moment there, when Mike mentioned *Top Gun*, I had their faces in mind but then let it go again. I thought it was just because we had played volleyball with them. But they fit Mike's description to a T. And think back: when that old woman started harassing us, Kieran already had his phone out to record everything because he 'had a feeling she wanted to stir trouble' because he saw her observing Bonny? Who keeps such a close eye on people while on vacation when it's not ingrained in you? That points to military. So, yes, it makes sense that it is them, and my gut feeling was right, I just didn't trust it and didn't put the picture together."

"Okay, stop putting yourself down for that. We didn't put it together, either," Ben told Josh and squeezed his hand for a moment. "It's weird though, right? That they are here?"

Bonny's expression darkened. "Not exactly, not if they're military and have orders to get somebody back. What's worse, though, and fits what they were saying earlier, is..." She looked at Josh to see whether he had come to the same conclusion, knowing he could read her perfectly.

"That they knew something would happen and left early because of a 'family emergency,' probably taking the day after our game with them to prepare their trip to here," Josh finished and silently agreed with her reasoning to put it out there now. Benicio had far too much on his mind to keep track of that, but it wouldn't do them any good if he came to that realization or the others admitted it outright when they were all sitting together.

Ben's step faltered for a moment, and Bonny and Josh saw him balling his fists, his nails biting into his palms. "*Chingando.* I'll kick their asses for this once we've got Val back," he mumbled just loud enough for them to hear.

A second later, Bonny and Josh enveloped him in their arms. "We'll help you," Bonny whispered and cupped his cheek in one hand. "Until then, will you be okay with them?"

"*Sí*, yes, I promise. As pissed off as I am right now, I want my sister back, and they're our best chance. I want to hear what they have to tell us."

<h1 style="text-align:center;">Chapter Twenty-Three</h1>

I t took a few minutes of greeting each other and the briefest of discussions to decide that, no matter what happened the next day, all of them would share the camp. Josh picked a spot and began clearing the ground for their tent, and Rhys offered his help to set everything up.

Meanwhile, Bonny and Benicio sat with the others and began preparing some of their own rations since the three men – not expecting company – had only made enough for themselves and had mostly finished their dinner already.

Finally, they all sat around the fire with the throuple facing the soldiers. Three men they had enjoyed a challenging but fun game with. They had seemed competitive but friendly with it, relaxed as much as the game had allowed. Now, they were on alert, tense. Kieran's bulk seemed more imposing in the darkness of the night. Jack and Rhys were leaner, yet their muscles were defined enough to warn people that they were quick and could handle themselves. In the few days since the throuple had last seen them, these two had cut their hair short, now each wearing a buzzcut. All three quietly studied the lovers in front of them over the dancing flames.

It was Benicio who spoke first. "Tell me whether you will help us get my sister back."

Kieran focused all his attention on Ben, looking him in the eye. "We will try. But I cannot guarantee it. I'm sorry, mate."

"Why, or rather, for whom, are you here, then?" Bonny wanted to know. "And don't get started with the whole 'We're not allowed to talk about it' bullshit. We aren't stupid. A small and – given your weapons – apparently well-equipped group of British soldiers in a foreign country isn't something you would get for just any tourist who went missing on a hike."

"Fair enough, and I know you aren't stupid. You managed to get this far. Tell me how you did that." He wasn't mean or intimidating per se, but his tone carried the authority of somebody who had interrogated a lot of people over the years.

Bonny wasn't giving in just like that, though. "Tit for tat, Kieran. Give us something here. We need to know what we're dealing with; it doesn't matter if we keep going with you or split in the morning," she insisted.

"Bloody hell..." Kieran seemed to weigh his choices, then shrugged. "All right. I cannot tell you everything. I know you understand that. What I can tell you is this: yes, we're soldiers. Part of the Special Forces. That's all you get about that. We're here to extricate a member of the royal family. Her relationship to the royal family isn't widely known, and she's kept out of the public eye to live a normal life. In that pursuit, she has been working as an entertainer on a cruise ship. She was abducted when the ship was docked in Cancún almost two weeks ago. It took some time, but we gathered intel pointing us in the direction of the people who've also abducted your sister, Benicio."

The group digested that information for a moment. Then Josh voiced his conclusions. "The kidnappers don't know who she is, either. There would have been a ransom demand and that would have been handled differently. And I'm not surprised the abducted cruise ship employee didn't get any media coverage, even without her relationship to the royal family and the palace's PR department keeping a lid on it. Cruises are kind of notorious; there've been several cases in the past where employees – usually female – vanished, and there's been barely any investigation into their disappearances. Ruins the cruise companies' joyful image if your employees vanish without a trace. And given her background, I assume it was a luxury cruise line, which would mean even bigger losses. So, silence."

Kieran cocked his head but didn't say anything. It was obvious Josh wasn't finished, yet.

"So, as you said, you gathered intel and somehow found out more about their plans and decided to follow them through the jungle, hoping they'll lead you to your target. My question is: are you prepared to get all the other girls out of there, too?"

Now all three soldiers sat up straighter. Josh could read on their faces that they hated to give away that they didn't know something. But then he could see the moment Kieran made the decision that he would rather admit to not knowing part of the problem and make use of a source instead of walking blindly into a dangerous situation. "All the other girls?"

This would be hard for his boyfriend to hear, so Josh slid his hand into Ben's, linked their fingers, before addressing Kieran and his men. "You don't know this, do you? Yes, Ben's sister was abducted near Cancún, it makes sense to follow these guys. I'm with you, they will very likely belong to the same group that took the woman you're here to rescue. But you're missing crucial information. Over the last several years, Ben has come across multiple cases that indicate a large operation going on all over Mexico, abducting young women." Josh succinctly laid out the cases and the conclusions for them. Then he finished with some news he had hoped he wouldn't have to tell Ben.

His plan had been similar to Kieran's: follow the kidnappers until they knew where the group would be going so they knew where to send the authorities. But then he would have gotten Valeria out before she would've even entered some guarded facility, only dealing with the small group who had been dragging her along.

He took a deep breath, then told everybody, "I did some more digging, looking not only into official, open missing person cases but also those where the police didn't open a case while the families were adamant their daughters, sisters, nieces had been kidnapped, and have taken everything they know to social media. All together, I have found forty-eight other currently missing women fitting the victim profile."

There was a sharp intake of breath from everybody, then a string of curses in both English and Spanish.

"Bloody goddamn hell," Jack huffed.

Rhys looked at Kieran with disbelief in his eyes. "How come we didn't know about this, boss? How can some kid know more about this after a quick Google search than we do?"

Kieran shot him a warning look, and Rhys picked up on its meaning. "Sorry, I didn't mean it like that, Josh," he mumbled.

Josh nodded in acknowledgement of the apology, then turned expectant eyes to Kieran once again.

"I'd say you're far more than a kid googling something, and given what you've told us before, I'm glad you're here to give us more information before this rescue turns into a complete clusterfuck. Unfortunately, with the lack of information and all of this not being treated as one large case, I'm not surprised our superiors didn't have more to give us. Now, I heard what you said, and I understand that you want Benicio's sister back. What you haven't told me so far is how you managed to track those guys so easily and why we should bring three civilians with us into such a dangerous situation."

"Fair, I'd ask the same," Josh admitted, then continued, "Here's why: we tracked them so easily because Valeria is wearing a GPS tracker. When she was picked with some others for lifeguard training, we didn't want to let her go there without being able to at least see where she was. She agreed, more or less reluctantly, to the tracker. The authorities didn't listen when we called it in. I'm in the lucky position that I could afford to get us a plane here quickly. We've been following the signal ever since." He held up a hand to stop anybody from interrupting, then he told them about his initial plan to pinpoint the destination but getting Valeria out before the kidnappers reached it. "We might have to adjust that part now that you're here. And if you need more reasons to bring us, then let me tell you, Bonny and I may not be as perfectly trained as you but we are proficient enough in self-defense and some hand-to-hand combat. We have friends, more like family, in law enforcement; we train regularly with them. I'm starting as a PI at a New York firm soon. And Ben is not only a native speaker who can help us calm down maybe fifty terrified young women, he also has at least some medical knowledge that we might need, depending on the state the women are in."

Jack looked between Josh and Kieran and snickered. "I hate to say it, boss..."

"Yeah, yeah, he has some valid points. I know it, don't I?" What followed was an immensely heavy sigh that clearly conveyed Kieran's deep unhappiness but also carried some resignation. "I suppose I can't persuade you to give me details on the tracker and let us go alone while you get back to civilization."

Each of the three lovers only glared at him, not saying a word in response.

"Didn't think so. I had to try. All right, I cannot stop you from moving along on your own, so let's agree on the smart thing to keep going together. I will not, at this point, blankly agree to take any or all of you inside with us when we find their destination. We don't know what we'll be running into, how many guards, how many women, anything. If I deem it too dangerous, you will have to wait while we work on taking the kidnappers down. For what it's worth, I want to know what you can do when it comes to training, survival tactics, and so on. And depending on how long we'll keep wandering through the bloody jungle – because our satellite scans didn't show any obvious destination in the direction they're heading – perhaps do some actual training with you. Apparently, you have some skills; you might have the tracker to follow, but you've made better progress than I would expect from somebody who's never been in a situation like this. And I will admit, I'm impressed that you could sneak up on us."

And so they talked. It took some time to update the soldiers on who would accompany them, but in the end, Kieran and the others seemed relieved to know they wouldn't end up babysitting the throuple. When Josh told them his future boss had made sure he would know how to handle some guns, just in case, Rhys took Josh to the side and let him show what he was able to do – cleaning, assembling, stance, aiming, and the like, minus actually shooting the gun to avoid any noise. From the look of it, Josh thought Rhys was satisfied.

Finally, after getting Kieran's word not to abandon them in the morning, Josh also shared the GPS tracker information with the man. He wasn't surprised that Kieran could easily access the tracker's position with his tech without the need to access Josh's boss' account. If his boss complained about the information sharing, he could take the money for a new tracker out of Josh's first paycheck and forget about the one Valeria was currently carrying.

<h1 style="text-align:center">Chapter Twenty-Four</h1>

The group was forced to march another two days through the rainforest. For all its beauty, the nature around them was harsh. Another storm system had come in and it had been raining nonstop for the past day and a half; the ground beneath them was soggy, either slippery with dead leaves or covered in almost ankle-deep mud that made each step that much harder and drained their strength. The pouring rain was loud and drowned out the sounds of the jungle they had gotten used to, leaving everybody on edge because it made it impossible to hear anybody who would be sneaking up on them, or each other on the rare occasions they were trying to talk while walking.

It was late afternoon when Josh and Kieran both got the impression from studying the tracker's signal that the kidnappers were calling it an early day. Jack studied a map and nodded. "Makes sense. If they keep going in that direction, they'll end up near a large waterfall in about an hour or ninety minutes. They probably found a better spot to set up camp and want to avoid the waterfall when it's dark and rather tackle it fresh in the morning."

It was tempting to keep pushing, to gain some ground. All

six were looking at each other, any of them ready to bring it up in a second, when the sky suddenly flickered bright white and deafening thunder rolled over them a heartbeat later.

Rhys looked at the sky, then back at the others. "I guess that's our clue to stay put for the night, too. If we head back a couple of minutes, we'll have a better spot to camp. There was an overhang by that rock formation we passed. It'll provide better shelter, and we might even be able to keep a fire going. With the rain and the altitude, it's bloody cold during the night."

The suggestion got a round of approvals, although Benicio thought the look of despair on his face must have gotten more obvious with each step away from his sister because not only were Bonny and Josh stepping closer but Rhys, walking next to him, slung an arm around his shoulder before his lovers reached Ben. "I know it feels wrong to turn back. But you getting at least some rest and keeping your strength for later is the best you can do for your sister right now, mate."

"*Sí*, I know. Thank you, Rhys."

"Sure."

As soon as the man had stepped away from him, Ben found himself in the middle between Bonny and Josh, each of them taking one of his hands and giving it a squeeze. The path was narrow, and they had to walk so close that they were constantly brushing against each other, but none of his lovers let go of Ben's hands. It helped to push back some of the desperation, warming the cold spreading inside him that had nothing to do with the weather.

They reached the overhang soon enough, and it turned out to be large enough that the throuple could set up their tent close to the rock wall at the back, while the other three put up theirs in a semicircle at the front edge of the overhang. In the middle was enough of a dry spot to start a fire, and they were all glad for it. The flames provided some much-needed warmth and a bit of light to lift their spirits, since the jungle around them and the sky were pitch black aside from the occasional flash of lightning.

During dinner, they were studying several maps, looking for potential destinations but still came up with nothing useful. Bonny shook her head at another set of satellite images that Kieran had brought up on a tablet. "There's nothing where they're going except what, some old ruins? What makes it worth trudging through the jungle for days with some kidnapped girls? I mean, realistically, if I kidnapped somebody, I'd want to get them to my hiding place quickly. Sure, the rainforest provides cover and all, but is this feasible?"

"I agree with you, Bonny. It sounds impractical and looks like they're heading to the middle of nowhere. We might know more when we finally know where exactly they'll end up. From a quick study of the terrain and weather during our flight from Mexico to here, I only know that there've been several severe storms lately. Maybe something prevented them from taking the usual route," Kieran speculated.

"Yeah, who knows?" Bonny shrugged.

She gathered her and her boyfriends' dishes, but Jack – after a quick look at Benicio – stopped her. "Leave it, Bonny. We'll take care of it."

"Oh, but..."

"It's no bother. We'll also take the watch shifts tonight. You three get some rest."

She knew what he was doing and why. Knowing exactly how Benicio felt and that he needed comfort, she smiled at the man for giving them the chance to retreat to the privacy of their tent early that night. "Thank you."

. . .

Inside their tent, Bonny and Josh moved in, enveloping Benicio in their embrace. Bonny's hands stroked soothingly over his back, Josh pressed his lips to his hair.

"How are you, baby?" Josh asked quietly.

Ben burrowed deeper in the embrace, taking comfort from their caresses. "Not great. I wish we could just go there, grab her, and get out of here. But then I think about all the other women you mentioned... We can't just leave them, and Val would kill me for even considering it. Of course I want to help them, too, it's not that I *want* to abandon them. I just want to get my sister back... It tears me apart, to be honest. And I know it's stupid, but every other moment I feel so guilty that she's been taken in the first place..."

"Babe..."

"No, *arañita*, it's okay. My brain knows that's ridiculous, and I'll get there. It's just my heart that is overwhelmed with everything and turns it into guilt. Logically, I know it's not my fault, and when my logic is louder, I'm so, so pissed and angry, I just want to hurt those bastards.

"And now there's this thunderstorm, and Val hates those. It's not like she's scared – or, at least, she wasn't before – who knows how she'll be after all this. But at home when it storms like this, we more often than not lose power, and once she had this whole essay written for one of her classes, but on her computer, not her laptop. And we lost power when she was nearly finished and hadn't saved her progress in a while... She had to do it all again, and ever since, she has *hated* thunderstorms. By the way, that's the family you two join, you know that, right? Some of us hate the weather with fervor." It was a weak attempt to lighten the mood, but Ben felt like he had to do something before he succumbed to his dark thoughts.

Bonny chuckled and gave Ben a kiss on the cheek. "Sounds

good to me; I like people who know what they like and what they don't."

Ben leaned into her and took a deep breath. "Thank you, *mi amor*."

Bonny brought up one of her hands and ran her fingers through Ben's hair a few times. "Tell us what we can do for you, sweetheart."

He hesitated for only a second, but then sighed, "Take me away from it for a bit. I don't want to think."

It wasn't ideal: the tent wasn't large, there were three people outside (who, admittedly, were likely used to intimacy happening near them in cramped quarters), and it was chilly even with the fire close to their tent. But one look at the despair in Ben's eyes had Josh and Bonny leaning in to bring their lips together in a three-way kiss.

Slow and sweet turned more urgent, coming together not just a want but a need. They hadn't had a chance to connect like this for days. Their touch, their kisses, were a reassurance that, no matter what happened, they had each other and always would be there for one another.

Hands began to wander, both Bonny and Josh focusing solely on Ben's pleasure for now.

Josh leaned forward, his lips ghosting over the skin beneath Ben's ear, traveling lower. His teeth nipped at the skin above Ben's collarbone.

Meanwhile, Bonny wiggled down Ben's body, her hands pushing up his clothes to get access to his skin. Her tongue traced his ribs, then ran over to his stomach and a little further down. She teased his happy trail while she slid a hand under his shirt, her nails scraping over one of his nipples.

Josh ran his hand up Ben's spine until he could get his fingers into his hair. He grabbed a fistful of hair and tugged Ben's head back. His mouth wandered, lips scraped along the stubble on Ben's jaw and cheek – more pronounced than usual now that they hadn't had the chance for a proper shave for a few days – then he caught Benicio's mouth in a deep kiss.

Their tongues tangled until Josh broke the kiss to keep making his boyfriend crazy. He brought his lips back to Ben's jawline, then kept moving until he found his Adam's apple and ran the tip of his tongue over it. Beneath him, Ben shivered.

Bonny let her hands explore Ben's thighs, leisurely kneading the muscles through his pants. Her mouth had made its way to just above his hip. Wanting, needing to tease and distract her lover some more, she opened his pants but only lowered them far enough to run her tongue over his hip bone, then shift a little lower to suck a small bruise on the line between hip and groin. From above, she heard a low groan.

Then Josh's voice reached her ear. "What do you want, baby? Do you want Bonny to get you ready for me?"

The initial response was a dark, hungry growl until Ben found his voice. "*Sí*, yes, god, yes!" It was gruff and deep, and Bonny thought it was a good thing that the rain and thunder were so loud. Ben's voice alone would tell everybody in hearing range exactly what they were doing and talking about.

Bonny didn't need to be told twice and, for once, the small tent came in handy since she could easily reach over and rummage through one of their backpacks and still keep pressing small kisses all over Ben's stomach.

They hadn't brought a lot with them on the flight, but the small toiletry kits from the hotel had been perfect for traveling light and contained some lotion. No lube but they already knew this worked as well.

With the small bottle in hand, she worked Benicio's pants further down and let her lips follow until she ran her tongue along the length of his arousal. Beneath her, Ben shivered. She loved drawing these reactions from him, and when she engulfed him in her mouth and he arched up in response, pushing further inside, she moaned around him.

Benicio tried to be quiet, but he couldn't stop the gasp and then his own moan when he felt the warm, wet heat of Bonny's mouth. He brought a hand to his face and covered his mouth, but Josh dragged it away.

"Uh-uh, I wanna be able to kiss you," Josh told him, then he leaned closer with a smirk on his face and whispered into his lover's ear, "and hear you. I want to hear just how wild she's driving you."

Hell, Josh was right, Bonny did make Ben crazy, but Josh's teasing comments and his hands running over Ben's skin did just the same. Combined, they made Ben lose his ability to speak. So he could only whimper when he felt a slick finger first circling his entrance, then slowly pushing inside. Bonny was so gentle it was almost too much; too much care, too much love, making him feel like his heart would burst. When she added a second and then a third finger he relished the slight burn – it helped ground him just as much as it built anticipation for more.

Then she curled her fingers, and Ben nearly exploded. He squeezed his eyes shut and for a second bit his lip hard. He reached out for his lovers, one hand dragging Josh in for a desperate kiss, the fingers of the other digging into Bonny's shoulder, torn between guiding her off and keeping her in place.

His heart raced, his mind was blank. Still, when Bonny let go of him and pulled her fingers out of his body, Ben managed a weak, "No... more."

He heard Bonny chuckle. "Don't worry, sweetheart, we aren't finished with you. Babe, come here," she ordered and tugged Josh closer by his hand. First, she gave him a deep kiss, then worked her hands between them, getting Josh partly out of his pants, too. Ben could see him grin at her, his arms running around her so he could grab her butt. The same smirk from before played around his mouth. "You know this is gonna be messy, right?"

Bonny replied with a smug grin. "With what I have in mind, not more than when you're inside me," she told him with a wink. Then proceeded to crawl over to Ben to kiss him deeply before looking at Josh again. "I think Ben is waiting for you, babe."

Benicio practically vibrated with need, desperate for any touch, any caress from the two loves of his life. He was unable to ask her what exactly it was she had in mind. And only moments later he felt the pressure of Josh entering him, making him forget about the question altogether. Josh's movements were slow and sensual at first, but Ben's hips soon began to move on their own, spurring his lover on to quicken his thrust.

Benicio couldn't stop the moans Josh drew from him, but then he caught Bonny's movement from the corner of his eye. He could see more of her skin than before. He realized she had pushed her own pants further down than his or Josh's, and a few seconds later he understood why.

She looked at him, smiling brightly when she saw his eyes on her. "Let's see if we can at least quiet the noise a little," she told him and then straddled his head. A tent made for two people was not meant for this, but Bonny managed to wiggle down Ben's body and maneuver Josh back far enough that she could take Ben into her mouth again while offering herself to Ben's lips and tongue.

Benicio arched his back, for a second overwhelmed by the dual pleasure of feeling Josh inside him and being inside Bonny's mouth. But once he found his breath again, he began to taste her, to make her as desperate as he was. She groaned around him, the vibrations only pushing him to tease her more. He couldn't see Josh like this, but he heard his murmured curses, then his voice telling them a little louder how beautiful they looked like this, how much he needed them.

None of them would last long, they all knew it. But when Josh hit the perfect spot inside Ben only a little later, Ben couldn't stop the climax exploding inside him. And he could feel how he dragged Josh over the edge with him when he clenched tight around his length. He barely realized how Bonny swallowed his release or how she used his mouth with a few gentle drags of her hips to bring herself to climax before his mind went blank.

Spent and satiated, their breaths came in pants, turning the air in the small tent humid. They were a pile of limp bodies, and it took considerable effort to untangle themselves from each other and get dressed again. Eventually, they managed it, each with a smile on their faces, then snuggled together to get some sleep.

Barely awake, Bonny mumbled, "See, no mess. We hardly needed to clean up."

It drew a chuckle from her men and, because they had ended with her lying in the middle that night, kisses to both her cheeks. She smiled, then managed a tired, "Night. Love you," and a quick kiss shared between all three of them before she fell asleep to the corresponding *Love yous* from Josh and Ben.

Chapter Twenty-Five

The next day had started early enough that the throuple was spared from any teasing comments about the night before, with all three soldiers functioning but not awake enough for social interactions. The rain had finally stopped in the early hours of the morning, and the group had then broken camp after rushing through morning routines and breakfast, hoping to get closer to the kidnappers. And it had looked promising for almost an hour. After that, the signal from the GPS tracker had begun moving as well.

In itself, that shouldn't have been a problem. But when the throuple and their military escort reached the waterfall Jack had mentioned the day before, everybody stared in disbelief at the screen and back to the scene in front of them.

Before them, the river was running fast, nearly flowing over the banks after the heavy rainfall. It rushed over the edge of the rocks, cascading over several plateaus into a pool of water nearly a hundred feet below, though they had to trust their terrain maps for the height. Thick fog hung in the air around them, and the mist from the churning, splashing water made it hard to get a good look. It was a beautiful scene and an impressive reminder of how powerful nature could be.

But none of them could appreciate the deadly beauty they were facing. Instead, they were all trying to make sense of what their devices told them. The GPS signal was moving along the river – but it was moving upstream, not following the river that came after the waterfall. And it was moving in a fairly straight line, like nothing the dense vegetation around them would allow, so it wasn't that Valeria was walking next to the river.

"How? They didn't carry a boat, the tracks weren't right for that, and there was no sign of one at their campsite. Any boat tied up here beforehand would've been swept away with the storm," Rhys told the group, almost yelling to be heard over the deafening roar of the water. He had looked at the kidnappers' campsite when they had passed it before arriving at the waterfall.

"And it would be too dangerous to just take a boat up the river when it's as bad as it is now. That water is treacherous on a good day, let alone after a storm," Jack added, then winced. "Sorry, mate," he muttered with a glance at Benicio.

But Ben shook his head. "No, it's okay. And you aren't wrong: taking a boat upstream sounds like too much of a risk. They go through all this trouble, then risk losing my sister by dragging her on a boat where she can easily fall into the water and drown? It doesn't sound right."

"So what, they fly and stay over the water, following the landmark? That makes even less sense," Kieran said. "For now, it doesn't matter. We need to follow them. Let's walk along the riverbank."

The group turned, the soldiers planning to take the lead. But when they took the first steps, Josh stayed in place. There was this nagging feeling again, something holding him back.

"*Arañita?*"

"Babe? Are you coming?"

"I... Wait, let me check one thing before we go."

A few feet away, Kieran became impatient. "Josh, come on, mate."

"I know, just one minute," Josh told him. He took out his phone again and opened the tracking app. But this time, he didn't confirm the live position but looked at the history of the tracker's movements.

It clearly showed the tracker first moving toward the water, then right to the edge of the cliff. From there, it neither moved upstream right away nor downstream. It only showed small movements back and forth, over and over again. There were no elevation readings, but it looked just like somebody climbing down a winding footpath that had been carved into the rock wall. Then the signal followed the river upstream again. And now that he focused on it, he realized a few readings were missing every once in a while.

Suddenly, it hit Josh. "They are not on the river. They're *under* it!"

"What are you talking about?" Kieran stomped over to Josh, staring at the younger man as if he had lost his mind.

"I mean what I said. Look at this," Josh insisted and pushed his phone into the soldier's hand. "They went down there, and it doesn't look like they came back up here. They're following the river upstream, yes. But there must be a cave system or something where they can just walk below the river easily."

Most of the group gathered around Josh and Kieran. Kieran wasn't convinced and was just about to order everybody to follow him once more, but Bonny, who had wandered closer to the edge of the waterfall, gave a sharp whistle and drew everybody's attention. "Josh's right. Look at this. There are steps going down here. There must be an entrance to that cave or tunnel or whatever."

"Are you bloody serious? You want to climb down there because you think there might be, maybe, some mysterious secret passage?"

"*Sí.* I agree with Josh and Bonny. If the kidnappers are in there, we should follow. If we don't, we risk losing them, depending on where the tunnel leads."

"We don't even know whether there *is* a tunnel at all!" Kieran huffed with all the frustration of somebody who was used to being in charge but was faced with people who simply didn't have to take orders from him but required convincing.

"Let's have a look, guys. It might not be anything, but it could also be the only way to keep up with them," Josh implored.

The men argued for a good ten minutes about their next moves and whether it was a waste of time to even check out the pool of water below. Then, Benicio turned around to ask his girlfriend to weigh in on the argument. "Bonny, what do you..." But his words died when he didn't see her. "Bonny?!"

A wave of frantic energy rushed through the whole group when none of the men could see her. Had she stepped into the bush to use the bathroom? Had she started to wander upstream on her own? Had she slipped and fallen down the waterfall? Pulse hammering, Josh and Ben both broke away from the soldiers, staring down the rock wall.

Relief washed through them when, through a thinning in the mist and clouds, they saw her at the bottom of the cliff, standing on a ledge right next to the waterfall.

She must have caught the movement overhead – there was no way she had heard their yells with the water masses rushing down – and looked up at them. A moment later, she brought her radio to her lips. Mike had packed one for each of them in case they were separated because even with a surprisingly good satellite coverage, there were spots where phones just didn't work.

As easy-going as he seemed, the guy had proven to have fore-sight, and right then Ben and Josh could have kissed him for it.

Bonny couldn't believe it. How could people waste their time discussing whether or not they were going to waste time? There was an irony to the argument she was witnessing, and if the situation hadn't been as time-sensitive as it was, she would've appreciated it and teased the guys about it. But that would have to wait. Right then, somebody had to do something to keep things moving. Yes, after seeing the data on screen, she agreed with Josh. But it wouldn't have mattered. Even if she had thought it better to follow the river above ground, she would've just started walking along the bank without the guys. All that the men were doing now was stalling their next move.

So she had given them another minute and once she had been sure that they were all caught up in the argument, she had walked over to the edge and had taken a closer look. The steps looked solid and relatively easy to climb. But just to be sure with the river as wild as it was after the rain, she had used her rope and a tree as a guideline. She wasn't in full gear, but if she slipped, she could hold on to the rope. The climb was surprisingly easy as long as you took care, and Bonny found herself at the bottom of the waterfall in no time.

Now for the interesting part, she thought and began studying the rock wall around her. There had to be some entrance here, it was the only thing that made sense. Looking around, she didn't see anything obvious. Still, she walked the ledge running along the edge of the pool to its end, pushing aside leaves and vines to make sure she didn't miss an opening.

After finding nothing, she walked back and then inched cautiously closer to the actual waterfall. This time, she tied the rope around her waist – the water was too powerful to not make sure she wouldn't just be dragged below the surface. There were still a good fifteen feet from the spot where the steps ended to the waterfall, but even here the air churned with the spray and she couldn't see perfectly because the air was so saturated with droplets that it was like she was standing in a thick fog bank. Step by slow step she walked closer to the waterfall, her hands running along the rocks and feeling for anything she might miss with her eyes.

The rock beneath her fingers was slippery, wet, and covered with moss or algae thriving in the wet conditions. The stone beneath her feet was shaking with the force of the water.

She was pressed closely against the wall, only an arm's length separating her from the water. This was getting too dangerous to try alone.

She was just turning her head back, wanting to turn around, when her fingers touched something strange. She lost it for a second and had to run her hand up and down to try to find it again. Where... where... There! There it was! She managed to bring her head a little closer and couldn't be happier. In a crack between two rocks, a piece of fabric stuck out, now wet and limp. But she had seen that pattern. Valeria had a blouse with these colors, and if she had been out with her colleagues, she might have been wearing it when she had been taken.

Now they only needed to find a way to move these rocks aside. But first, to get the guys down.

Bonny caught some movement overhead and, looking up, confirmed that Josh and Ben were staring down at her. Annoyed with the whole group, Bonny reached for her walkie-talkie. "If you all are done with your pissing contest, come down here. We need to find a way inside this tunnel because Valeria and the kidnappers are definitely in there."

Benicio and Josh were already convinced and began climbing down the steps leading them down to their girlfriend, and after another thirty seconds and the exchange of some frustrated yet considering glances, the soldiers followed.

The ledge was crowded, and Bonny had to yell to be heard over the noise of the water, but she explained the situation and what she had found in a few quick words. Kieran wanted to see the piece of cloth for himself and – after some shuffling to get there – had to agree with Bonny that it wasn't just some fabric stuck on a rock but indeed something that was clearly and deeply wedged between the stones.

"All right, Miss Marple, how do we get in there?" Kieran asked; his voice was teasing, but it carried the smallest hint of wounded pride with it. He seemed to regret his words instantly when he saw the furious way Bonny glared at him. Normally, she wouldn't have minded the teasing, but right then, they had been wasting precious time and playing with the life of a woman who was basically her sister-in-law. Of course, she wasn't up for some fun. "Sorry. You did a bloody great job finding this. I mean it. Let's figure out how to open this damn tunnel."

They all unsuccessfully looked around as much as they could or tried to push or pull the rocks around the piece of Valeria's blouse. Several frustrating minutes later, Jack kicked at the wall. Then he froze. "Stop, everybody. Look!"

His foot had hit a small rock, maybe the size of a man's fist, and had moved it deeper into the wall. Now they all could see that there was a groove beneath it, keeping it in its spot so that it could only move in and out of the wall.

"Keep pushing it," Kieran instructed.

Jack didn't have to do much more. A few inches, and the stone was so deep inside the wall that they could now push one of the slabs that kept the fabric in place to the side. It was surprisingly thin and – without the rock wedge preventing the movement – it slid in front of another part of the wall. A fissure opened for them, not a huge opening but enough for everybody to squeeze through.

Inside the tunnel, it was dark, with the light from the opening illuminating only a few feet. Josh carefully checked their surroundings as best as he could before he switched on his flashlight. In its light, they could see that the slab they had pushed aside was held in place by a chain mounted to the ceiling, giving it enough room to be moved but preventing it from toppling into the water outside. Somebody had also worked the stone to carve a simple handle into the rock to make it easier to open from the inside, and a look at the ground showed that the small stone wedge was sitting at the end of its groove. Studying it more closely, Josh could now see that it also had some ridges that would allow it to be dragged back and forth easily enough.

"They're well organized, it seems," Benicio spat and ground his teeth. The knowledge sat like lead in his stomach, and the grunts he got in response to his comment told him he wasn't alone. It didn't seem like much, just a few rocks, some metal chain, but it showed that the kidnappers had put effort into their organization and were extremely careful to keep things secret. And they knew the jungle. Nobody just stumbled upon a tunnel like this, even if they hadn't carved out the whole tunnel system. But they made it work for them. They had made the rainforest their home – and possibly their weapon.

As if reading his lover's mind, Josh ran the beam of his flashlight along the walls. "I don't like this. They know this place. Be careful, everybody. If they have secret tunnels, they might have traps, too. I think we're lucky, though. I don't see any cameras or anything. It's probably too wet to keep electronics here for long."

He wasn't wrong: as far as the light reached inside the darkness of the tunnel, it was obvious that there was a lot of water above them, even with a thick layer of rock separating riverbed and the tunnel. The ground wasn't swimming but there were small puddles everywhere: water ran down the walls in tiny streams here and there, and in other places drops fell from the ceiling continuously.

The tunnel itself seemed like it was mostly a natural structure, not running in straight lines and sometimes opening into small caves on the sides. The floor had been roughly flattened by human machinery, though.

"What is this place?" Bonny asked.

Benicio looked around once again, then shrugged. "There are some natural cave or tunnel systems below some rivers; some are dry like this here, I can tell you that much. And I don't really know for sure, but I think sometimes the original river ran underground at first but then a rockslide or something else forced it to the surface. If the terrain allowed, it followed the original path. The water finds a new way above ground, but the former riverbed stays and becomes a system like this. Other times, I would imagine it's like an underground overflow where water runs after heavy rainfalls, or snowmelts in some regions, when the water can't go anywhere aboveground. But don't hold me to it, I'm no cave explorer and I didn't study anything connected to this."

"I won't, but it at least makes sense, babe. Anyway, so this system was here, and they began using it to what? Stay hidden when they march through the rainforest with the girls they kidnap?"

"Likely. And to be faster, I'd think," Josh added. "Covering ground like this is a lot quicker than finding your way through the jungle. You've seen how tedious that can be."

Bonny nodded in agreement, but her attention, just like her boyfriends', slipped to the three other men with them. During the throuple's conversation, the guys had adjusted their gear and were now carrying their guns like they were ready to get into a firefight. Kieran gave some short orders to his men, then looked at Bonny, Josh, and Benicio. "We'll go first. We have no idea what they have down here or where this tunnel even leads. You three stay back. I want you about ten yards behind us so you can get away if things turn ugly. And you *will* get away, if that's the case. No playing hero. I let my superiors know where we are and I just sent you some contact information for them. Should we need it, you'll be our best chance to call for help and direct them to this tunnel."

Kieran took a deep breath, then reached behind his back. "And I can't believe I'm doing this, but here. Just in case," he said and handed Josh his holster and handgun with a second clip of ammunition while keeping his rifle for himself.

"From now on, we all stay quiet. We don't know how sound carries once we get further down the tunnel."

Chapter Twenty-Six

The tunnel was damp and dark, and as they moved away from the resealed entrance, the noise of the water flowing overhead got quiet enough that they could hear the constant dripping and the echo of their footsteps. With the gloomy light of their flashlights – dimmed as much as possible while still allowing them to see where they were stepping – the atmosphere was oppressive. That they didn't know what to expect at the end of it didn't help.

Like lambs to the slaughter, Josh thought fleetingly. As much as he wasn't a huge fan of guns, right now the weight of the borrowed weapon at his hip gave him a sense of security and the feeling that he would be able to protect the two loves of his life beside him. It was an odd sort of comfort.

They followed the tunnel and the signal in front of them for a few hours, gaining some more ground while doing so but still making sure to stay a safe distance away. It was written on Benicio's face how much the situation was wearing on him, and Josh could only imagine how hard it was for him not to charge ahead and grab his sister right then and there. He squeezed his boyfriend's hand in support just when Kieran signaled for everybody to stop.

Josh checked his phone and saw the GPS signal blinking in the same spot over and over for a few minutes before heading off to the right. Zooming out further, he had a look at the surrounding area. Most of it was still rainforest, the river veering away in the opposite direction from the signal. But then he saw it: deep in the jungle, still a good hour away given the terrain, the satellite image of the map showed a clearing with what seemed like ruins of an ancient building, better preserved than the other remnants of a long-gone civilization that they had seen so far. And although he couldn't say what it once had been from this image, he just knew that would be the kidnappers' destination. When Kieran waved them over, Josh showed the others his phone and whispered his conclusion after making sure Valeria's signal was far enough away and nobody in the other group would be able to hear him.

Studying the screen for a moment, all three soldiers nodded. "I think you're right. We'll still follow them rather than trying to get there first, keeping some distance between them and us, but it's a high probability. Let's go, then."

Everybody agreed quietly, and after making their way further down the dim tunnel for a little longer, they found themselves turning to the right and stepping into something that was more like a cave.

As far as they could see in the dimmed light of their flashlights, the ceiling was a little higher, and the walls grew farther apart. The air was still clammy, but the ground seemed dry. The sound of dripping water became more distant with each step they took, the quiet murmur of the river they had been hearing overhead before now faded away. A quick look at the map showed that the cave led them south while the river took a turn to the north. It seemed like they had covered a lot of ground, far more than the rainforest would have allowed. No wonder the kidnappers had found a way to conceal the tunnel and use it for themselves – covering such a distance while dragging along their victims could possibly add another day to their trip.

But it also meant that the group had to find the exit. The cave wasn't huge, maybe sixty feet in diameter, but it was large enough to have them split up to search the walls for any hidden mechanisms to get out from underground.

It didn't take long until they all met at the middle of the wall directly across from the entry to the tunnel, each with the same frustrated look on their face after checking their part of the cave wall.

"I don't suppose anybody here has magic hair that glows when they sing?" Rhys asked sarcastically.

Bonny cocked her head, her face caught between amusement and a frown. "Okay, first of all: we're not flooding this cave. And second, why the hell do you know *Tangled?*"

"My daughter is obsessed with that film," the soldier huffed with a smile.

"Guys, that does not help," Kieran told them.

"No, it doesn't exactly. But part of it might. Everybody, turn off your lights. This isn't a hermetically sealed bunker – we might get lucky and see something," Josh said.

Since they had been pushing and knocking against all of the walls before, Kieran agreed after a short moment of consideration and turned off his flashlight.

For a moment, pitch black darkness surrounded them until their eyes began to adjust. The last bit of light came from Josh's and Kieran's screens, each open to the map and GPS signal. It wasn't much, but it illuminated all their faces while they were looking around in hopes of finding a hint to where the exit was.

And still, it didn't seem to help any. No sudden ray of light shining on the floor, no glowing paint scribbled on the wall showing the way.

Frustrated all over again, they walked the walls up and down once more, just to still come up empty. Benicio leaned against the wall and cursed quietly before reaching for his water bottle. But when he tilted his head back to take a sip, something caught his eye and made him gasp. He ended up coughing for almost half a minute because, in his shock, he had swallowed wrong.

Bonny and Josh came to his side, even though they knew they could hardly do anything for their boyfriend. Once Ben had caught his breath, they asked what had happened. Since he didn't trust his voice just yet, Ben only pointed up to a spot near the ceiling at the other side of the cave. Following the line of Benicio's outstretched hand, Bonny and Josh both saw what had surprised their lover.

High up, almost under the ceiling, the dim shimmer of daylight was peaking through a narrow gap in the wall. And when Bonny switched on her flashlight for a few seconds to check something, she found her suspicion confirmed.

It was pure luck Ben had found the exit, because the gap was only visible from the specific position where he was leaning against the wall. Going a foot in any other direction would mean the small ledge was hidden from sight by other parts of the wall and ceiling. From where Kieran and his men still stood, it would look like the ceiling just gradually became the wall, the edge uneven with small overhangs and rough stone, not a sharp change from horizontal to vertical like at some other parts of the cave.

Bonny turned her flashlight back on and gestured for the others to come over as well before telling them, "Look. I think

Ben just found our way out. The only question is: how do we get up there?"

She made a good point. The ledge with the gap looked to be fifteen feet off the ground, and it didn't seem like there was a staircase leading up to it.

"It's too high to just give each other a boost and pull up the last person. There's got to be a way up there," Jack said after having a look for himself.

They all moved over to study the wall beneath and next to the ledge again. At first, they didn't see anything of interest, just like before. That changed when Kieran looked higher than they all had during their first search. He saw something that, at first glance, might just have been a small hole in the wall where a piece of rock had broken off. But when the light of his flashlight shone inside, a small shimmer of light illuminated the ledge above some more as well.

"Guys, wait. I think there's something. At least there's a connection between that space and the ledge. I want to have a look. Jack, give me a leg up," Kieran ordered. The hole wasn't as high as the ledge, only about eight feet above the ground, low enough to reach it after rolling a rock closer to use as a step if you were alone, but reaching in blindly didn't seem like a smart idea.

With Jack's help, Kieran stared inside the opening a moment later and snorted. "This is getting ridiculous. There's a bloody rope ladder in here, and what looks like a short hook and one longer one."

He reached inside and got out both the ladder and the smaller hook, handing them to Rhys before stepping off Jack's hands. "Can't get the large one, it's all too narrow to get it around the bend," Kieran explained.

"I don't think we need it; the small hook you found has a

telescopic rod. But more importantly: what are we supposed to do with this stuff?" Rhys asked the group.

While the soldiers had been busy retrieving the items, the throuple had kept looking around, and now Benicio pointed up towards the ledge once more. "I would suggest using the hook to hang the ladder on the small overhang there. It looks strong enough to be used for this."

Kieran checked what Ben had pointed out, then agreed with him. Meanwhile Jack was muttering, "Ridiculous, all right. What is this, some bloody escape room?"

The comment was more of a rhetorical question, but Benicio shrugged. "You might not be far off with that. One theory my boss and I have is that the missing girls are being kidnapped and used as drug mules. Which, unfortunately, wouldn't be the first time something like that happened. But since we work with law enforcement all the time, we hear more than most people and have heard some rumors and suspicions from the police in some of the individual cases. So my boss and I tried to come up with plausible suspects for running such an operation from all the possible ones that have been mentioned. One of them is actually a guy running a huge event company. They also cater to high-class hotels. He travels all over the country and into the US and also countries in South America, which would give him ample opportunity to run a drug business and use the event business as a front. About two years ago, his teenage daughter, who's a high-profile influencer herself, was diagnosed with cancer. Which is tragic, and I feel bad for her. She's apparently still fighting it, if the gossip channels are right for once. But what's really inter-esting regarding your comment? She's known to be a big fan of escape rooms; and after her diagnosis, her father added mobile escape room experiences to his event list so she can sometimes enjoy them when staying at the hospital for longer."

"Fantastic. So, what? If it's indeed that guy, we'll start running from huge boulders rolling at us while trying to solve some stupid riddle to get out once we get to their hideout?" Jack grumbled.

"No idea. Wrong movie for where we are, by the way, Indy. I just thought you all might want to know some more about the case, and this just fell into place with the rest that I know."

Jack smirked at the nickname. "Yeah, yeah. Good one, though. And you're right about the rest. Anyway, for now, let's get out of here," Jack said and turned to the others to check on their progress.

Ben did the same and caught Kieran balancing the top of the ladder on the extended hook, maneuvering it over the rock above their heads. As he finished hanging up the ladder, he shook his head, likely still at the ridiculousness of the situation. Benicio could understand him.

They all scrambled up the ladder moments later. With three muscled soldiers, their gear, and the throuple and all their equipment, the ledge was cramped, but they all took a moment to look around.

Next to their feet was an opening leading down to the hole where they had found the rope ladder. Kieran rolled the ladder back into a tight bundle together with the hook, then realized the reasons why there was another, longer hook. You would need it to get to the ladder up to the ledge to get down into the cave safely. And he also needed it to get the ladder back to the bottom of the hole without it ending in a knotted mess. Given that there were two hooks, and one that was designed to stay where it was, they all assumed somebody had just let the shorter one drop down in the past and people entering the cave from up where they were standing had had no chance of getting the ladder out of the hole to have something to climb down with.

With the ladder back in its hiding spot, everybody looked to where they had first seen the dim shimmer of daylight. To their surprise, they didn't come across another portal made of stone but were instead faced with a thick curtain of vines hanging over a narrow opening leading outside. The vines were entangled and covered the passageway so well that even standing directly in front of it, they could hardly see any light shining inside let alone make out any features of the jungle lying before them.

The throuple didn't complain when the three soldiers took the lead and, after a first careful inspection, pushed the vines to the side with visible effort. Kieran slid through the gap, then gestured to the rest of the group to follow him.

They found themselves at the foot of a small, rocky hill containing the cave behind them. The hillside was covered in climbing plants, their roots and vines all helping cover the cave entrance. Josh glanced back at the spot they had just come out of and found that he, indeed, couldn't see anything even hinting at a hidden entrance. "I think we better mark this spot on the map, Kieran. Finding it again, especially if we're in a hurry, might be impossible."

"Good idea, mate."

After making sure they'd be able to find their way back, the group began following the blinking dot on the map once more.

Josh's earlier estimate had been close. From when they had left the cave to the moment they came to a stop near a small plateau about an hour had passed.

The kidnappers had made another stop on the way. It had only been a few minutes, but it had allowed the group to get closer and make up for the time they had lost looking for an exit from the cave earlier. And it had made Ben's heart sing when he had heard his sister's voice cursing. Spitting mad, she was still yelling at her captors, even after days in the jungle. Benicio hadn't been able to make out all of it – they had still kept a good distance from the hostile group. But bits and pieces of her loudest swearing had carried to them. Josh and Bonny did the only thing they could when they saw their lover's tear-filled eyes: they both hugged him and pressed kisses to his cheek and temple, whispering reassurances.

After that, it wasn't long until the map showed the kidnappers nearing the structure Josh had seen earlier. Getting closer themselves, they now could make out what looked like a couple of ancient buildings on a small, elevated patch of land. Both structures were ruins, no obvious signs indicating that they were being used or that they were advertised to tourists, even though the larger structure showed the typical staircase architecture of an old Mayan temple, while the smaller one was made of stone and seemed to date back to the same time period.

Bonny wondered for a second why such a site wasn't open to the public, even if the ruins were a lot smaller than the more famous attractions. This had probably only been a small village, maybe cut off from others a lot of the time, so they had built their own small temple. She found her answer, though, when she glanced at the map Josh had still open. It showed a nature preserve running right along the borders of the plateau, also including the remains of an ancient civilization and protecting them from visitors. Naturally, an isolated place like this was an ideal hiding spot for a criminal organization. And if ever any possible ranger showed up, they could bribe him – or just get rid of him in the vast jungle.

But as valid as these considerations were, she also knew there was one far more important question. "Now, I don't suppose we'll just charge them and see how far we get, so how do we get in there?" Bonny asked in almost a whisper.

Josh looked over to her, then to Benicio. "I hate to say it because I know it's the last thing you or Ben want to hear, but you're right, we can't rush this. We'll get in by being not only careful but also patient. Kieran, I assume you'll want to check out the perimeter, right? I know you already did all the way here, but I guess you'll look even more thoroughly for cameras and motion detectors so close to their base, and check whether there are any guards posted."

Next to them, Kieran nodded. "That's the plan, yes. I didn't see any equipment before, so they're either bloody cocky, thinking nobody would ever find them in the first place, or they didn't want to leave any clues to their operation anywhere in case somebody stumbled upon the tunnel. I don't want to count on them doing the same here." After a short glance up through the thick canopy he continued, "It's getting late, too. Soon, it'll get dark. There's no time to plan anything properly today. Here's the plan: the three of you walk back to the large fallen tree we saw about ten minutes from here. Set up camp there for all of us. Jack, Rhys, and I will scout the perimeter, then come back and take shifts to see if there are any guards at night out here, if there's a pattern. We'll keep up the shifts, but whoever isn't on the lookout will rest. The best time to surprise them will be during the night."

"You think, since they dragged my sister here during the day, the base inside operates mostly during daylight hours as well," Benicio concluded.

"Yes. Most places do. People are more alert and do a better job during the day. You can get used to nightshifts, but most people function better during daylight hours, even when they're mostly inside or even underground."

"*Sí*, that is true. And even though I cannot say I'm happy

about the wait, I see your point. Let's go, then," Ben replied before looking expectantly at Bonny and Josh.

His lovers agreed, the same mix of emotions written on both their faces. Before they left, they each grabbed the camping gear from one of the soldiers so that the camp would be waiting for them. It might not have been the plan they wanted, but they all knew it was the smartest choice.

<h1 style="text-align:center">Chapter Twenty-Seven</h1>

"Is she secured?" asked the guy inspecting one of the cameras near the fence separating their destination from the rest of the jungle. His English was heavily accented, but he didn't seem to mind speaking to the other man in something that wasn't his native language.

"Yes, tied to a tree with a gag in her mouth. Peace and quiet for five minutes while we check on the cameras and traps here. That one is a bitch."

"She is. Sometimes I wish we were allowed to rough them up some more. But I think this time was also worse because of the storm and how long it took to get here."

As they went from camera to camera, trap to trap, making sure everything was as it should be, his associate agreed. "For sure. Haven't had to take the long route in a long time. Those were some massive storms hitting right here. Honestly, the march here was shit, but I'm relieved the pilot said he couldn't land closer by. I'm good with everything, but flying in stormy weather sucks. I crashed once during landing because of a storm when I was still in the military in the States; not something I need to experience again."

"I understand that. The location is a challenge."

Looking around, taking in the dense vegetation around them, his colleague agreed. "It is. But other than the flying during storm season, I can't complain. Never been paid better, and what's easier than snatching some chicks and keeping an eye on them here? It's not like they put up much of a fight. And however the boss does it, nobody's bothering us here."

"Nobody suspects us here. It is not always convenient, but it is smart. And with nobody expecting the girls to be targets, nobody has time to find us and follow us until we are out of the country already."

"That's true. Okay, all good here."

"Here as well."

The men walked back a few feet to where they had left Valeria. After untying her and – with a grim look on their faces – removing the gag, they each grabbed one of her arms and dragged her forward.

Her angry curses rang in their ears, but they seemed more ready to ignore them now that they would be able to hand her over to somebody else in a few minutes.

Chapter Twenty-Eight

A bit more than twenty-four hours later, Bonny woke Benicio by trailing gentle fingers through his hair. "Time to get up, baby. We need to get ready and break camp so we can get your sister back."

When she saw he had opened his eyes and gotten her message, she leaned over Ben and woke Josh the same way. Josh turned in his sleeping bag, first nuzzling Ben's neck and pressing a kiss below his ear, murmuring, "It's gonna be okay, Ben," before he looked up at Bonny and stole himself a kiss from her. With a small smile, she vanished from the tent again, leaving the guys to themselves while they got up. She would've stayed to comfort Ben some more but during dinner the night before, she had discussed a few things with Kieran.

At some point, realization had set in that she was the only female in their group. Sure, she knew that, but it hadn't sunken in before because neither her boyfriends nor the soldiers they were traveling with had treated her any differently. She had done some hand-to-hand combat training with the guys over the last few days when they had camped for the night – with nobody pulling a punch any more with her than a training situation usually called for – and she had carried her equipment like everybody else. There was no special treatment. It was exactly what she wanted.

But the previous evening during a quick bathroom break after dinner, she had heard some animal close by in the undergrowth, and she had suddenly felt a lot more vulnerable given her position than a guy likely would have. She had then gotten a quick glimpse at what looked like an anteater, which posed no threat to her; but that still had been the moment when it had struck her that there was a chance they would find dozens of terrified young women to whom men might have done god knew what. Returning to the camp, she had told Kieran she wanted to get basic first aid training the next day so she also could help the women. Some of them probably wouldn't want to be touched by yet another man. It hadn't taken long to convince Kieran of the idea, who then assigned Jack to teach her the most important things the following day.

So she had gotten up a few hours before her partners and had spent the time until she had to wake them up learning the best ways to stop possible bleeding, how to dress wounds until they could properly be treated, and getting to know the first aid kit so she would be able to find what she needed immediately. With her mother being a nurse, Bonny already had a good understanding of first aid. But knowing what to do to help until an ambulance arrived or having more medical equipment at hand was a long way from field dressings in the jungle.

Jack was just going over a few last details with her as she reorganized her gear to be able to carry a few more medical supplies on her own when Rhys came back from his patrol and Josh and Ben crawled out of their tent.

· · ·

Shortly after, the group began making their way towards the plateau. Rhys and Kieran had worked out a route that led them first a little farther away from the actual structure and along the border of the nature preserve.

The protected area was surrounded by a simple fence; it wasn't much and was clearly only meant to act as a visual tool to let people know where they were supposed to stop and certainly not to keep any animals inside. More importantly, though, the fence was somewhat broken in one place and allowed them to slip through, so they'd be able to backtrack and move closer to the plateau with the temple from the side instead of head-on inside the nature preserve.

The soldiers had thoroughly searched the jungle the night before and during that day and had found a few discreetly and well-placed cameras along with a few sharpened sticks, made to look like they had just been broken naturally to the untrained eye. Nothing obvious, but enough to make it too annoying for normal travelers to keep going in the direction of the plateau, and more than enough to decide not to get any closer to the plateau from that angle to avoid being seen on camera.

When they had been looking for another way in where they would be less likely to be spotted, they had found the gap in the fence and had scouted the jungle on other side of it and up to the plateau. They hadn't come across any cameras or deterrents on that side. When discussing it with the throuple, all had agreed that the kidnappers likely tried not to bring any attention to their operation in case a ranger should ever check the borders of the preserve. Finding cameras or traps inside the fenced-in area would only cause an investigation into illegal poaching activities – and the kidnappers certainly wouldn't value the extra attention. Thus, Kieran and Rhys had planned their actual approach of the temple from the back of the plateau while Jack had worked with Bonny.

The jungle was just as thick on the other side of the fence, and as they got closer to the plateau again they became even quieter than before. Finally, they reached the bottom edge of the plateau. They were lucky that the climb they were facing wasn't as steep as other formations. It was more of a challenging hike up to a flat mountaintop. It also meant that they weren't exposed while climbing on a steep rock wall but could instead make use of the dense vegetation to hide and help their ascent without the need to use their climbing gear. It was an arduous task, which took them longer than they would have liked. But climbing in the dark meant they could only turn on the barest, dimmest of light sources to avoid announcing their approach like a brightly shining beacon.

In the end, they crawled over the edge, staying low to the ground. All of them had gotten scratches from thorny plants or broken branches. On top of that, Jack had been cursing quietly for a good five minutes after he had accidentally placed his hand on a small anthill somewhere around the middle of the climb, causing the insects to attack him and leaving him with burning and tingling fingers. It wasn't pleasant, yet they had all been fortunate enough so far not to stumble over something more dangerous. *But we can't stay here forever with these open wounds, no matter how small, or we'll all have to deal with infections. They're just as dangerous as any wild animal,* Bonny thought and hoped they would be able to get out Ben's sister, the tourist, and perhaps even the other girls quickly.

Kieran diligently checked their surroundings to make sure nobody was waiting for them. Then he signaled the group to hurry along the thinning edge of the forest while staying behind the line of the last trees running around the plateau to get as close to the temple ruins as possible, using the jungle for cover.

But when they finally reached the closest point to one of the temple walls, they had no choice but to step out of their concealed position and to cross the few yards of open, grassy ground. There were still some larger plants covering the floor, but no trees had ever taken root on the rock bed below the shallow dirt cover closer to the structure.

As they ran, Josh tried to study as much of the temple as possible. Even from this close, there were no signs of life, nothing that hinted at the secrets hidden inside. Just an ancient structure left to itself, with large parts covered in moss and ferns clinging to places that didn't get too much direct sunlight during the day. An amazing site to explore – if you weren't there to rescue your boyfriend's sister from a criminal enterprise. But the closer they got, the heavier, more oppressive, the atmosphere got. It took him a second, but then Josh realized what left him with an uneasy feeling; it wasn't just that he knew why they were here, or all the ideas of what they'd find inside that his brain had come up with. It was the eerie silence.

Behind them, he could still hear the rainforest: leaves rustling in the wind, branches creaking, and the cacophony of animal noises. So many nocturnal species filling the night with their voices, the sounds of their movement. They were looking to mate, to rummage through the debris on the forest floor for food, to hunt. The jungle never was truly quiet. Life was happening everywhere.

But around the temple, there was silence. A dark, foreboding silence. Not even insects seemed to get too close to the ruins. Stillness hung like a bubble around the broken, weathered walls. Involuntarily, he shuddered.

Then he forced himself to focus on the task at hand: they had to scale the pyramid structure. Rhys had reported a side-entry at about three-quarters of the height of the building, hardly visible from below the plateau. It was on the other side of the structure from where they were leaving their cover, but it was still better to approach the temple like that and round the two corners than run across far more open ground.

The day before, they had seen the last of the kidnappers run toward the temple for a brief moment, but it had taken Rhys about thirty minutes from his position far away to find traces of their actual ascent up the stone steps and then around a corner to the entrance hidden behind a giant fern. He and Kieran had decided to follow as closely in their footsteps as possible to get inside. Entering somewhere else was not only no guarantee for secrecy, it also might end with them not getting to where they needed to be. A dead end in a dangerously dilapidated temple could be an easy death sentence without encountering a single enemy.

Instead, they were all pressing closely against the cold rock now and making their way to the corner that they had to turn around to get up to the main stairs. It would've been easy enough to climb the prominent stairs leading up the middle of the ruins, had it not been the middle of the night with clouds beginning to cover the moon. They went by feel, careful not to tread on loose stone or slippery plants. Using climbing gear was out of the question, and even with a temple like the one they were scaling, which was relatively small for a Mayan temple and measured around forty-five feet in height, it would still be a painful and possibly deadly fall should they slip. Carefully, they made their way up until they were almost at the top of the stairs. Then Rhys guided them to the side of the steps and over the edge onto the terrace-like wider platform running all around the temple. It was covered more densely in plants and they had to be careful when rounding the corner, but they managed to find the smaller secret entrance easily enough.

Up close, it was obvious that it was a new addition, the edges too smooth for centuries of the elements to have been battering them, and when a cloud let some moonlight through, they could make out what looked like more modern support beams hidden deeper inside the structure after Kieran had carefully checked the entrance first.

The fact that they still weren't seeing any guards, cameras, or obvious locks was unsettling, and Josh was grateful that he had talked to Kieran before breaking camp earlier. While the soldier had explained they had some emergency backup as well, Josh had managed to convince him that it would be useful to also let Josh's boss know the exact situation as they knew it and their target location. The man might not have a platoon of soldiers at hand, but if he didn't hear from Josh regularly in the following hours, he would still be able to get to Guatemala faster than Kieran's support. It was a small comfort, but Josh would take it.

Cautiously, the group inched inside. The side entrance had been created in the middle between the top floor and the one below, and the passageway they were following opened to a set of stairs connecting the original levels, so the angle was awkward since nobody had bothered to work on them. Worse, though, was the utter darkness staring back at them once they peered down the stone steps. It meant they would have to use their flashlights and potentially let people know their position, but night vision goggles hadn't been something the throuple could have easily ordered during their flight, and Kieran and his men hadn't expected to bring along three more people so they only had their own special equipment after buying camping basics locally as well.

The throuple watched as Jack slipped a pair of goggles over his eyes and tested his radio. They were all wearing earbuds – Josh could've kissed Bonny for her foresight in thinking something like that could come in handy when he had placed their order. It had taken a bit of finessing, but they had been able to connect them to the soldiers' equipment, and they all had a few basic signals memorized as simple click sequences for situations in which they couldn't talk. When they all gave Jack a quiet okay that his voice and the clicks came through, they observed him as he gingerly began descending the stairs. He'd be their scout, at least for now, and let them know when it was safe for them to follow.

Once he was lost to the darkness after a few steps, they heard Jack's voice whispering in their earpieces. "Watch out: every few steps, one is purposely littered with round pebbles or something. If you fall, it's gonna be bad."

Simple, yet effective and inconspicuous enough, Benicio thought to himself as he acknowledged the transmission with a click of his radio like the others did. Then he focused on Kieran, who was getting them ready to follow. They would have to navigate with the least bit of light possible and be careful not to blind the soldiers with their night vision goggles. Ben would carry his flashlight and walk with Bonny and Josh, one on either side of him. Bonny wanted her hands free as she was most comfortable with hand-to-hand combat; Josh checked the weapon Kieran had handed him before. This was not at all what Benicio had ever expected to happen, but he was incredibly grateful he didn't have to face the situation alone. *Scratch that: without them, I wouldn't even know where my sister was taken, let alone be here now. Let's get all out of here in one piece so I can spend the rest of our lives showing them how much I love them and how much I appreciate all their support.*

Then it was time to move.

Chapter Twenty-Nine

Beneath his feet, Benicio felt the rough stone of the stairs; in his hand, the metal of the flashlight still felt cool. From above them, a gust of wind pushed down the stairwell and left him with a shudder. He aimed the flashlight low to the ground, the beam of light dimmed as much as possible, and glanced from Bonny to Josh. Each gave a nod, and all three moved onto the steps to follow Rhys and Kieran down.

They had made it down several steps, avoiding the first one covered in treacherous pebbles, when Jack murmured in their ears, "End of first flight. Level clear. Going further down."

Kieran acknowledged, then pointed out another step to tread on carefully or avoid.

Once they reached the first level going down, they found themselves in an empty, square room. Dust and dirt covered the floor, but in the low light of the flashlight, Ben could not only see Jack's footprints but also several others, some of which were more smeared and uneven, like somebody had been fighting against being dragged further down. He and Josh took a quick look but both knew they didn't have time to check the tracks in detail. With Kieran turning to the next flight of stairs, they moved over as well when they heard Jack once again. "Tripwire, twenty-seven steps down."

So we've gotten to the obvious traps then, Ben thought fleetingly before moving with the rest of the group.

Moments later, Jack announced the next level clear and let them know he'd keep moving.

And so they went as well. Slow and careful, but at a steady pace. It didn't take too long to get to the tripwire, and only a few steps later, they were standing in the next room. This one was bigger to fill out the larger level of the pyramid structure, but just as empty. A glance back up the stairs made Ben stop in his tracks. He studied the tripwire from where he stood. Something was odd about it, but he couldn't pinpoint it. Bonny stepped closer and looked at him with a clear question in her eyes. He indicated the wire, then shrugged and mouthed, "Something's weird."

She studied the trap, and her face told him she felt the same but had no idea what exactly it was either.

The feeling stayed with both of them for the next three levels they descended. They encountered more loose pebbles, more tripwires, and, unnervingly, still no guards, no electronic security.

Added to that, the air got mustier, the darkness more oppressive with every step they took. They were so deep inside the structure that there was absolutely no sound from outside traveling down to them; all they heard were their soft footfalls, the rustling of their clothes while they moved. No forest breeze carried that deep, and every breath felt like they inhaled the grime of thousands of years of neglect and the remnants of lost, long-dead critters.

With the last steps they took down to the next level, Benicio thought they had just about reached the level of the ground outside, closed off from the outside world by thick walls of stone and earth. He could already feel the air clinging to the next flight of stairs getting cooler. They were about to go truly underground.

Next to him Bonny studied another tripwire, when her head suddenly jerked up. He saw her opening her mic and listened to her when she quietly explained to everybody, "Guys, the wires. They are all spun across too close to the back of the steps. I don't think their main purpose is to keep people out, but in. Anybody fleeing and running up the stairs in a panic would easily trip over the wire. They don't care who gets inside, they want to make sure nobody will get out again unless they're supposed to."

Kieran examined the wire on the stairs they had just come down and nodded in agreement, when they heard Jack coming through again. "Agreed. I reached some end point here; there are only walls. But at the bottom of the stairs is one more trip-wire. Looks like that one is connected to a trap mounted to the ceiling that overhangs the first few steps going up. Anybody running up and getting tangled in the wire gets a board with stakes mounted to it in the chest. Be fucking careful getting down here."

"Bloody hell," Kieran cursed soundlessly, then added in a quiet voice, "Copy that. Wait for us where you are."

They joined Jack soon enough and had to agree with him: the room seemed like a dead end. Another square space, empty, dark, and dank. Only the stairs leading down into the room, no others leading deeper. Aside from the trap, you'd think nobody had been here in a very long time.

That was, until you looked for the footprints on the floor. They led to the wall to the right of the stairs and seemed to vanish into the rock. Unfortunately, that didn't give them a clue as to where the opening mechanism was hidden.

While the others began to search for switches, Benicio looked up at the looming trap over the stairs.

It was simple enough: a sturdy wooden board with sharp, pointed stakes. If the tripwire was disturbed, the board would fling down forcefully, the kinetic energy driving the stakes through skin and into flesh. It would cause severe injuries at the very least, maybe even be deadly if the stakes burrowed deep enough into their victim to penetrate vital organs.

He couldn't stop the shudder running through him when images of scared, panicked young women swam into his mind, running away in a desperate attempt to get away, only to get impaled on their way to freedom. And he knew it could easily happen if there were indeed so many girls being trapped here. They could try to calm them as much as they wanted, but instincts would tell some of the women to run, no matter what. It wouldn't even be a conscious decision.

Making up his mind, Ben reached out to Kieran and pointed to the trap. He whispered as quietly as possible while still being heard, "We need to disarm this. If not, I guarantee you, at least one of the girls will end up with terrible injuries."

Kieran studied the contraption for a long moment, obviously picturing the same gruesome outcome. "Yes, likely. We can't just cut the tripwire or rip off the board, though. They might have hidden sensors somewhere."

Josh appeared next to them. "We've got rope. Let's tie some to the board and attach it somewhere on the floor above. I think I've seen some strong roots up there from some of the larger plants outside growing into the structure. That way, the board can't fall down, even if somebody trips over the wire."

"Grand idea, but how would you reach the bloody thing in the first place?" It was a good question, given that the ceiling to which it was mounted was about ten feet above the closest step, and that the board would be too far away from the edge to reach it from the floor above.

"We find a spot on the stairs and then can lift Bonny to attach the rope to the frame," Benicio said.

"Are you sure you can do that safely?"

Next to Kieran, Bonny jumped into the conversation after she had only been silently listening so far. "All we need is a good footing on the stairs. For the rest, don't worry, they know how to manhandle me safely," she said smugly.

Given the suppressed cough from Kieran, Bonny was sure she would've seen the big soldier blush if she'd had enough light on his face.

"We just need one of you to help us with the flashlight, since we'll all need both of our hands," Josh added, a smile carrying in his voice. He was grateful to his girlfriend for lightening the mood a little. The situation was bad enough and would only get more stressful soon; releasing even a tiny bit of tension wasn't a bad idea.

"I'll do that. Rhys, Jack, keep looking while we secure the trap," Kieran addressed his men, then held out his hand for the flashlight. He took a few steps up so he would be able to shine the beam to where they would need it without blinding them while conveniently being out of the way in case the trap activated accidentally.

The whole exercise could've been a circus act. After taking off their backpacks and finding their footing, Josh and Benicio lifted Bonny to sit on their shoulders. But she was barely touching the board, so she moved from sitting to carefully standing up, with each of the guys grabbing hold of a leg while she balanced between them. It gave her enough height to find a place where she could attach the rope.

With his position a few steps above them, Kieran took the end of the rope to keep gentle tension on it while Bonny was slowly brought back down. Then Kieran gestured for the throuple to stay where they were as he quickly took the remaining steps to the level above them and looked for the aforementioned roots. It didn't take him long to find them, and he managed to tie the rope securely to them.

The satisfaction the four of them felt then fled promptly when they joined Jack and Rhys again. The men were thorough in their search but so far hadn't found any hidden entrance.

They all kept looking, until all of a sudden a male voice spoke to them via their earbuds, "This is Anton Foss. Josh, precisely where are you?"

Everybody turned their gaze sharply to Josh, even though he was mostly hidden by the surrounding darkness. But he was as surprised as the rest of the group. Before Josh could say anything, Kieran answered the man with a tense hiss, "Who are you? This is a secure channel. How did you get on it?"

"I'm Josh's boss. I checked his location before his scheduled ping to me. He's been in the same spot for quite some time. As to how, I'm good at my job. Now, where are you and what's going on? I'm currently looking at the schematics of their security system and working on getting into their camera feed. Let me be your eyes and ears."

Completely baffled, Kieran mouthed a quiet, *What the fuck?*, but then addressed the young man next to him. "Josh, can you confirm?"

"Yes. That's Anton, I know his voice. And yes, he is that good. He can help us."

It was more than clear that Kieran wasn't happy about his supposedly secure line of communication being infiltrated that easily, but he begrudgingly talked to Anton, telling him which level they were on and what they were facing.

"Give me a moment, I just got into the schematics for the wiring," Anton told them, then fell silent for only a few seconds.

"All right. You're standing in front of the correct wall. To your left, directly in the corner, about a foot above ground, is a switch. I found some notes, seems like a pressure switch, likely a stone in the wall you can kick in. Wait before you press it. I can look at their cameras now. Give me three minutes to have enough of a recording that I can feed into their system to create a smooth loop, making you invisible for their cameras. I'll let you know when I'm ready. In case you're working in the dark, you can use more light where you are. There's no camera covering that part of the temple."

With silence from Anton's end, Kieran gestured for Rhys to look for the switch, and then made sure he wouldn't transmit it when he moved closer to Josh, nearly interrogating him in whispered tones, "Who the bloody hell is that? And don't tell me your boss, mate. I got that. What's his background?"

"I know he was military in the past. Some tech branch. He's still brilliant when it comes to tech; it's a big part of his business." Josh knew it was more than that, that it had been a secret military department specialized in gathering technological intelligence and infiltration of enemy systems, but he wouldn't just admit that. Then Anton's niece had been kidnapped. The police had been utterly unable to do anything, so Anton had quit the military, worked on getting her back – dancing along the line of legality but covering his tracks well – and then had opened his own PI firm. Josh had used his own skills to find out as much as possible about the man before applying for a job at Anton's firm. It had, in fact, become part of his interview. Anton had been impressed by how deep Josh had managed to dig before his alarms had alerted him that somebody was looking him up.

Given Kieran's hard stare, Josh could tell the soldier fully knew that that wasn't the whole story but was also aware there were more important things to focus on right that moment. "We will talk about this later."

Josh simply nodded. There wasn't much he could say or do, anyway.

Moments later, Rhys signaled to the group that he had found the switch. From what they could see, it looked like any other stone making up the wall, but Rhys highlighted a tiny smear of what looked like shoe polish, only visible in the right light. Having a way in eased the tension of the group somewhat, but they were all still far from being relaxed.

Fortunately, they didn't have to wait much longer. Anton hijacked their comms channel once again. "The feed is looped, but I still have the live view. I'll be assisting you. When you press the switch, you'll open up a wall inside a utility closet. I'll give you a signal when nobody is close by in the adjacent hall-way, so there's no chance any noise of the wall panel opening might alert somebody."

They were all sure they practically heard Kieran grind his teeth, but he copied. He also gave Anton a quick rundown on their agreed-upon click signals in case the group couldn't reply once they were inside the actual base.

Anton acknowledged the signals, then told them, "You're a go."

Chapter Thirty

With the push of a button – well, the press of a stone – a whole section of the wall swung open slowly towards the group. Once they could see the other side, they weren't surprised. There was no room inside for the doorway to open in the other direction. They were indeed looking at a small utility closet stacked high with a multitude of boxes and bottles. Next to practical things like light bulbs, toilet paper, and household cleaner, they found canisters with surface disinfectant usually used to clean surgical suites, a shelf with clothes in a variety of sizes, and different hair dyes. Even that small room painted a daunting picture.

Stepping through, they had to squeeze closely together to fit into the confined space.

"All right, I see you all now. Camera above the door. You can close the wall section. There's not only a switch hidden behind the shelf to your left, but I also managed to access their system: I'll be able to open it remotely."

"Copy that," Kieran whispered and gave Jack a nod to shut the entrance behind them.

The shelves attached to the doorway crowded back into the

room, making it an even tighter fit. *Herding a group of panicked women through here won't be fun*, Bonny thought.

She observed Rhys listening at the door, then glancing up at the camera.

"Still good. Surgical wing, barracks, and a security office, along with a room with a boiler, generator, and air and water filters to the left when you step out. To the right, toilets, an alcove behind which the holding cells are hidden, and a closet. A U-shaped corridor runs along everything. Directly in front of you is the kitchen and an office, both entrances toward the right corridor. The right part of the hallway ends at a door leading to some small but better living quarters with one bedroom, office space, and two undetermined rooms. Left part of the hallway ends at... something. Given the extra security, my best guess is a lab, weapons, something like that. FYI, I'm currently also working on getting more support for you. It will take a while, though."

Keeping as quiet as possible, Kieran used his radio to submit a click in acknowledgement.

"Hostile count as follows," Anton proceeded. "One person manning the security office. Six sleeping in the barracks. One patrolling the corridors. Two men in the office, one in the kitchen, one in another supply closet, looks like he's restocking backpacks. I assume some or all of them are the ones who just brought your boyfriend's sister here, Josh."

Another click.

"In the living quarters, two people are sleeping, sharing a bed. Supposedly hostile, but I can't say for sure. The two other rooms have no camera coverage. Status undetermined on those.

"And now to the poor women down there. I assume them all friendlies. I counted eight girls in total. Two in beds in the surgical wing, the others in the holding cells. Heads-up, the holding cells are hidden behind another secret door. Across from the kitchen is a small alcove with bookshelves and two armchairs. The shelf hides the access door. Haven't found the switch yet, as quite a few wires are running in that direction. Back to the girls: most are sleeping. Since Josh sent me a picture of Benicio's sister, I can tell you she's currently pacing her room, checking every inch for a way out. She looks unharmed aside from a few scratches that she probably got on the hike there."

Ben looked with gratitude at the camera and nodded, soundlessly mouthing, "Thank you."

"You're welcome. I'll let you plan for now. As long as you're talking quietly, you're still good. The guy patrolling just started talking to the one taking care of the backpacks."

"Thanks," Kieran whispered, then addressed the others. "I don't like those numbers. Any ideas how to balance the scales?"

For a moment, everybody took in the situation they were facing: a highly complex underground structure (meaning whoever was running the facility likely had also spent good money on security, including paying the guards well enough that they would put up a real fight); outnumbered by said armed guards; a group of likely terrified women (and the haunting implications about the number of women at their location compared to the number of likely related missing person cases); at least two wounded or recovering women. None of that inspired confidence. But everybody on the rescue team knew that a proper plan and a realistic yet positive attitude were important, no matter how bleak a situation might seem at first. Thus, all of them focused on finding solutions.

It was Bonny who spoke first. "Okay, tactically I would think we would do best if we managed to keep the sleeping guys asleep in their barracks."

"Of course," Kieran agreed. "But how do you plan to do that? Even if there's no alarm, I highly doubt we can get all those women out of here so quietly that none of the guys wake up and alert the others."

"There's apparently a whole surgical wing. For one reason or another, they operate on these women. They will have anesthetics here, most likely in the form of an anesthetic gas. If we can find a way to pump the gas into the barracks, the guards in there might sleep through the whole thing."

"Would that actually work?"

"It depends. I know that some of the gases can accumulate in a room and cause problems. My mom's hospital once had to cancel all surgeries for a day because a machine wasn't working and leaked gas, which they had to pump out of the air. Babe, what do you think?" Bonny asked Benicio, who had more medical knowledge than what she had picked up from her mother's stories.

Her boyfriend considered it for a moment. "Like you said, it depends. First on what gas they use. Some cause irritation to the airways and might wake the guys up if they start coughing. Also on how much gas we can find and how we can distribute it, its relative density and how the room or rooms are designed, whether they have bunkbeds, for example. It also depends on how much we care that those men will be left unharmed. Which is, frankly, not my biggest concern."

The rest of the group just shrugged in agreement. Given the horrendous situation they were dealing with, nobody made the kidnappers' well-being their priority.

"All right, I think it's at least worth a try. If we can manage the logistics. Anton, did you hear all of that? Can you support us getting into the surgical wing to start with?" Kieran took over the discussion again.

"I did, and I can," came over their earphones. "My advice is this: sneak to the boiler room. Then let me create an alert for the water filtration system. Either the guy in the surveillance office or the one patrolling will check out the room. Take out the one checking things. The others just got together in the kitchen; judging by the way they're raiding the fridges, they'll likely be busy for a while. That leaves you time to head to the surgical wing unseen."

"Okay. Let us know when we can move."

"Will do. Quiet now, patrolling guard left the others and is moving down your hallway again."

Kieran gave a click in response, and everybody fell into a tense silence. Outside the door to their closet, they heard the footfall of military boots on concrete. The steps were heavy but had a small drag to them. They hoped it meant the guy was tired and wasn't paying all that much attention to his surroundings.

For a long moment, the silence hung heavily in the tiny room until Anton spoke again. "Luck's on your side. The guy checked on the women in the surgical wing, then moved to his colleague in the security office to say *buenas noches* and just crawled into one of the empty beds in the barracks; no bunk beds, by the way. One of you, move quietly to the left down the hall. First door next to yours should be another closet. No camera, but the hallway camera shows a window in the door with some brooms visible. The door after that is the security office. Go low and be as quiet as possible. You'll head straight to a door at the end of the corridor. That door opens into the boiler room. I'll keep an eye on the one watching over security. Go now and click twice when you've found a good hiding spot in the boiler room."

Kieran silently copied, then ordered Rhys via hand signals to move, which told the throuple the man was likely extremely skilled when it came to silently disabling enemies.

While they waited, Josh turned his back to the door to the hallway to be able to brighten his flashlight some more. Bonny and Ben observed him when he found a piece of paper and a pen and began sketching the underground complex as he had understood it from Anton's description so far.

Once he was done, he took a quick picture and sent it to his boss. Then he waited with the others until they all heard the clicks confirming Rhys was in position.

"Copy that," Anton confirmed. "I'll trigger an alert for a blocked water filter. The logs show that happens regularly, they won't think anything of it." A few seconds of silence, then, "Triggered. Security guard looks annoyed and is getting up himself, not alerting others."

They all picked up the quiet click of a door, then there was more silence. Soon enough, though, they heard Anton whistling low-key in their ears. "Beautifully done, really. Guard is out. Your guy was hiding on a pipe running along the ceiling, reached down, and snapped the guard's neck in one smooth move. And... yeah, he's draping him over some of the machinery to make it seem like he hit his head when coming back up after checking something. Smart. Won't fool anybody once they get close, but it will buy you a few precious seconds. Also, Josh, yes, the sketch comes close. But there's a narrow, tiled hallway I didn't mention earlier, behind the wall with the alcove, running all the way along the entrances to the holding cells. I think that's where they let the women take quick showers. Just sent you an edited version."

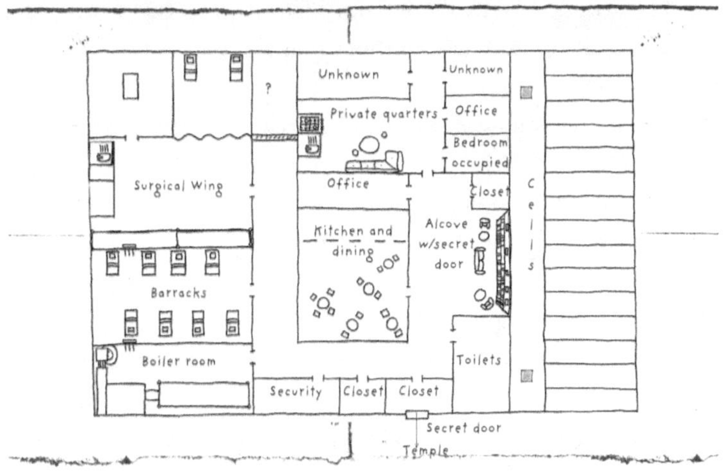

Instead of saying anything, Josh looked at the camera and gave Anton a thumb-up, checked his phone, and forwarded the picture to Kieran, who nodded.

"You can talk right now, but I would suggest moving to the surgical wing soon," Anton told them, then let them talk strategy once again.

Kieran took over. "Josh and I will stay here. Rhys, stay put in case somebody spots the dead guy. Jack, move with Bonny and Benicio, you three have the best idea of what to do with the medical equipment."

Everybody agreed, even though Bonny wasn't sure of how much help she would really be.

After cautiously peeking out the open door of the closet, Bonny could easily recognize everything Anton had told them about before. There had to be cameras everywhere for him to be able to paint them such a detailed picture just from the surveillance videos. If she leaned slightly to the right, she could look down the corridor that ended at the living quarters. Some brighter light shone from what had to be the kitchen, and quiet voices carried over to them. Too low to make out words, but constant enough to reassure them that those men were in deep conversation.

Then she followed Jack and Ben to the left, passing the doors to the other closet, the surveillance room, and the boiler room. It helped knowing Kieran and Josh were behind them to shield them, and Rhys could cover them as well if he opened the door. Still, Bonny was keenly aware of the fact that they were then creeping alongside a room full of armed mercenaries. They stayed low and on the far side of the corridor, away from the door, crawling around the corner and along the empty hallway Anton had described. The lights were dimmed for the night, but they could see well enough. Bonny studied the door in passing and was happy to see no gaps at the top or bottom. It would hopefully prevent the anesthetic gas from leaking into the hallway and affecting any of her lovers and friends, or the women they'd come here to rescue.

A few more steps down the corridor took them to the entrance to the surgical wing. They moved away from the wall and crossed the hallway, then Jack covered them as Ben oh so carefully pushed open the door. All three slipped through the door soundlessly.

Inside, they saw a curtained-off area to the right, the separations just open wide enough to show two sleeping women in hospital beds with one more empty bed next to them.

Behind that part of the medical bay, they could make out sinks directly across at the far end of the room, and a walled-off section with a set of doors pointing to the middle of the room. That had to be the scrubbing area and the actual operating room.

To their left, they saw multiple cupboards and shelves holding medical supplies, a machine to sterilize surgery equipment, and an ultrasound scanner.

Then, she did a mental happy dance and pointed to a spot high up on the wall. An air vent. The moment she showed it to Ben and Jack, they all heard Anton, who must've seen the gesture on the surveillance feed he was still hacked into. "Just checked. The air vents connect all the rooms on this side of the complex. Find a way to cover the vents in the boiler room and everything on the surgical side around the hose feeding the gas in there and you should be good."

Jack acknowledged it with a click, then they heard the answering click from Rhys.

Before any of that happened, though, Bonny turned around and tilted her head in the direction of the women. "We need to check them, and if possible, let them know what's going on," she whispered.

Jack nodded. He pointed at himself and the storage area, then at Bonny and Ben and the women.

Moving over to the beds, Bonny and Ben found both women sleeping with IV lines connected to their arms. Even in their sleep, there was tension written all over the girls' faces. *They must be scared to death and in pain on top of it*, Benicio thought and studied them for a moment longer. They seemed familiar, but he couldn't place them. It wasn't important right now, though. Instead, he placed a hand on Bonny's arm and smiled at her. "I think you should wake them, *mi amor*. They might react better to that. I'll translate," he offered softly.

He had a point, so she stepped over to the first bed. The woman lying in it seemed even younger than Bonny, and it broke her heart to think how utterly terrified the girl – and all the others – had to have been ever since having been dragged into such a place.

Bonny's touch was feather-light when she put her hand on the girl's upper arm, her thumb running over the skin in a soothing motion. She tried to put a reassuring look on her face, placing a finger over her own lips, hoping the girl would accept the request for silence.

At first, there was no reaction, just the girl's inhales and exhales. Then her eyelids began to flutter, only for a second, before she seemed to drift off again. Bonny gently put just a little more strength into her hold on the girl's arm. It seemed enough to get her back, fighting to wake up.

Agonizingly slowly, the girl opened first one, then both eyes. Confusion was replaced by pure terror within a heartbeat, and it was clear she wanted to open her mouth to get a sound out.

Bonny forced a smile on her face, her finger tapping against her lips, then pointed to herself and Ben and urgently whispered, "Okay. Help." That had to be universal enough to be understood by a young woman, even in such a frightened state, Bonny hoped.

The girl wasn't even fully awake just yet, but her head whipped frantically between the two people standing next to her bed, and her eyes grew bigger with every passing second. But she stayed silent.

Calmly and quietly, Bonny began to talk. "We're here to help. I'm Bonny, and this is my boyfriend, Benicio. What's your name? What have they done to you?"

Next to her, Benicio studied the woman. With her eyes open, he could finally place her. She was one of the missing persons Josh had shown them pictures of when they had been sitting around the campfire a couple of nights before. Same with the girl in the other bed. It was just more proof that everything was connected. For now, he focused on keeping his voice nonthreatening, though, when he translated, since the girl didn't seem fit enough to comprehend English very well.

When he had finished repeating in Spanish what Bonny had said before, the young woman quivered, and tears of obvious relief and hope ran down her cheeks. She answered them, first in Spanish, "Oh, thank god. I'm Isabella. I... Somebody grabbed me, I couldn't do anything. I was just on my way home from work. I think I remember a plane and a helicopter. And then they put me in a room. There were more girls, I heard them. It's all so confusing. I think they gave me something... Then they brought me from the other room here. I'm so tired, and my breasts hurt."

Ben quickly translated for Bonny, then looked at Isabella again. "Can we just take a quick look? We want to help, but we need to understand."

The girl hesitated for a second but then nodded and slowly pushed the blanket down. "Sí, all right. Please just get me out of here," she finally said, switching to English now that the sluggishness seemed to wear off bit by bit.

Bonny helped her, then lifted the gown Isabella wore as carefully as possible. She forced herself not to flinch as she revealed the woman's chest. It wasn't a real surprise, but the sutures running along Isabella's breasts made both Bonny's and Ben's blood boil.

It wasn't definitive proof what the women were used for, yet, but given the position of the stitches, it seemed unlikely that anybody harvested organs from the girls. Not to mention the location of the base in the middle of the jungle, meaning transport of any organ would take an unnecessarily long time. No, that wasn't what was happening here.

It left them with two other chilling possibilities: one was, somebody was operating on the women to prepare them to get trafficked. It didn't feel like it, though. Women being abducted and suffering such a terrible fate usually weren't all in the same age group or came from the same background. There was more randomness to the victims. And their bodies typically didn't show up like they did in the cases Benicio and the rest thought were connected to the base they were standing in. They were sold, and whoever bought them decided their fate. There wouldn't be a pattern to it like they had seen in the cases they had looked into.

The other possibility wasn't much brighter, but it fit better with what they knew. Even without a physical exam, it seemed more likely that somebody was forcing these girls to become their drug mules, like Benicio and his boss had already suspected. Surgically placing the drugs like this, covered up as breast implants, was unusual, sure. It meant a far bigger effort than making the women swallow the packages for body packing. But cops were trained to look for body packers crossing the border.

These young women didn't fit the picture of a typical drug mule – because they weren't. They wouldn't have chosen this voluntarily or because they desperately needed the money. And even if they were picked up, the sutures would look well-placed to a layman, like they'd just recently gotten standard breast implants. Add a few new clothes, a new hair color, and you had a young girl traveling and looking for some fun before life got too serious, perhaps trying to get over a bad break-up or visiting old friends or family in the US. It made for a simple but effective cover story.

And once border control got suspicious of any of the girls, one enforcer or another was told to get rid of them.

One quick glance shared between Bonny and Benicio showed them they had both come to the same conclusion.

They didn't have time to discuss it now, though. But they would have to update everybody as soon as possible. Girls with drugs in their bodies would require medical help, and they would have to keep a close eye on them and find a way to get them to a medical team as fast as possible in case any of the implants or packages – who knew what exactly had been put inside their bodies – burst or even just began to leak.

Bonny helped the girl with the gown and squeezed her arm in support. "We'll do what we can to get you out of here soon. For now, we need you to stay quiet, okay? We have more people here, like the guy over there," she said and pointed over her shoulder towards Jack. "Do you think you can wake up the other girl while we help our friend?"

Isabella glanced over to the other bed and considered it for maybe half a second. "You bet your ass. Help me sit up and bring the beds closer together, then I'll talk to her and make sure she'll stay quiet, too," she told them with determination written over her face.

Bonny assumed her accent was a little thicker than under normal circumstances, but she was glad Isabella seemed to be fluent in English. That would make it easier later in case they needed more than one translator.

"Perfect," Bonny said, then she and Ben did as Isabella had asked. After a last quick check, they left her and moved back to Jack.

The man hadn't wasted any time, it seemed. He had found several large gas cylinders with anesthetic gas (Ben gave them a look and nodded that the gas should work well for their purposes) and had those lined up next to two anesthesia machines he had rolled over from the OR. He had laid out different surgical drapes as well.

Jack gave them a questioning look when they stepped over. "Forced drug mules," Bonny informed him quickly and quietly. She could see him swearing internally, but he controlled himself.

After that, the three of them worked together to come up with the best way to make sure the soldiers in the next room would stay asleep through any ruckus caused by getting the women out.

At some point, Rhys whispered to them. There was some

background noise, so they assumed he had taken cover behind the boiler or one of the filters to cover his voice, but they could make out his words easily enough. "Found a plastic bag and tape. Vent's covered here."

Bonny clicked to let him know they had heard him, then they focused on their own task again.

Jack had picked up some of the drapes to get to work covering their air vent. Luckily, there were also some incise drapes, and they hoped the synthetic material would provide a better barrier for the gas than a lined cotton drape. It was also easier to attach the incise drape to the wall than to try to tape a cotton sheet to it. So far, everything had worked in their favor.

Meanwhile, Bonny and Ben were working on the anesthesia machine, which turned out to be the bigger challenge. It had sounded simple enough, but they quickly realized it was more than just picking up the hose and pumping the gas into the barracks. They had to adjust the pre-determined gas concentration (making an open room full of people fall asleep or keep them sleeping deeply was vastly different from maintaining a safe gas and oxygen concentration for one patient with a mask over their face, after all), make sure there wouldn't be an alarm beeping when the oxygen concentration the machine measured was too low, and prevent another alarm alerting the person usually controlling the machine when the anesthetic gas can was almost empty. All useful safety features in a normal surgery setting, but the noise would be detrimental to their plan.

Once they were done with the first machine, they moved to the second one, taking the same precautions, and then fiddled with the flow rate. One machine would need to pump the gas faster, but the second one would work to deliver the gas more slowly to keep up the concentration for a longer time and let the soldiers sleep deeply for longer.

At least, they hoped things would work like that. Yes, Bonny had some knowledge she had picked up from her mom. And Benicio had studied in the medical field and knew the basics better. But that didn't mean they were even remotely skilled anesthesiologists. Then again, what Ben had said before was true for everybody in their group: as long as it knocked their enemies out, they didn't care too much about possibly harming them.

A couple of minutes later, Bonny climbed down to the guys again after she had cut two small holes into the drape covering the vent and inserted the hoses, then had used some tape to keep everything in place.

Benicio turned on the machines. "Here goes nothing."

A gentle hiss through the lines told them the gas was flowing. After hearing it, Jack made a gesture toward the camera, and Anton confirmed for them to the others, "They did it. Gas is flowing now."

That got acknowledging clicks from Rhys and Kieran, respectively.

It would take several minutes to flood the room next door enough to have an effect on the sleeping guards, so they took a few steps away from the vent to check on the women.

The second woman, Sofia, was awake as well and stared at them in wonder. "*Gracias*," she whispered. Then her gaze drifted off and she stared at a wall, a smile tugging at her lips. It seemed her drug pump had just delivered another dose of pain meds.

All they could do now was wait and hope the other guards would stay busy with their meal a little longer.

Chapter Thirty-One

The wait was excruciating, but finally Anton spoke up again, "No promises, but it looks like the guards' breathing patterns in the barracks are leveling out, deep and slow. Those who looked like they were dreaming before seem to be far away now, too, even the guy who was patrolling earlier. If you want to make a move, I suggest doing it now. The others are still in the kitchen. No, wait, one of them is just wandering over to the bathroom next to you, Josh."

For a few seconds, everybody was silent and figuring out a plan, recalling the layout of the corridors and where the door to the bathroom was. Then Rhys addressed the group, "Stay put. I'll get him. I should be able to get in without being in line of sight of the kitchen."

Kieran confirmed the plan with a click, and they all listened for an update from Rhys or Anton.

Once they were rid of that guard, too (Rhys had apparently managed to sneak up on him and break his neck as well, then had stashed him in one of the stalls, as Anton informed them), Kieran took over the mission again. "Well done, Rhys. Jack, stay back as backup in case anybody wakes up. Rhys, you and I move to the kitchen area. Josh, stay back around the corner, but be ready to engage if you have to. Bonny, Ben, keep the women in the beds safe."

Everybody acknowledged their roles, and Josh followed Kieran to the door leading into the hallway. He tapped the soldier on the shoulder before they stepped out. "Let me check the barrack door real quick when we get out."

For a second, he could see that Kieran wanted to argue. Then the man seemed to think better of it, interest as to what Josh had planned written all over his face. "Twenty seconds."

"Okay."

In the hallway, Josh moved with Kieran to the wall across from the closet they had just come out of, then slid quickly and quietly to the left. He grinned when he saw the basic lock that would only require a regular key. His hand moved into one of the pockets of his cargo pants and he came up with a set of lockpicks.

Josh was aware of Kieran waiting behind him at the corner, looking in the direction they had come from but glancing over his shoulder every few seconds. But this wouldn't take long.

Josh had learned to pick locks for fun and games first, presenting his friends with a live challenge during a pen and paper campaign. Then he had deepened his knowledge during his studies because it had been a nice way to keep his hands busy when going over his notes while studying for exams. It had come in handy as he had been able to impress Anton with his skills when he had been interviewed for his first job.

What they were facing now called for the opposite, though. He carefully worked the lockpicks in the other direction from what he'd normally do until he heard the quiet, satisfying click of the lock engaging. He retrieved the picks and selected a smaller, finer pin and wiggled it a few times until the metal gave way and broke apart, leaving a piece of the destroyed lockpick in the lock, making it harder to just unlock it again. It wouldn't make it impossible for anybody waking up inside the barracks to open the door with some force, but it would slow them down.

Apparently, Kieran had realized what Josh was doing; when Josh got back to him, the soldier gave him a nod and a quick smile.

Once they were back at the corner leading to the section of the corridor with the door to the kitchen, Kieran let the others know with a series of clicks that they were in position.

It took Rhys only a few more seconds to cautiously open the bathroom door and join them. Josh observed him and Kieran exchange a few quick hand signals, and Anton gave them some additional information over their comm channel. "Two of them are sitting at one of the tables to the right side of the door. They have their backs to you, but they'll probably still see you before you reach the table. Number three just stepped further into the back towards the cooking area."

Again, Kieran acknowledged the input, then gave a few visual orders to Rhys before turning to Josh. The gesture to stay put was clear, and Josh agreed without arguing. He wasn't bad when it came to hand-to-hand combat and he could shoot, but by no means was he – or did he ever intend to be – a fighter like the men helping him get his quasi-sister-in-law back.

Josh was left alone, and only a few seconds later he could hear the noise of a scuffle breaking out. There was cursing, the scratch of furniture on the floor, then the clattering of a chair falling over. The voices grew more agitated, there were sounds of fists hitting flesh, the crunch of cartilage and bone, huffing like somebody had been punched in the gut. Then Rhys' voice carried to him, "Knife!"

Josh heard Kieran's grunt but was relieved when the sound seemed to carry more than pain – there was a distinct quality to it that was more annoyed than anything else, and the "Fuck you!" that followed was clear enough that Josh hoped any wound wasn't life-threatening.

But he didn't have time to process it any further. In his ear, Anton let him know, "One's coming your way, Josh. Get ready."

"Keep it quiet, if you can," Rhys rushed to add. Which made sense. There had been some noise, but nothing as loud as a gunshot that could be enough to wake any of the drowsy guards in the barracks.

So Josh hurried to find a good footing while staying close to the wall. Even though he kept hold of the gun Kieran had given him, he angled his hand in a way that would allow him to lash out with it before having to shoot it.

The footfalls had already been close, and only a second or two later the harried guard ran around the corner, clearly trying to make his way to the barracks to gather help from his colleagues.

Josh swung his arm up, putting enough force behind it to make sure it would at the very least slow the guy or stop him, if not incapacitate him right away. He didn't need to worry. The barrel of the gun hit its target and connected with the other man's throat, the speed of his running only propelling him harder into the sudden obstacle. There was the distinct sound of soft tissue tearing, small ligaments snapping, and even with the metal of the gun acting as a barrier, Josh could still feel bone and cartilage being displaced.

The guard only managed to croak helplessly as he first stumbled a step back, then began to fall forward to his knees, reaching for his throat. Josh brought his own knee up, his free hand pushing the man's face down on it, adding a broken nose to his injuries.

Admittedly, when the guy hit the floor with a dull thud, it wasn't as silent as when Rhys had taken out the other two guards. But he hadn't managed to shout or otherwise alert his colleagues to what was going on. Josh counted it as a win.

In his ear, Anton sounded like he had a grin on his face. "Nicely done. I'm glad I hired you, Josh."

Suppressing a chuckle, Josh peeked at one of the cameras covering the corridor and shook his head with his own grin on his face. Then he stepped towards the feet of the guy he had knocked out and began dragging him towards the kitchen. The sounds from there had quieted down a few moments ago, and all Josh heard was Kieran and Rhys murmuring to each other in low tones. Checking to make sure he was good to come in, he let go of the guy's feet and met the soldiers' eyes. They nodded to him. Josh scanned the room: the two other guards were lying on the floor, either unconscious or dead, he couldn't say from where he stood, and Rhys was looking at Kieran's arm where a blade stuck out of his muscle.

"You okay?"

"Yeah. Bloody idiot grabbed a kitchen knife and got me on his way out of here. It's deep enough that the blade got stuck, but I don't think he got any major arteries or anything. Jack can have a look. What about you?"

"I'm all good. Last I checked, the guy was still breathing, not sure how long that's gonna last, though. I hit him in the throat with the barrel of the gun. Even if I didn't destroy what anatomical structures he needs to keep breathing, I'm pretty sure once the swelling has reached its max, he'll have a hard time getting some air," Josh said with a tinge of regret in his voice.

"I know it's hard but remember: he signed up to be part of this shitshow. Let's get these bastards out of the way, then keep moving. We have women who actually deserve our sympathy to rescue," Kieran said, and in that moment Josh realized just how good a leader the man must be to his team.

"Yeah, you're right," Josh replied solemnly. It didn't take

away the gravitas of possibly having taken a life, but it put it into perspective.

Meanwhile, Rhys had a look around. "Kieran, why don't you go to Jack, have him check the injury. I don't think the guards here will get up anytime soon, if at all, but Josh and I can move them to the walk-in fridge in the back, stuff them in there, use some zip ties on the doors, just as a precaution."

After a moment's consideration, Kieran agreed and left them behind.

Josh and Rhys had secured the guards in the fridge (for once, the base in the middle of nowhere came in handy as it meant there had to be enough storage room for food to last between longer delivery intervals) when they heard soft steps coming into the kitchen. Turning around, they found Jack and Benicio looking at them.

Ben took a few quick steps over to Josh and enfolded him in his arms. "Are you okay, *bebé*?" he murmured, his voice offering warmth and safety.

"Yeah, or at least I will be. I know you and Bonny will help me."

"We will. And if it's not enough..." But Ben stopped mid-sentence, not wanting to put even more to think about on Josh's mind.

"I know; if not, you two will drag me to therapy. You wouldn't have to drag me, I'd go voluntarily. But for now, let's make sure we all get out of here safely, and we'll figure out the rest later."

"Okay," Ben agreed and pressed a kiss to Josh's temple.

In the meantime, Jack had updated Rhys that Kieran would stay with Bonny but thought it wise to have somebody with two fully functional arms around to keep clearing the rest of the base and help with the women. He had sent Benicio along with Jack to translate but had given Jack orders to keep Josh and Ben as much in the background as possible.

Which meant the two soldiers ordered them to wait in the kitchen while they would move to the living quarters to get a handle on the situation there. "Wait till we call you, but we might need you to translate, mate," Rhys said to Benicio just before he slipped out of the kitchen area behind Jack.

Moments later, Anton let them know he had managed to disengage the electronic locks to the living quarters.

Then Ben and Josh were alone, and Josh ran his hand up and down his lover's back, whispering in his ear, "How are you holding up with all this?"

"Better than expected, to be honest. But that might be because the last few days have been exhausting and I don't have the energy to rage. Bonny is furious, I could see it in her eyes the moment we saw the wounds on those poor women. It also helps that I know they didn't have time to do that to Val, yet."

"I swear to you, they won't get a chance to even try."

"I know. Thank you."

It wasn't long until they heard muffled sounds from the closed doors of the living quarters. They lasted for about a minute, then the door was opened a little bit and Jack gestured to them and asked quietly, "Benicio, could you help translate?"

"Of course."

As Ben walked out of the kitchen, Josh shot a glance to the right to make sure everything was safe, then walked a step behind his boyfriend to make sure he had his back in case anybody tried to sneak up on them.

A few quick steps took them to the slightly open door where Jack was waiting for them. He let them in, and the young men took in their surroundings.

As Anton had mentioned before, they saw what he meant

by "better living quarters." To the left of the door was a small living space with a comfortable-looking couch. The space was shared with a small kitchen area and a dining table with four chairs. There even was a TV mounted to the wall across from the couch.

To the right were three rooms with the doors open. The first held a middle-aged couple in their night clothes, both standing there with huge eyes looking at Rhys, who watched over them with his gun in hand, looking menacing enough to keep them quiet. The second door led to what looked like an office space, and the third door opened into another bedroom. While the rest of the living quarters were done in darker colors, polished wood, and sleek steel, the last room on the right seemed brighter with soft yellow walls and colorful highlights.

Across from that was one more room. It was larger than the other ones and seemed to be the master bedroom. Ben and Josh couldn't see a lot from where they were standing, but it was once again done in dark colors with what looked like an expensive throw over the one corner of the bed visible to them, and one wall held a sitting corner and a large desk.

A glance also told Josh that Rhys or Jack had broken the locks of the unoccupied bedrooms. The wood on the door frames looked splintered, and the door to the master bedroom hung crookedly on its hinges.

But then Jack ushered them closer to the bedroom with the couple inside. "Would you please help us talk to them?" he addressed Ben, purposely leaving out the young man's name this time, Josh would have bet.

"Sí, of course," Ben said and got a little closer, mindful not to step in between the soldiers and the people staring between all of them with huge, shocked eyes.

He studied the couple for a moment; they were both showing signs of their age – gray strands in their hair, visible wrinkles around their eyes and mouths – and had obviously been awoken from a deep sleep. The woman looked terrified, but deep lines in her face and an unusually pale complexion seemed to indicate that she had not only been in a high-stress situation for a longer period of time, but had presumably also stayed below ground for quite some time already. The man showed similar signs of stress and lack of sunlight, but where his wife (Ben concluded that's who she was after he spotted matching rings) looked frantic and maybe even a little bit hopeful, with her eyes drifting towards the camera in an upper corner of the room in a panic every few seconds, he looked nervous but also almost annoyed about people barging into the complex and interrogating them at gunpoint.

It didn't take long for Benicio to understand why: during their questioning, it became clear that the man had been hired as a surgeon to operate on the kidnapped young women, placing the drugs inside their bodies. His wife was a surgical nurse, thus he had brought her along. He very obviously hadn't mentioned to her that he was getting paid (and paid well, Josh assumed) to do it but had told her that somebody had threatened their own daughters if he wouldn't cooperate. He had tried telling the group that story at first as well but had soon ended up in a tangled web of lies. He was not a good liar under pressure.

His wife listened to her husband's explanation, her face clearly showing the shift from panic to disbelief to anger and rage. Irate as she was in the end, she surprised everybody when she turned towards her husband far quicker than any of them expected and slapped him across the face before bringing her knee up to his groin. She watched him crumble to the floor, then spat on him. Benicio decided not to translate the tidal wave of curses she threw at the man, but apparently this wasn't the first time he had lied to her, even if the previous affairs she mentioned weren't nearly as terrible as his latest lies.

With her husband curled up and groaning, she turned back to the others, pleading with Ben to take her with them and help protect her daughters. She wasn't naïve; it was clear to all of them that she knew there would be repercussions, even if the initial threat might have been made up by the man she had been married to. When they promised to help her escape at the very least and, if possible, help her family, she nodded, resolution clearly written all over her face. She spat on her husband once more, checked in with Ben, who quickly confirmed with the soldiers that it was okay that she could get dressed and grab a few small items. Once she was assured it would be all right, she got ready, not minding the people standing around while she changed her clothes. Jack kept an eye on her, just in case (although the woman would deserve an Oscar if the last few minutes had been an act, Ben thought).

Meanwhile, Rhys asked Josh to keep his gun on the whimpering bundle on the floor while Rhys went through his pockets for some zip ties. They didn't need to kill everybody in the facility, and even if the bastard got out of the restraints at some point and called for help, it would take a while. They'd be long gone by then.

Carmen – she had taken a second to tell them her name – moved as quickly and efficiently as one might expect from a nurse. She was ready to leave in barely three minutes, only grabbing one small bag and a photo of her daughters from a bedside table. When she passed her husband, she swore once more and kicked him in his kidneys for good measure. This was a woman who had reached her limits. She stomped out of the bedroom, looking from Ben to Jack, and gestured them to follow her, while Rhys and Josh began to drag her – likely former – husband up and heave him onto the bed to tie him to the frame.

Done with the task of securing the man, Rhys was about to leave the living quarters again when Josh stopped him. "Wait, there might be medical files that could be useful in the office. And I want to have a quick look at the master bedroom. If we can find something that gives us a definitive name, or perhaps just something with fingerprints on it, we might be able to force the authorities to do their job after all when we present them with evidence of who runs this operation."

"Fair point. All right, mate. Let's do a quick sweep."

In minutes, they gathered up several thumb drives and two external hard drives in the office space used by the doctor. The master bedroom didn't give them any useful paperwork or IDs, but they carefully gathered a watch and several cufflinks, hoping that they would be able to pull prints from them, then grabbed a toothbrush and a few hairs from a brush out of the ensuite. Storing everything in a couple of small plastic bags they had also found in the bathroom, they got out of there and joined the others in the hallway, making sure to also take a short video of the parts of the facility around them.

Jack was quietly updating Kieran over the radio, and Benicio was doing his best to calm Carmen down. His gaze went from the woman to the alcove with the reading nook, and Josh was pretty sure his lover hoped the woman could help them get to the girls quickly. When he saw her shaking her head, he figured they were out of luck.

Ben confirmed it as soon as Jack stopped talking to Kieran. "Carmen says they were never allowed to talk with the girls outside of medical issues or interact with them in any other way, including walking them from the surgical suite to the cells. The guards brought the girls in, kept an eye on everybody in the medical bay, and then Carmen and her husband had to make sure the girls could get out of bed. As soon as they could, the soldiers would bring them back to the cells. They would also escort them back and forth for check-ups until they were taken away from here."

"Fucking assholes," Rhys muttered, to which the others agreed with grunts or nods.

Then Jack spoke up, "Not sure what you all got of the conversation. Kieran says he'll stay with Bonny and to send Benicio back with Carmen, so she can check on the girls in the medical bay. He wants us to find a way to get to the cells and get the girls out asap."

Another round of agreements followed, then Ben gave Josh a quick peck on the cheek before leaving with Carmen. His face made it obvious that he'd rather be there when they got to Valeria, but he also knew it would be wiser to have somebody else with at least some amount of medical training there to lend a hand to the nurse should she need it. Also, he wasn't needed for translating for the girls – Valeria would soon be free, and as they had seen with the women in the medical bay, they had all worked in a field that had required them to speak at the very least basic English, and their age would mean they likely were more proficient as well.

Chapter Thirty-Two

The remaining three men turned their attention to the alcove with its bookshelves.

"Anton, are you any closer to finding out how we can get in there?" Josh asked hopefully.

"Unfortunately, no. I can tell you that it looks like there are multiple switches, one on each shelf, based on the wires. This might be some kind of combination lock. But I can't even see to which books they might connect."

They all let out an annoyed groan or a sigh. This was turning more and more into an escape room, indeed.

"Can you see any kind of failsafe? Will there be fucking lasers shooting out of the walls if we get it wrong?" Rhys wanted to know, apprehension evident in his voice. Given the despicable operation they were dealing with, he had every right to be cautious.

"No *Resident Evil* setup that I can see," Anton replied. "I will say, there are wires running to somewhere I can't pinpoint a hundred percent right now, but none of it looks like a typical weapon or explosive trap, or anything like that, not even a standard alarm."

"Guess that's got to be good enough. Guys, should we just pull out all the books? I think we all expect it to be some weird shit like that, right? And I don't think we have enough time to try figuring this out," Rhys said.

He was right, they didn't have time to try finding the right books, the right combination, so Jack and Josh agreed to the plan, and each of the men began taking books off the shelves and piling them on the armchairs, so they wouldn't be in the way when they'd lead the women out of their cells.

When they pulled the last book from the shelves, they heard a click and metal sliding over metal from behind the shelf. "Uh, Anton?" Josh addressed his boss, hoping he could tell them what was going on.

"Well, shit. The camera feed is still running. Apparently, not pulling the right books in the right order triggered an extra lock. The other side of the shelf you're all standing in front of is designed as a fairly simple door with a fingerprint lock. But now a metal bar slid across the door, adding another layer of security to keep the door closed. Looks like that one needs a physical key to be unlocked, or possibly another combination entered via the switches. You won't be able to just push the door open now."

"Bloody hell," Jack cursed.

Josh kicked one of the armchairs in frustration before looking at the empty shelves. "Yeah, I can make out the trigger plates now. They're well hidden. But I couldn't tell you the right combination from where we're standing, either."

"I didn't think you would be able to," Anton replied matter-of-factly.

Rhys balled his fists a few times, then cocked his head studying the shelf. "Anton, quick question: it's still a wooden shelf or door or whatever you want to call this bullshit, just with a metal bar running across the middle now, correct?"

"Yes, that's right."

"Then let's just kick a hole into it and rip off pieces until we can get through. The guards are dead or deeply asleep by now, and Kieran is keeping an eye on the corridor there anyway, should anybody wake up. We'll have to duck under it, but at least we'll get to the cells and get the girls out."

They all considered it for a moment but finally had to admit that neither of them had a better idea.

They decided Jack would kick at the door, as he had the best height to aim his kick between two of the lower shelves. Since he wasn't going to kick the door open like he normally would, he positioned himself with his back to it and gave the wood a hard mule kick. His second attempt produced a small hole that allowed them to widen it with their hands.

It worked surprisingly well, until they heard Anton loudly cuss. "Fuck! You need to hurry."

"What?" All of the men asked simultaneously.

"The wires I was talking about earlier and didn't know what they were connected to? They were running between the wood panels of the door. Ripping the door open, you came to a point where you damaged them. They are connected to a water system. There are sprinklers running on high now, and there's water being pumped into the closed-off area. The water is already covering the floor. There's your failsafe in case any woman gets out of her cell and tries to get through the door from that side."

Cursing, they began to rip at the broken shelf more forcefully, and Rhys vented his anger while throwing pieces of wood behind him, "Sick bastard. No *Resident Evil* shit, but instead we get a *Kingsman* reenactment? Who's this asshole? Some sick movie freak on top of everything else?"

"Seems so," Josh said, then mumbled, "Damn, I liked that movie. Not sure I'll be able to enjoy it anymore."

They knew it was ridiculous talk between them, but it

helped distract them from the splinters ripping open their skin, and kept the rising unease at bay when they got their first good look behind the door.

As soon as the hole was large enough, Josh ducked through. "I'll get started on the cell doors. You keep working on this; we don't want the girls injuring themselves, who knows what has already been done to them."

He could see the other two men weren't happy for him to go off on his own, and even less for him as a civilian ordering them around, but they bit their tongues given that he made a valid point.

It hardly took Josh a second to get a picture of his surroundings. He stood in the middle of a narrow corridor with tiled walls and a tiled floor. Behind him was only the one door leading out of there, and across from him were fifteen solid metal doors, each with a small, round window and a hatch just large enough to pass a tray with food through. All of them were secured with electronic locks similar to the one on the door of the living quarters. The water was already reaching his ankles. A quick look confirmed Anton's remark that water wasn't just coming from overhead; it was also being pumped into the corridor from below through what usually would be the drains on the floor. He checked and saw the sprinklers above him were actually showerheads. Just this corridor alone made the situation so much more appalling. They were forcing the girls to shower in the small corridor in front of their cells, likely all at the same time, and probably under the lecherous gaze of a guard or two.

Josh's blood boiled with rage, but he had no time to dwell on that. Instead, he opened his microphone. "Anton, can you open the locks on the cells remotely? If so, can you start on one side of the row of doors, while I take the other?"

"Already on it," was Anton's short reply.

Josh had never been so thankful to have interviewed for the job at Anton's company: his boss was a genius when it came to electronics, and with the water rising as fast as it did, they would need to be quick to get all the girls out. He ran to the left and started at the outermost door. His hand dug out the utility knife from his pocket, and he began unscrewing the paneling of the lock so he'd be able to short-circuit the mechanism manually.

He had hardly loosened the first screw, when a face appeared in the window.

"¡*Dios mío!* Thank fuck you're here," Valeria cheered, her voice muffled by the door but still easy enough to understand. "Anything I can do?"

"Not right now. I'll let you know if there's something once I get you out of there."

"Okay." After that, she let him work in silence. He very much admired his future sister-in-law's ability to keep her head and understand what a situation called for.

Josh worked quickly, opening the casing and revealing the wires underneath. He studied them for a moment but was relieved to realize it was a fairly simple layout that would only require him to cut two of the small cables and crosswire them. As soon as he had, he heard a satisfying click and the bolt inside the lock sliding to its open position. He hurried to pull the door open – the water already hindering the motion – and had his arms full of Valeria.

"¡*Gracias!* Thank you so much! Are my brother and Bonny okay?"

He hugged her back for a second while telling her, "Yes. They're helping two other women."

"Good. Now, tell me what I can do," she said fiercely as she let go of him. Her face was pure determination, and in one hand she was carrying a flat piece of metal that she must've ripped from the old bed frame in the cell, he concluded. She was smart and resourceful. He was very proud to call her family.

He studied the piece of metal, then pointed at the broken lock. "Can you pry open the paneling on the other locks so I can open them?"

"Sí, I can," Val replied and strode to the next cell.

She was just about to get started, when Anton spoke up in Josh's ear, "Not that one. The cell is empty. There are five more occupied cells. Skip the one Val is standing in front of and the next. The one after that needs to be opened."

"Copy that," Josh said and relayed the info to Val. They made their way over, and Josh could only think, *Thank fuck it's only five more, not all of them; we would never make it in time.* The water was already almost knee-high. As he neared the door he had come through, he heard Jack explaining the situation to Kieran over the radio, likely on a one-on-one channel to keep communication with Anton open, and telling them to get the girls out of the complex already, as they had no idea how quickly the water would fill everything. Then he saw another door at the other end of the hallway pop open. Rhys just crawled through the now mostly open, broken shelf, and Josh pointed to the open cell. "Check on the girl, get her out. We'll keep working on this. Anton is also opening locks remotely."

"Done."

It was a good thing they could split the work. The water was rising incredibly fast; and by the time they got the last girl out of the cell, they had to actually submerge themselves to get back out through the broken door as the water had already reached chest-level for some of the smaller women. Jack was acting as a guiding light, literally, from the other side, waving his flashlight to illuminate the gateway. Rhys had already guided each girl to the exit and was now waiting for Valeria and Josh, who were the last ones inside the corridor. Josh pushed Val to duck through first while steadying himself with a hand against the wall. The pressure and drag of the water rushing through into the rest of the facility was no joke. As soon as Val was clear, he followed Rhys' nod to go next. Jack, who was holding on to the remains of the shelf himself to keep his own balance, offered his wrist to quickly help Josh back up before doing the same for his fellow soldier when Rhys dove through the hole as well. The girls were waiting for them across the hallway, hovering against the wall next to the kitchen entrance with water rushing around their legs. All but Val, who was already checking them for obvious injuries while talking soothingly to them, stared with huge eyes at their rescuers. Behind him, Josh heard Rhys confirming to Kieran that they had found the woman they had actually come to rescue, alive and reasonably well. Seeing Valeria in the same condition, he could imagine the weight falling off the shoulders of all three men.

There was no time to explain every detail to the girls. Instead, Josh planned to let Jack lead them towards the supply closet through which they had originally entered the complex. It wasn't far, only a few steps really. Yet getting a group of terrified women to move, especially with another group of military-type males, wasn't easy. With Jack waiting at the corner and Rhys getting in position to secure the back of the group, Josh moved to the group of women and explained to them the very basic details: they were here to rescue them, the guards were taken care of, there was more help on the way, but they needed to hurry. There was still a moment of hesitation to move until Valeria gave Josh a sideways hug and told the girls in Spanish that he was one of the good guys, and if he worked with the others, they had to be, too. The women finally began turning to Jack to follow him, and Josh had never been happier that he and Bonny had made sure to get onto Val's good side, to befriend her as a person, not just see her as their boyfriend's sister whom they had to somehow get along with.

She and Josh helped keep up the momentum of the group. Jack brought them to the passageway leading back to the temple, and they found Benicio waiting on the stone staircase. He was obviously guarding the wire running across the steps, making sure none of the women would trip over it and get hurt. Josh could feel Valeria brimming with excitement and relief to see her brother, but she held back to hug him until the last girl had stepped safely over the wire.

The siblings exchanged a few hurried words of reassurance in Spanish before following the others up the stairs toward freedom. Behind the group, Rhys pushed the hidden door closed and cursed, "Bloody hell, we need to hurry. I heard movement from the barracks. Sounded like they weren't happy about the locks and started kicking the door."

Ben looked over his shoulder and explained, "Yeah, the gas was running low after filling up a whole room."

They did their best to climb the stairs quickly, but some of the girls were weak and it took time to get them to the next level. Enough time, it seemed, for some of the guards to reach the temple. Footsteps echoed below, and Josh and Rhys fell back to get a better angle to shoot at their pursuers.

Meanwhile, Benicio ran over to the rope keeping the trap in place. When his sister asked him what the rope did, he explained in a few quick words, "Securing a board covered in spikes in place."

She apparently instantly understood and hurried to be the one to pull open the quick-release knot Kieran had used to tie the rope to the roots. Her menacing smile was something that frightened even her brother for a second, before he reconsidered and came to the conclusion that she deserved a bit of gleeful revenge for what she had been through.

"My turn," Rhys said and shot his rifle several times down the stairs. They only needed one of the guards to trigger the trip-wire – be it in their haste to follow them or because they were still drugged or hit by a bullet, it didn't matter – but Rhys wanted to make sure one of the bastards did indeed set off the trap.

The gunshots were almost deafening in the confined space, but they could still make out a yell when one of the mercenaries was hit. A dragging sound joined the footsteps, noises of some-body stumbling, breathing heavily because of pain. There were also more footsteps from another person now. Then two things happened simultaneously: the stumbling noises ended in a dull thud, like somebody falling over, and a click echoed around them.

After that, they heard the whoosh of something heavy rushing through the air, and part of a curse reached their ears. The voice had to belong to the second guard following them, the other man still moaning in pain, and even the little bit they heard from the new guy's speech was slurred. He was clearly still under the influence of the gas, his reflexes far too slow to evade the spike trap. His curse was abruptly cut off, and the crunching sounds of breaking bones and the wet noise of blood squelching out of large wounds reached Josh's and Rhys' ears.

There was no time to relax, though, and Rhys made sure to get everybody going. Ben, Josh, and Valeria were in good shape and could climb the stairs rapidly by themselves, but as soon as they caught up with Jack and the other women, they could see that it would take too long for them to ascend all the way up to the top. So Valeria hooked her arm around a struggling girl's waist while two more helped each other. Benicio and Josh each ended up carrying a girl piggyback. Understandably, the soldiers wanted to keep their hands free if at all possible. Jack joined Rhys at the end of the group to provide protection against any possible guards following them.

If the way down had felt like an eternity, the way up the stairs wasn't any better. The only improvement was the fact that they now didn't care as much about staying in the dark. They had turned on their flashlights, making sure to remind the women and themselves to watch out for loose pebbles and more tripwires. This was exactly what they had hoped to avoid.

With every level up, the girls seemed to slow down, the quiet from behind them lulling them into a false sense of security combined with the emotional exhaustion of the whole situation kicking in and dragging them down. Both Ben and Josh could understand them – though for them it was the physical exertion of the previous days and more so the last hours combined with the additional weight on their backs – but they actively fought against themselves, keeping up their speed as best as they could. Still, they did their best together with Val to push the women to keep going.

Soon enough, bitter voices and the bubble of water combined with the splatter of wet footsteps carried up to them, the sounds distorted, but distinct enough to put a new wave of fear into the girls. It was a terrible thing to be thankful for, yet neither Josh nor Benicio could stop their relieved sighs when the women moved faster again.

Finally, after what seemed like ages of climbing the dark, ominous stairs that made the temple feel far too much like a grave, Benicio softly called out to the girls to stop and turn left to the hidden entrance to the stairwell.

Freedom was so close now; they already felt the first breeze of fresh air on their faces. Only a few steps left before they could run into the jungle, into hiding, before they could make their way to the location that Anton had sent them. To safety.

That's when they heard a shot and screams outside.

Chapter Thirty-Three

Bonny was not happy to leave the others so far behind, but with Isabella and Sofia fresh out of surgery, it took them forever to move up inside the temple staircase. They had decided Bonny, the girls, Carmen, and Kieran would get out of the base before the others to save some time. So, after a quick check of Kieran's arm back in the medical bay, Carmen had done her best to help get the girls on their feet and support them on the way up.

Once they were finally out of the building, still high up on the old stone structure, the jungle stretching out below them as far as the eye could see, tears began running down the nurse's cheeks, which only led to the two wounded women crying as well. They hadn't been outside for who knew how long, had either been terrified for their own lives or the lives of their children. To finally feel a fresh breeze on their skin again, to know they were with people who were trying to rescue them, had to be one hell of a shock.

But as much as Bonny would've loved to give them a moment to adjust, she knew they had to keep moving. The way down the outside steps of the pyramid wasn't as long as the climb inside, but the stairs were more weathered, partly over-grown, and slippery. It hadn't been a problem for Bonny and her men and the group of healthy soldiers on the way in; but guiding down the injured women, still drowsy from their pain meds and weakened from everything they had been through, wouldn't be as easy.

Bonny glanced at Kieran and asked, "Will you keep watch from up here while Carmen and I help the girls down?"

"Yes, I planned to."

"Perfect."

With Isabella's help, Bonny managed to convey the plan to the rest of their small group. Then they began the careful descent.

Getting into the temple and taking out the guards had started in the middle of the night, but morning had crept up on them. Light was spilling over the stairs, the mist hanging over the trees below was glowing brightly. All around them, the jungle seemed to wake up, more and more bird calls reached their ears, insects began buzzing with the rising temperatures. It was stunning, and under other circumstances, Bonny would've taken the time to marvel at it. But right then, she was only glad that it was bright enough for everybody to see on the way down the stairs which left her with both her hands free without the need for a flashlight.

They were just stepping off the last steps onto the plateau when Kieran contacted her. "Get down and hide, you've got company. Three men dragging two women out of the trees to your right."

Shit, Bonny thought but had already reached out to gently push the other women behind a few large plants at the foot of the temple, hopefully shielding them from view in time.

Luck was not on her side, though. Not entirely. She must've managed to hide the others, but the men then had apparently spotted her. At least, that's what the snippets of their surprised calls to each other seemed to indicate. She couldn't make out all of it, but it sounded like they were only mentioning one woman. Great, now she had to get them away from the others and make sure Kieran had a chance to get to the men without accidentally shooting the two new girls they had brought along or the other women in their hiding place.

With the rescued women behind her, she made a split-second decision and darted to the right. It brought her closer to the newly arrived enemies, but only until she could round the corner of the temple and run toward the steeper edge at the back of the ruins where they had climbed up earlier in the night.

She heard a few shouted commands, some more commotion, and then running footsteps following her. As much as she wanted to know what was happening, she knew it would be a mistake to turn around. Instead, she kept running. *Move and get them away from the others,* she repeated in her head.

Only a few seconds into her sprint, she heard the loud *pop* of a gunshot. With the layout of the area, it was impossible to say where it had come from, its boom echoing seemingly from everywhere around her, then mixing with the cries of hundreds of birds when a huge swarm of parrots rose into the air.

It was hard to make out over the noise, but Kieran updated her over the radio. "One down, one still following you. One with the new girls. I'm on him."

To save her breath, she acknowledged his words with a few quick clicks. She focused on her steps, on the ground before her, making sure not to trip. Most of the plateau was clear of trees, but there were enough smaller plants to make the ground uneven. She hoped to get around the pyramid, maybe even to the back corner of the side with the side entrance. That way, if Josh, Ben, and Kieran's men exited from the hidden entrance, they'd see her easily and hopefully be able to help her should she need it. But right then, while she ran, she mentally shifted gears, getting herself ready for a fight.

She concentrated on the footsteps behind her. Good, the guy was still running. She had been zigzagging until then, not giving him a steady target. Small movements, but enough to make it too hard to shoot her while she was fleeing. And that didn't even take into consideration that he no doubt thought she would be easy enough to grab and drag back to the underground compound and into a cell until it was time for them to use her as the next unwilling drug mule. He would be in for a surprise, Bonny swore to herself.

Then she was nearly where she wanted to be: almost in the middle of the larger clearing at the back of the temple, the slope to one side of her, the ancient structure to the other, with enough open space around so she would be able to move freely. She deliberately slowed her steps just a little bit, giving her pursuer the impression she was getting into his reach. In front of her body, out of his sight, she balled her fists, the muscles in her arms tensing, then clenched her jaw – hopefully, he wouldn't get a hit to her face in, but she would do her best to prevent herself from cracking her teeth or biting off part of her tongue.

Only a couple more steps, letting him come just a little closer. When her feet landed where she wanted, when she thought him the perfect distance away, she abruptly stopped and pivoted on one foot, then let herself drop on one knee, her face tilted down a bit with her left arm shielding it, her right arm pulling back.

The guy was completely startled, surprise written all over his face. He had no idea what to do, nor could he react in time. His speed carried him directly to her and into her attack.

Bonny released the punch, her right fist finding its target in his stomach. When she heard him cry out and was sure his knee wasn't coming up to her face, she used her left fist to deliver a forceful strike against the guy's thigh, further unbalancing him.

More on instinct than anything else, the man tried to get a hold of her; one hand landed on her shoulder, pushing her away, the other grabbed the large bun she had tied her hair into, so he could pull her up.

The pain in her scalp was sharp but nothing she couldn't handle. Instead of giving in to his maneuver, she brought her hands together, interlacing her fingers and making sure the knuckles of her thumbs pointed up. Then she brought up her hands with as much force as possible, violently driving the hard bone of her thumbs straight into the guy's groin. Above her, the man let out a painful moan, his grip on her momentarily loosening. Yep, that usually worked; a low angle could very well be an advantage in a fight.

Not relying on the hope that that had been enough, Bonny rolled backwards from her kneeling position and sprang to her feet. When she was standing, she saw him stumble towards her, and even through the pain, the idiot managed to hurl a few swearwords at her. But he was out of it and apparently enraged enough that he wanted to use his hands on her, ignoring the weapon hanging at his side. Bonny was supremely grateful for that. Fighting somebody who actively pointed a gun at you was something she could do without.

Instead, she found herself evading a few attempts by him trying to grab or punch her. It wasn't easy; the guy had surprisingly long arms, and Bonny had to be watchful. So far, she had managed to jump out of the way every time, though. And while he continued cursing her, taunting her, she kept an eye on her surroundings. His eyes looked wild, and he clearly was still in pain; she knew he'd be too desperate to get to her and would do something stupid sooner rather than later.

Bonny found out how right her assessment of him was only

a moment later. They had been circling each other, but then the guy charged at her. She had about a heartbeat to decide what to do. Evading could possibly save her from the hit, but would probably end with him getting a grip on her arm at least, possibly dislocating her shoulder, or he could turn around and ram the handle of his rifle into her back if she wasn't fast enough. Or she could take the hit, end up on the floor with him and try to throw him behind her or find a better position to fight against him when they were closer to each other again. And maybe there was one other solution, she just had to be quick about it when he barrelled into her. She decided it was worth the chance.

His charge hadn't entirely been a surprise to Bonny, but her standing her ground was to her attacker. Still, he ran into her and followed her movement when she turned them a little as they fell into the dirt.

Bonny grunted when her back hit the ground, the guy heavy on top of her, his shoulder digging hard into her ribs. That would be painful once the adrenaline wasn't keeping her from feeling most of it. For now, though, she did her best to ignore the dull throbbing sensation and instead fisted her hands once more before hitting the guy's ears hard with the outer edge of her hands. She wasn't hoping to rupture his eardrums, she just needed him to get off her enough to give her some room to slide back and hitting his ears would still be painful enough like that, and with a bit of luck even cause some mild disorientation.

Bonny got her wish when her attacker sat up to get away from her punches and brought his hands to the sides of his head, the movement automatically lifting him more onto his knees, far enough for her to push herself backward on the ground. She drew her knees up to her chest, gave the area behind them one last glance, and kicked with all her might against his chest.

While they had been dancing around each other, Bonny

had realized just how close to the edge of the slope they had gotten. And when the bastard had charged her, she had made sure she'd end up in a position where he would have the hill behind him while she would fall towards the safety of the plateau.

Now, he faced the consequences of not paying attention. Bonny's kick toppled him over backwards, and even from his kneeling position, he was pushed too far to catch himself. With a cry of surprise and terror at the sudden feeling of falling, he crashed down the steep hillside.

Bonny was vaguely aware of more shouts and the sounds of another fight, of women screaming and crying, carried over to her from where she had come from. Her attention, though, was still focused on the mercenary she had fought with. She heard him crash through the underbrush, tumbling further down the side of the plateau. His startled yelp from the fall was replaced by more pain-filled and angry groans. Then there was a thud and a grunt, and she assumed a larger tree had stopped his roll further down.

She had to find out whether he still presented a danger, though. So Bonny knew she had to check. But she was smart enough not to make herself a target by just getting up and looking down at him. The guy still had a weapon, after all. She carefully crawled closer to the edge, keeping her head down.

She had barely moved when the man started screaming in pain all over again. What the hell? She had assumed he had hit his head and was knocked out, or perhaps was lying in the dirt, dizzy with a concussion. Her movements got a little faster, and even though her instincts still made her more cautious the closer she got to the first trees, deep down, she knew she wouldn't be shot at. Those screams were filled with agony, creeping deep into her bones and making her shiver. Whatever was happening to him had to be horrifying, excruciating.

Moments later, she managed to get a glimpse of her attacker. Her fingers dug deep into the earth beneath her hands in sympathy. Nevermind the fact that she had fought with the man only minutes ago, that she would've hurt him badly herself if she had been forced to – nobody should suffer like he did in that moment. He had indeed ended up against a larger tree, and he was covered in snakes. Many of them slithered over him, trying to get away, but multiple others were also biting him. They all seemed relatively small, except one large snake that was anxiously fighting to get out from underneath the man's leg, and in its agitated state, bit his hand more than once as he mindlessly tried to push it away.

From what Benicio had told them days ago, Bonny put together what had happened. This had to be a female fer-de-lance. Bonny had read up on them one evening when she had a bit of a signal on her phone and found the snakes interesting enough, although she was glad they hadn't come across any before. From what she had found out, the females didn't lay eggs but instead gave birth to live young. She hadn't thought this would be the right time for them to produce offspring; then again, the females could store sperm for some time before fertilizing their eggs, and conditions might have been in her favor. Also, Bonny wouldn't have expected one so high up in the mountains, as the nights could get chillier than the species' usual preferred temperature. But her human senses were far less accurate than the animal's, so maybe the underground complex was producing enough heat and the female had found herself a less contested territory.

No matter the cause, she obviously had just given birth to a fairly large number of young snakes, which were said to be even more venomous than their adult counterparts, if Bonny's research had been correct. And they all felt threatened when a huge enemy had fallen onto them. Of course they were defending themselves and trying to get away. The man had to be covered in dozens of bite wounds by then, each of which was causing him severe pain. Bonny couldn't even begin to imagine how terrible it had to be for him. But there wasn't anything she could do to help. She neither knew whether the medical bay below her feet contained any antivenom nor could she even go down the hill and get him away from the cluster of agitated snakes without risking her own life. And if there wasn't any treatment nearby, he was doomed anyway. Not that she thought his chances were all that good to begin with, given how much venom had been injected into his body. He would very likely die a painful death. She knew it had been his own choices bringing him to this point, but it still wasn't a way to die she would wish even onto her enemies.

She had no time to contemplate it further, though, when she heard two pairs of feet running over to her and then found herself dragged away from the edge and into the arms of her lovers.

Chapter Thirty-Four

"Are you okay, baby?" Josh asked frantically.

"*Mi amor*, are you hurt?" Benicio was desperate to know.

For a couple of seconds, Bonny only bathed in the warmth of their connection, in their love and concern for her. That's when the adrenaline rushed out of her system and she crashed. She began to shake, and the deep breath she dragged into her lungs made her hiss when her ribs ached sharply and then kept throbbing.

Her lovers quickly loosened their grip on her, studying her with fear in their eyes. Bonny rushed to reassure them, "I'm okay. It's the adrenaline wearing off, and yeah, I think I bruised my ribs quite a bit, but I don't think there's anything broken. That idiot down there is doing a lot worse." With both men intently staring at her, she sighed. "I swear, it's not too bad. I'm gonna hurt for a bit, but I wasn't shot or anything. It's the bruised ribs and a few scrapes and scratches, that's all."

"We'll have you properly checked out as soon as we're out of here," Josh declared, and Ben nodded in agreement.

"Yes, of course," Bonny said. She knew when it was a lost

cause to argue, and if it made her men feel better, she had no problem obliging them.

"What happened? We were almost outside when we heard a shot, and then somebody screamed."

"They nearly managed to run outside to find you before Jack and I could get a hold of them to see what was going on first," Rhys added, and Bonny nearly jumped in surprise. She hadn't even seen him until that moment, but he had apparently checked on the guy Bonny had been fighting with and was now standing next to the huddle she and her boyfriends formed on the grass.

Bonny looked from Rhys to her men, a half-smile on her face. "Guys, that's sweet, but also not smart. You know I can take care of myself, and I know you want me to be safe. But I want the same for you, so you gotta be more careful and think things through first, okay?"

Begrudgingly, Ben and Josh gave her their word to be more careful the next time – while they all hoped there wouldn't be a next time like this. None of them had ever expected a vacation or even a few weeks of watching out for family would turn into the mess they had found themselves in. It was time to finally go home.

Bonny gave each of them a kiss before telling them, "I'll remind you of your promise if I have to." She turned to Rhys. "Kieran?"

"Not sure, yet. Jack moved there, I came here. Boss, Jack, you okay?" he asked via their radio, and it was clear he wouldn't be at ease before he knew, either.

It was Jack who answered them. "We're good. Kieran shot one of the guys following Bonny, then ran to the other who was guarding the women to avoid shooting into the group. I reached them just when Kieran was ending the knife fight with the asshole. The boss has a few more scratches, luckily nothing too bad. We're now gathering all the women to get out of here. Since you didn't call for backup, I assume all's good there, too. So you better get moving, we've all seen enough of this damn place."

Truer words have never been spoken, all three of the throuple thought and picked themselves up from the ground. Josh and Ben made sure to keep Bonny between them should she need support, but not to bump into her, and she softly smiled at them for it.

But as much as everybody wished to just snap their fingers and be home, they still had to make it to the extraction point Anton had provided them with.

They decided to head out within minutes, not taking any chances on more of the guards inside the temple waking up and following them. All of them purposely ignored the anguished whimper from the guy suffering from the snake bites, although Bonny had a feeling the sounds might haunt her for some time to come.

But for the moment, she focused on helping guide the girls through the jungle to get away as fast as possible, that time luckily without having to pass through much of the nature preserve as the group took the direct path from the front of the temple toward the trees. The slope down the plateau was less steep there as well, making it a little easier for the terrified, exhausted women. Backtracking the path the new arrivals had taken, they found a part of the fence that was designed to look normal but could actually be opened to let everybody through – an easier way in for the kidnappers that the soldiers hadn't seen before because it was in the area they had avoided during their scouting due to the cameras.

Yet, even after leaving the plateau behind, it was all still far slower than when only the six of them had hiked to the temple, but they were lucky that most of the girls were physically well enough and could walk on their own without too much of a problem. Mentally, they were understandably barely holding it together, though. The young woman Kieran and his men had originally been here to rescue clung to them once she understood they would take her all the way home to the UK, and most of the other girls kept their distance from Carmen. The woman might have left with them, but they were far from trusting her. It meant that Benicio, Josh, Bonny, and even Valeria were constantly encouraging them to keep going, and calming them when they cowered at the sound of a twig breaking somewhere in the forest or a bird calling loudly when it spotted them.

They walked for a couple of hours, Rhys leading them, Jack covering the back, and Kieran navigating them through the thick vegetation next to Rhys, with the throuple, Valeria, and the other women forming a group or walking in pairs between the soldiers depending on the terrain.

At first, the women were too excited to be free, too pumped on adrenaline to realize their own exhaustion, but after a while, with the biggest danger now farther behind them, the group was forced to take more breaks. During one of those breaks, Kieran seemed impatient, and the throuple understood him: they weren't far from the extraction point, and he wanted to get people out asap. Apparently, he had said the wrong thing to get the girls moving, though, because Valeria stood up from the crouch she had been in to help one of the girls retie her shoe when the woman's hand had been shaking too much. Valeria confronted Kieran head-on and slapped him across the back of his head. "You can wait two minutes longer! In case you forgot: we were fucking kidnapped. They, even more than me, have been through hell. Without any military training in advance to prepare us for anything like that. We all want to get out of here, but rushing them like the guys who dragged them here in the first place is not going to help, *maldita sea!*" she growled at him.

Kieran was smart enough to look properly chastised. "I'm sorry, you're right. Take your time." Then something passed over his face and he smirked. "You know, that's no way to talk to a guest, though. I'm not sure I can leave the hotel a five-star review after you just assaulted me," he told her, clearly trying to lighten the mood and get back on her good side.

Benicio thought the man was a lucky bastard when Valeria glared at him for a second but then huffed out a small laugh. His sister could hold a grudge if she wanted, but it seemed she knew the situation was a mess for everybody and was okay with forgiving him. He was incredibly proud of her for standing up for herself and others like that.

Josh and Bonny must've thought something similar because they both moved closer to him, Josh with his arms around Ben from behind and Bonny leaning her temple against his shoulder, and studied Valeria.

"She's going to be an epic sister-in-law, I'm so glad she'll be part of the family," Bonny said.

Josh hummed in agreement and added, "I can't wait to meet the rest of your family."

That had Benicio snorting. "You say that now, *arañita*, but believe me, my mother will skin us alive for not letting her know what was going on. As much as I admire Val, she got that stubbornness and temperament from somebody, and it wasn't our father."

"And you think Bonny's parents are going to be any different? Or my brother and Scarlette? Or even Bea? I'm pretty sure we'll get our asses kicked more than once in the foreseeable future."

"Josh is right. It's not like our families are so much different from yours in that aspect."

Ben smirked. "Good, then you at least know what you're getting yourself into."

He got quick kisses from his lovers, but then it was time to keep moving.

At last, they reached the larger clearing to which Anton had directed them. Josh had no idea how his boss had managed it, but not only was a helicopter waiting for them, large enough to carry all seventeen members that their group had grown to, but Anton himself stood next to the machine. Given what favors his boss had called in to get here as fast as he had, and with a military-looking helicopter no less, Josh thought he might have to offer to work his first year unpaid. That was something to discuss later, though.

In that moment, he was more concerned with getting all the women on board their transport out of the jungle. Some of them looked terrified all over again, their eyes huge, their knees locked so they wouldn't buckle. This didn't come as a huge surprise – they had already heard that some of the girls had been brought closer to the temple by a helicopter if the weather allowed for it. But with some gentle coaxing and reassuring words from Valeria (and her display of confidence when she strode directly to the helicopter and climbed in), they got everybody on board in a few minutes while the pilot was running his pre-flight checklist in the background.

As soon as everybody was settled, the pilot started the motor again. The massive rotor blades began turning faster and faster, sending rumbles through the whole aircraft and all its passengers. There was a split second where they could feel engineering fighting gravity, but then they lost the ground beneath them as the chopper began climbing in the air. It was thrilling and humbling at the same time, and Benicio spoke into his headset to be heard over the roaring noise all around them. "I don't know about you, but I thought a helicopter ride would've been a more romantic date than this."

Grinning, Josh nudged him with his elbow. "No idea what you mean, isn't this perfect?" He looked around the cramped surroundings, the basic seats – far more practical than comfortable – and the shell-shocked faces of most of the other people on board. "But yes, next time it's just gonna be the three of us, and the pilot, if you want."

For a while, they all gave in to their relief to get back home. Some people were joking around or just holding the hand of whoever was closest, holding onto the reality of freedom. The soldiers just looked right at home, relaxing in their seats as much as they allowed. Bonny was glued to a window and reveled in the thrill of the flight, and Josh and Ben were talking with Valeria.

But once they were on a course bringing them to Mexico and at a safe cruising altitude, the cabin came alive: the medic Anton had also thought to bring along checked on the women; Josh, Benicio, Anton, and Kieran moved closer together to discuss next steps. Benicio would have to talk to his boss, and with the evidence Josh had gathered, he hoped together they would be able to convince people higher up the chain to finally run a proper investigation.

Kieran squeezed Ben's shoulder. "Don't worry; we, or rather our government, will put pressure on your authorities as well. After all, it's obviously not only Mexican women going missing."

Next to them, Anton nodded. "He's right. On the flight to Guatemala, I did some more research. I have also found several US cases that could very well be linked to this. We'll talk to our authorities; Josh and I both have ties to several agencies and branches of law enforcement. As much as the Mexican police might not want to work this case properly, I guarantee you they want an international conflict about it far less. Plus, we'll also have to involve the Guatemalan authorities, and I don't assume you have connections there."

Benicio was overwhelmed. Rendered speechless, he pressed his lips together and shook his head at Anton's comment, then tipped his head at them all in silent thanks. He never would have expected to get this kind of support on top of everything else the soldiers and Josh's boss had already done to help. When Josh saw him struggle to keep it together he drew him close, and Benicio buried his face in the crook of his boyfriend's neck until he got his emotions back under control. They still had so much to talk about, video evidence to back up and make it available for all parties, and photograph the physical pieces of evidence they had brought along, just so they wouldn't "accidentally" get lost without a trace of their existence.

After that, they still had enough flight time left that Jack and Rhys said they'd try to get some sleep and shut off their headphones. It seemed to have been a sign for the girl they had come for that she could speak to Kieran again without interrupting. But instead of the questions about her family or what would happen next, she came up with an idea that could potentially turn out to be important. She spoke slowly at first, not sure how her input would be taken, but once she saw everybody was listening and not interrupting, she became more confident. Her plan included taking videos of each woman telling her story in a few short sentences while they were still in the air, so there wouldn't be any cops interfering or trying to coerce them into saying what they wanted to ditch the investigation. Clearly, the woman had heard a lot of their previous discussion. And she had a point. With their reluctance to investigate, the authorities had been far from trustworthy. "Also, if the case officially goes nowhere, you will have the videos and you can upload them on social media to get the public involved, have them add more pressure on the cops," she finished.

It didn't take much to convince the group of rescuers to do it. Explaining it to the former kidnapping victims was easy enough with Ben and Valeria translating. Some of the women agreed right away, a few others seemed wary at first; they were still skittish, still petrified by the whole experience. But once they listened to the others telling what had happened to them, they understood bit by bit that they weren't alone, and how valuable these unfiltered first comments could be in the end.

Filming the reports wasn't easy with the engine noise, but they made it work. Who knew how much time they would have with the women on the ground without being interrupted? They already had to inform several people so they'd get clearance for the flight after all, so their arrival wouldn't exactly be a surprise for anybody. In the end, they got everybody's statement on tape along with contact information for each woman, and the men shared the files between them as well just in time for the pilot to let them know they were approaching their destination.

What followed seemed like pure and utter chaos. Apparently, somebody had not only made sure there would be enough ambulances (the sheer number of which had also brought police to the airfield) to transport the women to a nearby hospital, but had also let Benicio's boss know to show up so he could be looped into the investigation right from the start.

With the EMTs around the women, the cops that had shown up were getting antsier by the minute as they pushed for access to the girls. Luckily, the medical personnel stood their ground and made it clear that all of the girls needed to be checked out at a proper hospital first and some would likely have to go into surgery, even more so if the police wanted the drug packages in their bodies as evidence. The only one getting out of it was Valeria, since she hadn't been operated on and was physically fit enough.

Benicio wasn't happy about her refusal, but she glared at him. "What are they going to do? Put me on an IV? Give me something to calm me down? I can drink water instead, and I don't need any medication. As much as I hated the tracker idea at first, once I was taken, it was what kept me sane. I *knew* you'd come for me, that I just needed to hold myself back from antagonizing the *gilipollas* too much, just cursing them, so I wouldn't end up being beaten or whatever. I'm pissed, but I'm not in shock or anything. I do not need to go to the hospital," she told her brother in English to make it easier for Bonny and Josh, who stood with Ben between them, each with an arm around his waist.

Then there was no more time for the siblings to fight about it when Benicio was dragged away by his boss, while Valeria was cornered by a police officer and three more cops crowded Josh and Bonny. To say the police seemed less than eager to acknowledge the scale of the problem would've been a compliment. Everybody was asked half-hearted questions, and the cops noted their names and phone numbers, but that was about it. Especially Bonny and Josh were asked almost no questions above the basics – not without a reason. They had demanded to either have a translator present, as they weren't fluent enough, or they'd give the cops their identification only. There was no need for them to end up as any kind of suspects because somebody twisted their words or they failed to give enough of a detailed report to convey that they were part of the cavalry. No translator was called. Instead, they showed their passports, had the cops take some probably blurry photos of them, and then were left alone again.

Nobody seemed to see them as important in this investigation, Josh thought. He took Bonny's hand and guided her a few steps away, discussing it with her. That's when they heard snippets of the other cop's conversation with Valeria, and from the sentences they could make out and translate, it sounded a lot like the man did his best to pressure Valeria into saying that she voluntarily boarded the plane to Guatemala. What had happened in another country was obviously not a case the Mexican police could investigate. It sounded oddly familiar to what they had been told on the phone days before by the Guatemalan police.

"Are they truly that careless or self-centered and just want to save their asses because nobody looked into it before, or are they on somebody's payroll?" Josh wondered when he looked back at Bonny.

She shook her head and sighed. "No idea. Neither would surprise me. I think Ben and the others will have a lot of work to do to get somewhere. Well, Ben's boss. I think Benicio is done with all of this."

"He is, and he has done all he can do in his position. I think he meant it when he said he'd be okay to let the case go. He helped blow it wide open – if the authorities are willing to act on what we've brought them."

"You're right." Then she got a glance at Benicio, who appeared to have finished talking to his boss for the moment, and the glare he sent towards Kieran. "Oh oh..."

"What?" Josh spun in place, looking for any sign of trouble.

"I think now that we're back in Mexico, that Valeria is safe, and the adrenaline is wearing off, Ben remembered that he still wanted to kick Kieran's ass."

"Hm? Ooh, because they seemed to know something was going to happen even before Val had been taken?"

"Yep."

Chapter Thirty-Five

"This should be interesting," Josh chuckled. He checked his surroundings and found what he was looking for. He couldn't wait to see Benicio confronting Kieran because the whole situation still left a sour taste in his mouth too, but they shouldn't be discussing that out in the open air next to the helipad they had landed on and where they were all still standing, minus the women who had been brought to the hospital and the police who had vanished already. He took a few quick steps to a door and held it open, just when Ben reached Kieran and put his hand on the other man's shoulder.

"Ben, babe, let's do that in here. There's an empty office right inside."

Benicio looked over at his boyfriend and grunted, then gestured with his head for Kieran to come along.

Moments later, two of the soldiers (Jack had accompanied the British woman to the hospital), the throuple, Valeria, Anton, and Benicio's boss squeezed into the room inside the airport building. The office wasn't tiny, but it was also not meant for that many people. As soon as the door was closed, Benicio turned to fully face Kieran.

"What's up, mate?"

Benicio gathered his thoughts for a second before talking. "Let me say first that I am incredibly grateful for your help in getting my sister back, and for helping rescue all the other women. And for the offer to put pressure on the authorities here. I appreciate that. I really do. That's why I hope you won't change your mind after this."

Kieran looked curious, his eyebrows rising higher and higher. But he kept quiet, letting Ben get off his chest whatever it was he needed to say.

"When we found you guys in the jungle, we realized something: you left early for some 'family emergency.' You said your target was taken well before Val, but you stayed at the hotel. You *knew* something else was about to happen, didn't you? And you let it happen. My sister got taken and was put in danger because you did fucking nothing to stop it!"

For a second, Kieran looked lost; it was clear that he had not expected this. He recovered quickly enough, though, and began to explain. "Okay, yes, we knew *something* would happen, but..."

"You goddamn asshole!" Benicio exploded, then fell into a stream of swearing in Spanish, his voice getting louder with every word.

When he was raging so much that Josh was afraid he'd lash out with his fists as well, he brought his arms around Ben from behind and laid his chin on his boyfriend's shoulder. "Sweetheart, I know it's hard, but let him talk." Then he nuzzled closer and whispered into Ben's ear, "Not that it's not incredibly hot to see you this passionate." Was it the time for a comment like that? Maybe not, but Josh knew it would steer Ben away from punching Kieran in the face.

Kieran pinched the bridge of his nose and squeezed his eyes shut for a second. "Look, mate, I get why you're pissed off. But believe me when I say we had no clue that they targeted your sister."

"So what? It wouldn't have made it better if it had been any other girl!"

"No, it wouldn't have. Look, some lass way, way down the ladder in the organization had realized just who had been kidnapped from the cruise ship. Probably some bloody social media connection or blog or whatever, no idea. I just know she reached out to somebody and asked to get paid for information. Along the chain, we were briefed on where to meet her and to give her the money she asked for so our woman wouldn't disappear completely without a trace. Wouldn't have been my choice to do it like that, but I don't question the orders as long as they don't put innocent people in danger."

"But they did!"

"Bloody hell, yes, I know that now! But when we met with the girl, she only told us our target had already been flown out of the country, but she didn't know where to exactly. But that we should wait because something had come up and she would find out more soon. So, because we had no other way to find our target, we waited."

Grumbling, Kieran went on, "Initially, she was tight-lipped and didn't tell us anybody else would be kidnapped, it all sounded vague. Only when things got more concrete did she let us know what would happen. But she never mentioned who would be taken."

"You put it together immediately, though, when I showed up at your camp," Josh concluded.

"Yes. But, as you found out, we didn't know the scale of the operation, and frankly, we weren't sent to Mexico to investigate it."

Anton cleared his throat. "If I may? I have been digging ever since Josh contacted me, and I think I've found out a few things.

I think it was more or less spontaneous that they decided to take Valeria when they learned about Benicio and her befriending a US couple. With that, Val got onto the radar of somebody picking victims for their sick scheme. If I had to guess, I'd say they have people in all kinds of positions in high-class hotels, clubs, and so on. That's pure speculation, though," he said with a shrug. "Once Valeria became a target, they formed a plan to isolate her after seeing how well she was protected by her brother and his partners. They drugged the lifeguards – and yes, I confirmed that via the medical records – and created a situation where they could get Valeria away from the hotel. You heard her, she was grabbed from her room at the training facility in the middle of the night after she had fallen into bed in her clothes and everything, way more tired than the evening out with her colleagues called for. My guess? Her roommate was your informant or something, and was there to make sure people could get in quietly, maybe even slipped Valeria a light sedative at the end of the evening. And before you ask what makes me think that: I'd say somebody knew she had ratted them out. Otherwise, it would be a big coincidence that she was found dead with a gunshot wound to her chest two days after you made your way to Guatemala. I'll keep digging, though, trying to get my hands on some more surveillance footage from their hideout. And with some luck, I'll find some videos from Mexico, maybe even with sound now that many businesses have updated their systems. I'll let you know what I find," Anton finished with a look at the throuple.

All color drained from Benicio's face. "I... This is..."

But his sister was right in front of him in a heartbeat and grabbed his chin, forcing him to look into her eyes. "If you say this was your fault, I will slap you. I could have ended up as a target for any reason. If it wasn't my connection to you and Bonny and Josh, it would've been Dad. Or perhaps a course on Tourism at the university in cooperation with a US school later on, or anything else. This is *not* your fault, do you hear me?"

"But, Val..."

He couldn't finish when she – lightly – slapped his cheek. "Stop it, damn it. You are a good brother. The damn best brother ever. You flew to another country and hiked through the jungle. You fought your way into a drug lord's lair. You made sure you knew where I was in the first place. I'm here, I'm alive and safe because of you. I will not have you blaming yourself for something that some criminals did to me, especially not when I know you'd ultimately blame yourself for falling in love. And if you do that and even consider breaking up with Bonny and Josh, I will not only slap you, I will kick your ass so hard you won't be able to sit for a month. They are perfect for you, and you loving them is not a mistake, and it most certainly did not cause any of this shit."

From one side, Bonny told him, "Listen to your sister. She's right."

"They both are," Josh said from his other side.

They both framed Ben, who let his head hang with a heavy sigh but then nodded. "*Sí*, okay. I know it. It's a lot to process." Then he looked back at Kieran. "I guess I should apologize for yelling at you. Sorry."

But the soldier just shook his head. "It's all right, mate. I know everything has been crazy, and from your point of view, without knowing what we did – or didn't do in time – I would've been angry too."

"Okay."

After that, they all kept talking some more. Josh made sure to get Benicio and Anton together for some conversation so they'd already get an impression of each other. Just when the group was about to disperse, Anton bumped his shoulder against Josh's. "Am I right when I assume you'll pitch hiring Benicio to me soon, boy?"

Josh chuckled. "You know me so well already, boss."

"Hmm, thought so. We'll talk about it when you're back in the States. For now, as fucked up as things have been, enjoy the rest of your vacation."

"Thanks, we will. And thank you for everything, Anton. Truly."

"You're welcome, Josh. See you soon."

Anton was the first out the door, making sure he'd get on the helicopter to get back to the US with his pilot and medic. Kieran and Rhys followed; they still had to organize a flight back home but would need to contact Jack first to find out what the hospital had said.

After that, the throuple and Valeria decided they'd just rent a car to get back to the hotel. They'd drive for a good three hours from where the helicopter had landed, and they just wanted to get it over with.

During the drive, Valeria told them she would get home to their mother as soon as possible. It wasn't like she trusted the hotel anymore.

"Don't get me wrong, I still like working with people and all, but not when I don't know what will be done about the case. The industry doesn't seem safe at the moment if Anton is right and there are people working for them everywhere."

It was a valid reason, but it made Bonny think. Suddenly, she sat up straighter. "Val, would you be okay with working in the States? And are you at all interested in history?"

"Um, *sí*, to both of that. Why?"

"Well, aside from the company Josh's family is running and where I'll start working, the museum they've been putting together on the West Coast opened a few years ago. We're always looking for people who would want to work there on a long-term basis. Actors between gigs do a great job during short jobs, too, but there's a need for permanent staff. You could probably start right away, or study first and maybe work there during semester breaks."

"Oh, wow. Ah, let me think about it, okay? That's something I need to consider once my mind functions normally again."

"Sure thing."

In the front passenger seat, Josh chuckled. "Epic idea, baby. Now we just need to convince your mother to come to the States, too, Ben. She can join the clan kitchen in New York. With your dad working there already, we'd have all your direct family over in no time, babe," he said and laid his hand on Benicio's thigh and gave it a squeeze.

Ben grinned first at Josh, then in the rearview mirror at his girlfriend and his sister. "If *mamá* lets us all live once she learns what happened, we can mention it sometime in the future."

At the hotel, Valeria first packed her own things in a rush, then accompanied the throuple to their bungalow to collect their belongings – none of them had a desire to stay any longer at the hotel and Ben's invitation to come home with him sounded perfect. Not that Bonny or Josh would ever have let him face his mother alone: even if he seemed relaxed about telling her about his lovers and plans for the future, he did not seem like he was joking all that much when he said the woman would skin him and Valeria alive for not telling her what had been going on.

With their bags packed, they made their way over to the front desk and explained to the clerk that they'd all check out early.

Meanwhile, Valeria slid behind the counter, assured her

obviously worried colleague that she was fine, then knocked on the door to the manager's office. It almost took her less time to quit than it took to check the throuple out. Val would have to send in a written termination, but she had been assured she'd get the highest recommendations and that her manager fully understood why she had to leave. Who knew whether the man meant it or just wanted to avoid any further problems for himself or the hotel? A dead employee and a kidnapped one weren't something you'd want to advertise.

Another few hours and a drive through a larger city and into its adjacent suburb later, Benicio pulled his own car into the driveway of a bright yellow, two-story house with pink flowers on each side of the door. It wasn't a huge house, but it was detached and had a garage next to it. The neighbors were close, but the houses were arranged in a way that you wouldn't constantly feel like you were under surveillance. Compared to some of the cramped neighborhoods in the country, his parents had been lucky to find a property like this.

"There's a guest apartment above the garage; that's where I usually stay when I come by for a few days. We'll have our privacy," he told his partners with a soft smile. Then he looked seriously at his sister. She swallowed audibly but put on a brave face, then followed her brother's lead and stepped out of the car.

Chapter Thirty-Six

The sun was just vanishing below the horizon when they stepped into the house. Inside, the temperature was refreshing compared to the lingering moist heat of the day outside.

Bonny and Josh found themselves looking everywhere at once, taking in the mix of white walls and archways along with some traditional Mexican art pieces, modern furniture, and multiple digital picture frames hanging and standing all over the short hallway they were in and the living room.

When Ben saw their curious glances, he told them, "Like I said, we're a large family. We started giving our parents the picture frames because there would not be enough room on the walls for all the pictures the family constantly shares. I'll give you a tour later or tomorrow."

Both his lovers smiled brightly at that. They were keen on getting to know even more about Ben: where he came from, his family. In that moment, though, their boyfriend had more important things to do.

"*¿Mamá? ¿Estás en casa?*" he called out, although he was pretty sure she'd be home by now. It was her usual time to go over the books of her food trucks, to check if any of her employees had sent over a request for more ingredients or supplies that needed to be ordered.

A moment later, his mother came into view from further back in the house. Yes, she had been in her office. Seeing her always made Benicio happy. She was a middle-aged, small woman, her long, dark hair tied into a bun that day, but she was still pretty, still quite fit, with only her hip acting up sometimes. And fierce, he knew. A quality he deeply admired, even if it scared him at that particular moment.

Her surprise at seeing them was obvious, but she greeted both children with a hug. That's when she first noticed Bonny and Josh, who had stayed in the background so far.

Instead of a hug, she held up her hand and greeted them with a friendly, "*Hola.*"

When they both had said hello as well, Benicio's mother turned her attention back to her son with more than one question in her eyes. Showing up unannounced fairly late in the evening with his sister and two strangers in tow would do that. Ben cleared his throat and glanced at his sister, asking her if she could get coffee for everybody. He would get started with what for him was the positive news of his new relationship. It would also make it a lot easier later for his mother to understand why his lovers had just jumped on a plane and helped him rescue Valeria.

With his sister vanishing toward the kitchen, Ben asked the others to get comfortable in the living room. Once all of them had found a place to sit, he introduced Bonny and Josh to his mother. First only by their names, and introduced his mother as Catarina Pérez to them. Then he took a deep breath and told her he was dating both of them. He talked in Spanish, but Bonny and Josh could tell he was speaking slowly, so they'd have a chance to catch most of what he was saying.

His mother only seemed more confused, looking from her son to the strangers and back. Clearly, she didn't grasp what he wanted her to understand, so he took both his lovers' hands and pressed a kiss to each, before he phrased his news differently, telling her he was in a relationship with both of them, loved them both. That got through to her, and she studied her son with thoughtful eyes. When she asked him whether he was joking, he shook his head vehemently and told her he most certainly was not.

His mother sat with that for a few minutes until Valeria entered the room with a tray full of colorful coffee mugs. For good measure, she had also brought along a bottle of some cream liquor to top off the coffees. *Not the worst idea*, Benicio figured, thinking about how much more he had yet to tell his mother.

With a coffee in hand, Catarina focused on her son again, and Bonny and Josh could make out enough to hear her telling Ben that she needed him to explain to her how he had ended up with two people at once because she couldn't understand how that had just happened.

They all had to give her credit: she wasn't outright dismissing her son being in a poly relationship, and she seemed comfortable enough with the fact that part of that relationship was another man. She just needed the full story to comprehend it. There was no meanness behind her request; that came through clearly. And Bonny and Josh thought she doubtlessly would even accept her son's relationship without understanding it – but for her, it seemed to be important to understand it, just so she'd be able to support him in more ways. On top of that, it was obvious that she wanted to know how he had fallen so quickly for two people at once, and of course wanted more information about the people who had captured her son's heart.

Understanding where his mother was coming from, Benicio glanced at Bonny and Josh to make sure they were okay with sharing their story. When he got a shrug and nod from both of them, he began to tell his mother how he had met them, had fallen for them.

Every once in a while, Bonny or Josh added a few details from their perspective, doing their best to keep it in Spanish, or had Ben or Val help out when they weren't sure how to phrase things correctly to get their point across. Especially the last few hours had brought back a lot of the language skills they had acquired in the past, but school had never prepared them for such a conversation.

For what it was worth, with everything Benicio told her, Catarina seemed more relaxed and genuinely happy for her son – and they hadn't even added the liquor to their coffees, yet. She admitted freely she might not be able to see herself in a relationship like that, but all that she cared about was that her children were happy. Ben hoped her generous mood would stay, because he was getting closer to the part of the story he wished had never happened.

He cleared his throat and looked from his mother to his sister and then back again. "Things were good, really good. Then Val knocked on the door of our bungalow one evening and told us that she was supposed to do some extra training," Benicio told his mother in a dark tone, sticking to Spanish.

Bonny and Josh could follow him well enough. Both reached out to touch their boyfriend and to help him go on. Catarina observed them and gave them a bemused smile, not understanding why her son had suddenly become so somber.

Before he could say anything else, Valeria reached for the liquor bottle. "I think we can all use a bit of this for what comes next," she said, also in Spanish, and began adding some of the creamy liquor to everybody's coffee.

Benicio figured his sister was on the right track and held out his mug to make it easier for her. After a small sip, he turned back to his mother and began recounting what had happened next. "None of us were happy with the situation, but *mamá*, you have no idea how lucky our family is that I met Bonny and Josh. You've been kind not to ask us why we all look like hell, but you need to know."

She indeed hadn't asked out loud why her son and daughter – who were both supposed to be at the hotel – had suddenly come home, nor had she mentioned the group's appearance, even though they had all seen better days. But back at the hotel, they had decided all they wanted to do was leave. Ben had promised a shower and a change of clothes once they explained everything to his mother.

"I wondered about that, but I figured you'd have a good reason. Go on, tell me," she encouraged her son.

From there on out, it was about as bad as Benicio had expected. At first, his mother gasped and grabbed onto her daughter, clinging to her like she would never let the young woman leave the house again. The more Benicio told her, with his lovers and his sister adding more details here and there, the scarier the look on Catarina's face became. She was furious on behalf of her daughter and terrified for her, of course, even with Valeria in her arms now. But the longer she listened and asked questions in between, the angrier she got. In the end, when Ben finished with them landing in Mexico and the police's approach at playing down the case and trying to hand the responsibility to authorities in other countries, Catarina nearly yelled at her children.

Some of it was too fast for Bonny and Josh to catch, but they got the gist. She was horrified, but she was also unhappy, very much so, that nobody had contacted her to let her know what was going on. What followed was a long lecture and more than one curse about how she had a right to know, how she would've raised hell until the officials started to move their asses and made any cop sorry who would try to dismiss her or the case. When she moved on and said she would've come to Guatemala with them, Ben held up his hands. So far, he had shrunk down in his seat under the heated speech, his eyes fixed on the coffee table sitting between him and his mother.

But now, he whipped up his head. "*Mamá*," he said in a stern voice, "I love you, and I know what you would've done. But that wouldn't have done any good at that moment. And as brave as you are, as much as I admire you for all you've achieved, you have a bad hip. There was no way I would've taken you into the jungle with us, nor would you have been able to walk the distances we had to cover each day, much less with the terrain we had to deal with."

He had talked to his mother in Spanish again, but then quickly recapped anything they might have missed for Josh and Bonny. They smiled and thanked him, then looked at Catarina, hoping she wouldn't be just as mad at them. Those were idle hopes, if the look she gave them was any indication. She glared at them, shaking her head, then addressed them directly. It cost her, but she forced herself to speak slowly so they would understand her. "Seeing as you're family now, let me say: what I told my son goes for you, too. I am sure I will not be the last person to be angry that none of you called anybody. Don't misunderstand me, I am beyond grateful to you; you helped bring my daughter home. You helped save so many innocent women. But your families also should have known what was going on. I understand you informed your employer, Josh, and I think, or hope, that you would not have done something stupid like that without speaking to your families if you didn't have such strong backup. Even though I think Benicio did not tell me exactly when you knew the man would show up to get you home." She gave her son a knowing glance before talking to Bonny and Josh once more. "If anything had happened, how would your families have ever really under-stood why you went on such a dangerous mission without knowing what my son is to you, or how much you care for his sister. Your employer knows and could explain, but it would never carry the same weight as coming from you. I do under-stand why you want to share such news in person. But walking into the jungle like that without letting families know where to and why was a foolish thing to do, even under the circum-stances and with the need to act quickly. But imagine what you would've put all of us through if anything had gone wrong. I hope all three of you learn from this and take this to heart."

The woman didn't pull any punches. All three of them mumbled their apologies, not daring to object to anything. Seeing all her children, even the new family additions, looking appropriately guilty, Catarina let out a righteous huff. She had said her piece, and she knew it had reached them.

Benicio sighed and ran a hand through his hair. "All right, *mamá*, we'll do better in the future. Now, we do have more to tell you, more plans to share. But it's late, and we've had more than a couple of long days. We all need a proper shower and a good night's sleep. The guest apartment is free, *sí*? No cousins visiting or anything?"

"No, it's free. And of course you need to rest. Get ready and have a good night. But we will keep talking in the morning," Catarina ordered, then got up from her seat and gave all of them a kiss on the cheek before sending them off, telling them she'd take care of the dishes.

A shower and sleeping in a real bed again sounded like heaven to all of them. Valeria slipped away towards the room she still lived in after hugging her brother and his lovers. Her steps were slow, her feet dragging across the floor a little. It was obvious how exhausted she was.

After a quick detour for their bags, Benicio guided Bonny and Josh around a corner and through a door behind which a narrow staircase led up into the guest apartment. Under other circumstances, the two of them would've taken their time to take in the small suite, to appreciate the details making it part of the home, not some random condo that was used as an Airbnb. But that evening, all any of them could think about was getting clean and crawling under some fresh, clean sheets.

Days in the jungle with no time to properly prepare for it had left their marks on them. Blisters on their feet from walking for hours in the moist air, scratches here and there from branches, mosquito bites despite being covered up as much as possible. None of that was pleasant. Adding to that, they all felt gross; real showers hadn't been an option, only cleaning up with some water and a cloth. And even Josh and Benicio couldn't wait to wash their hair again. It was so much worse for Bonny. She had done her best to detangle her wild curls every day, but without the right tools and products, she'd known her hair would be a mess in no time, so she had mostly worn it in a tight bun. Loosening the hair tie would be annoying and a relief at the same time. She smiled when she saw Ben maneuvering Josh toward the bathroom while she was crouched next to her suitcase to retrieve her brush, comb, and the shampoo she'd need to tame her hair.

Any other time, she would join her men who were just stepping into the shower when she entered the bathroom. But not only was the shower smaller than the one at the hotel, she would need time and some room to work on her hair. So, as she told them to enjoy their shower together, she slipped out of her clothes and leaned against the counter while she watched her boyfriends. It wasn't a hardship at all. Although observing Josh and Benicio told her there wasn't any fun to be had that night. They were gentle with each other, trading small kisses as their hands wandered cleaning the other. The love between them was easy to see. But utter exhaustion almost had their eyelids drooping. They barely managed to wash their hair before Bonny told them to get out.

Her own shower took longer than theirs, but once she was done, she finally felt human again. She had found a thin bathrobe in her bag and slid into it after toweling off, then sighed happily as she walked back into the bedroom. Earlier, she had considered hunting up underwear for a short moment, then had shrugged it off. Falling into bed with her waiting men, she found she wasn't the only one who hadn't bothered with any clothes.

All three of them cuddled close, and would have even if the bed had been bigger than the queen-size one in the apartment, and somehow Bonny ended up between Josh and Ben. From some deep recess, Josh found the energy to joke. "You need to crawl behind Ben; we're no real color gradient like this."

Ben snorted, and Bonny pinched Josh's hip. "Shut up," she mumbled, then giggled, too.

The tiny burst of energy didn't last long, and after saying goodnight to each other and sharing a kiss, all three of them tumbled into a deep sleep in no time.

A shower and a full night's sleep had been amazing, not to mention the relief that they were out of the jungle in one piece and with so many women finally freed. It caused a new endorphin high for her only moments after Bonny woke up. The rush was enough to ignore her bruised ribs and try to get both of her lovers closer. When both of them started nuzzling her neck and cheek, she smiled even brighter. "Morning, you two."

"Morning, baby."

"Good morning, *mi amor*."

Bonny let herself enjoy the kisses they pressed to her skin for a moment, until she turned her head and captured Benicio's lips with hers. Seeing them together like that drew a quiet moan from Josh, and Bonny began roaming her hands over each man's body; first their backs, their arms. When Ben broke their kiss to trace her collarbone with his lips and tongue, she shivered. It had taken him no time at all after they had gotten together to find out how sensitive she was at that spot. Moments later, Josh was there to steal himself a proper good morning kiss as well, first from Benicio then from her.

Sparks crept up Bonny's spine as the hands of her lovers were teasing her. She had no idea how she had gotten this lucky, but she wouldn't question what those two men could do to her. Her own fingers got tangled in Benicio's hair as he was making his way slowly down her body, her other hand dancing across Josh's ribs and further down, caressing his abs. When she reached his length and closed her hand around him, Josh gasped. It was always such a thrill to know what she in turn could do to them, what pleasure she could give them. Her hand moved up and down him in slow, seductive glides, her fingertips ever so slightly massaging him. She considered for a moment to take her time that morning, but then Ben sucked on the skin along her hip crease, causing her to arch her back and whimper with need. Such a small move, but it was another spot she reacted to instantly. Her blood suddenly was on fire with a desperate need to have her lovers, to feel them as close as they could be. An image floated up in her mind, making her shudder with want.

She tugged on Ben's hair so he'd look up to her; the hand around Josh's length released him and wandered to his thigh, trailing along his muscles. "I want you in me, both of you," she told them in a voice harsh with arousal.

For a second, she was certain they'd ask her whether she was sure, then they both seemed to think better of it. After all, she had already told them she would want that one day, and they trusted her to know herself enough.

Instead of questioning her, Josh leaned in for a deep kiss, his fingers following the outlines of her breast before drawing a spiral on her skin until he reached her nipple and gave it a gentle squeeze. He let go of her mouth to ask, "Do you want Ben to get you ready?"

Bonny nodded. "Yes! Wanna taste you, Josh," she added between heavy breaths. She ran her hand around Josh's thigh to pull him closer until she could wrap her lips around his hardness. That was the moment Ben lowered his head between her legs and began teasing her with his tongue. All she could do was moan around Josh. His groan only spurred her on, and when she felt him quiver beneath the hand she had moved to his butt, she took him as deep as she could. It didn't take long for Josh to run shaking fingers through her hair while he was panting hard above her.

The noises they made, so heavy with lust and desire, were like a drug to Ben, and Bonny's taste only drove him higher. He kept pleasuring her, kept pushing her closer to the edge with every stroke of his tongue. Then he slid his finger into her wet, throbbing center to nudge her just a little further. From the corner of his eye, he saw her stilling. The movement of her head stopped for a couple of seconds until a loud moan escaped her as she contracted around his finger. A short glance at Josh told Ben how much he enjoyed the sounds vibrating around his shaft. Almost too much, if how hard he bit his lip was any indication. Ben would need to start prepping her if they wanted a chance to fulfill her wish to feel them both inside her. Because seeing them, hearing them, lost in their pleasure like that was almost enough to tip Ben over the edge. He repositioned himself a little onto his side to reduce the friction of the sheets below his body and kept his hands on Bonny to prevent himself from giving in to the temptation of touching himself.

Slowly, he withdrew his finger and let it wander farther down, circling her at first. Using the proof of her arousal to smooth the glide, he soon pushed inside her, careful to take his time. His eyes wandered up to Josh, who watched intently what Benicio was doing. Ben didn't have to say a word; Josh already pointed at the nightstand, a question in his eyes because he seemed too lost to form the words. Ben only hummed his confirmation, his tongue still busy making Bonny wild. In seconds, Josh handed him a bottle of lube from the nightstand drawer so Ben could add first one more finger, then a third to make sure Bonny would be ready.

It didn't take long before Bonny was pulling away from Josh to tell them in a hoarse voice that she was okay, that she wanted them – right now.

"Okay. How do you want us, *mi amor?*" No matter how much she wanted it, Bonny would be the one who had to adjust to both of them inside her. Benicio would do everything to make her as comfortable as possible, and he knew the same went for Josh. They would let her make all the decisions.

Bonny had a hard time concentrating after her first orgasm and being opened up, but with some effort, she shook herself out of it and directed Ben to lie on his back. Once he was in position, she straddled him and sank down on him with a deep sigh. She would never get tired of having any of her lovers inside her. That morning though, she wanted more. Needed more. Needed a connection they hadn't shared before to exorcise the stress and terror of the previous days.

Leaning back a bit, she reached behind her to pull Josh

closer and kiss him. "Now you," she whispered with a smile when their lips parted. In a fluent move, she turned back to Ben and laid almost completely on top of him to offer Josh a better angle. Before she felt him push inside her, though, he leaned over her shoulder to kiss Ben, then pressed a quick kiss right in between her shoulder blades. A bone-deep shudder ran through her. Ben had learned to read her in no time, but Josh knew all those secret spots, too, and both men loved to tease them to drive her crazy.

Goosebumps still covered her skin when she felt the first hint of pressure at her entrance. When Josh had managed to get his hands on the lube, she didn't know, but at that moment she couldn't care less. All she wanted was for him to keep going.

"Okay, baby?"

"Yeah."

Josh was gentle as always when he entered her like that. That time, he moved even slower than he normally would, giving her time to relax, to let her body adjust to a second person entering her. Bonny was grateful for it. She wanted it, and so far it was amazing; she barely felt a burn after the prep Ben had treated her to. But she also knew why she had asked for Josh to be the one to slide inside her from behind. Before they had met Ben, they hadn't had anal sex for a bit; and after they had come together, they had experimented with so many ways to pleasure each other that she hadn't felt Ben like that, yet. With him being wider than Josh, she wasn't sure she could've taken him as easily with Josh inside her already, at least the first time they came together like this. Because the deeper Josh moved into her, the more certain she was that they'd do it again.

Beneath her, Benicio had started panting, his hands restlessly running up and down her thighs. His eyes were huge and unfocused, and she felt him harden even more inside her. She was not the only one enjoying the way Josh worked his way farther inside.

It took a couple of minutes until not only Ben but also Josh were sheathed inside her completely. Once he was, Bonny felt Josh melt down onto her back, holding still there, his breath heavy. They all needed a moment to absorb all of it and settle. Bonny was almost overwhelmed with everything she felt. The physical sensation alone was heady: deep inside, she noted the heat radiating from both of her lovers, could make out the pulse waves of even more blood filling them. She could feel where they lay against each other, pressing her between them. And the fullness. Gosh, had she ever felt this full? But it wasn't just physical. Emotions rolled over her: love, lust, happiness, and so much more, filling her heart with pure joy. Had she ever experienced such bliss from having one of them inside her? Yes, she loved it, no matter how they were having sex, but what they shared in that moment was something else. It left her speechless, a whimper all she could manage in her current state.

"All good, baby?" Josh asked next to Bonny's ear, turning her face just a bit so he could look her in the eyes. He needed to make sure this was still what she wanted, that he wasn't hurting her, although if her wide pupils and the soft moans following her whimper were anything to go by, he doubted she wanted to stop. He desperately hoped she wouldn't want to, because being inside her like that, so tight around him, and then also feeling Benicio next to him – the sensation softened by the layers of her body separating them but still able to make out the shape of his boyfriend as he filled her – was incredible.

"Great," Bonny managed with a soft smile. "Need you to move."

"Good. I'll move in a second. Ben, babe, are you okay, too?" Josh asked. Their boyfriend had gone so, so quiet, and as Josh ran one hand over his biceps, he noticed how much Ben was trembling beneath them. The other man's muscles were all tense, his breath shallow, but the look on his face spoke of nothing but pleasure.

Ben's gaze found Josh, and he gave a small nod. "*Sí*, all is good. Just need you to move, too, *arañita*. Please," he pleaded.

Josh didn't fare much better than his partners, his mind clouding more and more already by just being connected to them like he was, but they were right, he was in the best position to move; he'd better sit all the way up again to give them room to breathe. Before he did, though, he leaned in a little closer, kissing first Ben, then Bonny.

After that, he wiggled into a better spot behind Bonny and oh so slowly began to slide out of her, then glide back in. Fireworks erupted inside Josh. He didn't think anything had ever felt that amazing. The groan that escaped him started deep inside, rumbling through his whole body. *Oh god! This is...* Josh's brain shut down on conscious thoughts as he completely lost himself in experiencing his lovers like that. So much heat surrounding him, the tightness of Bonny's body holding on to him whenever he was almost slipping out; the glide against Benicio's length, so familiar after weeks of being together, but also nothing like he had felt him before. There was no way he would last long. It was all too much: being joined with them that way, his racing heartbeat, the pulse he heard thundering in his ears that still wasn't enough to drown out the sounds his lovers made. Because they were not quiet at all. Bonny's loud moans hung heavy in the air, and Ben's curses in a wild mix of Spanish and English, which had begun the moment Josh had started to move, wound their way into Josh's brain, spurring him on to go faster with each thrust.

Bonny couldn't come up with any thoughts. Her senses were overloaded with the push and drag of Josh in and out of her, of Ben being pressed hard against that perfect spot inside her, the sounds around her, even the smell. She couldn't even form words to beg her men to go on, the only thing escaping her were dark, desperate moans. Her nerves were on fire; her body tingled all over. Her teeth ended up marking the skin of Ben's shoulder more than once. And when her lovers were nearing their climaxes, she just knew it would be a moment like nothing she could have ever imagined.

Beneath both of them, Benicio tried not to lose his mind. From the moment Josh had pushed inside Bonny, Ben had been right at the edge. So much so that his entire body went taut, his hands dropping to the sheets and grabbing handfuls of fabric in his clenched fists. Breathing had turned into a near-impossible task, not because of the two people on top of him, but because breathing against his strained muscles was just too much to ask in that moment. He needed some form of relief, so he had almost begged his boyfriend for more. When Josh had started to move? There was nothing Ben could compare that feeling to. Bonny enveloping him with her wet, soft heat, the press of Josh against Ben's arousal; it was the most intoxicating thing he had ever experienced. The string of curses falling from his mouth was involuntary, but he couldn't stop it. Nor could he stop his body from taking over when Josh picked up the pace. Planting his feet, Ben's one hand came up to Bonny's hip, gripping her hard enough to probably leave even more bruises on her, his other reaching for Josh's hand and interlinking their fingers in a vise-like grip. Then his hips began to thrust up into Bonny, dragging along Josh, the friction increasing to a near-unbearable level and pushing him the last little bit until he erupted inside her with a roar. Only seconds later, she clutched even tighter around Ben, screaming her with her own climax, just as Josh began to pulse inside her so much that Ben could feel the waves of his release running along his length.

The second Ben positioned himself so he could join him in

moving in and out of Bonny, Josh knew he was lost. In seconds, his heart beat so fast he thought he might pass out. Then he felt Ben's orgasm hit him, heard his lover's deep roar, and was squeezed unbearably tight by Bonny's muscles. All he could do was fall with them, let their ecstasy drag him over his own peak. Once the spasms of his release stopped, Josh sank down on Bonny again, all muscle tone leaving his body, his lungs burning in their attempt to drag in some oxygen.

Caught between her boyfriends, Bonny was utterly blissed out. Feeling them grow that bit harder and pulse inside her was more perfect than she had ever imagined, and as they had swollen the last little bit with their orgasms, they had filled her in a way she couldn't even begin to describe. It left her in a deep euphoric state, a rush of endorphins drugging her from head to toe. She was completely out of it. She heard Josh say something, felt one of them brush her hair aside to study her face, but she couldn't make sense of the words or what her eyes were seeing. She could only lie there and float on the cloud of bliss that was fogging her brain. Her muscles were lax, and her mind was empty of any rational thought. She had never felt better in her life.

Bonny had no idea how much time had passed, but it seemed her boyfriends had maneuvered her onto her back at some point. She had an ice pack on her ribs, and they were sitting on each side of her; Ben was lovingly running a tissue over her face. Had she cried? She had no idea. She hadn't even realized when they had slipped out of her or whether they had spoken with her. Josh was cleaning her gently of their release. No surprise – she hadn't been able to move, let alone walk into the bathroom; she was grateful, though, and tried to smile at them. That was when the shivers started. Not too bad, but she felt the high of the hormones vanish from her body and leave her quivering and nearly on the verge of tears all over again.

Damn, she needed them closer. With some effort, she lifted a hand and mumbled, "Hold me, please."

There was no hesitation, both Josh and Benicio crawling to her and laying down on each side of her, enveloping her in their embrace and holding her through the moments of her system crashing, making sure she felt safe and secure and loved. She sighed, happy and satiated, and felt her eyelids droop. The last thing she heard was their chuckles before she drifted off to sleep.

With Bonny deeply asleep, Benicio and Josh wriggled out of bed to take a quick shower together.

They hadn't done much before except caring for their girl-friend. After the epic conclusion of their morning fun, Josh had jerked up when he had realized how much weight he was putting on Bonny and her bruised ribs. But when he'd asked her whether she was all right, she hadn't answered. Concerned, he and Ben had taken a closer look at her. She had been awake, but there was no way of reaching her. Benicio had checked her vitals just to be sure but had decided she was safe, just needed time to come down from her high. With that assessment, it had taken about three seconds of Josh and Ben staring at each other for them to break out in wild giggles. It had been amazing for them, too, no question. But they hadn't expected for it to hit Bonny quite that hard. They were pretty sure it wouldn't be the only time they would indulge in such a mind-blowing way to come together.

Showered and dressed, Benicio grabbed Josh's hand and led him back into the main house. They decided they would let Bonny sleep off her endogenous high but left her a note on the bedside table.

As soon as they entered the kitchen, his sister looked up

from the laptop she was working on and rolled her eyes. "Brother of mine, there are things I do not need to know about you. How you sound having sex is one of them," she told him, the smirk appearing on her face winning over her attempt at seeming annoyed.

Josh coughed, and Ben stared at her for a second. "*Mierda*, we never closed the window."

"You didn't. And the window in my room is closest to the garage."

"Sorry, Val," Josh mumbled, while Ben ran his hands down his face.

"I don't mind hearing *you*, Josh. I told my brother already that I think you're hot. It's just him I don't need to hear."

That caused another coughing fit from Josh, while Ben stared at his sister. "Hey, stop..." he managed, but she was already yelping in surprise and pain.

"Behave!" Catarina told her daughter as she pinched her ear. She had just come in and had apparently heard at least the last part of the conversation so far.

"*¡Ay, mamá!* What? He's family, I should be allowed to tease him like any family member. He knows I'm joking."

"He is, but he also helped rescue you, so be nice. Good morning, Josh. Good morning, *mi'jo*," Catarina addressed the last part to the two men, focusing her attention on them with a smile.

Josh was surprised to hear mother and daughter speak in English with each other and him and Ben, and it must have shown on his face when he greeted her. He had known Valeria was fluent, of course, but he hadn't expected Catarina to have almost as little of an accent as her children.

"Is something wrong?" There was honest concern in Catarina's voice, and it made Josh smile. She had obviously accepted him and Bonny without any fuss, just as long as they made her son happy.

"No, all good. I was just surprised by the language. Please don't think Bonny or I expect any of you to speak only in English with us. We're a bit rusty, but we're both happy to brush up on our Spanish."

Catarina tilted her head to the side and studied him for a second, then she took a step closer and gave Josh a motherly kiss on the cheek. "Oh, right. You'd be surprised by that. You're a sweet man. But speaking in English doesn't bother me. With their father working in the US, and my son over there for lectures every now and then, I have already made sure to know the language well enough, in case there ever is an emergency and I need to travel there. And some of the suppliers for my business are based in the US. I only find it easier to speak in Spanish when I am more worked up, like I was yesterday with all the things you told me."

Josh considered that for a moment, then nodded. "That makes sense. I'd tend to use my native language in such situations, too. Still, thank you, Catarina," he said and gave her a wide smile. He and Bonny had addressed her as *Señora Pérez* exactly once, the day before when they had said good night. Catarina had told them in no uncertain terms she wouldn't allow that from the people who were so clearly important to her son.

"You are very welcome. Now, Benicio, haven't I taught you any manners? Why haven't you made your man some coffee already?"

Ben gave up the argument and turned to the coffee machine, hoping his mother wouldn't see him rolling his eyes. "Sorry, *mamá*. I'll get right to it."

Satisfied to have her son back on track, Catarina stepped over to the small breakfast table next to her daughter and quickly flipped through a planner that lay on it. "You do that. I called your father last night to let him know what happened. If he had his way, he'd be here already. I told him I wasn't sure what your plans were for the next few days, but I assume they'll involve checking in with Bonny's and Josh's families. You mentioned the New York area yesterday when you talked about Josh's boss, so I take it you'll be somewhere around there soon. That works: your father is more or less close, and he'll want to see you, too, Benicio. And meet you and Bonny," she added with a glance at Josh. "Now, I have to check on two trucks this morning. As long as you tell me all four of you are all right, I would rather not reschedule the checks."

"We're all good, *mamá*. You can do what needs to be done for work," Valeria assured her mother.

"Good. And once I'm back, I would love to hear more about your plans for the future. Not just the near future, but in general. From the bit you said about it last night, it sounds like you have it all planned out. But I would love to have Bonny with us for that discussion, too."

Both men shared an indulgent smile, but Josh turned back to Catarina quickly. "We can do that, Catarina. And I'm sure Bonny will be awake by then."

"Good. Enjoy some breakfast, all of you. I will see you later," she told them before vanishing out of the kitchen with determined steps.

There wasn't much else to say, so they did just that. At some point, Josh went back to the guest apartment for a minute, checking on Bonny and grabbing his tablet so he could book their flights back to New York for the next day.

So once Bonny was awake – still too happy to be shocked or embarrassed by how out of it she had been – and Catarina was back, they spent the rest of the day explaining what their long-term plans were exactly. From the looks of it, it was pretty much what she had expected. But having her blessing at the end of it still felt good.

Of course, she made them promise to visit often. "Oh, and don't forget your cousin's wedding is in three months, *mi'jo*. I'm expecting to see all three of you there, so you can meet most of the family. Almost everybody will be there. And don't worry, I will let them know you will need one more seat at the table. I am helping with the seating order anyway."

After that, the conversation drifted over to more family stories, and Bonny and Josh couldn't help it when they burst into laughter at the horrified look on Ben's face as his mother produced an old photo album from somewhere.

It was the perfect way to end their visit with Ben's mother.

Chapter Thirty-Seven

With everything that had happened, none of them had really checked a calendar against their original plans. But as things were, it turned out they landed in New York only two days earlier than they would have, had Bonny and Josh just stayed at the hotel for the duration of their vacation.

After collecting their luggage and a stop at the small apartment he and Bonny held in the city to pick up their own car, they first drove to Bonny's parents. But the closer they got to Hope, the more nervous Bonny seemed to become.

Josh was driving, so Ben reached between the front seats from the back, his hand rubbing her arm in an attempt to calm her. "*Mi amor*, what's wrong? Do you think your parents won't accept us?"

Bonny vehemently shook her head. "No, that's not it. I mean, there's no guarantee, and they might need a little time to wrap their heads around it, but I think they'll be okay with it once they realize how happy you make me, make us. It's just... they won't be happy about me ending up in the jungle, or getting injured, even if it's just minor stuff. It doesn't help that the first time I brought Josh around was the night his car was blown up in my parents' driveway. I wasn't allowed to go over to his place for days until that case had been closed."

Next to her, Josh hummed his agreement. "Hmm, yes. They liked me fine; they just hated that you might be dragged into some dangerous situation. On the other hand, perhaps we can sell it that you just have... unusual first dates with new partners. Something like, 'Look how safe we are now. Nothing bad has happened to Bonny since that explosive evening. Until we met Ben. But we checked the danger part with him off the list already, and we don't plan to include anybody else in the relationship, so all good for the future.'"

"Uh-huh, sure. What about the Halloween party where I wrestled with the guy pointing a gun at Leroy a few years ago?"

"Let's just not remind them of that," Josh said, reaching over to give her thigh a quick squeeze.

"That would be best. Anyway. They won't be happy, we know that. But at least we can say we won't just end up in the jungle again now that Val is back home." Bonny took a deep breath, then nodded to herself. "And hey, even if they don't like it, I'm an adult now, they can't tell me not to go back home with you."

Josh chuckled. "That's the spirit, baby. Though they will try, you know that."

"Let them try. Won't happen, I'm gonna go home with my boyfriends."

Behind them, Ben drew up his eyebrows. "Should I be concerned?"

Bonny half-turned in her seat to face him better. "No, don't worry. My parents are actually great. Sometimes they can be a little overbearing, but that's only until I remind them that I'm not a teenager anymore. They just want all of our family to be safe. That includes Josh, and will include you, too. They might read us the riot act for acting the way we did, just like your mom, but I think they'll just have to get it out of their system once."

For a moment, Bonny thought about her own words and realized that was likely exactly what would happen. It helped a lot to calm her jittery nerves.

The relative calm lasted until she was out of the car and at the door of her childhood home. She knocked once out of courtesy but then opened the door right away to step inside. Her parents should be at home. Her mother had been working as a nurse part-time for as long as Bonny could remember and had always scheduled her shifts at the hospital in a way that she could help her husband with some of the things that went hand in hand with the farm. That day would usually be their preparation day for the market the next morning.

Back when she had been living at home, Bonny had helped, and her father had kept working outside. With her moving out to go to school , her siblings had helped their mother at first. Then it became clear that her brother was interested in taking over the farm later, so over the years a new routine had evolved: her father would help at home, saving him from some of the hard manual labor, and her brother would take over the farm on those afternoons. He enjoyed being outside, and he was eager to learn and take on more responsibility step by step. Bonny was immensely proud of him. He had already implemented a few changes that made processes more efficient, and he was always looking into ways not only to generate more money but also to make the farm more sustainable. She was already planning to use him as a consultant once she took over the wine and breeding business to see what methods could be transferred.

First, she needed to talk to her parents, though. She guided her lovers through the house back to the kitchen, where her parents would be sorting through things to pack for the next day. As expected, she saw them checking their list against the items stashed in several boxes. Good, she wouldn't interrupt them right in the middle of packing; the final review they were doing was something that could be skipped once.

Upon hearing footsteps coming closer, her parents looked up. There was surprise written over their faces for a second, but then her mother smiled and came over to give Bonny a hug. "Hello, sweetie! I'm so happy to see you. We didn't expect you until the day after tomorrow. Did we get the dates wrong somehow?"

Bonny tightened the hug for a second – surprised herself by the sudden wave of emotions crushing her – before stepping back and smiling at her mother and shaking her head. "Hey, Mom, hey, Dad. No, you didn't. We came back a little earlier than planned," she explained.

By then, Bonny's dad had joined the group and hugged his daughter as well.

Next to them, Bonny's mom was already dragging Josh into her arms. The woman had basically adopted Josh in a heartbeat back when Bonny had brought him home the first time. Which hadn't surprised Bonny – it hadn't been long after Josh's parents had died, after all.

It had taken considerably longer until Josh had managed to call her "Mom" as well. Understandable, given how raw the loss of his parents had still been. But after years of being part of Bonny's family, the word fell from his lips easily enough when he greeted her. "Hi, Mom."

"Josh, honey. We missed you, too. You have to tell me all about your trip." That was the moment she took notice of Benicio, who had stayed a few steps behind his partners and looked more than a little unsure. "Oh, hello. I'm sorry, I was a little distracted. Are you a friend of Bonny and Josh?"

"Ah…" Benicio had no idea what to say and hoped Bonny or Josh would help him out, because Bonny's dad had released his daughter and had reached over to give Josh's shoulder a quick squeeze but was now also looking curiously at the other guest in their kitchen.

Bonny came indeed to his rescue. "Kind of. Mom, Dad, this is Benicio. He is our boyfriend."

It took a moment for the words to compute, then her mother looked back and forth between all three of them. "Your… your boyfriend. What? You and Josh broke up? But you love each other!"

"No, Mom, we haven't broken up, don't worry. Ben is *our* boyfriend. We're both dating him."

At that, her mother gasped, and her father cleared his throat. "You're *both* dating him. Both? How… what the hell happened?"

At least they aren't yelling or having a heart attack, Bonny thought. "Uhm, why don't we sit down, and we'll tell you all about it," she suggested.

"Uh-huh, good idea," her mother stammered.

"Yeah, sitting down is a good idea. Why don't you do that, and I'll get us all some coffee?" Josh asked. He knew the kitchen by heart as much as his own, and he thought Bonny's parents might do better with something like a mug to busy their hands with. Josh knew them both to be able to handle pretty much anything, but the announcement of her daughter dating two guys seemed to leave even them in a bemused state.

Bonny directed her parents to the table and was almost glad for the clutter, because it gave her something to do while she waited for Josh with the coffee. She began making some room, putting packed boxes for the market to the side and rearranging some chairs around so she, Ben, and Josh would be able to sit together as they faced her parents to tell them everything that had happened over the last weeks. Wherever he could, Ben lent her a hand to avoid just sitting there and staring at Bonny's parents. He couldn't positively say how things were going so far. Mostly, Bonny's mother and father looked confused at that moment.

Minutes later, Josh carried a tray with five steaming mugs over and distributed the coffees to each person. He had already prepared them to everybody's personal taste, and despite everything, Ben smiled at the consideration. He thanked Josh and, in what was almost a reflex, gave him a quick peck on the cheek when his boyfriend sat down next to him. On his other side, Bonny leaned forward and winked at Josh as she thanked him as well.

Across from them, her parents both gasped, and Bonny decided it was time to get started with her report.

There was a heavy silence hanging in the air when they finished.

Bonny had done most of the talking, but like she and Josh had done with Ben's mother, her lovers had jumped in and added some details for her parents as well. At first, her parents had interrupted. They weren't judging her, but they obviously had a hard time understanding how she – and Josh – could have fallen in love with another person while they were as happy as they had been before their vacation. Once Bonny had taken Ben's hand and Josh had put his own on top of both of theirs, and all three of them had radiated more joy than ever before, her mother had sighed and just said, "All right, all right, we see how happy you are. Just give us a bit of time to get used to the situation. We're happy for you, sweetie. It's just that we've been used to seeing you only with Josh for the past seven years."

After that, when Bonny had gotten to Valeria's abduction, they had mostly stayed quiet, her father only mumbling the occasional curse.

But now, after Bonny had finished the whole story, they were deadly silent, when all of a sudden, her dad erupted, "You flew to the damn jungle and didn't tell us?! What on earth were you thinking?!"

Yep, here we go, crossed Bonny's mind as she tried to open her mouth to answer.

But her father was faster. "I can't believe you. None of you. How can you do something like that without any authorities with you? Without letting your families know? Ty will kick your ass, Josh, I hope you know that. And I can't even imagine what Scarlette will have to say."

"I'm more worried about her, too," Josh mumbled.

"You better be, boy. Holy hell. I won't blame you two for dragging my little girl into this..."

"Dad," Bonny tried, but was interrupted.

"No, you let me finish, Bonny. Like I said, I won't blame either of you. Even if she had been alone and just met and befriended your sister, she would have followed her all by herself. I'm glad you were there to go with her. But how... how could you be this reckless?"

Her dad went on like that for a good five minutes. It wasn't like Bonny couldn't understand him. And she knew he'd accept it once he got the terror he felt at that moment out of his system. She was more worried about her mother; the woman was a force to be reckoned with.

Once he had calmed down somewhat, her mother fixed her eyes on her, and Bonny shuddered. "I have never laid a hand on you, girl, but this time you would deserve it. What the hell were you thinking? I should put you on house arrest for the next ten years. And if you even dare to tell me you don't live here anymore, you better know I have no problem dragging you back and locking you in your old room. You will *never* do something this foolish again, do you hear me?"

"Yes, ma'am," Bonny muttered.

"And you will come to the hospital with me. All three of you. You need to have all kinds of tests run to make sure you didn't pick up anything from some bug bite. I also want X-rays of your ribs."

"Mom..."

"Non-negotiable. You can drive over to Josh's house, drop off your bags if you haven't already, then follow me, or you all come directly to the hospital." She didn't give them any chance to object when she just stood up and grabbed her car keys from where they were lying on the kitchen counter. "Now!"

It took most of the afternoon until Bonny's mom was convinced that they were all okay. Finally, she declared they could all go home. Some of the tests would take longer, but after getting clearance from all of them, she told them she'd check for the results when she was back for her next shift and let them know.

Finally, after interviewing Benicio in detail during their stay at the hospital, she was satisfied with him, too. When fatigue caught up with them, she allowed them to go home to rest.

On the drive, Ben looked at Josh with a smirk. "Don't get me wrong, *arañita*, I want to meet your brother and sister-in-law, too. But I won't be mad if it isn't today. I'm not sure I can take a second round like that. I absolutely understand your parents and I like them, baby," he addressed Bonny, "but that was a hell of a day."

In the front seat, Bonny giggled and reached back to take Ben's hand. "All good, I get you. I'm glad it's over, too."

Josh agreed wholeheartedly. "Yeah, no, I don't need a second round today, either. And we'd get one. I get your parents, babe, but still, that was intense. And don't worry, Ben. I checked the family calendar we share with Scarlette and Ty; they're in the city and will stay there. Some meeting with Vi – that's Ty's agent – and later tonight a meeting with Scarlette's mom, Cynthia, to plan some charity function. And Lorraine, our housekeeper and basically my second mom, and her husband always have their date night on this day of the week. We'll have the place to ourselves for the night. Honestly, we are rarely all in the same place at the same time. Ty and Scarlette have the apartment in the city they call home just like the house here, and it's the same for Bonny and me – and now you."

"Okay."

As soon as they reached the gate at the beginning of a long driveway and Ben got his first look at the building, he gaped. The house was huge enough that he was sure that even if Josh's brother had been home, they could've easily hidden from him and his wife.

Josh must've caught Ben's reaction, because he cleared his throat, a flush creeping along his cheeks. "Guess I should've warned you. Uhm, yeah, it's big. Comes with the business. With the horses and the winery, the family never had an office building or anything. We have some stables for our older horses here at home, and there's a small winery building, too, where we bottle wines we're experimenting with that aren't ready for the market yet," Josh explained as he pointed down a hill while he was driving up to the house. "The actual breeding stables are really close by, too. The larger winery is only a little further away. And my dad was a lawyer. There have always been dinners and stuff like that being held here for business partners, and later, when my mom and dad took over the house, his clients were invited to dinners, too."

Reading his boyfriend's discomfort, Ben leaned forward and pressed a gentle kiss against Josh's cheek as soon as he turned off the car. "There's nothing to be embarrassed about. Yes, your family has money, and yes, this estate is huge. But from all I have learned over the last weeks, you all do good things with the money you make. And you are neither arrogant nor do you treat anybody with less money like they were less. I love you, and I'm proud to be part of your family. And let's be honest, I like the fact that the place is big – with your brother and sister-in-law around, it still will give us privacy."

Ben had hardly finished when Bonny snorted. "Yeah, keep dreaming, baby. You have no idea how often I have run into Scar and Ty making out somewhere. Word of advice: never, ever just enter the pool house without knocking – loudly – and waiting a minute or two before opening the door."

"Good to know."

They got their luggage out of the car, and Josh let them in through the main door. "I hope it's okay if I give you a tour tomorrow instead of tonight. Honestly, right now I just wanna take a shower and crawl into bed, make love to you both, and then sleep like a rock."

"That sounds like heaven. I don't think I could take in a lot right now, anyway," Ben admitted.

Bonny also nodded, then held out her bag to Josh. "Would you take that with you? I'll detour to the kitchen, get us something to drink so we won't have to get down here again later."

"Sure, that's a good idea." With Bonny leaving, Josh began climbing the stairs and gave a bit of information. "So, first floor is mostly the 'official' or public part of the house: formal dining room, parlor, pretty living room. But some of our family places, too, like our family dining room and the kitchen with our breakfast nook. Oh, and we all love to spend time in the library we have down there. Second floor has a guest suite for friends or family who stay for longer. That's also the floor where Scarlette and Ty have their home offices. And we have our less official family room there. The third floor has the master bedroom that Ty and Scarlette share, a couple of smaller guest rooms, and…"

"Your room," Ben said with a bright grin when he saw a door that was designed to look like a Tardis.

"Yep," Josh confirmed with a chuckle as he opened the door.

"I love that. And from the glimpses I got so far, I think I'll love the rest of the place, too. It looks well taken care of and incredibly cozy with lots of personal details. I can't wait for the tour tomorrow. Do you have a home office here, too?"

"Not yet. Ty and I are looking into remodeling part of the attic, though. We'll have to figure it out as we go, because we'll also need to find a solution for Bonny and Scarlette. Scar took over my mom's old home office when she moved here, but once Bonny takes over the company, she'll probably need that one. Luckily, Scar doesn't need a huge office space for the work she's doing from home, and she has her actual business space in the city for storing crates and stuff, so we should be able to make it work."

"I'm sure you will find a way," Ben said.

Then he looked around and took in Josh's room: colorful lights highlighted all kinds of comic and SciFi collectables, but everything looked ordered and as if it had been placed with consideration. Sure, the room was a testament to the nerdy part of Josh's personality, but it didn't look like a teenager's room just stuffed to the ceiling with the hobby of the week. There were also pictures of him and Bonny, and a wall held shelves with her camera equipment. It was a welcoming mix of the two people he loved so much. The large bed with its dark green covers made it perfect and was luring Ben in right away.

As if he had read his lover's mind, Josh took Ben's suitcase and put it aside with his own and Bonny's. "We'll take care of that tomorrow, too. For now, come. Let's wait in the shower for our woman before we break in the bed as a throuple," he said with a grin and dragged Ben through the door of the ensuite.

Epilogue

"And that's pretty much all that's happened since we left for our vacation, and what Anton emailed me about early this morning. He found some footage from various sources to support his theories after running a facial recognition software for the dead girl from the hotel and going from there," Josh finished.

They were all seated in the breakfast nook, the food mostly gone, and everybody was on their second cup of coffee. Looking at Tyler's and Scarlette's blank faces, the throuple had no idea what kind of reaction would bubble up.

The silence was a little nerve-wracking, and Benicio began to realize what kind of first impression he must've made and how it might not have improved with him dragging Josh and Bonny into all the drama that had happened. He took a deep breath and looked over to Tyler. "Ah, I want to apologize for yelling at you like that earlier, Ty. Josh is right, he told me you have bi and gay friends, it's just... Well, when I was younger, the first boyfriend I had had a brother, and honestly, that guy looked a bit like you, and he ran into us holding hands. Nothing more, really; we were fifteen, there wasn't much happening. But his brother started yelling right away, too. Contrary to you, though, he turned out to be deeply homophobic, and he almost hit his brother and me. That's when their mother came in and threw her older son out. He wasn't living at home anymore, anyway, so she just shut the door in his face. But it was kind of a déjà-vu, and I just wanted to protect Josh."

Ty studied Ben for a moment, then nodded. "Apology accepted, Ben. Wasn't my finest moment, either. I'm sorry, too, for yelling at you guys without knowing what's going on. And I appreciate that you wanted to protect my brother."

"Ty's right, it's sweet that you want to protect them. Almost as sweet as you guys blushing or looking between the three of you whenever you edited out some of the more private content of that story. It was kind of obvious, but also funny to watch," Scarlette said with a grin. Then she grew more serious. "But that doesn't save you from us kicking your asses for being that stupid."

"Didn't think so," Josh sighed.

The lecture that followed was a lot like what they had heard the previous days already, but was sprinkled with a few of Scarlette's more creative curses. Once she and Ty were done, she shook her head one last time. "I hope you know you'll hear more of that from the rest of the clan, too. There's dinner with everybody planned at Granny's restaurant for tomorrow. Anyway, listen, because I will only say this part once, so you don't get any crazy ideas of repeats: we're proud of all three of you. You did something amazing."

Since Josh seemed at a loss for words at the unexpected compliment, Bonny smiled at Scarlette. "Thank you, Scar."

"You're welcome."

That's when Ty cocked his head. "Ben? Are you okay? You look a little terrified."

At the question, Benicio shook himself. "Uhm, yes, all good.

I was just not prepared to meet 'the clan' so soon," he explained while making air quotes.

That made Scarlette laugh. "Oh, you might've been nice enough to not dump your whole family on them right away, but that's not gonna work here. We originally had planned to pick Josh and Bonny up from the airport as a surprise and have dinner with everybody. Ty and I haven't been back long, either, and have only seen a few people so far. We're under strict orders to all come to the restaurant and tell everybody about our respective trips. I figured surprising you with meeting the whole clan would be a bit unfair, but you won't get out of it, believe me. Welcome to the family," she told him with a smirk.

Whatever Ben had expected, it hadn't been the easy acceptance from everybody the next evening. The restaurant was cozy, but at least on that night, it was also utter chaos. There were so, so many people he was introduced to, so many kids running around, and just so much laughter and joy. That was, after everybody had gotten over the initial shock when they had recounted their story once again. Scarlette's grandmother Bea had been the first to react – by giving all three of them a (somewhat) gentle smack to the back of the head and forbidding them from doing anything like it again. The woman was in her eighties now, but she was feisty. Benicio's father, who had managed to time his tours so he could meet his son's lovers and had of course been invited to join the dinner, agreed with Bea wholeheartedly. Then Benicio was dragged into all kinds of conversations, and at some point even handed Michelle's and Leroy's youngest daughter so they could go collect their other two kids, who were running around with some of Scarlette's cousins. But when things slowed down a bit with families with young kids leaving and Luke taking July – heavily pregnant with their first child – home to get some rest, and Bea ordered Ben to help clear the tables like he had always been part of the chaos, he knew there was no place he'd rather be. And nobody he'd ever love more than the woman and man next to him who were also carrying plates back into the kitchen and each dropped a kiss on his lips as they passed.

THE END.

Author's Note

Let me just get two things out of the way before we get into some more details about this trilogy.

Some of you might have wondered since when we have an HIV vaccine – well, that's unfortunately still fiction. Even though researchers are working hard, hoping to make it a reality despite it being quite difficult. Science is amazing! The fact that I mentioned a character still using PrEP (Pre-Exposure Prophylaxis) despite getting a vaccine usually should not be necessary, I'm aware. But since the vaccine is so far only made up, and we don't know how actual medical protocols will look like in reality until the effectiveness of a possible vaccine has been determined (even after countless tests during its development), I used some artistic freedom here (and for some other things).

The same goes for the unusual use of anesthetic gas. It's not that easy, and modern anesthetic machines are built to support the anesthesiologist in keeping patients safe. But you have to get rid of the bad guys outnumbering your heroes somehow, right?

Okay, enough of that; let's get started on the bigger picture after wrapping up a trilogy.

Some of you might have wondered who, in this day and age, still writes romance novels with characters who fall in love at first sight (or at least within a few days). Well, some of that has probably been answered in this book. But another reason is just personal experience. Yes, believe me, you can fall incredibly fast and hard for somebody – and it can last. It has been more than twenty years for me now.

I'm not saying to throw caution to the wind or that relationships don't require work.

But sometimes I indeed hear people around me talking, who listened to their friends' and even a strangers' opinion more than to their hearts, and they sound so unhappy about being with the people they're "supposed to be" with rather than with the ones they wanted to be with, and that's just sad.

So, perhaps I just wanted to open people's eyes a little to the fact that maybe there's a reason why we sometimes click with somebody, and giving it a chance, even when the other people think it doesn't fit, might just be worth it.

And if you wonder why I chose to write this trilogy around low-angst relationships, then all I can say is, maybe I'm a sucker for a Happily Ever After, and I just feel like we always imply it's going to be that way after we close a romance novel, but we so, so rarely get a good glimpse of it.

I wanted to change that a bit. Why not show how happy people can be together without having a big third-act-breakup, just to bring them together again on the last few pages? (And frankly, sometimes you wonder, if they broke up over something minor, can it really be a *HEA* in the end?). Yes, we're talking romance here, but why does that mean the drama must stem from the relationship between the protagonists? Or even just one character's reaction to something, like discovering they're attracted to their own gender, too? Don't get me wrong, I'm not saying that can't be a surprise, or that other books showing a shocked reaction are bad. They are not. If your story focuses on that, awesome! I'm just saying, again from personal experience, I know there can be other reactions, too, and I've missed reading about those.

So, I guess that's why I wrote the *Couples & Crime* books the way I did. In no way to discredit other approaches to story-telling, but to have something out there that shows it can also be different for characters, and to give readers something to choose from when they are in the mood for a whole lot of love without relationship drama.

And now let's end this at the beginning. I thought coming up with a dedication for this book would take me forever – after all, there are so many people who are important to me that choosing one would mean ignoring the others.

Then I began thinking about why I started writing this trilogy in the first place. Sure, part of it was the wish to write stories that show that not every love story needs to thrive mostly on the drama between lovers. But I realized that wasn't the only reason. Instead, I've begun to understand why I not only started writing romance novels, but why so many of us also *love* to read them.

And there we are: Love.

Don't get me wrong, I enjoy the steam and spice as much as the rest of you.

But.

I've come to think romance novels are often more than just some light entertainment. Yes, I am aware I'm not writing the next *Pride and Prejudice*, and I'm not aspiring to do so. But not every romance novel needs to be a great masterpiece to touch readers. I think part of why we find romance books so intriguing is because they give us a glimpse into society in a way no other genre does. They often deal with everyday people and show

how life and society is or was in a specific time. And moreover, they deal with their emotions in a way other genres don't. You can read a political thriller – and it can be an amazing book! – but you will rarely get that deep insight into a character's feelings, of what it does to characters living their ordinary lives.

And still, even without the stage set for a huge political play or a mission to save the world, we love romance. Not because of the danger or adventure. But because it deals with one of the strongest emotions that almost everybody can relate to. It equals us, it makes us root for the characters in a way hardly any other emotion can. Because most of us know what it is to love someone. And yes, in this case I'm talking about romantic love.

But the dedication is meant to address Love in all its forms: romantic love in all its various expressions, of course, but also love for family, for friends, for pets, for yourself and your dreams.

Love is a driving force for us every day, even if we don't realize it. We get up and maybe go to a job we aren't as excited about as we could be about another, but it brings in money to provide for the family at home that we love. We go out in the rain and the cold because our dog needs to go, because we love our pets. We'll drag ourselves to a bar with a friend to keep an eye on them, even if we prefer staying on the couch, so we can make sure they're safe while looking for a date because we love them.

So much love, no matter what it looks like.
Thus, *To Love.*

Acknowledgments

As always, I have so many people to thank now that this book, this trilogy, is finished.

My amazing husband, for not only keeping up my coffee supply and feeding me, but also his constant encouragement and feedback. And, of course, for letting me put his face online for my writing adventures. Most important, though, for his love!

My wonderful editor and friend Jessica Scott Romano for all her hard work and help in improving my books!

And of course, my epic family and friends for their support! I can't name you all here, but I'm so grateful for all of you, no matter where in the world you are – your input helped give my books more details, and made this one specifically so much more authentic (let's just say, all of you being called "bad-spoken" or a little vulgar out there: it can be incredibly helpful to your friends in need of a translator to get the Mexican Spanish right)!

Bonus Content

Want to dive deeper into the world of *Couples & Crime*? Visit
the link below for special bonus content from the author.

www.lyvlamere.com/bonus-content

Lyv Lamere grew up in Germany and still lives there with her husband and her snake, even though they might relocate in the future. Lyv successfully studied veterinary medicine and worked at a laboratory. The pandemic had her following another interest of hers, which gave her the chance to work as a contractor in the tech industry for a while.

One day she found she had developed yet another passion – writing – and her first novel was completed sooner than expected. Currently, she is focusing on her literary adventure and loves coming up with new stories and meeting new people while promoting her books. She's always writing and hopes to bring a smile to people's faces with her work.

To learn more about Lyv, visit
www.lyvlamere.com.

<h1>Also by Lyv Lamere</h1>

Couples & Crime Series:

Generational Payment

Pieces of a Murder

Treacherous Paradise

www.ingramcontent.com/pod-product-compliance
Lightning Source LLC
Chambersburg PA
CBHW051440190726
48289CB00001B/268